CRITICAL ACCLAIM FOR
THE SORCERER'S LADY

"A marvelous tale with a grand maze of twists and turns that will mesmerize you and spark your imagination. . . . A keeper!"

—*Rendezvous*

"*The Sorcerer's Lady* is a warm and touching love story evoking the magic and beauty of a fairy tale."

—*Romantic Times*

"Debra Dier takes myths and turns them into a magical, mystical world. . . . Here is laughter and love wrapped up in a marvelous, memorable story."

—*The Paperback Forum*

"A magical story with one of the most charming, caring heroes encountered in a long time."

—*The Heartland Gazette*

THE SORCERER'S LADY

DEBRA DIER

LOVE SPELL BOOKS NEW YORK CITY

LOVE SPELL®

April 1999

Published by

Dorchester Publishing Co., Inc.
276 Fifth Avenue
New York, NY 10001

ISBN 0-505-52305-1

Printed in the United States of America.

THE SORCERER'S LADY

"You called me. That's why I journeyed a thousand years. To be with you."

"I don't know what you are, or who you are." Laura drew a deep draft of air into her lungs. "I do know I want you to go back to where you came from."

"No, you don't." Connor leaned down and kissed the tip of her nose. She jumped as though she had been stung by a bee. "And I intend to prove to you just how much you want me to stay."

Laura's lips parted, her breath rushing out in a heated gasp that warmed his cheek. "Why you arrogant—" She hesitated, denying her own anger, as though it were indecent to feel good, honest rage. "I assure you, I do not want you to stay."

Connor frowned. "If you wish to scream at me, why don't you?"

"A lady does not scream."

Connor considered this a moment. "A lady is still human, is she not? And humans are ruled by emotion."

"It is apparent you know nothing at all about ladies."

"Tell me, is a lady a woman?"

"Of course."

He grinned. "Then I do know something of ladies."

To Kim, who understands my search for the perfect word.
Thanks for sharing your thoughts and your friendship.

Prologue

Erin, A.D. 889

"There is no need to be embarrassed, Connor. We're fortunate none of your other abilities are impaired. Indeed, I would say it's a miracle you have any abilities at all." Aisling glanced from her nephew to her sister, one golden brow curving upward. "Given your bloodline."

Ciara's cheeks flushed under her younger sister's gaze. "There is nothing wrong with his bloodline."

Connor crossed his long legs and leaned against the tall back of an oak throne chair, studying his mother and his aunt over the steeple of his fingers. They stood face-to-face in a golden pool of light spilling from the hearth, both tall and slender, their shoulders stiff with indignation.

"Your marriage has produced one child with limited ability, and five mortals." Aisling shook her head, clucking her tongue in disgust. "It would seem our blood does not mix well with that of your potent Viking. As I recall before you married, I did mention the folly of following a reckless heart."

"In ways we are fortunate the other children were not as gifted as Connor. Raising a boy with his abilities without letting his father know of my legacy has not been an easy feat."

"If you had married your own kind, you would not have needed to keep your true nature from a mortal."

"I couldn't help falling in love."

"How long can we keep diluting our bloodlines before the power dissolves into mist?"

"Love is stronger than all the power we possess!"

"Nonsense!"

Flames danced on the stone hearth behind the women, flickering higher with their rising anger. Even the flames of the candles danced to the rhythm of their rage.

"We are the *Tuatha De Danann*. We once ruled as powerful sorcerers in Atlantis and here in Erin." Aisling twitched the medallion she wore on a golden chain around her neck. "And now we are hunted, shunned, feared. We hide our powers, for fear of being destroyed."

"And I suppose I'm to blame for destroying our people."

"If we do not alter this path we are on, the future will see few of us on this earth." Aisling stared into the fire as though she were looking beyond the flames into the future. "In a thousand years, there will exist only a handful who truly understand the ancient ways, and a scattering of children who do not even know they possess the power of Mother Earth."

The cold chill of winter seeped through the stone walls of the tower room, setting intricate tapestries shivering on the walls, seeping into Connor's blood. Aisling's gift of divination was powerful. What she foresaw would come to pass if something was not altered. Yet he could not turn his back on the woman in his dreams to marry one of the *Sidhe*; to do so would be to sacrifice his very soul.

"If you are so concerned with our bloodline, why is it you have not chosen a mate, Aisling? Is it because you can't find one of the *Sidhe* who will have you and your sharp tongue?"

Aisling twitched her pendant between her fingers, the emerald eye of the bird carved into the ancient gold medallion winking in the firelight. "Careful, Ciara."

"And what shall you do, fill my bed with toads, as you did on my wedding night?"

Aisling smiled. "Perhaps."

"Why you . . ."

Connor sighed, weary of this argument. With a wave of his hand both women floated upward toward the thick beams of the ceiling like butterflies gently taking flight, scarlet and ivory, emerald and gold, their gowns fluttering as they lifted.

"Connor!" they screamed in unison.

He looked up at the two women who hovered three feet above the floor. They were as different in coloring as midnight and morning, his mother's black hair as dark as Aisling's was light. Yet both women shared delicate features and skin as smooth and unlined as a ten-year-old child's; the passing of time meant little to his people. Like two angels they hovered in the room, staring at him, silvery blue eyes shimmering with rage.

"Get us down, young man!" Ciara shouted.

"So it seems I have your attention once more." Connor tapped his fingertips together, smiling up at them. "I realize my destiny isn't nearly as important as a thirty-year-old argument. But I had hoped the two of

13

you might help me sort through my problem."

Both women glanced at each other, guilt dampening their anger. They had gathered here tonight to decipher the dreams that had been plaguing Connor since he was a boy.

"He does make his point." Ciara forced each word past her lips as though they were pennies pried from a miser.

"I've never turned my back when Connor needed me." Aisling tossed her hair over her shoulder, the cascade of silvery blond curls shimmering to her knees, swishing against the scarlet silk of her gown. "I was there for him even when you were too busy playing mortal wife to teach him the ancient ways."

Ciara crossed her arms at her waist, the gold trim of her wide emerald sleeves glittering in the firelight. "I appreciate the time you spent with my son, but if you think I shall—"

Connor lifted his hand. The women glided closer toward the ceiling.

"Very well!" Ciara shouted.

"Enough, Connor!"

"Think you can behave?" Connor asked, halting their upward progress a foot from the ceiling beams.

"Yes!" both women shouted.

Connor snapped his fingers. The women floated in swirls of emerald and scarlet silk to the rushes that covered the floor.

"Impossible Viking," Aisling said, the smile tugging at the corners of her lips spoiling the severe tone of her voice. She smoothed the wide scarlet sleeves of her gown, as though she were repairing her dignity, before withdrawing a piece of amber from a gold silk bag dangling from the thick gold chain she wore around her waist.

14

"I should do the reading," Ciara said, reaching for the amber. "I'm not at all certain why he wanted to see you about this."

Aisling clutched the talisman in her hand. "Because you have never been as good as I am at divination. And since you've been suppressing your powers, you're blind."

Ciara lifted her chin. "I can certainly—"

Connor waved his hand. Ciara glided upward.

"All right!" Ciara glared at her son. "I shall give her the first chance."

"Thank you." Connor gently lowered his mother to the floor. Ciara flicked her emerald skirts as she marched toward the opposite end of the long oak table, firelight glittering on the golden threads running through the shimmering silk. She sat in a carved oak throne chair and pouted.

Later he would appease his mother. Now he needed to know the answers lurking in the shadows beyond his reach. He watched, uneasy with what she might see in his destiny as Aisling held the amber before the flames. His gift of precognition had never been strong, and when it concerned his own future he was painfully nearsighted, a fact Aisling attributed to his tainted blood. "Do you see anything?"

"Patience, son of Setric," Aisling said, reminding him of his Viking heritage. She stared deeply into the precious amber she held before the flames of the stone hearth, the ancient talisman half the size of her palm.

Connor pressed the tips of his fingers together, conjuring in his mind the image of the woman who had haunted him for so many years. Why hadn't he been able to find her? In the past year he had searched every sanctuary and village scattered around the world. He hadn't found a trace of her. He was beginning to believe

15

the woman lived only in his imagination.

"In a time of trouble she will call to you," Aisling whispered.

The breath settled in his lungs as she spoke of his destiny. "Then this woman I have seen in visions is real."

"You have always known this woman was real, Connor." Aisling looked at him, her blue eyes piercing him as though she looked straight into his soul. Light twisted like flame itself through the golden amber she held, illuminating a smile as mysterious as her powers. "From the day you were seven and she first came to you in your dreams, you knew you would find her one day."

The dreams had been with him for 20 years, since the night a girl with green eyes and hair the color of warm honey had come to him while he slept. Since that night, when the pull of the moon was most powerful, one night in every earth cycle, she came to him.

They had played together as children, in a valley he had never found on this earth. Through the years, as she blossomed into a woman and he grew from boy to man, the bond had grown between them until his need for her was elemental, like the air he breathed. Somehow he had to find her. Somehow he had to claim her, in a way he had never claimed her in his dreams: completely, irrevocably.

"Carved as from the finest marble, she glows and shimmers, ice in sunlight," Aisling whispered, her dark voice seeping into every corner of the large room. "Yet embers simmer deep within her, waiting for the breath of a lover's kiss."

Connor released his breath in a long sigh. They were connected, he and this woman he had seen only in dreams, bound together like links in a golden chain. She was his. He was hers. And somehow he would find her. Nothing would keep him from finding her.

"Be forewarned, Prince of Wexford, this maid will know you and deny you to her own heart." Aisling smiled into the amber as though she gazed upon a beguiling child. "The cold hand of logic is her master now. Still, when the river of time bends back upon itself, logic will yield. In this you will find your triumph, or your defeat."

"Tell me, great sorceress. When shall I see her?"

Aisling looked up from the amber, a smile curving her lips. "Come, dark warrior. See your destiny."

In long strides Connor crossed the distance. Rushes scented with pine and herbs stirred beneath his boots, their fragrance melding with the spicy scent simmering from melting candles.

"Look into the amber," Aisling whispered.

Connor did not touch the gem; to do so would be to disturb Aisling's link with the vision. He stared into the golden depths of the amber, seeing the shifting shapes of the flames beneath, searching for the face of the woman who wove through the fabric of his destiny like a golden thread through a rich tapestry. She was his *Edaina*, his soul mate; of this he was certain.

Flames danced in the amber, sparking light that parted like golden petals and blossomed into a living image. Connor drew a deep breath as he stared into the lovely face that haunted his dreams. Golden waves framed the ivory oval of her face. Tears shimmered in her eyes like dew welling on the first tender leaves of spring. He felt the pain within her sinking into him like the talons of a falcon.

"Why do you weep, my *Edaina*?" he whispered.

"To know your answer you must abandon all else and travel farther than you have ever imagined." Aisling twisted the amber, dissolving the image of the woman Connor knew in his soul, leaving him craving the sight of her. "If you go to her, the faces of your family will

17

live only in your memory."

"What nonsense is this, Aisling?" Ciara stood, staring at her sister.

"Your son must choose. His family or this woman he sees in his dreams."

Ciara crossed her arms over her chest. "What game are you playing?"

"I speak only the truth."

"A truth of your making. My son is not going anywhere."

Connor smiled as he looked at his mother. "I have to find her."

Ciara lifted her chin. "You would leave us?"

"What did your parents say when you told them you intended to marry a Viking?" Connor asked.

"But that was different. I was . . ." Ciara hesitated, studying her son. Connor's chest tightened with emotion as he held his mother's gaze and saw understanding swell with tears in her eyes. "I think you should take time to consider this, Connor."

In his mind Connor saw the faces of his father, his brothers and sisters, a vise squeezing his heart when he thought of never seeing them again. Still, he knew what he must do. "Tell me how I can find her, Aisling."

Aisling smiled. "When her need for you reaches into the mists of time, she will summon you to her side."

The look in Aisling's eyes told him she knew more than she was saying. He had the sense of being manipulated in some subtle way. Yet it didn't matter. Nothing mattered except finding his *Edaina*. "When will I be with her?"

Aisling smoothed her fingertip over the amber. "Soon."

Chapter One

Boston, 1889

"Come to me."

Laura Sullivan hesitated on the threshold of the library. The turmoil that had brought her looking for her Aunt Sophie dissipated as she stared at the small, dark-haired woman standing in the center of the room. What in the world was her aunt doing?

Sophie Chandler stood with her eyes closed, her hands outstretched toward the wall across from her. "Come to me," she said, her voice unnaturally deep, as though she were trying to draw the words from the tips of her toes.

Laura looked at the wall, wondering who her aunt was summoning. Although the glass doors to one of the walnut bookcases built into the paneled walls were open, she could see nothing to command save the leather-bound volumes that lined the shelves.

Sophie opened her eyes, her expectant look dissolving into a frown. "Oh, bother."

"Is something wrong? Are you all right?"

Sophie glanced at Laura, her frown replaced with her quick smile. "Nothing, dear. I'm quite fine."

Sophie fluttered toward a wing-back chair near the hearth, muttering something about books that wouldn't cooperate, her skirt of sapphire blue wool swaying like a bell on Sunday morning. She plucked an open book from the burgundy velvet–covered seat and stared at one of the pages.

"Isn't that the journal Ridley found last week?"

"Yes. The journal of Rachel Paxton." Sophie ran her fingertips along the upper edge of the scarlet leather binding the book. "Remarkable, isn't it?"

The journal had been found when a floorboard in the wine cellar had given way beneath their butler's foot. "I'm sure poor Ridley doesn't think it's remarkable. He was limping for days."

"Poor man. But think of what he found. This journal is more than two hundred years old, and it scarcely looks worn."

Paneled walnut shutters were tucked behind the undrawn burgundy velvet drapes at the windows. Laura crossed the room, drawn to the windows and the quiet beauty of the snow that lay beyond. There was a full moon tonight, as she knew there would be, round and lush, shimmering silver in a black sky.

Would he come?

In her mind, with every logical thought, she wished he would stay away. Yet in her heart, she begged for him to come, to whisk her away from reality. Still, she knew the problems of this world would not go away, even if she chose to ignore them. She had to make a decision. Soon.

"Looking at this journal, I wonder just how it could

manage to look so untouched after so many years."

"The iron box it was in, I suppose."

"Perhaps. Then perhaps it's magic."

Laura glanced at her aunt. "Better to believe in the iron box."

" 'The power of the Earth Mother shall reside in each generation descendant from me.' " Sophie read from the journal she held. " 'To my descendants this book of enchantments is bequeathed, for only with their power can they be enacted.' "

"Aunt Sophie, you don't really believe all that hocus-pocus."

"Think of it, Laura. Rachel Paxton was our ancestress, a direct line through my mother. Your great-grandmother was a Paxton." Sophie's expressive blue eyes grew wide. "I remember Grandmother had an uncanny way of seeing things in her dreams, predicting the future. Now I understand."

"You don't really believe she could predict the future?"

"She was right too many times for it to be coincidence." Sophie stared at the journal. "Why, we could have 'the power of the Earth Mother' inside of us, just like Rachel."

"Careful, Aunt Sophie. Rachel was burned at the stake because she believed she was a witch."

"A white witch. And it says in the journal that those with the power of the Earth Mother cannot harm anyone with their magic. Rachel was only trying to help heal a neighbor who had broken his leg." Sophie shook her head as she stroked the old journal. "Poor child. She was barely twenty years old, with three young children, when they snuffed out her life."

"Yes, it was unfortunate." Laura stared through one square pane of glass into the gardens behind her home, where the roses and flowers lay sleeping beneath a thick white mantle. If only answers to her questions could be found written in the glittering moonlight scattered upon the rippling snow. "Pity Rachel believed in enchantments and all that nonsense."

"Nonsense?" Sophie sounded startled by Laura's common-sense attitude. "Have you never believed in magic, Laura?"

The chill of winter crept through the windowpanes and seeped through Laura's emerald cashmere gown, a pale reflection of the chill she felt in her soul. "I believe in what I can see and touch."

"But there is so much more to the world, things just beyond our reach, mysteries as old as time. We all have a little magic inside of us."

"Do we?" If there were truly magic in the world, she wouldn't be facing the decision she must make.

"Think back to when you were a child, Laura; remember what it was like to play make-believe with your friends, when you could look at a tree and imagine it was a knight in shining armor. That magic still lives inside of you."

Laura pressed her hand against the windowpane, watching the heat of her skin radiate across the glass. "I never played make-believe."

"Never?"

"Never." That wasn't entirely true. Still, how could she explain to Sophie that she had played such games in her dreams, with a boy who had existed only in her mind? "Mother needed her rest, not a noisy child running about the house."

"But you must have gone to play with other little girls?"

Laura shook her head. "You know how frail Mother was." *Quiet now, your mother is resting*—she had heard those words every day of her life.

"Yes. I know exactly how *frail* your mother was."

There was a tone in Sophie's voice, a subtle shading of disgust that startled Laura. She glanced back at her aunt, searching her expression, seeing only a gentle concern in Sophie's face. "Mother was afraid I would catch some illness and bring it home."

"I see. So you spent most of your time alone."

Laura cringed at the pity she could hear in Sophie's voice. She didn't need anyone's pity.

"I should have visited you more often, my beautiful child."

"I read and studied. I assure you, my childhood was well spent."

"It's never too late to learn how to believe in magic."

Laura slid her fingertip over the windowpane, smoothing the steam that had collected in the shape of her hand, beads of moisture sliding like tears down the glass. "I believe you are an incurable romantic, Aunt Sophie."

"I suppose I am." Sophie laughed, a sound that rippled with the crackle of the fire on the hearth in the quiet room. "For instance, I believe there is one special person in the world for each of us. Two halves separated before birth. And somehow we are meant to find each other in our lifetime."

Laura turned to look at her aunt. Sophie was watching her, a keen understanding in her dark blue eyes. Sophie knew her better than Laura's mother had ever known her, but then Eleanor had never tried to know her daughter. "And what happens if you never meet?"

Sophie smiled, the curve of her lips hinting at a long-suppressed sadness. She was 39 and had never married. "In that case, as my Aunt Millicent taught me, we plunge forward and try not to think of what might have been."

"Did you ever meet him, that special man?"

"Oh, yes." Sophie's gaze flickered to the portrait

above the mantel before resting once more on the journal she held open in her hands. The glance had lasted an instant, only an instant, but it was enough to reveal a lifetime to Laura. "But I'm afraid it was the wrong time, the wrong place. I was far too young to catch his eye. And by the time I was old enough, he was married."

Laura glanced to the portrait hanging above the mantel. The painting had been done 15 years ago, when her father had been 31. From the confines of a carved rosewood frame, her father gazed down at her with dark brown eyes, his thick, dark brown hair framing a handsome face that could capture the hearts of many a romantic maiden. Had he captured Sophie's heart?

Sophie had left her family home when she was 18, to live with her widowed Aunt Millicent in New York City. Laura had always assumed Sophie had gone to keep Great-Aunt Millicent company. Yet suddenly she wondered if there had been another reason Sophie had escaped Boston.

"Do you still love him?" Laura's breath stilled in her chest as she waited, both afraid and anxious to hear the answer.

"It doesn't matter."

"Are you certain? Perhaps it isn't too late."

Sophie waved away Laura's words with one slender hand. "Enough of me. It's you I'm worried about."

"There is no need to be worried about me." Laura glanced out the window, watching the wind carve patterns in the snow.

"Your father is a man who wears responsibilities as men once wore armor. He still feels an obligation to my father, God rest his soul, for taking him in after his own father died. Father raised him like a son, gave him the hand of his daughter in marriage, and the helm of a great shipping company. And for that, Daniel feels a great responsibility. Even though I suspect Father had

24

his own reasons for his kindness."

Sophie was quiet for a moment. In the glass Laura could see her aunt staring up at the portrait above the mantel. "I know how much Daniel wants an heir, someone to carry on the Chandler tradition. I hope you don't feel pressured to marry someone who might not be right for you."

"Father has mentioned how much he would like me to marry. But I'm certain he doesn't mean to pressure me into anything."

"From what I've seen, he scarcely spends enough time in this house to tell you anything."

It was true; her father was a little better than a stranger. "He has a business to run." A business Laura owned. A business her father expected Laura's husband and children to run one day.

"I'm afraid the business has become his life."

There were times when Laura wondered if his office had become a sanctuary, a place to be free of a wife who had been little more than a ghost, and a daughter who craved his attention. And then there were times when she wondered if he hoped for an escape from the crushing responsibilities of his business. She knew his only escape from Chandler Shipping would be if she married and her husband took over the business.

"Philip Gardner spent a long time with you in the parlor after dinner."

Laura nodded, realizing there was no avoiding the decision confronting her. "He asked me to marry him."

"I'm not surprised."

"When Father returns from New York tomorrow, Philip wants to ask for my hand."

"What did you tell him?"

"I told him I wanted to think about it."

"Good. It gives me at least a little time to talk you out of the idea."

Laura turned to face her aunt. "Why don't you like Philip?"

"I don't think he is right for you."

"But he's from one of the finest families in Boston."

"I'm certain he hasn't hesitated to elaborate on his breeding."

Laura pursed her lips, searching for Philip's attributes. "He is very handsome."

"If you like that smoother-than-pudding look."

"He is . . . responsible."

Sophie crinkled her slim nose. "Stuffy."

"Aunt Sophie, he's a respected gentleman, one of the most suitable bachelors in the city. Any woman would be honored to become his wife." Laura hugged her arms to her waist, feeling chilled suddenly. "I'm amazed he would even find an interest in me. After all, I must be the oldest debutante in the history of Boston."

"You're one of the most beautiful debutantes Boston has ever seen. Now don't shake your head. All you have to do is look in the mirror to see the truth of what I'm saying."

Laura glanced at her father's portrait, remembering how anxious he had been for her to enter society after their period of mourning had passed. "Father was worried I would be an outcast because of his lack of family. You know how thrilled he was when Philip took an interest in me."

"In the eyes of this town you are a Chandler, Laura. Our family is one of the oldest, most influential in the city. Never let anyone make you feel less than what you are."

Laura felt the responsibility of that name sitting upon her shoulders. "I want you to know you truly helped ease Father's fears when you agreed to come home to sponsor me."

"I'm afraid your father knows how it feels to live in

this town and not carry the right surname, even though he is worth a dozen of those blue-blooded Bostonians." Sophie glanced up at Daniel's portrait, the look in her eyes whispering of wishes that had never come true. "Boston is a society more concerned with who your great-grandfather was than who you are."

"I know." And she knew how much it meant to her father to see her settled properly, with one of those proper "blue-blooded Bostonians." Philip Gardner's blood was as blue as it came. "I'm sure you will like Philip when you get to know him better."

"I know his mother well enough, and he is every bit as arrogant as she."

Laura shivered when she thought of Philip's mother. She had all the warmth of a granite statue. But she was one of the most influential women in Boston society.

"It's only been two months since you entered society. You need to take your time, Laura."

"I'm twenty-five years old. I can't keep waiting for a man I see only in my dreams."

"Is there a man you see in your dreams?" Sophie asked, her voice far too gentle; it spoke of a woman who understood the magic that could be found in dreams.

Laura didn't want to talk about him. She was certain people left imaginary friends behind when they stepped over the threshold from childhood. Yet he was still with her, a boy who had grown into a magnificent man in her dreams. For 20 years he had come to her one night every month, when the moon was at its fullest. She had always believed they would find each other in the world outside of the mystical valley where they met. Yet they never had.

Dreams.

Fantasies.

Foolishness.

It was useless thinking about a man who did not ex-

27

ist. And yet she knew his face, the sound of his voice, the touch of his hand. She knew him in ways she had never known another human being. Did he live only in her imagination? "I learned a long time ago that dreams don't come true."

"Marriage lasts a lifetime. Think very carefully. You will live each day with your husband. Share his bed, bear his children."

With each word Laura felt the knot of apprehension pull tighter in her chest, squeezing her heart. She knew everything her aunt was saying was true. And yet she also felt the weight of responsibility that lay across her shoulders like an iron yoke. "Not all marriages are love matches."

"They all should be. Every woman should wait until she meets that special man who fills the empty places in her."

Laura drew a deep breath. "I'm afraid I don't believe in fairy tales."

"Well, I do. And if I have anything to do with it, you will have your happy ending." Sophie leafed through the old journal as she spoke. "Now where did I see that?"

Laura frowned as she watched her aunt search through the journal. "Aunt Sophie, just what are you looking for?"

"An incantation."

"An incantation?"

Sophie nodded. "One to bring to you that which you most desire."

Laura stared at her aunt. "You are joking."

"Not at all." Sophie rested her finger on a page near the center of the book, studying the words for a moment before she looked up at Laura. "I intend to bring him to you."

"Who?"

"The man in your dreams."

Laura released her breath in a long sigh. "You can't be serious."

Sophie waved aside Laura's words. "Be still, dear." She stared at the open book, her lips moving as though she needed to feel the shaping of the words as well as to see them printed on the page.

Laura shivered at the sound of the wind whispering against the windowpanes. She watched her aunt, admiring her determination even as she wondered how anyone could live to be 39 and maintain such innocent beliefs.

Laura's mother had been Sophie's older sister. Yet the two women bore little more than a nodding resemblance in looks, and had been complete strangers in temperament.

Although her health had never been robust, Eleanor had become an invalid after Laura's birth. She had spent each day in her sitting room, reading, doing needlepoint, staring out at the gardens, not wanting or needing company. And finally, 15 months ago, she had passed away in her sleep, congestion of the lungs draining her last reserves of life.

Sophie had returned to Boston three months ago to help launch Laura into society. A bundle of energy, vibrant with life, always finding light where others saw only darkness, that was Sophie. There had been no discussion about when Sophie might return to New York, and Laura hoped there never would be, even if her aunt had the ridiculous notion she was a witch.

Sophie glanced up, pinning Laura in her dark blue gaze. Laura caught her breath. Never had she seen her aunt look so intense, as though the fate of the world rested upon her slender shoulders. Sophie believed. With all of her heart and soul Sophie believed every word that was printed in that journal; Laura could see it in her eyes.

Faith radiated from Sophie, the kind of faith that pulled people through when life was crumbling around them, a faith strong enough to penetrate Laura's defenses and touch the dreams hidden deep inside of her. Laura held her breath, watching Sophie, waiting, wondering if the power of faith could move mountains.

Sophie spoke, her voice singing like crystal touched by a blade. "Hear me, Lady of the moon. Your pull is great. You move the tide. Now bring Laura's beloved to her side."

The words rippled in Laura's head like a distant echo, both familiar and strange all at the same instant. The fire from the carved walnut fireplace cast a golden glow behind the small, dark-haired woman who repeated the incantation over and over again, each time the words coming from a place deep within Sophie, a place where innocence dwelled, sheltered and nourished through the years.

Sophie fell silent, her eyes closed. Laura waited, the fine hair on her arms tingling beneath soft cashmere.

Click, click, click, click. The pendulum of the grandfather clock standing against the wall across from Laura marked the seconds as they passed. She stared at her aunt expecting . . . what? Did she really expect the man of her dreams to materialize out of thin air?

She released the breath she hadn't realized she had been holding. She was falling under the spell of Sophie's enthusiasm. It certainly could be contagious, this faith in make-believe nonsense, especially when you wanted so much for it to come true.

"Aunt Sophie, perhaps we should retire for the evening. It's getting late and—"

Sophie raised her hand, silencing Laura. She drew a

deep breath and spoke the incantation, her voice vibrating in the room.

In her mind, Laura conjured the image of the man she had known since she was a child. Lost in the rhythm of Sophie's voice, Laura silently repeated the words: *Hear me, Lady of the moon. Your pull is great. You move the tide. Now bring my beloved to my side.*

Sophie spoke the incantation three times, the ancient spell rippling in Laura's brain, the words silently shaping her lips. Even when Sophie stood silent, the words seemed to hover in the air.

Laura held her breath, staring at the journal in her aunt's slender hands. The scarlet leather had captured the glow of the fire, that was all, Laura assured herself, the only reason the book seemed to glow with a light all its own.

The wind whipped against the windows, rattling the panes. Laura started with the sudden sound. She pressed her hand to her racing heart, stumbling toward her aunt. The fire blazed on the hearth, flames leaping upward, as though the wind were coaxing the fire to escape the bounds of the hearth.

"Something is happening," Sophie whispered. "Do you feel it?"

Laura couldn't speak. The air pressed against her like a lover's arms wrapping around her, warm, seductive. A fragrance drifted in the air, the smell of pine and herbs, the pungent scent of burning candles. Yet there were no candles in the room.

The electric lights in the crystal-and-brass fixture overhead flickered; they pulsed with a brilliant glow before fading to black, all the energy draining into the room.

Moonlight streamed through the windows in a brilliant column of silver. So beautiful. Laura couldn't look away from the light even when the fear inside of her begged her to flee. As she stared, particles of light gathered, glimmering, shimmering, coalescing, as though a celestial artist were shaping the moonlight, gathering the brilliance, sculpting the sparkling glow.

"Oh, my," Sophie whispered.

Laura couldn't form a single word.

A figure materialized from the sparkling light. A man. Tall. Broad shouldered. Laura stared, each beat of her heart thudding at the base of her throat. This couldn't be happening. Logic told her this was a dream, all a dream.

The moonlight faded. Electric lights flickered overhead, flooding the room with a golden glow. And still he stood there, pulsing with vitality.

Laura had seen his face a thousand times; she knew each strong line and curve. Pride etched his high cheekbones, the slim straight line of his nose, the sensual curve of his full lips. Power radiated from him like heat from the sun.

Hair darker than midnight tumbled in waves to the wide expanse of his bare shoulders, ebony touched with sapphire highlights, wild shimmering silk. Eyes the pure blue of a summer sky regarded her with a warmth that whispered of days and nights spent in her arms. No stranger's gaze this, but the gaze of a friend, of a lover. The warmth in those blue eyes triggered a response in her, an unfurling of emotion, like a rose opening to the sun.

"Look at him," Sophie whispered, grasping Laura's arm.

"You see him too?"

"He's magnificent." Sophie's fingers bit into Laura's arm.

How could this be? How could she feel the bite of Sophie's fingers in a dream?

"*Edaina*," he whispered, moving toward her. Supple

black leather molded his long legs, where thick muscles rippled with each step that brought him to her.

This had to be a dream!

He paused inches from her, so close she could feel the warmth of his bare skin radiate against her, so close she had to tip back her head to look up into his handsome face. Words rippled from his lips, his deep voice spilling over her like dark summer rain, in a language she had never heard. Still, the words did not matter, only his voice, his eyes, his touch as he brushed his fingers over her cheek, only these mattered in this moment in time.

She touched his chest above his heart. Warm skin, soft curls, thick muscles shifting beneath her fingertips, a heart beating strong and sure. She took a shaky breath; the sharp tang of citrus and musk filled her nostrils in a way that made her want to press her face against his neck and breathe deeply of his essence.

Although logic argued against it, she could not deny her senses, and right now they were filled to overflowing with this man. Laura drew back, staring up into the pure blue of his eyes. "You're real." The full import of the fact hit her like a clenched fist. "Oh, my gracious! You're real!"

Chapter Two

He frowned, looking at her lips as though he were trying to decipher her words, as though they might reveal the reason behind her sudden change in behavior.

Laura stepped back from this half-naked barbarian. "Aunt Sophie, he is real!"

Sophie looked down at the journal as though she held the secret of the ages in her hands. "I'm a witch," she whispered. "I am truly a witch."

"You cannot be a witch. You are a Chandler!"

Sophie looked up at Laura, her delicate features drawn into serious lines. "And a Paxton."

"This cannot be happening." Laura felt the blood drain from her limbs. Her head reeled, darkness clouding her vision. She had never fainted, but she was certain this was what it must be like, a draining of strength, darkness closing in around her. For heaven's sake, she couldn't faint. Not now. Not with a barbarian in her library.

Strong hands gripped her arms. She drew deep breaths, an intriguing scent of musk and citrus filling her senses. When the darkness lifted, she looked up into his eyes, those beautiful blue eyes that were filled with warmth and a tender concern. He smiled, a smile that embraced her, a smile that seemed to say everything would now be as it should be, as it had been destined to be from the beginning of time.

Laura jerked free of his grasp. He frowned, tilting his head, studying her as though she were a puzzle that needed solving. "Aunt Sophie, do something!"

"What would you like me to do, dear?"

Laura trembled. "Send him back."

"Isn't he the right man?"

Laura looked at her aunt, certain Sophie had lost her wits. But then perhaps she was the crazy one here. She seemed to be the only one upset over what had happened. "What do you mean?"

Sophie looked up at the raven-haired barbarian who stood quietly watching the two women, a frown marring his wide brow. "Is he the man you've seen in your dreams?"

"What difference does it make?"

"Is he?" Sophie asked, as though the answer made all the difference in the world.

"Did you pluck him out of my mind? Is that it? Is the man no more than a figment of my imagination?"

Sophie pressed her fingertips against the barbarian's shoulder. He smiled as he looked down at her, quietly amused. "He certainly seems real enough to me, Laura."

"He certainly seems real enough to me, Laura." He imitated Sophie, his words tinged with an accent that might have originated in Ireland or Wales. He glanced at Laura, one black brow arching upward as though he were waiting for her response.

"Do you think he understands?" Laura whispered, afraid suddenly to raise her voice.

"I don't know." Sophie smiled up at the man as though it were the most natural thing in the world to have a half-naked barbarian in the house. "Do you understand English?"

He looked from Laura to Sophie and back again, black brows drawing together. When he spoke, he pronounced each word carefully, as though he were testing to see if Laura understood him. The words were not spoken in the same language he had used before, but in a language Laura could read as fluently as she could read Greek, French, or German.

"Latin," Laura whispered. "He speaks Latin."

"My Latin is not what it should be, Laura, what did he say? I caught the word Connor; is that his name?"

"Yes." Laura stared at him. "I've never heard anyone speak Latin so fluently."

"Since you know Latin," Sophie said, patting his arm, "it shouldn't be difficult to teach you English, my dear young man."

"Aunt Sophie, he isn't going to be here long enough to teach him more than the word *good-bye*. Send him back!"

Sophie blinked at her niece's strident tone. "But, dear, he's only just arrived."

He seemed to have lost interest in their conversation. He was looking around him, staring at the carpet with its urns and flowers stitched in shades of red and ivory. He looked up at the fixture overhead, as though fascinated by the frosted bulbs of glowing light. A gold medallion dangled from a gold chain around his neck to nestle against the black curls that covered his wide chest. In the center of the disk a square-cut emerald winked at her as it captured the light.

Laura watched him. He looked around as though he

were a child discovering the world for the first time. There was something utterly appealing about this man, an intriguing blend of strength and gentleness, a warmth that made her want to slip her arms around him and hold him until the end of time. He was a man who could steal her heart with little more than a smile. Perhaps he already had.

What was she thinking? He was a figment of her imagination. How could she possibly fall in love with him? "Aunt Sophie, you have to send him back immediately."

Sophie leafed through the journal as though it were a cookbook and she needed to find something interesting for dessert. "Now where did I see that spell?"

Laura held her breath, watching him, willing Sophie to hurry. He walked toward the open bookcase as though the row upon row of leather volumes were beckoning him, the sheathed broadsword hanging from the black belt slung around his narrow hips brushing his thigh. A broadsword!

"I wonder if I might cast a spell to teach him our language," Sophie said, studying a page in the journal.

"Cast a spell and send him back." Heavens! Did she really believe in all of this hocus-pocus? She glanced to where her barbarian was looking at a book he had taken from the shelf. Did she really have a choice but to believe in this magical nonsense?

"Laura, dear, why don't you show Connor the Latin-to-English dictionary. It will have to do until I can work up a spell to teach him English."

"Aunt Sophie, are there words coming out of my mouth when I move my lips like this?"

Sophie looked up at her, startled by the question. "Why, yes, dear."

"If you can hear me, then tell me why you won't try to send him back!"

37

"Because he is your other half." Sophie patted Laura's arm. "The part you were meant to find in this world."

"My other half is a barbarian?"

Sophie's lips quirked into a mischievous grin. "So it would seem."

Laura moaned. "How do you suppose we will ever explain this man to my father, to anyone who sees him?"

Sophie pursed her lips. "I'll think of something."

"I can't believe this is really happening. I'm going to wake up and find this is nothing more than a nightmare."

"I don't know about you, Laura, but I think he looks much too good to be a nightmare." Sophie stared at the dark-haired giant who stood quietly leafing through a book. "I must say, you do have a way with dreams."

Laura looked at the man who had stepped from her imagination, a dream made flesh and blood. Light tumbled from the fixture overhead, sliding golden fingers along the smooth curve of his shoulder. How many times had she nestled her head against that strong shoulder in dreams?

Memories surged from hidden corners of her mind, memories of strong arms closing around her, keeping her safe. Warmth flickered inside of her, the heat of longing seeping into her blood, tingling her skin. What would it be like to feel his arms close around her and know the reality of her fantasy?

Connor looked up from the book he held as though he sensed her watching him. With his gaze he touched her, every feature of her face, as though he had been away from her a lifetime, as though he needed the sight of her as much as he needed air to breathe. Yet, caught in the strong tether of his gaze, she could not draw breath into her lungs; she felt the emotion inside of him, a mirror of the emotion dwelling inside of her, reaching for her.

"Aunt Sophie." She turned away from him, frightened by the intensity of her feelings for this man. "Send him back. Please make him disappear."

"Laura, I don't understand. Why would you want him to disappear?"

"Because he isn't real. At any moment he could disappear, fade, vanish, dissolve in the sunlight."

"He isn't a snowman, Laura."

"Aunt Sophie, please. You have to send him back."

Sophie sighed, her gaze lingering on the man who stood watching them as though he were trying to absorb everything they said. "All right, I'll send him back. But I believe you're making a mistake."

"And I believe I might be losing my mind," Laura said, rubbing her fingertips against her throbbing temples.

"Laura," Connor whispered, moving toward her, smiling as though he wanted to ease her fears.

Laura backed away as he drew near, avoiding the warmth of his touch when he reached for her. He dropped his hand to his side. There was no anger in his eyes at her rejection, no surprise, only patience and an infuriating trace of amusement. "Aunt Sophie, please get rid of him."

Sophie studied a page in the journal, then glanced up at the man. "Hear me, Lady of the moon. Your pull is great. You move the tides. Now pull Laura's beloved from her side."

Laura held her breath and waited. The breeze whispered against the windows, tossing snow against the glass. The fire crackled on the hearth. Connor smiled down at her.

"Try again."

Sophie cleared her throat and tried the incantation

once more. Connor winked at Laura.

Laura glared at Sophie. "Why isn't this working?"

"I don't know." Sophie leafed through the book. "Perhaps I'm not using the right incantation. I am rather new at this."

"Aunt Sophie, you do remember Salem, that little town just a few miles from here? Can you imagine what might happen to us if anyone suspected we were dabbling in witchcraft?" Laura looked straight into her aunt's wide blue eyes. "Perhaps you should try something else."

"Yes, of course." Sophie leafed through the journal. "I remember reading something about creating one's own incantations. Let's see." She pressed her fingertip to her chin and closed her eyes.

Laura glanced up at Connor. He was watching her in that quiet way that spoke to her more eloquently than any man had ever spoken to her. She was certain they had spoken in her dreams. She remembered telling him things she had never told anyone. "Strange, I thought he could speak English," she whispered.

"Pardon me, Laura?"

"Nothing." Laura shook her head, dismissing her thoughts as sheer folly. "Go on with it, please."

Sophie cleared her throat. "A man sublime, yet wrong in this time."

Connor crossed his arms over his chest, studying Sophie as she fumbled for words. Laura watched him, feeling a moment of regret when she realized he was about to disappear. She curled her hands into tight balls at her sides to keep from touching him one last time.

He had to leave. He couldn't possibly stay. No, they must send him back. Quickly.

"So back you must climb," Sophie said, "while the clock finds its chime. So fly away, fleeting as the day."

40

In a carved niche between bookcases, the grandfather clock chimed, deep, resonant tones pealing, brass hands reeling around the clock's face.

"Oh, bother!"

Laura ran to the clock. Brass hands flew around the polished face, clicking off Roman numerals, spinning like a pinwheel in a gale.

"Do something!" Laura shouted over the deep chiming of the clock.

"Let's see."

Laura glanced back at her aunt. "Stop it before someone comes in here to see what's wrong."

"Ah, clock by the wall . . ." Sophie leafed through the book.

"Aunt Sophie!"

Sophie pointed at the clock. "Stop! I command you to stop!"

The mainspring popped, hitting the mahogany case like a gun exploding. The chimes faded on a sour note. Delicate brass hands wilted like daisies in the sun, swinging together over the elegant brass VI.

"I did it!"

Laura turned toward Sophie. "This clock was made by a nephew of Nathan Hale."

"Yes, dear, I know." Sophie glanced down at the open journal. "Perhaps I can fix it."

"No!"

Sophie looked up from the journal. "But I'm certain if I—"

"Please don't try." Laura had visions of the elegant old clock bursting into a pile of splinters. "Not now."

"Very well, dear. I'll concentrate on our other problem." Sophie looked up at Connor. "Now what shall I try?"

Laura glanced at Connor. He was watching her, a smile lingering on his lips, curiosity aglow in his beautiful eyes. What must he think of all of this? "Aunt Sophie, you don't think anything you do will harm him?"

"Oh, no, I'm certain it couldn't. It says right here that the power of the Earth Mother cannot be used to do evil."

The sound of the mainspring exploding echoed in Laura's ears. "Not on purpose."

Sophie smiled. "Do you want him to stay?"

"No. Of course not. I simply . . ." Laura glanced away from Connor, staring at the moonlight glowing against the windows. "Please be careful."

"I will, dear. I'm certain I can come up with the right incantation, if I just take a moment to read a few of these pages once again."

Laura halted in the center of the library. She glanced at the watch pinned to her bodice. Three o'clock in the morning. And all was not well. She sighed and plunged back into her pacing, her circuit pulling her toward the windows she had shuttered hours ago.

"Laura, dear, I'm exhausted just looking at you. Why don't you sit a while?"

"I can't." Laura pivoted on her heel. She stared at the man who looked more at home in her library than she did, watching him flip the pages in a book. She believed he was now devouring a hefty tome on the history of Massachusetts.

"I must say you are wonderfully clever, Connor." Sophie lowered the journal to her lap, sighing as she dropped her head back against the ivory and burgundy stripes of the silk-upholstered armchair in which she sat. "I am amazed at how quickly you've picked up our language."

Connor glanced up from the book, smiling at Sophie. "This language you call English, it comes from pieces of other languages, those I have already made my own."

Earlier, while he dashed through the Latin-to-English dictionary, before he consumed Webster's Dictionary, Aunt Sophie had slipped her shawl over his naked shoulders, afraid he might catch a chill.

So there he sat, this beautiful figment of her imagination, in a burgundy velvet wing-back chair near the fire, his black mane tumbling in thick waves to the delicate ivory cashmere shawl covering shoulders that tested the breadth of the wide chair. He sat as regal and straight as a prince, with his long legs crossed, open book perched on one muscular thigh, flipping pages as though all he needed to do was glance at a page to know the contents. And Laura was beginning to believe that was true.

Connor glanced up from his book, smiling at her in that soft, embracing way that made her want to trace the curve of his lips with her fingertips. Oh, they really had to find a way to send him back.

"I need your assistance," he said, his words tinged with an intriguing lilt.

She had spent the past few hours pronouncing words, thousands of them, that Connor had pointed out to her in the books he was reading, this on top of naming every object in the room. She drew a deep, steadying breath before she moved to his side, firming her resolve to remain unaffected by this man. "What do you need?"

He pointed to a word. "Pronounce, please."

She rested her hand on the back of his chair and leaned closer to see the word he indicated. Citrus and spice, an intoxicating scent drifted with the heat of his skin, ambushing her best intentions.

She tried not to notice the way the firelight slipped into his midnight hair, mining sapphire in the ebony strands. Her fingers curled against the burgundy velvet. Was his hair really as silky as it looked?

"Laura?" he asked, tilting his head toward her.

"What?" she whispered, looking into the bluest eyes she had ever seen.

A glint of mischief lit those blue eyes as a far too knowing smile curved his lips. "The word."

He knew. She jumped back from him as though he were a cobra about to strike. The rogue knew exactly what wayward paths her thoughts had taken. "Transcendentalism."

He frowned. "Traan . . . sinden . . . lism."

Laura dragged air into her lungs. "Transcendentalism."

"Tran-scen-den-tal-ism." He laughed as though pleased with the sound of the word as it rolled off of his tongue. "And this means?"

Laura glanced over her shoulder, looking for help, more than just the meaning of transcendentalism. Sophie was watching her as though she were fitting together the pieces of a puzzle, a smile lifting the corners of her lips. There would be no help from that quarter.

Laura glared at Connor. "What is transcendentalism doing in a history of Massachusetts?"

"The book speaks of a man named Emerson, his poetry, and this tran-scen-den-tal-ism."

"It's a way of looking at life, a certain mysticism. Those who believe in transcendentalism hold to certain spiritual laws. They believe in the openness of the human mind to unseen powers." Laura rubbed the stiff muscles at the back of her neck, staring down at Connor, for the first time in her life seeing some reason in Emerson's theories. "They believe in miracles."

Connor nodded. "I understand these things."

Laura turned away from him, marching until she had put the space of the room between them. She took refuge behind the heavy mahogany of her father's desk, where she sank to the soft brown leather chair. "Aunt

Sophie, have you found anything in that journal that might help?"

"Darling, I'm numb." Sophie closed the journal. "Perhaps we could get back to this later, after we've both had some sleep."

"But what are we going to do with him?"

"Since I'm certain Fiona is in bed, we'll have to prepare a guest room."

"And what do we tell Fiona and the other servants when they discover our guest is a barbarian? And what about Father? He'll be home tomorrow evening."

Connor looked from Laura to Sophie, as though he were following every word of their conversation, amusement glimmering in his beautiful eyes.

"I've been thinking about that." Sophie tapped her forefinger against her chin. "We can say he is a cousin who arrived late last night from England."

"England?" Connor asked.

"It is a country across the ocean from us." Sophie stood and offered Connor her hand. "Come, my dear young man, let me show you."

"How can we possibly pass him off as English?" Laura watched Sophie lead Connor to the globe perched in a carved wooden stand near the desk. "He can scarcely speak English."

"I'm sure it will take him little time at all to master the language." Sophie turned the globe with the tips of her fingers, studying the land masses as she spoke. "Until then we can say he is ill, and keep him secluded."

"Secluded." Laura drummed her fingers on the green desk pad. "Much more of this and I shall be secluded, in the lunatic hospital."

"Think of how he must feel, Laura. Whisked away from his home, plopped down in a strange place, where people don't even speak the same language he does."

Laura looked at Connor, wondering if he did feel a

trace of fear. He stood beside Sophie, his weight balanced evenly, his feet slightly apart, his arms folded across his wide chest, as though he were accustomed to command—a man born to lead warriors into battle. Only the lacy shawl draped over his broad shoulders spoiled his regal stance. And his eyes—there was amusement in his eyes, intelligence in the stunning blue depths, but not a trace of fear. "If you ask me, this man is enjoying every second of this."

Connor nodded. "I do enjoy this time with you."

Laura dragged her gaze from his face, feeling heat rise in her cheeks. "The man is nothing short of infuriating."

"Now, Laura, I think we should try to make him feel comfortable and welcome while he is with us." Sophie tapped her finger against the globe. "Here, Connor. This is England."

Connor glanced down to the globe. "England," he whispered, tracing the outline of the country with his fingertips. He moved his hand. "This place, this is from where I came."

"Laura, dear," Sophie said, looking at her niece. "He has pointed out Ireland."

"How could he be from Ireland?" Laura stood and walked to Connor's side, looking down at the place on which his finger rested. "He's a figment of my imagination."

"Figment?" Connor lifted one black brow in question as he gazed down at her. "Explain this figment."

Laura drew in a breath. "It means something you've made up."

He frowned, obviously not understanding her completely.

"A vision in my mind." Laura tapped her temple with her fingertip. "You aren't real."

He shook his head. Before she realized what he was

doing, he closed his warm fingers around her wrist and brought her hand to his chest just above his heart. "Real."

Laura caught her breath at the feel of his skin beneath her hand. He was so warm, infinitely alluring, an abundance of tempting male textures. Heat flared inside of her, a scorching wave that started at her waist and surged upward until her ears tingled.

She jerked her hand back, curling her fingertips against her palm. The smile he gave her told her he knew exactly how much he intrigued her. "Oh, you are an infuriating creature. I don't know how I ever could have imagined anyone so . . . so . . . unmannerly."

He laughed, a resonant sound that came from deep in his chest.

"You know, Laura, perhaps he didn't come from your imagination after all."

"If he didn't come from my imagination, then just where did he come from?"

Connor tapped the globe. "Here."

"Ireland," Sophie said. "But you're not from the Ireland of today, are you, Connor?"

47

Chapter Three

"This is the year 1889." Connor stared down at the globe, words of prophesy whispering in his memory. *You must abandon all else and travel farther than you have ever imagined*—Aisling had spoken those words last night—a thousand years ago.

He spun the globe with a flick of his fingers. A soft hissing sound issued from the brass rod as the globe rotated wildly. "It seems I have traveled a thousand years."

"A thousand years." Laura shook her head as though she wanted to clear her senses. "I don't care where he came from. I only want him to go back."

Connor glanced at Laura, a smile curving his lips. How odd it was to look upon her, to see her both as a stranger and a woman he had loved all of his life.

"Aunt Sophie, you must get rid of the man."

"We'll work on it later, dear. I need some sleep." Sophie patted Laura's shoulder, then looked up at Connor. "If you're to be my cousin, I'm afraid you will have to be from England. Now what do you think of the name Paxton? Connor Paxton?"

"It is the way of things here? This second name?"

"Yes," Sophie said, smiling up at him. "Just as my second name is Chandler, and Laura's is Sullivan."

"I understand. It is a way to identify families."

"My, but you are clever," Sophie said.

He knew he would need all of his resources to survive in this century. "Tell me, where is here?"

"We live in Boston, which is in the state of Massachusetts." She touched the small dot of Boston on the globe. "We are one of the United States of America."

"I have been to this place before." Connor studied the globe, turning it on its axis. "This Boston was not here. Only scattered villages, and people of a different tongue."

"You've been here before?" Laura asked.

"Yes." He looked at her, sensing the confusion and fear inside of her. "When I searched for you."

"You searched for me?"

He brushed the back of his fingers over the curve of her cheek, her skin softer than he had ever imagined. "I had to find you."

"This is nonsense." Laura stepped back from him, the color draining from her face. "You are no more than an illusion."

"An illusion?" Connor grinned as he gazed down at her. "Perhaps you are the illusion, my beautiful *Edaina*."

Laura released her breath in a hiss between her teeth. "Aunt Sophie, do something with him."

"I think we can all use some sleep."

"Sleep?" Laura stared at her aunt as though Sophie had lost her mind.

"Yes, dear." Sophie smiled as she slipped her arm

through Connor's. "Oh, it will be a marvelous adventure, teaching you all this century has to offer, Connor. Don't you agree, Laura?"

"An adventure? This is nothing short of disaster."

Sophie shook her head. "Really, Laura, you must start looking at the positive aspects."

"I would if I could see any positive aspects."

Sophie glanced up at Connor before casting Laura a meaningful look. "Open your eyes, dear."

Connor didn't need his power to perceive emotions to read what was in Laura's green eyes—she was terrified of him.

He resisted the urge to touch her, to reassure her in any way he could, knowing she would spurn him. Aisling had warned him of the difficulties and the risks he would face if he chose to go to Laura. Yet he would risk his very life to claim this woman.

He glanced down at Sophie as he walked beside her across the library, wondering what part she had played in his journey to this century. Sophie cradled the journal against her chest as though it were a babe. The book intrigued him. It seemed she needed the journal to conjure, and from what he had seen the lady needed all the help she could find. She fiddled with magic like a drunken Druid. "How did you come to have that book?"

Sophie smiled as she looked at him. "A few days ago our butler discovered it hidden away beneath the floor of the wine cellar."

"So it only recently came into your possession." She was a fledgling; that explained her wayward incantations. Still, it didn't explain why a book of enchantments was in a mortal's wine cellar. His people guarded their magic well; it was the only way they could survive.

"Without the journal, I would never have been able to bring you here."

"And we wouldn't be in this tangle." Laura walked

beside Sophie, looking like a prisoner being led to the stake.

"It will all work out for the best, I'm certain." Sophie patted Laura's arm. "Think of it this way, if Ridley hadn't found the journal, I would never have realized I was a witch."

"Aunt Sophie, you cannot be a witch. There are no such things as witches." Laura halted at the door and turned to face her aunt. "There has to be some logical explanation for this."

"There is more to life than logic," Sophie said, tapping the journal. "And since we are both descendants from a Paxton, perhaps you're also—"

"I am not a witch!"

Sophie shrugged. "You can't really be certain until you try one of the incantations."

"I am quite certain I am *not* a witch."

"You have to admit, Laura"—Sophie glanced up at Connor—"it is all truly remarkable."

"Remarkable is one way to describe it. Catastrophic might be a better word."

Connor laughed, winning a chilling glare from Laura. "Perhaps you will let me read the journal," he said, opening the door for the ladies.

"Of course," Sophie said, offering him the leather-bound book.

"Aunt Sophie!" Laura snatched the journal from Sophie's hand. "I don't think we should let anyone read this thing."

"But only a Paxton can make the enchantments work."

"All the same. I think we should put this in a safe place."

"Very well, dear." Sophie looked up at Connor, an apology in her huge blue eyes. "I hope you don't mind."

"I understand." There were other ways to get a

51

glimpse at that journal, he thought. He glanced at Laura. She stood hugging the book to her chest, staring at him as though he had just stepped from a dragon ship wielding his sword. The lady was certainly the most intriguing challenge he had ever encountered.

"Laura, dear, if you want me to create a spell to send him back, I need the journal."

Laura hesitated a moment before she handed the journal to Sophie. "Please be careful."

"I'll be careful." Sophie fluttered from the room.

Very careful, Connor thought. Each time Sophie got that determined look in her eyes and started tossing together an incantation, he got the uneasy feeling the sky was about to fall.

Laura gave Connor a wide berth, her back brushing the door casement as she sidled past him into the hall. Did she think he would bite?

The lady was going to prove only one of many challenges he must face. To win his lady, he must first master this century.

Connor ran his fingertips across the carved wooden panels covering the walls as he walked beside Sophie and Laura down the hall. They used much wood here, the walls, the floor, all smooth and polished. He paused, examining three candles that were fitted against the wall in a brass holder. Yet they were like no candles he had ever seen. It was as if a bit of sunlight had been captured, contained within small glass chambers fitted atop metal cylinders.

"Incandescent light," he said, recalling the words Laura had taught him. "Energy from electricity."

"Come along," Laura whispered, her words a hiss in the long corridor.

He glanced down at her, smiling into her serious face. Incandescent light glowed golden upon her delicate features. She was even more beautiful than in his dreams. And the dreams had not prepared him for the reality of her: the warmth of her skin reaching out to him as she stood before him; the luscious scent of her, spring flowers warmed by the sun. It was all he could do to keep from taking her in his arms. He wanted to feel her softness pressed against him, brush his lips across hers. . . .

"Don't just stand there smiling." Laura tugged on his arm. "Come along before someone sees you."

"Now, Laura, think of how extraordinary this must be for him."

"He can study the lights later. If someone should happen to see him, we could never explain his appearance. Why, the man looks like a marauding Viking."

Connor grinned. "My father is a Viking."

Laura muttered something about a nightmare under her breath. From the look in her eyes, he was glad she was not carrying a weapon.

"It's three in the morning," Sophie said. "I doubt anyone is up and about besides us."

"If one of the servants has trouble sleeping, we're doomed." Laura tugged on Connor's arm. He smiled down at her. "You might find this amusing, but I don't intend to end up burned at the stake just to satisfy your curiosity."

"Salem." Connor covered her hand with his, frowning as he recalled a dark chapter in one of the books he had read. "I will allow no one to hurt you."

Laura snatched her hand from his arm and the shelter of his hand. "Will you just come along!"

"As you wish, my *Edaina*," he said, watching her cheeks deepen to a dusky rose.

"Stop calling me that!" She turned on her heel and marched down the hall.

"Give her time, Connor," Sophie said, resting her hand on his arm.

"I have given her a thousand years. I shall give her a thousand more if that is what it takes to win her heart."

Sophie smiled. "I have a feeling it won't take you that long."

Laura was buried, encased in ice, Connor thought, admiring the slim line of her stiff back. Yet even ice melted in the heat of the sun. And like the sun he would warm her.

The corridor opened to a large entry hall dominated by a broad staircase with carved and twisted balusters. A brass fixture dangled on a thick chain suspended from the ceiling, a dozen of those strange candles tossing light against the polished wooden floor and walls.

He pivoted in a circle. Paintings hung from the paneled walls: landscapes, portraits—all so real. Doors stood open on either side of the hall, and a dark corridor ran back from the staircase where more doors opened into the shadows. Where did they lead?

"Come along." Laura tugged on his arm, urging him up the stairs.

Connor caught a glimpse of the full moon through the arched window at the top of the landing before Laura prodded him to hurry along. She threw open one of the doors at the top of the stairs. She touched the wall just inside the room, conjuring light to flow from a crystal-and-brass fixture suspended from the ceiling. Connor followed her into the room, staring at the riches held within.

Shades of blue and ivory mingled in the carpet beneath his feet, intricate wreaths of flowers and medallions stitched in wool, stretching to all four corners of the room. The sofa by the hearth, the chairs, all had carved arms and legs of a red-brown wood, the seats and backs covered in dark blue velvet. Dark blue velvet draped the three windows and formed a canopy over a large bed.

"Your father is king of this Boston?" Connor asked, touching the wall near the bed, his fingertips sliding against blue-and-white-striped silk.

"The United States of America is not a monarchy," Laura said.

"Yes, I remember this now. I read of the tea dumped into the harbor." He turned to look at Laura, smiling, hoping to coax a smile in return. He failed. She stood with her hands clasped at her waist, staring at him with eyes the pure green of meadow grass in spring, looking as though she wished she could strangle him. "Because of this revolution, everyone lives in luxury during this century?"

Laura shook her head. "Unfortunately, everyone cannot afford a house such as this."

"Laura's father runs a great shipping company. His wealth allows such luxuries," Sophie said.

"It was the same in my time." Connor sat on the edge of the bed, smiling as he sank into the soft mattress. "Though even a king did not possess luxury such as this."

"There are many wonders to show you, Connor," Sophie said. "Tomorrow we shall start. For now, I'll fetch some fresh linens so we can prepare your bed."

"Wait!" Laura said as Sophie headed for the door. "You aren't going to leave me alone with this man?"

Sophie waved her hand, dismissing Laura's protest. "I'll be right back. Do show Connor the sitting room and the bath," she said, her skirts swaying as she hurried from the room.

Laura stared at him, one hand at her throat, the other clenched into a fist at her waist. She looked as though she were torn between the need to run and the need to stay and face her demon. He being the demon, of course.

"Are your chambers located near mine?"

"Where my chambers are is no concern to you."

Not a good beginning, he thought, rising from the bed. "You have no need to fear me. I would never do anything to harm you."

Laura tilted her chin. "I'm not afraid of you."

"I'm glad." He moved toward her as though he were approaching a wild swan poised for flight, his booted footsteps silent against the thick carpet.

"What are you doing?" she asked, stepping back as he drew near.

"I want only to touch you," he whispered, running his hand down her arm. "I've waited a lifetime to touch you."

Her emotions flooded him as he touched her: fear and anger, doubt and desire; he perceived all that he had only sensed without this physical contact. She stared up at him, green eyes wide. As he slid his hand back up her arm, her lips parted on a startled sigh. Yet she stayed, trembling, like a wild swan, both entranced and frightened by his touch.

Her glorious hair was swept back from her face, caught up in thick coils on top of her head. Golden light glowed on the rich, dark gold tresses. From his dreams he knew her hair would fall thick and waving to her waist once freed from pins and combs. He wondered what it might be like to slip his hands into the carefully fashioned curls, releasing the heavy mass to fall against his bare chest. His muscles tightened in response.

"You shouldn't look at me that way. It isn't proper."

"In what way do you mean?"

Laura moistened her lips, a quick slide of the tip of her tongue that left an inviting sheen. "You're looking at me as though you're thinking of . . . things gentlemen in this century do not think around a lady."

He stared at her lips, tracing the trembling curve with his gaze. Would she taste as sweet as he imagined?

"Will you teach me how men of this century behave around a lady?"

"I can assure you they do not behave like a marauding Viking."

"And would you believe me if I said I have never gone raiding, that I have never raped or pillaged?"

She glanced to the sword dangling at his side. "I suppose you need that sword to weed your garden."

"A man must always be prepared to defend himself against attack."

"Not in this century. Men are civilized now."

"I am glad there is no need for weapons. In my time even a peaceful man used a sword to defend his home."

She looked up at him, her eyes narrow with suspicion. "And your home is Ireland?"

"My home was the island of Erin. What is now called Ireland. But I have spent much time traveling the world. My people have always been traders, shipping goods to distant lands."

"You speak of Vikings as though they were simple traders, shipping merchandise much the same as my father does."

He smiled. "We have much in common."

She shook her head as though she couldn't allow herself to believe him, as though she needed to hold on to some shred of logic. "This cannot be."

He wanted to take her in his arms, to chase away her fears, to convince her everything was now as it should be. He stroked his hand upward along her arm, because he sensed it was all she would allow, absorbing the tremor that rippled through her. "You have nothing to fear, my *Edaina*."

"Why do you call me that?"

"Because it is what you are to me." He stroked her arm, learning the curve of her elbow, the slim line of her forearm, the delicate bones of her wrist. "My *Edaina*, my soul mate."

She drew a ragged breath. "Who are you?"

"You know me." He cupped her cold hand in his warm grasp. She stared at him as he lifted her hand to his lips. The delicate fragrance of her skin filled his senses as he pressed his lips to her damp palm, reminding him of the flowers in their secret place. "You've known me since we were children and we played together in a lush green valley that was always filled with wildflowers."

"This is insane." She stepped back, breaking away from him.

"No. It's not insane."

"You aren't real."

"I am real. I am Connor, Prince of Wexford, son of King Setric. I was born in 862 A.D., on the island of Erin."

Laura shook her head. "How can this be?"

"I can't explain how you and I are joined, but I know we are. Joined in a way that defies time itself."

She clasped her hands at her wrist as though she needed to contain the emotions he sensed swirling like a whirlpool inside of her. "There has to be some logical explanation for all of this."

"You called me. That's why I journeyed a thousand years. To be with you."

"I don't know what you are, or who you are." Laura drew a deep draft of air into her lungs. "I do know I want you to go back to where you came from."

"No, you don't." Connor leaned down and kissed the tip of her nose. She jumped as though she had been stung by a bee. "And I intend to prove to you just how much you want me to stay."

Laura's lips parted, her breath rushing out in a heated gasp that warmed his cheek. "Why, you arrogant . . ." She hesitated, denying her own anger, as though it were indecent to feel good, honest rage. "I assure you, I do not want you to stay."

Connor frowned. "If you wish to scream at me, why don't you?"

"A lady certainly does not scream."

Connor considered this a moment. "A lady is still human, is she not? And humans are ruled by emotion."

"It is apparent you know nothing at all about ladies."

"Tell me, is a lady also a woman?"

"Of course."

He grinned. "Then I do know something of ladies."

Laura's lips pulled into a tight line. "I suppose you have known more than a few women."

"None who compare to you," he whispered, brushing his hand across her shoulder. He flicked his fingertips over the tiny curls at her nape. "And none I wish to know the way I want to know you, in every way imaginable."

Laura gasped and slapped away his hand.

"So it seems the two of you are getting on splendidly," Sophie said, breezing into the room, her arms loaded with white linen crowned with a small pile of blue sapphire silk.

"Please excuse me for not helping, Aunt Sophie. But I find I cannot abide this man a moment longer."

Chapter Four

Connor watched Laura march from the room, admiring the way her odd gown hugged her narrow waist before flaring into a small bundle of material projecting at the rear that twitched with each step she took. "She is like a flickering flame trapped in crystal, all emotion contained inside of her."

"Yes." Sophie dropped her bundle on the chair by the bed. "I'm afraid Laura was taught from the time she was a small child to suppress her emotions. She was never allowed to play as other children were."

Was this the reason she had reached out to him when they were children? He remembered the mischievous little girl who had played with him in their secret valley, as though she were a wild swan skimming the wind. "It is strange; she is at once the same and different from the woman I know from my dreams."

"There's a certain freedom in our dreams, the freedom to be who we want to be. I'm afraid Laura has never known that freedom outside of her dreams. She was taught to be quiet and docile, even though it's clear there is a fine fiery spirit hidden beneath that carefully constructed facade."

"Yes, I can sense her fire." And he could sense the woman he knew and loved buried deep beneath the icy veneer of this Laura of Boston. He had traveled a thousand years to claim that woman.

"All of my life, I've been called a dreamer, a hopeless romantic. I suppose I've always believed in miracles, and here you are. Living proof." Sophie smiled up at Connor. "I believe you and Laura were meant to find one another. I hope you can free her from the prison that has been built around her emotions."

"But you will try to send me away from her."

"I'm afraid I did give Laura my word." Sophie squeezed his arm. "You do understand."

Connor nodded. "You are honor bound."

"Yes." Sophie gave him a reassuring smile. "Still, I have a feeling my feeble attempts at magic will not be able to tear you and Laura apart."

In truth he was not certain what her wayward incantations might bring. "I will do everything in my power to stay. Nothing must take me from her side."

"I'll put my faith in you." Sophie patted his arm. "Now let's see about getting you settled."

After helping Sophie cover the bed with white linen and blankets, Connor followed her into the adjoining bath. White marble squares covered the floor and walls, and there were porcelain basins of various sizes. Sophie rattled off the names of each object in the room: bathtub, sink, and the "necessary."

"This is for . . . ah . . . it's . . ." Sophie pulled on the brass chain attached to a porcelain box above the seat of the necessary. Water rushed into the porcelain basin beneath the oak seat, swirling, gurgling, like a small

61

whirlpool, finishing with a loud *whoosh*. A small amount of water trickled into the basin and it was still once more. "It's for when you need to . . . nature and all."

Connor smiled as a blush rose to stain her cheeks. "I think I know what it is for."

Sophie sighed, rolling her eyes toward the ceiling. "Thank goodness."

He followed her back into the bedroom, wondering about the nature of this woman who was Laura's blood relative. Was she one of his people without knowing it? What about Laura? *There are no such things as witches*— her words echoed in his mind. Magic terrified her. He terrified her. She thought he was a marauding Viking. What would she do if she realized he was one of the *Sidhe*? He released his breath in a long sigh as he imagined Laura's reaction when he told her the blood of his mother's people, the *Tuatha De Danann*, ran through his veins.

It was best to keep his own abilities concealed until he was certain how Laura would accept them. At the moment he was faced with the difficult task of making her accept him solely as a man.

"I took the liberty of borrowing some clothes from Laura's father." Sophie lifted a tunic and trousers of dark blue silk from the chair beside the bed. "Pajamas," she said, offering the clothes to him.

"Pajamas." Connor took the garments from her hands, the silk cool against his skin. What had men become that they would wear such feminine garments? "This is what men wear in this century?"

"Only to bed."

He released the breath he had been holding. "But why would they wear garments in bed?"

Sophie looked up at him, color rising in her cheeks. "You don't?"

"No."

"Not even in winter?"

"Never."

"I see." She cleared her throat, and he was certain she was trying to cover a giggle. "Well, I suppose there really isn't any need for them."

"Yes, I see no need for them," he said, handing her the pajamas.

"We'll see if Daniel's clothes fit you tomorrow." She turned and walked toward the door, the pajamas dangling over her arm. "If you need anything, just tap on my door. I'm just two doors down on your right." She turned and smiled at him, her hand resting on the brass door handle. "I hope you have a pleasant night."

"Thank you." He thought of the moon glowing full and bright, the dreams awaiting him. "I'm certain I will."

It never rained here, in this valley Laura had only visited in dreams. The surrounding mountains pierced a sky that was forever blue, looking like jagged black diamonds, crystals trapped in the stone sparkling in the sunlight. Yet water tumbled down the side of one of the rugged mountains that cradled the valley, splashing against the black stones, plunging toward a lake in a glittering crystal cascade.

"Connor." Laura turned, searching for him. Fear seeped like ice into her blood when she couldn't find him.

"Connor!" Emerald grass and bright wildflowers of blue, white, yellow, and pink bowed to her as she ran toward the lake that spread in a glistening crystal pool from the base of the falls. She stood on the smooth black stone edging the lake, searching the water for a lone swimmer, finding no one. "Connor, where are you?"

"I'm here with you."

Laura pivoted at the sound of Connor's voice. He stood a few feet away from her, dressed in nothing except a pair of breeches, black leather hugging his narrow hips, the long, muscular length of his legs. "I was afraid you hadn't come."

He smiled as he moved toward her. "Nothing could keep me away from you."

She ran to him, and he opened his arms, catching her as she threw her arms around his neck, lifting her until her feet dangled above the ground.

"My *Edaina*," he whispered, holding her as though he were afraid someone would tear her away from him.

"Promise me you'll always be here for me."

He brushed his lips against her ear. "Always."

She pressed her lips to his neck, breathing the intoxicating scent of citrus and musk deep into her lungs. She wore no corset or petticoats in this place. Nothing but a veil of white silk protected her from the thrust of hardened muscles and potent male heat.

The warmth of his bare chest seeped through her gown, drenching her skin in his radiance. Finely etched muscles flexed against her breasts as his sigh warmed her cheek. He shifted her in his grasp, slipping one arm beneath her knees, lifting her in his powerful embrace.

Cool strands of emerald grass cushioned her back as he lowered her to the ground. He settled on his side, planting his elbow in the soft grass, propping his chin in his hand as he smiled down at her, his long body stretched beside her.

She touched his cheek, traced the curve of his smile with her fingertip. "I've always felt safe here."

"Nothing can harm you here."

There was a lure to this place. Deep inside it pulled on her, as though she belonged here more than she belonged in the real world. It was bewitching. And in ways it was frightening.

"You're troubled." He slipped his hand into her hair, lifting unbound waves to the sunlight, letting the golden strands spill through his fingers. "Tell me what's wrong."

How could she tell him when she couldn't find the answers inside herself? His warmth reached out to her, stroking her through the white silk of her gown, making her long for something she couldn't even name. She wasn't certain when their relationship had altered, when innocence had been consumed by desire, but it had been consumed like a log on a hearth, succumbing to the flames.

Heaven help her, she wasn't sure of herself.

She wasn't certain of what she might do if she surrendered to temptation and touched him as she longed to touch him. And she wanted to touch him, to learn every texture, every smooth curve and hard line of his body. What were the consequences of surrendering to desire?

"I wonder sometimes"—she brushed her palm over a daisy that swayed in the breeze beside her—"if one day I shall be forced to choose between this place and the world beyond this realm."

He cupped her cheek in his warm palm, coaxing her to look at him. Sunlight glowed like a soft golden nimbus around him. "I love you, Laura."

"I love you." She stared up into his eyes, seeing the promise of forever in the endless blue depths, feeling each beat of her heart throb at the base of her neck. "So much it frightens me."

"I would never harm you." He brushed his lips against her cheek. "I would give my life to protect you."

She tried to breathe, the air catching in the emotion squeezing her chest. "Never leave me, Connor," she

65

said, sinking her hand into the soft hair at his nape, squeezing the silky black strands in her fist. "Promise me you'll never leave me."

He ran his fingertip over her brow, smoothing away her frown. "Where would I go without you?"

"Stay with me forever."

"Forever." He lowered his head, pressing his lips against the pulse beating wildly in her neck.

Laura held her breath, enchanted by the gentle touch of his lips. He spread kisses upward along her neck, lingering when he reached the sensitive skin beneath her ear, his breath warming her, his lips soft and firm against her. Tingles radiated across her skin, gathering like shimmering embers in pools at the tips of her breasts.

"Be mine, Laura." He splayed his hand across her ribs, his long fingers grazing the underside of her aching breast. "For eternity."

The longing in his dark, velvety voice whispered to the need inside of her. Could they be together for eternity?

"You're the missing half of my soul." He brushed his lips across hers, a delicate graze that left her craving more.

She slid her hands across his shoulders, absorbing the heat of sun-drenched skin, needing him in ways she was only beginning to understand.

"I must have you, Laura." He pressed his open mouth against her neck. She whimpered as he swirled the damp heat of his tongue over her skin. "Yield to me, my beautiful *Edaina*."

She shivered, realizing the woman she knew as Laura Sullivan would vanish if she should give her heart and soul and body to this man. He would alter her in some irrevocable way.

"Become one with me."

Slowly he slid his hand upward, over the curve of her breast, cupping her, lifting the plush weight of her. Through the silk of her gown he squeezed the tip of her breast. Sensation splintered within her, skittering in all directions like embers shooting upward from a raging fire. He would consume her in the fire he kindled within her. She could feel the flames licking over her skin.

"Yield to me, Laura."

Laura sat up in bed, breathing hard, as though she had been running for miles. She glanced around her bedroom, latching onto each familiar sight, a lifeline dragging her from the pool of her dreams.

Sunlight peeked through the cracks where the jade green brocade drapes met at her windows; it fell in strands of golden light, slipping across the Aubusson carpet of green and gold and ivory. It was morning.

Laura fell back against her pillow, staring up into the dark folds of the canopy above her bed. The chaste white flannel of her nightgown clung to her damp skin. She tingled all over, as though Connor's hands were still stroking her.

What was wrong with her? How could she imagine such wicked things? Or was she imagining them?

You've known me since we were children and we played together in a lush green valley that was always filled with wildflowers. How had Connor known of the valley?

"That man," she whispered, throwing back the covers. She scrambled from the bed and snatched her sapphire blue velvet robe from the chair beside her bed. He was doing this. She didn't know how, but that Viking marauder was invading her dreams.

She shrugged into her robe as she marched toward the door. When she got her hands on him . . . Oh, he was going to regret the day he was born!

67

Chapter Five

Erin, A.D. 889

"I want to know what you've done with my son." Ciara paced in front of the stone hearth in Aisling's tower room. "His servant told me he disappeared soon after coming home from here last night."

Aisling shifted on the oak throne chair near the fire. "I have helped send Connor where he most wants to be."

"Where?"

"It matters not where he is, Ciara. You cannot reach him." Aisling drew a deep breath. "And I'm afraid you shall never be able to reach him again."

"What have you done?" Ciara grabbed her sister's shoulders, leaning over her, her ebony hair spilling over her shoulders, falling across Aisling's lap. "How could you send him away from his family?"

"It was for his own happiness." Aisling tried to

shield herself from the tempest of her sister's emotions, rage and fear throbbing in the air between them. "I have never turned my back when Connor needed me. And I will do what needs to be done to help find his *Edaina*."

Ciara shook her sister. "What have you done with my son?"

"I have helped send him to the woman destiny meant him to find."

Ciara straightened, staring down at Aisling with eyes narrowed by suspicion. "Who is this woman?"

"Her name is Laura, daughter of Sullivan."

"Laura. Such an odd name." Ciara flicked her ruby-colored skirts as she paced a few feet away from her sister, rushes stirring beneath her feet, releasing the scent of pine and herbs. "And you say you sent him to this woman because you believe destiny meant for their love to flourish?"

"Yes."

Ciara pivoted to face her sister, pinning Aisling in her sharp blue gaze. "I thought you didn't believe in the power of love."

Love. Aisling had never met a man she had considered loving. Still, she acknowledged an emptiness inside of her, a dark place waiting to be filled with light, a loneliness that wouldn't remain banished, no matter how hard she tried. "I believe in destiny."

"You believe in manipulating destiny. What reasons did you have for sending Connor to this woman?"

Aisling glanced away from her sister's stare, shielding her thoughts from Ciara's insistent probing. There were things her sister need not know. "As I said, I seek Connor's happiness."

"So you have. But I know you well. And I know you would not send him away without a purpose that suits you. He means too much to you."

"Yes, even though only a handful of years separate us, he is like a son to me." Aisling glanced at her sister. "If I were his mother, I would want him to be happy."

Ciara released her breath in a frustrated sigh. "Why can't I at least see him? Why must he become an exile?"

"It was the only way he had a chance for happiness. Even now I cannot be certain he will succeed in winning his lady's hand. But I know he had to go to her. He had to try. You must understand, this is for Connor's welfare."

"And I suppose I shall never see his wife, never look upon his children."

"You have two daughters and three other sons. Content yourself with them."

"How dare you! How dare you think I could cut Connor out of my life!"

A winter chill crept into the tower room, as icy as Ciara's stare. Aisling passed her hand over the fire, commanding the flames to leap on the stone hearth, dry logs crackling as they succumbed to the golden flames licking over them. "Take heart in knowing he is where he should be, Ciara."

"You don't understand. Connor is the only one of my children who shared my secrets, the only one who bore my gifts."

Aisling looked at her sister. "You were the one who always thought of Connor's gifts as annoyances, something to be kept from your other children and that Viking you call mate."

Ciara waved aside her sister's words. "Connor is my son, and I won't let you steal him."

"You must release him. You must let him find his own happiness."

Ciara shook her head. "Where is he, Aisling? I want to see my son."

"He has journeyed far, Ciara. You cannot reach him."

"How can this be?" Ciara stared at her sister. "I may have suppressed my powers, little sister, but I can still fly. I am still every bit as capable as you."

"Are you?" Aisling twitched the pendant she wore, the glitter of firelight on gold and emerald striking her sister's face. "As I recall, you cannot journey through time. You were always far too frightened to try."

Ciara stepped back, pressing her right hand to her heart. "You didn't send him on that journey?"

"He is in a place called Boston, in the year of 1889." Aisling smiled at her sister's look of horror. "It was where his destiny beckoned him."

"Aisling, you know it's forbidden by the Inner Circle."

"What right does the Inner Circle of Avallon have to dictate to me?"

"In case you forgot, sister, Avallon was created to protect our people."

"I do not need reminding." Every *Sidhe* knew of the colony that had been founded 5,000 years ago. Avallon was a sanctuary high on a secluded mountaintop in the heart of the great western forest, a place for those who had once lived in Atlantis. Within that sanctuary a coven had been formed by descendants of those who had once ruled that island nation, in an effort to protect the gifts of the *Tuatha De Danann*. Yet Aisling knew they would fail.

"The Inner Circle of Avallon cannot protect us, Ciara. In time even they will cease to channel the power of the goddess, because there will be too many who fear that power."

"We must obey the rules, Aisling."

Aisling waved aside Ciara's words, anger growing inside of her, resentment for the rules that kept her people prisoners. "I don't recognize rules made by the Inner Circle of Avallon. It is our right to move through

71

time the way a bird moves through the air. I shall not be denied my birthright."

"You must bring him back. Connor cannot stay in this Boston of 1889."

Aisling leaned back in her chair, her hands curling around the smooth wooden arms. "I must let him have his chance at happiness."

"What shall he do in this distant place? He shall be lost."

"He is intelligent, resourceful. He will make a place for himself."

"He is in this place alone, with none of his own kind. If anyone should suspect his true abilities . . ." Ciara rubbed her fingertips across her brow. "He could be destroyed. There would be no one to help him."

Aisling felt a hard hand squeeze her heart as she recalled the shadows she had seen lurking in Connor's future, the dark spots her power could not penetrate. "Connor will surmount any difficulties. You must have faith in him."

"He is all alone." Ciara pressed her hands to her face as though she intended to weep. Yet when she looked at her sister, there was steel glittering in her eyes. "I will not allow you to do this."

"You have no choice."

"We shall see, little sister." Ciara smiled, a slow curve of her lips that sent a chill seeping into Aisling's blood. "You are not the only one with the ability to alter destiny."

It was nothing more than bluster, Aisling assured herself. Her sister could do nothing to stop her plan. Yet she shivered as she watched Ciara storm from the room. Had it been a mistake to reveal Connor's location?

Aisling leaned back in her chair, staring into the flames, feeling a sense of impending disaster settle over her like a heavy cloak. She would have to be careful with Ciara, very careful. Nothing would upset her plans. Connor was right where he should be, and she intended to make sure he stayed there.

Chapter Six

Laura pounded on the door to Connor's bedroom. No answer. She hesitated a moment before she grasped the brass handle and threw open the door. Bright winter sunlight poured through the three large windows, casting squares of gold across the blue and ivory carpet.

He was gone.

A chill settled in her belly when she realized he had disappeared with the light of day. Had he ever truly existed?

She glanced around the room, looking for some trace of evidence to assure her he had once been here. The bed covers were thrown back, revealing the rumpled sheets where he had slept. For a few hours he had entered her life, this maddening man who had stepped from her dreams. She had touched him, felt the warmth of his skin. And now he was gone.

It was for the best, she thought, resting her fingertips on the pillow that had cradled his head, tracing the impression he had left in the soft feathers. Her throat tightened with an emotion she refused to acknowledge. She refused to grieve for the loss of a man who had no place in her life. He couldn't possibly have stayed. How could she ever have explained an Irish Viking to her father? And yet . . .

"Laura."

She jumped at the sound of that dark voice. Connor was walking toward her, the bathroom door open behind him.

His wet hair was slicked back from his brow, emphasizing the finely chiseled lines and angles of his face. Water dripped from the thick hair resting against his broad shoulders, droplets sliding down his chest, clinging, glistening in black curls. Aside from the white towel wrapped around his slim hips, he was bare. He looked for all the world a statue come to life, personified male perfection. Dear heaven, she couldn't breathe.

"Oh, my gracious!" Laura held up her hand as he drew near. But in that moment she wasn't sure if she meant to ward him off or touch him.

"Good morning." He took her outstretched hand as though she held it in invitation, strong fingers embracing her.

Laura couldn't form a single word. Her dream from the night before conspired with the reality of this man standing before her to ambush her senses. All she could do was stare. All she could think about was how it might feel to be held in his arms, to feel the strength of his body close around her, to taste those lips that were tilting into a wide, embracing smile.

"Did you sleep well?"

"Fine," she said, appalled at the breathless sound of her voice. It suddenly seemed unwise to discuss the dream from the night before. No, it definitely would not be wise to acknowledge the intimacy they had shared, not when he was standing so close, dressed in so little.

"I too slept well," he said, his smile tipping into a devilish grin.

Did he know? Was it possible for two people to share a dream? Before she could form a protest, he turned her hand and pressed his lips against the soft skin below the heel of her palm. Soft lips, a teasing scrape of beard, intriguing contrasts, intensely masculine. Warm breath spilled across her wrist, kindling flickering flames deep inside her. She jerked her hand free of his grasp, appalled at her own reactions.

"Just what do you think you're doing?"

"Greeting a beautiful woman."

She tried to keep her gaze fixed on his face. She refused to notice the way his skin glistened as sunlight streamed over the curves of his damp shoulders. Yet those broad, bare shoulders were there, at the edge of her vision, as were the dark curls that spread like eagle wings across his wide chest. "Do you always greet women dressed in nothing more than a towel?"

"Only those I find in my bedchamber when I leave my bath." He smiled, mischief lighting the depths of his blue eyes. "Is this a custom of your century? Do you greet all of your guests in their bedchambers?"

"Certainly not." She turned away from him; the blatant impropriety of the situation scalded her cheeks with shame. "I would appreciate it, sir, if you would put something on."

"Of course. If you would hand me the trousers that are on the chair."

Laura looked at the leather breeches that were tossed over the back of the Chippendale armchair beside the bed, a slash of black across the blue velvet. Memory flashed in her mind: supple black leather hugging long, muscular legs. Heat flickered low in her belly. "You can't go around Boston wearing those."

"They are not proper?"

She pressed her hand to her neck, feeling her pulse race beneath her fingers. "Not at all."

"Still, I'm afraid my wardrobe is somewhat lacking."

In his voice, she could hear the smile he was wearing. In her mind she could see the devilish tilt of those sensual lips. She sensed him move toward her, felt the heat of his body bathe her back. When he spoke, his lips brushed her ear, sending shivers skimming down her neck and across her shoulder.

"It is the leather trousers or"—he dangled the towel in front of her—"this towel."

"Oh, my gracious!"

The deep rumble of his laughter followed her as she dashed from the room. She slammed the door behind her, but it couldn't block the deep rumble of his laughter.

"That maddening, insufferable . . ." Oh, she wanted to strangle him!

Sophie stood in front of the bureau in Daniel's room. Under ordinary circumstances she would never have dreamed of doing what she was about to do, but the circumstances were hardly ordinary.

She pulled open the top drawer. Her face grew warm as she stared at the contents. As she suspected, his underthings lay in neat folded piles in this drawer, white linen separate from ivory wool.

"Pardon me, Daniel," she whispered as she removed several undergarments, two each of linen and wool. Connor could decide which he preferred. If the man preferred either, she thought, smiling as she remembered the pajamas from the night before.

She was about to close the drawer when something caught her attention: the edges of two photographs peeking out from beneath an undervest of white linen.

Why would Daniel hide photographs in the bottom of a drawer? She lifted the garment and stared down at her own likeness.

The girl in the photograph stood in one corner of the ballroom downstairs, dressed in ruffles and white silk, looking into the camera with eyes that were far too solemn for her years. It had been taken on her eighteenth birthday, the last she had ever celebrated in this house. For on that night, during her birthday ball, she had danced with Daniel for the first time—a dream come true, a reality she could not continue to face.

She had loved him. A deep, penetrating love that filled every vessel of her body and reached to the very center of her soul. A love that sliced into her heart every time she saw Daniel with her sister. A love that would not give her peace, even now. For she knew the life he had lived with Eleanor—cold, empty.

Perhaps it had been the fever she had suffered as a child that had ruined Eleanor. Perhaps it was the constant attention and concern lavished upon her by their parents. She had been cosseted and protected from the time she was five, kept like a golden-haired porcelain doll wrapped in cotton wool.

Whatever the reason, Eleanor had not possessed the capacity to love anyone or anything beyond her own lovely face and selfish whims. Father had provided Eleanor a husband bound to him by loyalty and honor, a man Eleanor wanted but had never loved, the man Sophie had always adored.

She moved her portrait, revealing the photograph beneath it. "My goodness," she whispered, staring down at a family gathering.

They were all there—Mother, Father, Eleanor, Daniel, gathered in the drawing room on Christmas day, the year before she had left home. Sophie was also in the photograph, standing beside the fair-haired

Eleanor—at least part of Sophie was there; her head and shoulders had been carved out of the photograph, leaving behind a neat oval hole.

Why in the world would someone have removed her from the family portrait?

"Aunt Sophie."

Sophie jumped at the sound of Laura's voice. She pivoted, slamming the drawer, guilt bringing the blood hot into her face. "I was getting a few things for Connor."

"That man!" Laura threw open the closet door. "Do you know he was parading around with nothing but a towel wrapped around his hips?"

"Oh?" Sophie hugged the linen and wool garments to her chest, her mind lingering on the image of the family photograph, and her missing head.

"I never thought I could do bodily harm to another human being. Until I met him." Laura turned, her arms laden with clothes. "I could strangle the man."

Sophie glanced up at her niece. "That's nice, dear."

Laura frowned. "Aunt Sophie, are you all right?"

"I'm fine."

"You're pale."

"I need something to eat, that's all." Sophie managed a smile. "After I take these things to Connor, I'll have Fiona send our breakfast up to his sitting room."

Laura had always considered her father tall, until now. Her father's dark blue striped trousers halted a full three inches above Connor's ankles. The white linen shirt wasn't any better. It stretched across his chest, and the sleeves ended an inch before they reached his wrists. "He looks like an orphan."

Connor grinned as he held up shoes that were too small for his feet. "In need of a good home."

Laura nodded. "The one from whence you came."

Connor turned his grin down in a mock show of injured feelings. It was all Laura could do to keep from smiling. The rogue!

"I wonder if I might try something," Sophie said, fingering a cuff of Connor's shirt.

"Try something?" Laura had an uneasy feeling about this.

"Yes." Sophie tapped her finger against her chin. "All I need do is coax the shirt to stretch a little, and—"

"You don't mean you're going to try magic?" Laura asked.

Sophie's smile was as bright as the sunlight pouring into the sitting room. "In a wink I could—"

"No!" Laura said.

"But, Laura, if I'm ever to become an accomplished witch, I really must practice my spells."

Spells. Witches. Vikings traveling through time. Laura pressed her fingertips against her temples, feeling the blood pounding beneath her touch. "Aunt Sophie, you really must stop this . . . magical nonsense."

"Now why would I want to do that? I'm only just beginning to learn how it works."

"This is Boston. People are scandalized if you read the wrong books. What will they do if they find out you're a witch?"

"But no one would have to know, if I'm careful."

"You mean as careful as you were in bringing this man into the house?" Laura asked, gesturing toward Connor.

"You and I are the only people who know how Connor got here."

"I'm still not sure how he got here. I only know I want him to go back to where he came from."

"Careful, dear," Sophie whispered. "You're going to hurt his feelings."

Laura glanced to where Connor was standing, gazing out the window of the sitting room that adjoined his bedroom. The sunlight pouring through the glass embraced him, slipping golden fingers into his thick hair, wrapping shimmering arms around his wide shoulders, worshiping him as though he were its master. Even dressed as he was in ill-fitting garments, he was the most intriguing man she had ever seen.

A glint of amusement sparkled in his blue eyes as he watched her, making her painfully aware of each thud her heart made. Well, she would not fall victim to his blatant charm. "The man is far too arrogant to let anyone hurt his feelings."

"I'm sure you would find him quite charming if you only gave him a chance."

"A chance for what? To completely destroy my life?"

Sophie smiled, her blue eyes sparkling. "A chance to make your dreams come true."

Laura shivered as she remembered the shameful spectacle she had made of herself in her dreams. "I don't want my dreams to come true."

"You don't?"

"No." Heaven help her if she allowed those wicked images to come true. "I much prefer to live in the real world."

"I see."

Something in the tone of Sophie's voice made Laura think she really did see the reason Laura wanted the man to disappear. Was she truly that transparent?

"Well, I'm afraid I will have to use magic to send him back."

"That's different."

"It is?" Sophie asked.

"That's necessary." Laura glanced at Connor. He smiled at her, a wide, embracing smile that conjured memories inside of her. She could feel his arms around her, his lips on her neck, his hands stroking her through the silk of her gown. Heat sizzled across her breasts, rising along her neck, her cheeks, until her ears tingled. The longer he stayed, the stronger the danger she would do something utterly ridiculous. "Absolutely necessary."

Laura jumped at a knock on the door. "Now what?"

"It must be one of the maids with breakfast." Sophie walked toward the door as though she didn't have a six-foot-four-inch Viking to hide.

"Wait." Although Laura had whispered, the harsh sound brought Sophie up short.

Sophie turned. "What is it, dear?"

"Him." Laura pointed toward the door to the adjoining bedroom as she directed her words at Connor. "Go back and stay in your room until I tell you it's safe to come out."

He lifted one black brow as he looked down at her. "You want me to hide?"

There was another rap on the door.

"I want you to disappear." Laura grabbed his arm and tugged him toward the door leading to his bedroom, trying to ignore the warmth of his skin radiating through the smooth linen. "Until then, I want you to stay out of sight."

He paused on the threshold to his bedroom, smiling down at her in a devilish way no gentleman would ever smile. "Will you keep me company?"

"No! Please just get in there and stay," she said, pushing against his chest. It was like pushing against a granite wall.

"As you wish." He winked at her before he turned and left the room.

"That man!" Laura slammed the door.

"Now?" Sophie asked, her hand poised on the brass doorknob.

Laura smoothed the rose merino wool of her skirt. She took a deep breath and tried to pull together the scattered pieces of her wits. "Yes."

Fiona was frowning when Sophie opened the door. Laura stared at the housekeeper, wondering why she had decided to serve breakfast instead of sending one of the kitchen girls.

"I was beginning to take the notion you had changed your mind about breakfast."

"We were so deep in conversation, we didn't hear you knock." Sophie glanced at Laura. "Isn't that right, dear?"

"Yes," Laura said, avoiding Fiona's keen brown eyes.

Fiona glanced around the room. "So you say Mr. Paxton arrived late last night," she said, pushing a serving cart to the round mahogany table that stood in a corner by the fireplace.

"That's right." Sophie sat on the edge of the sofa.

Laura held her breath as she noticed Fiona glance toward the door to the adjoining bedroom. Curiosity had brought Fiona with breakfast.

Stay in there. Silently Laura pleaded with the Viking on the other side of that door. *Please just stay in the bedroom until after Fiona is gone.*

Fiona flicked open a tablecloth, the white linen settling over the table. "Seems odd, him not letting you know he was coming."

"He wanted to surprise us." It wasn't exactly a lie, Laura assured herself. Connor had indeed surprised them with his visit.

"And you say he isn't feeling well?" Fiona asked, setting the silver tea server in the center of the table.

"He caught cold on the voyage from England," Sophie said.

"Well, I'll be sending up some of my tonic for him."

Laura crinkled her nose, remembering the taste of Fiona Kelley's special tonic. The short, plump woman with her keen brown eyes and curly brown hair had been the Sullivan housekeeper for the last 14 years. She had come to work for them soon after her husband had died, bringing her 15-year-old daughter, and a strong maternal instinct that had wrapped around Laura like a comforting shawl in winter. She had always been able to confide in Fiona, until now.

Laura remembered the Irish folk tales Fiona was fond of telling, of fairies and Druid magic. Fiona believed in wicked witches, mischievous fairies, and magical people she called the Shining Ones. She even wore an amber talisman around her neck to keep the Dark Folk at bay. Dear heaven, Fiona would be reciting scripture if she discovered Sophie was dabbling in witchcraft.

"And if you'll be asking the gentleman in." Fiona lifted a lid from a silver serving dish, allowing the aroma of roasted ham to filter into the room. "I can be serving you before it gets cold."

"Thank you, Fiona," Laura said. "But we can serve ourselves this morning. I'm certain you have better things to do."

Fiona smiled. "But I don't mind."

"I won't hear of it." Laura took Fiona's arm and led her toward the door.

Fiona glanced at the door leading to Connor's room. "Are you sure?"

"Positive."

Fiona looked up at Laura, curiosity and a glimmer of suspicion in her eyes. "I'll be going then."

Laura leaned against the door after Fiona had left. "She won't be satisfied until she gets a look at him."

"I can't say I blame her," Sophie said as she walked toward the door leading to Connor's room. "He is quite pleasant to look at."

"Aunt Sophie, if I didn't know better I would say you were smitten with that barbarian."

Sophie smiled as she knocked on Connor's door. "Perhaps I am."

"After breakfast, the man disappears."

"I'll do what I can, dear."

Still, Laura had the uneasy feeling Sophie intended for that Viking to stay.

Chapter Seven

Avallon, Brazil, 1889

"It seems clear to me what must be done," Fraser Bennett said.

Rhys Sinclair glanced up from the ancient scroll he held, a message written a thousand years ago, a plea for help that had materialized in this chamber this morning. He stared across the polished surface of the round table, meeting Fraser Bennett's blue eyes. "And what do you propose we do, Fraser?"

Fraser folded his hands on the table. "This man must be found. He must be . . ." He moistened his lips, glancing down at his hands. "He must be destroyed."

Rhys pressed his fingertips together and stared at Fraser over the steeple of his fingers. "We have no reason to believe this man is dangerous."

"He is one of the ancient ones, a *Tuatha De Danann*." Fraser glanced around the table. "You know as well as

I do what that means. They were sorcerers, shape changers, conjurers. We can only guess at the power he can channel."

Rhys rubbed his fingertips together, searching for inner balance as he stared at Fraser. "In case you have forgotten, Fraser, the *Tuatha De Danann* were our ancestors."

Fraser tapped his clenched hands on the table. "He was one of the renegades who decided to live outside of Avallon. You know what the ancient records show of these people. They refused to follow the laws set down by the Inner Circle. Their own lack of common sense sent many of them to the stake as witches."

"Isolation is not for everyone." Rhys rubbed his fingertips together. He knew to those in this chamber he looked calm. No one could glimpse his growing anger. "Even today, there are those who prefer to live in the Outworld instead of this mountaintop. Should we punish them for wanting their freedom?"

Fraser flicked his tongue between his lips like a nervous lizard. "If they threaten Avallon, then yes, I believe they should be forced to live here, or be destroyed."

Rhys wondered if Fraser remembered how his own son had threatened Avallon two years ago. Only those with unquestionable honor were allowed to enter the Inner Circle, and only if they had been born of the bloodline. Yet there were those who changed over the years. Ambition had a way of twisting a man, and Fraser was one of the most politically ambitious men Rhys knew. "We have no proof this man Connor will threaten Avallon."

"Great Alexis! The man is running wild in Boston, with who knows what type of powers." Fraser swept a hand through his light brown hair. "Why, he could decide to fly across Beacon Hill. What if he is caught? He could tell the Outworlders all about us."

Rhys stared down at the scroll. It was a mother's plea for the return of her son. He understood Ciara's pain; he had lost his own son years ago. He also knew she had not realized her plea might cause her son's destruction. "None of our people, including the renegades, have ever revealed Avallon to the Outworlders."

"We can't take the chance," Fraser said.

"Think of what this man could teach us." Rhys glanced at the people gathered in this hidden chamber. They were the governing council of the Inner Circle, 15 people descended from the ruling class of Atlantis, 15 souls who would decide the fate of one young man.

Crystals embedded in the black stone walls of the mountain chamber glittered like silvery stars shining in a black sky, their cool radiance commanded in a spell cast ages ago, a spell none of the nine men and six women who sat at the round rowan table that dominated the chamber could cast. For the past 4,000 years, the Inner Circle of Avallon had met in this hidden place. Yet they were no longer the powerful sorcerers they had once been.

"Our abilities have been eroded through the ages." Rhys looked at each person sitting in judgment. Their expressions were carefully masked, their emotions well shielded. "We are now pale reflections of what our ancestors once were. Even the most gifted of our number can channel a mere portion of the power of the earth."

"There was a good reason why our ancestors abandoned their gifts," Fraser said.

"There was a reason." Rhys stared into Fraser's eyes, seeing that reason clearly defined. "Fear."

Fraser sat back as though Rhys had slapped him across the face. "Are you implying our ancestors were cowards?"

"No. I'm suggesting what each of us already knows. In Avallon, as if it was in Atlantis, there always existed a separate group, a sect of individuals who possessed knowledge and skills far beyond the scope of the majority. These people once ruled, until fear and prejudice nearly destroyed them. Their gifts could not be used to defend themselves. The power cannot be used to destroy." Rhys looked at the others, judging their reactions, no matter how slight.

"In Avallon we allowed the scientists to flourish, because science was something all of our people could understand. The gifts our ancestors possessed, the magic they could conjure, set them apart, made them different, incomprehensible to those without the gifts. People fear what they do not understand." Rhys stared across the table at Fraser. "They seek to destroy what they fear. For us, that fear meant we would in time abandon our special gifts. Little by little we suppressed our abilities until they became dormant. In some of us the gifts may never be awakened. In others, there is a chance we can learn to use them once again."

"And how would we ever maintain order if there were people running around casting spells, turning things upside down?" Fraser clasped his hands together on the table in front of him. "Our powers are dormant for a reason. We cannot risk this Connor coming here, upsetting the natural order of things."

Rhys drew air deep into his lungs, trying to cool the anger simmering inside of him. "We cannot justify destroying this young man."

Fraser leaned forward, his shoulders curling in a silent show of fear. "What do you suggest?"

"I suggest we have our emissary in Boston investigate Connor." Rhys glanced around the table. "Once we have more information about the nature of this young *Tuatha De Danann*, we can decide if he should be allowed to stay in the Outworld, or be brought to Avallon. We should not even consider destroying him. For if we do, we are no better than those who destroyed our ancestors."

Fraser shook his head. "This is far too dangerous to ask our emissary to handle. Henry Thayer is an old man, scarcely capable of dealing with a creature with that type of power."

"The emissary of New York is more than capable of aiding Henry," Rhys said.

Fraser huffed. "As I recall, your son Austin is the emissary of New York."

Rhys smiled. "I'm certain Austin would have little trouble securing Connor, no matter what powers the man possesses."

"It's too dangerous. This man is a renegade." Fraser bounced his clasped hands on the table. "We can't be certain he won't use his powers to suit his every whim."

"I believe there are others who must decide this issue." Rhys looked at each of the other members of the governing council of the Inner Circle. "I submit we investigate Connor, son of Setric, to determine if he is a threat. Who among us would destroy this young man without giving him a chance?"

Fraser raised his hand and looked around the table for support. "We must protect Avallon from this menace," he said, trying to persuade others to join in his witch-hunt. Yet he stood alone.

"You have reconfirmed my trust in your judgment." Rhys smiled as he looked from one member to the next.

Fraser lowered his hand, glaring across the table at Rhys Sinclair. "You're making a fatal mistake."

Rhys held Fraser's angry stare, the veil of his emotions parting, revealing all to Rhys—fear, bordering on panic; envy so strong it reeked with a rotten stench. If he could, Fraser would find a way to destroy the young man.

Rhys would have to keep vigil on the other members

of the council. He didn't intend to let Fraser persuade anyone to vote for Connor's death. He only hoped Connor did nothing to cause the Inner Circle to betray him. Wayward magic in Boston might cause the council to alter its decision and issue a death warrant.

Chapter Eight

"Oh, bother!"

Connor brushed feathers from his shoulders, only to have more settle on his shirt. Now he understood how Aisling had felt when he was a neophyte testing his developing powers.

"I don't think I should have mentioned birds in that spell," Sophie murmured, brushing feathers off the open journal she held.

"Aunt Sophie, make them stop!" Laura held up her hands, gesturing to the hundreds of small white feathers drifting from somewhere near the ceiling to cover everything in the sitting room.

"Yes, of course." Sophie looked up and sneezed as a feather nestled beneath her nose.

"Aunt Sophie!"

"Yes, dear." Sophie cleared her throat. "Feathers of white, stop this plight!"

That was better, Connor thought, brushing feathers

from his hair. Feathers settled like snowflakes on the blue velvet of the sofa and chairs, the polished table-tops, and the three people standing in the room. Yet the storm was over.

"I did it," Sophie said, bouncing on her toes, feathers fluttering from her hair and clothes. "I made them stop."

"I suppose we should be happy for small blessings." Laura sank to the sofa as though all the strength had been drained from her limbs, feathers billowing up on either side of her.

Feathers nestled against the golden curls piled on top of her head, settled on the slender width of her shoulders, the bodice and skirt of her gown, flecks of white against dusky rose. She looked lost in the midst of a winter storm, bewildered by all she saw around her, determined to hold together the pieces of her logical world.

"Are you all right?" Connor sat beside her, kicking up feathers with the movement. "You're pale."

"I have a right to be pale." Laura glanced to where Sophie sat in a Chippendale armchair near one of the windows, studying the journal. "My aunt is a witch."

"Now all I need to do is clean up this room a bit," Sophie whispered, oblivious to Connor and Laura.

"Heaven help us," Laura whispered. "There is no telling what disaster will come of her attempt to clean up a bit. I can just see all the furniture disappearing."

He rested his arm on the back of the sofa, careful not to spook his wary swan. She sat stiff and straight on the edge of the cushion, ready for flight. "Your aunt has been given a great gift."

Laura tilted her head to look at him, feathers dripping from her hair. "A curse is more like it."

"Sophie doesn't look at her new abilities as a curse."

Laura dusted feathers from her hair. "Aunt Sophie is

a dear lady who is far too naive to realize we are on the brink of disaster."

He brushed the feathers from her shoulder, absorbing the warmth of her skin through the soft wool of her gown, allowing her emotions to crest over him like a crashing wave. She stared at him, her leaf-green eyes wide and wary.

He felt her fear buried beneath the strength of her will, fear of the other emotions inside of her—the longing for him she couldn't disguise, the confusion she had rarely known in her life. She wanted him and denied him all in the same instant.

"Is there no place for magic in your century?" he asked, brushing a feather from the soft hair above her ear. The sweet scent of spring flowers wafted with the warmth of her skin, tempting him to press his lips against the smooth curve of her neck. He settled for tracing the curve of her ear with his fingertip.

Laura swatted away his hand, her lips drawing into a thin line. "Was there a place for magic in your century?"

Connor shook his head. "People fear what they do not understand. They fear those who are different. Sometimes that fear can lead to violence, as in Salem."

"Then you can understand why I'm concerned for my aunt."

"I understand the need for caution." He stroked her shoulder with his fingertips, wanting so much more. The dream from the night before haunted him. The memory of her, soft and warm in his arms, triggered a response in him, tightened his muscles until his blood throbbed low in his belly. "I don't understand the need to deny the gifts she has been given."

"She simply can't be a witch. There has to be some other explanation." Laura curled her shoulder, drawing away from his touch. "Witches are evil. They worship the devil. There isn't an evil bone in her body."

"The devil of Christianity has no place in the gifts Sophie has been given. The power comes from all we see and all we cannot. It is the power in nature, the very heart of the Earth Mother. It is as old as time itself."

She stared at him. "How do you know so much about these gifts?"

For one moment he considered telling her the truth. Yet, as he looked into her eyes, he realized she was not ready to accept him for who he truly was. He needed time to win her, time to show her he was not an evil creature of darkness. "These beliefs were common in my century."

She drew a deep breath. "I suppose they still had Druids in your day."

"Yes. There were those who practiced the Druid rites." And there were those who had practiced the black arts, but he was not one of them. *Trust me. You have nothing to fear from me.*

"I'm not frightened of you," she responded, without noticing his words had only whispered in her mind. "I simply don't believe there is a place for you here."

He smiled, a smile he hoped might win a smile in return, just a small one. *Smile for me, Laura.* But her lips remained drawn in a tight line. "My place is with you."

She released her breath. "Don't you have a family back in Erin?"

"I do have a family." He couldn't be this close and not touch her. He lifted her hand. He slid his thumb over her knuckles, slowly and steadily, hoping to soothe his wary swan. "I left behind my parents, my two sisters and three brothers, as well as my aunt."

She stared down at her hand, watching the slow slide of his thumb back and forth across her skin, the color returning to her cheeks. "Won't they miss you?"

"Yes." His chest tightened with emotion as he thought of his family, their faces now only memories. "But I knew I had to find you, no matter how far I had to travel."

She parted her lips, yet no words escaped. She glanced down at her hand resting in his, staring for a long moment before she spoke, her voice soft and breathless. "It was a dreadful error, bringing you here, dragging you away from your home. I'm sorry, but you don't belong in my life."

He took her chin in his fingers and coaxed her to look at him. He knew she believed every word she had said, even though he could feel the turmoil inside of her. He could see the doubt shimmering beneath the surface of her logical thoughts, like a spring running clear and swift beneath a coat of ice. Her doubt was his hope. "Look inside your heart, my *Edaina*. There you will find the answers."

"You must return to your own time." She pressed her hand against his chest as he leaned toward her, her palm resting over his heart. "There can be no other way."

"I'm here for you." He slid his fingers along her jaw, into the soft hair behind her ear, smiling as her lips parted on a startled sigh. "And here I shall stay."

Laura closed her eyes as though she needed to shut out the sight of him. "You cannot stay here."

"I cannot leave you."

"You must." She looked up at him, denying him with her words, beckoning him with her eyes. "It's for the best."

"How could I ever leave you?" He pressed his lips to her temple, feeling her pulse throb beneath his lips, breathing in the fragrance of her hair. "It would mean leaving behind my heart."

"Oh." She curled her fingers against his chest. "Your family will—"

"Understand." He drifted down her cheek, spreading soft kisses. "Your skin, it's softer than down, warmer than summer."

"Oh, my gracious," she whispered.

He wanted to wrap himself in the soft warmth of her skin, feel her arms curl around his shoulders, her legs entwine with his. He slipped his arm from the sofa to her shoulders, holding her as he had only dreamed of holding her.

"You mustn't do this." Yet he felt the supple shift in her muscles, the sweet yielding curve of her body against his.

"You are more wonderful than I ever dreamed possible." He nuzzled the sensitive skin beneath her ear, breathing in her fragrance, tasting her with the tip of his tongue. A soft sound escaped her lips, a startled moan of pleasure that rippled across the pool of longing deep inside of him.

He pulled back to look into her beautiful face, needing to see her desire for him in the forest green depths of her eyes, the desire he felt pulsing inside of her, the desire that gave him hope of melting the ice surrounding her heart. She looked dazed, a child drifting into a pleasant dream. Her lips parted; her breath drifted like a sweet, moist mist against his lips. "Do you have any idea how long I've wanted to kiss you?"

"Kiss me?" She blinked, awakening with a start. "Oh, my gracious!"

Connor sighed, realizing he had taken one step too far.

She pushed away from him, holding him at arm's length, dragging air into her lungs like a drowning woman who had popped to the surface of a pool. She sat up, smoothing her skirt, glancing toward her chaperon as though she expected to be sent to the pillory for her behavior. Sophie was reading the journal, blind to everything else.

Laura squared her shoulders as she looked at Connor. "This type of barbaric behavior might have been accepted in your day, but here gentlemen do not maul ladies."

"It seems you have much to teach me about your century." Connor smiled, tracing the curve of her tightly pursed lips with his gaze. "How does a man show the woman he desires how he feels?"

She stiffened; her lips parted, then closed, then parted once more as she found her voice. "A gentleman does not feel that emotion toward a lady."

"No desire?"

"Certainly not."

"What has become of men in this century?" He gazed at her, absorbing each delicate line and curve of her face, the elegant sweep of her neck. He traced the slope of her shoulders, the full swell of her breasts, imagining the pale skin hidden beneath rose-colored wool. "How can they look at beauty such as yours and not want you?"

"Oh." Laura pressed her hand to the base of her neck. "It's clear you shall never adapt to this century."

"I shall do what it takes to win you."

"You don't seem to understand. I don't want you here."

"Ah, my lady," he said, brushing the back of his fingers across her smooth cheek. "I'm going to enjoy showing you just how wrong you can be. And desire, I shall take special pleasure in teaching you what it means to feel this emotion."

"Why, you . . ." She shot to her feet, feathers flying in every direction. She batted the feathers away from her face and stared down at him, eyes narrowed, like a cat about to strike. And yet she halted her tirade before it truly could gain control of her.

She closed her eyes, her lips moving as though she were silently counting. When her thick, dark lashes lifted, she looked down at him with that icy control she so worshiped. "Your behavior makes far too evident the impossibility of your ever remaining in this time."

"I will make a deal with you: You teach me to be a gentleman, and I will teach you how to scream when you are angry."

"I assure you, I don't care to be taught the manners of a barbarian."

Connor shrugged. "Are you frightened of enjoying the lessons?"

"Certainly not!"

He leaned back against the sofa, smiling as though he knew her mind better than she did.

Laura stared down into his smiling face, resisting the urge to slap him. She could feel her control slip away from her like drops of water leaking from her cupped palms. Never in her life had she met anyone more infuriating. She clenched her hands into fists at her sides when someone knocked on the door. "Now what?"

"It's probably Fiona with her tonic," Sophie said, glancing up from the journal.

"Wonderful." Laura looked around the feather-strewn room. "I suppose I can tell her we had a pillow fight, and the pillows lost."

Sophie glanced around, her eyes growing wide. "I don't suppose she will just go away."

Someone rapped once more on the door.

"I don't suppose she will." Laura spun on her heel, kicking up feathers as she marched toward the door.

"Be careful," Sophie whispered.

Laura drew a deep, steadying breath. She brushed feathers from her clothes before she cracked the door open a few inches. Fiona was standing in the hall, looking at her with those keen eyes that Laura felt certain saw more than she was willing to reveal.

"Mr. Philip Gardner is here to see you, miss. He's waiting in the drawing room."

Philip, that was all she needed. "Thank you, Fiona." Laura moved, blocking Fiona's attempt to look into the room.

Fiona frowned. "I brought this for the gentleman."

Laura stuck her hand through the crack between door and casement, taking the green bottle from Fiona's hand. "Thank you, I'll be sure he gets it." She would like nothing better than to force the entire contents down Connor's throat.

"And if you'll be letting me by, I'll be clearing away the dishes."

"We aren't ready," Laura said, pushing against the door when Fiona tried to open it wider.

"Not ready?" Fiona stared at her, suspicion carving deep lines into her face. "Well, then I'll be coming back in a bit."

What must Fiona be thinking? she wondered, watching Fiona walk away. Laura released her breath in a sigh as she closed the door.

"Who is this Philip?" Connor asked, watching her with the look of a lion protecting his territory.

That proprietary look sent a ripple of excitement through her blood. "Philip is none of your concern." She marched to Connor and thrust the bottle with its bitter brew at him. "Here, take a good long drink."

"Thank you," he said, smiling as he took the bottle. "But I feel fine."

She crinkled her nose at him before turning to face her aunt. "I'd better see Philip."

"Yes, dear. I'll stay here and keep Connor company."

"I'll try to get rid of Philip as quickly as I can." Laura

glared at Connor's smiling face. "See what you can do about getting rid of the Viking."

Laura paused in the hall outside of the second-floor drawing room, checking her skirt for feathers. Be calm, she told herself. There was no way Philip could know she was hiding a Viking down the hall. Was there? She drew a deep breath, trying to ease the sense of impending disaster.

Philip turned from one of the windows as she entered the room. Tall and slender, his short-cropped dark brown hair neatly brushed back from his wide brow, his dark gray coat and striped trousers impeccably tailored, he looked handsome, proper, so sane and ordinary she wanted to hug him. Philip, of course, would have found that behavior quite scandalous, so she merely extended her hand in greeting. "Good morning."

"Laura," he said, taking her hand in his grasp, barely touching her. "How very good it is to see you this morning."

She looked up into his dark eyes as he brushed his dry lips over her fingers, hoping for a tingle, a spark, even a small one. She needed to feel something, anything to help cool the embers still burning from Connor's touch. She felt nothing, not even a faint glimmer of heat.

"Is something wrong?" Philip asked, releasing her hand. "You're frowning."

"Am I?" She managed a smile. "I can't imagine why." It couldn't possibly have anything to do with an infuriating barbarian.

"What is this in your hair?" He plucked a white feather from one of the curls piled on top of her head and held it up for inspection.

Laura swallowed hard. "It looks like a feather."

"It is a feather." Philip frowned, studying her as

though she were a new rock he had added to his mineral collection. "Though I don't understand what it was doing in your hair."

"It must have come from my pillow." Laura stared at the pearl stickpin in the crisp white folds of his cravat, cursing Connor for the lies she had to tell. "I had a bit of a headache so I took a short nap after breakfast."

"I hope you're feeling better. I thought we might take a stroll through the Natural History Museum this afternoon. Dr. Hallshall has part of his mineral collection on display. I understand he has some particularly fine pieces of malachite."

"Oh, that sounds fascinating. But I'm afraid I can't go this afternoon. You see . . ." She hesitated as Philip looked past her. She glanced over her shoulder. Oh, my gracious! She was doomed.

Connor strolled toward her into the pool of sunlight cast by the windows. Laura's breath caught at the sight of him. He had changed into his black breeches, her father's white linen shirt tucked into the black leather; the sleeves rolled up to his elbows, revealing strong, tanned forearms; the first few buttons were unfastened, exposing a vee of golden skin and black curls. The man looked every inch a pirate.

She looked at her aunt, who walked beside Connor, her arm through his, as though strolling with a ninth-century Viking were the most natural thing in the world.

Philip wrapped his hand around Laura's upper arm. She glanced up to find him staring at her, frowning. He turned his dark gaze on Connor as though he sensed a predator approaching.

"Philip, how nice to see you," Sophie said as they drew near. "I would like you to meet my cousin, Connor Paxton."

A smile curved Connor's lips as he extended his hand

in greeting. Yet his eyes glittered with a feral gleam, a lion issuing a silent warning. "Mr. Gardner," he said, glancing to where Philip held Laura's arm.

Philip tightened his grip, then released her. "Mr. Paxton."

Laura watched as they shook hands, one quick pump before breaking the greeting. The men stood staring at one another, silent, except for the crackle of energy she could sense rather than hear. Philip was frowning, Connor smiling, if one could call that cold twist of his full lips a smile.

Philip stood nearly as tall as Connor, yet he didn't fill out the shoulders of his coat nearly as well. Both were handsome, in divergent ways. Philip was pale and smooth, his features finely drawn, a man who preferred the confines of a library to the expanse of the world beyond four walls. Connor was vibrant, his black hair touched with blue highlights, his skin kissed by the sun, his features carved with strong lines and angles, a man four walls could never contain.

Philip would ask for what he wanted.

Connor would take it.

"Laura didn't mention she had company," Philip said.

"I arrived last night."

"I see. And where might you be from?"

Laura felt ice water trickle into her veins as Connor began to respond. If he started spouting the truth, they were ruined.

"I come from—"

"Cornwall," Sophie said, patting Connor's arm. "He surprised us all by popping in late last night."

That was an understatement, Laura thought.

"Cornwall." Philip lifted one dark brow as he studied his rival. "You have a rather strange accent. I would not have placed you in Cornwall."

"From the time I was a child, I've traveled a great

103

deal." Connor looked at Laura, mischief twinkling in his blue eyes. "My father was in shipping."

As well as pillaging and plundering, Laura added silently.

"I see." Philip smoothed the thin line of his mustache. "And did all of this travel give you a fear of barbers, Mr. Paxton?"

"Barbers?" Connor frowned as he glanced at Laura. "And what does he mean by these Barbers?"

Laura laughed, hoping Philip couldn't hear the hint of hysteria in her voice. "Oh, Connor, you're always so amusing."

Philip frowned as he looked down at her. He didn't look at all amused.

"You see, Connor has been on an archaeological expedition. I'm afraid he often loses track of the present when he is delving into the past." All eyes turned to Sophie as she spoke. "He's quite an expert in ninth-century Vikings. Particularly in Ireland."

Stunned, Laura could only stare at her aunt.

"Vikings." Philip tilted his head, giving Connor a look of sheer arrogance. "And is it your fascination for the ninth century that has you going about in that strange costume?"

Connor's eyes narrowed.

"Connor's trunk hasn't arrived yet," Sophie said.

"I see." Philip picked an invisible piece of lint from his tailored sleeve. "I must say, I don't see why anyone would be fascinated with a pack of bloodthirsty barbarians."

Laura cringed, silently willing Philip to tread softly around bloodthirsty barbarians.

"Vikings are masters of trade." Connor smiled, but Laura could see the icy glint in his eyes, a look that chilled her blood. She had little doubt he could lay Philip low with a single blow of his hand. "They are hardly bloodthirsty barbarians."

Philip lifted his brows. "You speak as though they still exist."

"Only in spirit."

"Not in the spirit of any civilized man," Philip said, his voice filled with an annoying note of superiority.

"Perhaps man has lost much in this process of becoming civilized."

"I would hardly think a Viking would be welcome in Boston society, Mr. Paxton. We long ago abandoned the practice of solving our differences with a sword and battle-ax."

Easy, Philip, Laura thought. Connor still had a sword.

"As I recall, the men of this century tried solving their differences with sword and cannon only a few years ago." Connor paused as he held Philip's dark gaze. "I believe it was called the Civil War."

Philip sniffed loudly. "You can't possibly compare the noble fight to rid this nation of the blight of slavery to the wholesale slaughter the Vikings spread."

"I merely wish to point out the fact that beneath the polished surface of civilization"—Connor glanced at Laura—"man has changed little in a thousand years."

Laura stared, unable to draw her gaze from Connor's blue eyes. Her skin grew warm, as though she stood naked in the summer sun. What lay beneath the surface of this man? She was tempted to explore every layer, tempted to delve deep inside his soul to see if there truly was a place for her there. Heaven help her, she was definitely losing her mind.

"Perhaps you haven't evolved from your beloved Viking barbarians, Mr. Paxton, but I can assure you, I have."

Connor looked at Philip, a devilish grin curving his lips. "In that, I must heartily agree. You, Mr. Gardner, would not survive a week in the ninth century."

Color slid upward from the starched white collar of Philip's shirt until his face flushed purple with rage. "I believe it is time I take my leave." He turned to Laura. "Would you see me to the door?"

"Of course." She was only too anxious to get Philip out of this room away from one thoroughly infuriating, far too fascinating Viking.

Chapter Nine

Connor stared out one of the drawing-room windows, watching Philip Gardner march down the brick-lined walk leading from the house to a wide street. With the tip of his cane, Gardner poked at one of the white ridges that rose on either side of the walkway, punching holes in the shimmering snow. "This Philip Gardner, he is typical of the men of this century?"

"He is quite typical of the men in Boston," Sophie said.

He watched Gardner pass through a wrought-iron gate and mount a black conveyance that stood behind a pair of gray horses in the street. The man walked with his back straight, his stride stiff, as though someone had rammed a pole through the top of his head straight down to his toes. Was this truly the type of man Laura preferred? "He smells like a sultan's harem."

Sophie's giggle brought him around to look at her. "Most of the men in this century wear a scent, Connor."

Connor considered this fact for a moment. "I don't think I will wear such perfume."

"No." She smiled, her blue eyes sparkling with humor. "I doubt that sweet scent of Philip's would suit you. But you might try bay rum. It has a most appealing . . ." Sophie paused as Laura rushed into the room.

Laura closed the door behind her, leaning back against the oak panel, her heart racing. She stared at the Viking and her aunt, the two people who had turned her life upside down.

"You look as though a thousand raiders were chasing you," Connor said, a smile curving his lips.

"One Viking is more than enough to threaten me."

"I would never do anything to harm you." Connor pressed his hand over his heart. "You are my heart."

Laura's breath grew heavy in her lungs as she held Connor's gaze. He stood in front of the windows, framed by gold velvet drapes, sunlight painting a golden glow around him—a portrait of potent masculinity.

Laura stared, absorbing the sight of him, like the frozen earth absorbing the first warm rays of sunlight in spring. Possibilities whispered to her; the promise of dreams come true beckoned her like a siren call.

She glanced away from him, clenching her hands into fists against the solid oak at her back. She could not allow herself to imagine life with this man. It was dangerous. Far too dangerous.

"Aunt Sophie, did you really think it was wise, bringing Connor in here to meet Philip?"

"He insisted on meeting Philip." Sophie looked at Connor, obviously seeking an ally. "Isn't that right?"

"I wanted to see this man who wishes to steal my woman."

"Your woman?" Laura glared at the rogue, fury rising within her, warring with the excitement she refused to acknowledge. "I am not your woman."

"You're mine." He lowered his gaze, sweeping her figure in a bold, hungry gaze that made her tingle, as though he had peeled away her clothes and stroked her bare skin with his hands. "In time you will come to realize we belong to each other."

"Why, you arrogant barbarian." She marched toward him until she could stare straight up into his face. "Understand this, Viking, I do not belong to you or anyone."

"This Philip Gardner. He believes you are his property." His eyes narrowed as he stared down at her. "I could see this by the way he touched you."

"The way Philip behaves toward me is none of your concern," she said, managing to speak in a level tone.

"Do men in this century no longer protect what belongs to them?"

"I am not a piece of chattel. It's obvious you haven't the slightest idea how gentlemen of this century behave."

"You're right. I don't know how these *gentlemen* behave." He stepped closer, the enticing scent of his skin teasing her senses. "But I do know how a man should act around the woman he loves."

Laura gasped as he caught her upper arms. "Let me go!"

"I could never let you go," he whispered, his dark voice brushing over her like warm velvet.

"I demand that you . . ." Her words dissolved in a sharp intake of breath as he nuzzled the soft skin beneath her ear. Shivers shimmered across her skin. "Stop this!"

"Do you have any idea how beautiful you are to me?"

In his arms she felt beautiful, cherished. He made her feel as though she were the only woman he wanted to touch, the only woman he wanted to kiss, the only woman he wanted to possess. She struggled in his far too tempting embrace, fighting the dangerous desire dawning inside of her. "Let go of me!"

"You are the breath that sustains me." He slid his arms around her, imprisoning her waist with his left arm, slanting his right upward across her back. The heat of his body reached for her, wrapping around her, enveloping her in an inviting warmth.

"This is not at all proper," she said, her voice dwindling to a whisper.

"Ah, but it is proper to show a woman how much she is desired." He opened his lips against her neck, flicking the tip of his tongue against her skin, the fiery touch spiraling like a flaming arrow all the way down to her toes. "I want you in every way."

"Oh!" Laura swallowed hard, trying to marshal the defenses she could feel dissolving in the heat he kindled inside of her. "You must . . ."

"Taste your lips."

"Oh, no." She stared up at him, the heat in his eyes evaporating her will. "You couldn't possibly."

"Oh, I think it's quite possible." He looked down at her, smiling, a slow curve of sensual lips that stole the breath from her lungs.

She stared up into his eyes, sensing as well as seeing what simmered in the endless blue depths—desire and something far more frightening, a warmth that whispered of eternity. "You must release me."

"Must I?" He slipped his hand into the hair at her nape, cradling the back of her head in his big hand, drawing her toward him. "This is how a man should show his beloved how much he wants her."

Laura pressed her clenched fists against his upper arms. "You mustn't—"

"I've waited a lifetime to kiss you."

She stared as he lowered his head, those smiling lips moving closer, closer, his breath falling soft and sweet upon her cheek. "You shouldn't—"

He drank the words of protest from her lips. At the first touch of his lips, she felt her heart stop, then start with a headlong rush. His kiss—so soft, so gentle, like warm honey sliding sweetly across her lips.

How many times had she imagined this? How many mornings had she awakened hugging her pillow to her chest, warm and restless, taut with longing for this man?

The soft touch of his lips upon hers, his strong arms holding her as though she were the most precious gem in the world, his warmth chasing away the chill of winter—this was reality where only fantasy had existed before. Still, her imagination paled beside the reality of this man.

Promises dwelled in this kiss, promises waiting for her to claim them, if she found the courage to make them her own.

Dangerous! her mind screamed. This kiss was dangerous. This man was dangerous. He threatened to steal her away from the world she understood. He threatened to change her in unseen ways.

Still, she had waited a lifetime for this man to take her into his arms. He was here, in her world, holding her, and he was more than she had ever dreamed possible.

She opened her hands upon his arms, arching her fingers against the thick muscles stretched taut beneath white linen, craving the feel of his skin. He slanted his mouth across hers, his beard sliding against her chin in a delicious tease. Tingles spiraled down her spine as he touched the tip of his tongue to the seam of her lips, coaxing her to open for him.

A sorcerer weaving magic, spinning a golden spell around her, enchanting her, this was Connor, this was the power of the man who knew her better than any living soul. A moan escaped her as she surrendered to his magic, sipping light and warmth from his lips.

He tunneled his fingers through her hair, dislodging pins and combs, allowing her hair to slide through his hands. She sighed as the heavy weight of it fell against her back.

"Beautiful," he murmured against her lips. He held her closer, her soft breasts nestling against the hard thrust of his chest. Never had she realized such pleasure could ripple through her at a mere contact.

He dipped his tongue into her mouth, tasting her, allowing her to taste his spicy essence. He was sleek heat, damp and firm, flicking against her teeth, her tongue, teasing her, tempting her to join him in this sensual game.

She slid her hands upward, along the smooth linen covering his broad shoulders. She slipped her hands into his long hair; ebony strands of silk curling softly around her fingers—softer than she had imagined.

The fragrance of his skin, citrus and an intriguing spice all his own, enticed her senses. She drew his scent deep into her lungs, and still it wasn't enough. She glided her lips against his, snuggling against his hard frame, needing to feel his arms tight around her, needing something she sensed only he could give her.

When he lifted his lips, she moaned, curling her hands into his soft hair. It was too soon to stop. And yet a part of her wondered if it was far too late. She stared up into his eyes, seeing his hunger for her, unaware of the desire shimmering in her own eyes.

"Tell me you feel these things when Gardner kisses you," he whispered, his hands flexing against her waist beneath her hair. "Tell me this passion flares between you and that man."

"Oh!" She stepped back, escaping his warm embrace, his words lashing her cheek like a physical blow. "How dare you think I would allow Philip or any man such liberties!"

He smiled, a slow lift of his lips that spoke of pure masculine possession. "And yet you kissed me as though you drew your breath from me."

"Why, you . . ." She pressed her hand to her lips, catching her scathing words before they were spoken. The man had the most uncanny way of making her want to scream like a hoyden. "I have never met a more provoking man."

"And I have never met a more alluring woman."

Laura turned away from him, looking at Sophie. "Aunt Sophie, did you see what this man did?"

"Yes, dear." Sophie stood a few feet away from them, watching their exchange, smiling. "It would seem men were far more forthright in expressing their emotions back in his time."

Laura combed her fingers through her hair, snatching the few remaining pins from it. "You must do something with this Viking."

"I thought I would send for your father's barber."

Laura stared at her aunt. "Father's barber?"

"This Barber who is supposed to frighten me?"

Sophie waved away his words with one slender hand. "I'm afraid that was only Philip's weary attempt at levity. A barber is a man who will trim your hair and shave you. Nothing more."

Connor ran his hand through his hair, plowing furrows in the thick black waves. "He will make me look more like a man from this century?"

"Yes." Sophie turned the corners of her mouth down into a frown. "But I have to admit I will hate to see all of that lovely hair cut off. Won't you, Laura?"

Laura cast Connor a contemptuous glance. She bent, searching the carpet for pins amid the intricate pattern of leaves and flowers. "If you were to send him back to his own time, there would be no need to cut his hair."

"Yes." Sophie tapped her forefinger against her chin. "But I'm afraid I haven't any luck in that direction."

Connor crouched beside Laura, who was sitting on her heels. "I like your hair loose and flowing," he said, lifting a handful of the disheveled locks. "It's far too beautiful to keep it locked in tight coils."

Laura snatched her hair from his grasp. "A lady certainly doesn't go about with her hair hanging wildly around her shoulders."

He grinned at her, his eyes sparkling with a light that was pure mischief. "Not even at night?"

Laura stood and glared down at him, trying to ignore the heat shimmering through her at the look in his eyes. "That is none of your concern."

He stood and winked at her. "Not yet."

"Oh, you . . ." She pivoted, her hair spilling around her shoulders as she faced Sophie. "Philip reminded me of the birthday party for his mother we are to attend next week. He invited this Viking to join us."

Sophie nodded. "Philip may be a pompous bore, but he is unfailingly polite."

Laura stiffened, feeling a sudden need to protect Philip, and her own century, against this marauding Viking. "Philip is not a pompous bore."

Sophie rolled her eyes. "His idea of a fascinating evening is staring at a collection of rocks."

"Rocks?" Connor looked at Laura. "This man collects rocks?"

Laura lifted her chin. "He happens to be very interested in geology."

"Rocks." Connor grinned.

Laura twisted her hair into a tight coil. "I happen to find his rock collection fascinating."

"Yes," Connor said, his lips tipping into a wide, mischievous smile. "I'm sure it is quite fascinating."

Laura turned away from him, staring at the large gold snowflakes that marched in orderly columns across the ivory silk wallpaper. Perhaps Philip was dull. But at least Philip was a gentleman. He would never have dreamed of kissing her. A fresh wave of heat rose from her waist, searing her breasts, her neck, her cheeks.

She clenched her jaw when someone rapped on the door. They didn't need another visitor. At Sophie's invitation the door opened and Fiona entered.

"I was wondering if you might be liking a little tea," Fiona said, her dark gaze drifting from Laura to Connor.

"Not now, Fiona," Laura said, her nerves making her impatient. They had to find a way to get rid of this Viking. "I'll ring if we need anything."

Fiona nodded, her gaze never leaving Connor. "Ah, but you must be Mr. Paxton, I'm thinking."

Connor smiled. "And you are the kind lady who gave me the tonic."

"Aye, Fiona Kelley, I am. And I'm glad to be seeing my tonic has done the trick. You're looking fit as a thoroughbred in May, you are."

"I'm feeling much better, thank you."

"My pleasure, I'm sure." Fiona stood smiling at Connor as though she intended to stare at the man all day.

"Fiona, don't you have something to do in the kitchen?" Laura asked.

"Why, it's sure I do, now." Still Fiona made no move to leave. The woman was beaming like a candle under Connor's smile. "Is there anything that you're liking for dinner, sir?"

"I'm certain anything you fix will be delicious."

Fiona giggled. "Well, I'm hoping we can please. I'm thinking we'll have some nice roasted lamb, with a little raspberry sauce." She crossed the room, pausing at the door to turn once more and smile at Connor. "And I'll fix a nice chocolate cake."

"I'll be looking forward to it."

Laura glared at Connor as Fiona left the room. Did he have that disturbing effect on all women? But of course he did. What woman could look into those mischievous blue eyes and not feel her heart trip? No doubt the man had long ago lost track of his conquests. "Aunt Sophie, do you think you shall be able to send this Viking back to where he belongs before he serves us up for ridicule?"

Sophie drew a deep breath. "I'm afraid we must face the possibility I might never be able to send him back."

She was going to scream. Laura closed her eyes. Slowly she counted to ten, then 20. When that didn't help she kept counting, reaching a hundred and beyond, hoping to contain the horrible urge she had to scream.

"Laura, it's only a possibility," Sophie said, touching her arm. "I've been thinking a great deal about this. And I wonder if the spell will only work during a full moon. He came to you on the night of the full moon; perhaps he will leave on the night of the next full moon."

Laura thought of the dreams, the nights Connor had come to her. It had always happened on the night of a full moon.

"And if I can't send him back, then he will indeed become my cousin."

Laura looked down into her aunt's smiling face, seeing the hope in her dark blue eyes, the optimism Laura couldn't manage. "How do you hope to ever pass this Viking off as a gentleman? Why, he eats with his fingers."

"This is not acceptable?" Connor asked.

Laura glanced to where he was leaning against an arm of a wing-back chair, his arms crossed over his wide chest, his black leather breeches stark against the mint green velvet upholstery. No modern man could manage to look so commanding, so utterly untamed, so impossibly appealing. Her skin tingled from the memory of his body pressed against hers. "Like most of your behavior, it is not acceptable."

Connor nodded, accepting her words without argument. "I shall learn what is proper."

"It's only one of a thousand things you must learn."

He grinned. "And I shall learn all of them."

"All he needs is a little polishing, dear." Sophie moved to Connor's side. "With the right clothes, his hair trimmed, the proper etiquette, he will do splendidly in this century."

"We don't have years to train him. Father will be back tonight."

"Laura, your father doesn't spend enough time in this house to even notice Connor is here." Even though Sophie spoke the words gently, the meaning jabbed Laura like a hot poker. "I wouldn't be surprised if he went directly to his office from the train station."

"Father is busy, but that doesn't mean he wouldn't notice a Viking in the house." Her father loved her. He did, Laura assured herself. He had priorities, that was all. Business engagements. Important issues to be resolved. "And even if Father didn't notice him, there is still the matter of the Gardners' party. We have a handful of days before Connor is thrust into the lion's den. It's a ball, for heaven's sake, Mrs. Gardner's ball."

"Why do you fear this woman?" Connor asked.

Laura straightened, startled by his perceptiveness. "I don't."

"You speak of her as though she were a queen who could lop off a head with a wave of her hand."

"I do not." She turned away from him, looking at Sophie for support. "Do I?"

117

"It's true, dear. You do speak of Esther Gardner as though she were a queen."

Laura sighed. "Perhaps I do think of her as a queen."

"I thought Boston was no longer part of a monarchy," Connor said.

"You don't understand." Laura walked to the windows, staring out at Boston Common. "My father is Irish, and that means there are those who look at him as though he were a peasant."

"These people are ignorant." Connor shifted on the arm of the chair, turning to face her. "They don't realize the Irish are a proud race. They knew the love of art and history, the great writings and poetry, while most of the world was still in darkness."

"These people don't care. To them history began when the first settlers landed on Plymouth Rock." Laura pressed her hand to the window, absorbing the icy feel of the glass. "And heaven forbid if your ancestors cannot trace their roots in this country at least as far back as the dawn of this century."

"Why do you care what these foolish people think?" Connor asked.

"On my mother's side, my family is one of the oldest, most respected in Boston. Aunt Sophie and I are the last of the Chandlers. My father wants me to take what he believes is my proper place in society." Laura turned to face him. "Mrs. Gardner *is* society in Boston. If she accepts you, then you are deemed worthy. If she spurns you, you are a social outcast."

Connor shook his head. "From what you've said of Boston society, I think I might prefer to be a social outcast."

Laura lifted her chin. "I didn't expect you to understand."

"But I do understand." Connor studied her as though

he were looking beyond her face, straight into her mind.

Regal—for the first time Laura truly understood the meaning of the word. Power radiated from the man, the absolute power that decided the fate of nations.

"I'm the son of a king and an Irish princess. Still, I would be considered no better than a peasant of dubious heritage if Sophie had not given me the name of her English ancestors."

"Not in my eyes," Sophie said.

Connor smiled. "Thank you."

Laura felt like a bigoted boor. "I didn't say it was right."

"No." Connor held her in a steady gaze. "But you did say you wanted to be a part of this society."

"You don't understand." Laura glanced away from him, staring out the windows. Snow spread across the common, trees lifting supplicating arms toward the sun. "It means a great deal to my father to know I've been accepted. He feels he owes it to my grandfather to make sure I marry into the right family."

"In my time there were many arranged marriages. Few of them were happy."

"This is not your time, Connor." Laura hugged her arms to her waist, a chill of anxiety seeping into her blood when she thought of her future. "I will not disappoint my father."

Connor was silent for a moment, and when he spoke his deep voice betrayed none of his emotion. "I look forward to meeting your father."

"Daniel is due back in town tonight." Sophie smiled as she looked at Connor. "I have a feeling you and he are going to get along just fine."

"Connor, you must not go with us to the Gardners' party. We can say you took ill."

"I'm feeling fine." Connor grinned. "And I'm anxious

119

to meet the queen of Boston."

Laura groaned in frustration. "Aunt Sophie, tell him about the people that will be there. All of Mrs. Gardner's friends. You know what those women are like." She rubbed her arms, trying to chase away the shivers that skittered across her skin when she imagined how Mrs. Gardner and her friends would pick Connor apart, piece by piece. She might not like the man, but she certainly didn't wish to see him humiliated. "He can't possibly attend."

"I will learn what needs to be learned," Connor said. "I will go with you to this party."

"Aunt Sophie, help me talk some sense into his thick head."

"The only way we are going to keep him from going to the party is to tie him up and lock him in his room." Sophie glanced at Connor, her lips tilting into a smile. "I think it would be easier to polish the rough edges."

Laura sighed, knowing they had no choice. He would have his night at the ball.

"I'll have Ridley send for your father's tailor. In the meantime, we'll send one of the footmen to purchase a few ready-made clothes for him." Sophie patted Connor's arm. "I'm certain you will do just fine."

Connor smiled. "I will make this century mine."

Laura frowned, wondering how she would make certain the Viking did not get them banished from polite society. There was no hope for it; she would make a gentleman out of him if it was the last thing she ever did.

"This is extraordinary." Henry Thayer squeezed the handle of his atomizer, misting one of the dozens of orchid plants growing in pots in his conservatory. "A *Tuatha De Danann* in Boston. It boggles the mind."

Austin Sinclair stood by one of the glass-lined walls,

staring past the moisture beading on the panes, looking at Boston Common, thinking of the young sorcerer who was living nearby.

"According to the report I received this morning, he's staying with the Sullivans," Henry said.

"Apparently he came here to meet Laura Sullivan."

"I don't understand how this could happen."

Austin had his own theories of how this had happened, none he cared to share with Thayer. He drew his fingertip over his brow, wiping away the moisture, pushing back his damp black waves.

"This is simply extraordinary," Henry mumbled.

In the corner of his eye, Austin could see Henry moving along the black wrought-iron shelf that curved through the banana and palm trees crowding the room, their green leaves pushing against the glass ceiling and walls. Henry bent over the orchids that stood in pots, lined up along the shelf like soldiers awaiting a general's attention.

"How would he even know of Laura Sullivan?"

"That is one of the things we must discover." Was Connor here to find his *Edaina*? Could two souls be linked in a way that defied time? Austin thought of Sarah, his wife. Although he had not traveled through time to find her, he had defied every rule of his people to make her his own.

Henry squeezed the handle, mist hissing from the metal tip, adding to the humidity clouding the sultry room. "Do you think he could be dangerous?"

A bead of sweat trickled down Austin's neck. "There are those who believe he could be."

"Yes, I know. I spoke with Fraser Bennett a few hours ago." The atomizer hissed in Thayer's hands. "Tell me what you think."

"I think I'll know more after I meet the young man."

"You do know the governing council has given me

discretionary power to handle the situation any way I deem necessary."

Austin clenched his jaw. He wasn't sure he had faith in Thayer's judgment. "Yes."

"If I believe this man is dangerous, I will eliminate the threat."

Austin turned to face the emissary. Henry stood beside a banana tree, watching him, his brown eyes undimmed by age, a frown drawing together his white brows. "I don't believe we'll need to destroy him," Austin said.

"I can assure you, I would only destroy the young man if I had no other recourse. But make no mistake, I'm still the emissary of this town." Henry snapped off a pink orchid, the petals edged in brown. He frowned at the ruined blossom before tossing it to the gray flagstones lining the floor. "I know there are those who think I'm too old to handle this problem, but they're wrong. You might be an English marquess and the emissary of New York, but just remember, you're here as my assistant. I'm running this operation."

"Of course. And I'm certain you will do what is best." Austin intended to make sure of it.

Chapter Ten

Although she hid it well, Connor could see Laura was upset about her father. It showed in her eyes each time she glanced at the empty chair at the head of the table. What type of man visited his office before visiting his daughter?

"I'm certain Daniel had very important business to attend to," Sophie said, as though she too could see Laura's hidden wounds.

"Of course he did." Laura looked at Connor across the table, burying her hurt and disappointment beneath an icy veneer. "He has a business to run."

"This business keeps him from spending time with you?" Connor tugged at the collar of his shirt, the starched white linen scraping his neck.

"Don't fuss with your clothes," Laura said, ignoring his question.

He decided to allow this change in the direction of the conversation, sensing her reluctance to discuss her father. "This collar feels like hemp around my neck."

Laura pursed her lips. "You can't go around with your shirt unbuttoned; it isn't civilized."

"It seems society expects men to be as stiff as their clothes in this century" He pulled his white tie loose and tugged open the first few studs fastening his shirt, sighing as he rubbed his neck.

"A gentleman does not go about exposing his person." Laura tapped her fingers against the skin below her collarbone. "I can assure you a lady does not wish to see a man's naked chest."

"Although I don't care for the cut of a man's clothes in this century"—Connor grinned, lowering his gaze to the smooth, pale skin rising above the burgundy silk of her bodice—"I do approve of the way your gown reveals the curves of your shoulders, and hints at other delicacies."

The flickering candles in the silver candelabra illuminated the color rising from Laura's bodice, streaming crimson upward along her neck and cheeks. She turned toward Sophie, who sat on her right, at the head of the table. "This is impossible. The man will never learn proper decorum."

Sophie patted her arm. "Give him a little time to get accustomed to everything. We've spent the entire day filling his head with rules."

"We don't have time." Laura drew in a sharp breath and glared at Connor. "Mr. Paxton, if you don't conform to society, you will hold Aunt Sophie and me up to ridicule. Is this what you want?"

Connor grimaced at the thought of fastening the stiff white linen around his neck. Yet he knew he must fit in to her delicate little world of manners if he were going to have the chance of winning Laura. Slowly he fastened the shirt.

"Thank you," Laura said, her words closely clipped.

He slid the silk tie through his fingers, trying to coax it into a neat bow like the one Sophie had tied before dinner. "I would do nothing to humiliate you, my lady."

"Perhaps not on purpose." Laura frowned as she watched him fumble with his tie. After a few moments she tossed her napkin beside her plate and walked around the table. "Let me," she said, snatching the tie from his hands.

"My pleasure." The scent of spring flowers settled over him like a warm mist as she leaned toward him, the heat of her skin brushing his cheeks.

Her brows tugged into a frown as she crossed the ends of the tie and began to repair the damage he had wreaked upon the silk. "You must learn the proper way to tie your neckcloths. Men in Boston don't fancy the use of valets like the English do."

He grinned up into her frowning face. "But I'm supposed to be English."

Her lips flattened into a tight line. "And it looks as though you lost your valet on the way here."

He stared at the soft swells of her breasts rising above her bodice, her flesh pressed against the snug burgundy silk as she leaned toward him, the enticing valley mere inches from his lips. "From where I sit, I can see some advantage to losing my valet, no matter what this valet might be."

Laura straightened, slapping her hand over the top of her bodice. "A gentleman would never take such a loathsome advantage."

He winked at her. "Then a gentleman is a fool."

"And you are quite crude." She stormed away from him, the burgundy silk of her gown swishing with each indignant sway of her hips.

Connor smiled at her as she took her place across from him. "Shall we continue, teacher?"

She took a deep breath, and he could see her silent

125

struggle for control. In some respects he wished she would lose that fight, explode in a glorious display of temper. When she spoke, he knew she had once again hidden her emotions deep inside of her.

"You must hold your fork like this," she said, lifting one of the forks from the side of her plate, the silver glittering in the candlelight. "Do not crook your elbow and bring the fork around like this. People will think you're shoveling food into your mouth. And make sure you don't overload your fork or spoon. We certainly wouldn't want people to think you're vulgar."

"Of course not." He stared at the bewildering array of china and silver and crystal laid out before him on the white linen that covered the table: a half dozen glasses for water and wine, a small knife and fork for fish, a small fork for oysters, three large forks, three knives, two spoons. "Why do people of this century need so many implements to eat?"

"Because . . ." Laura hesitated, staring at her own place setting. "I don't really know."

"Perhaps all the rules of this society have been created by people with money and power as a type of barrier, a way to keep the classes separate."

Laura looked stunned. "That's ridiculous."

Connor lifted a fork, shifting it in his fingers until he was a portrait of proper etiquette. "Is it?"

Laura glanced at Sophie, but her aunt kept her own counsel. "The people of Boston society are well known for their charity."

"As long as the peasants stay in their place," Connor said.

Laura glared at him. "And was it so different in your time?"

"Only the rules were different. But people have changed little in a thousand years." He lifted an oyster with the proper fork. "I will learn your rules and make this century my own."

Laura swallowed hard. Her eyes revealed her thoughts, the uncertainty, the fear and longing.

You're mine, he whispered into her mind.

She sat back in her chair, staring at him, her lips parted as though he had kissed her hard and let her go too soon. "Did you say something?"

He smiled as he shook his head.

She frowned, tapping her finger against the stem of her water goblet, looking at him with a provocative blend of desire and fury that made him wonder just what it would be like to release all the pent-up emotion inside of her.

Nothing would keep him from making this woman his, even the ridiculous excesses of Boston society.

Laura looked up from the book she was reading, glancing at the rosewood clock on the mantel in her bedroom. Midnight. And she still couldn't go to sleep. Was she so worried about meeting that Viking in her dreams again? Or was she more worried about what she would do if she did see him in her dreams?

"That man!" He had no right to make her feel this way, as though every rule, every piece of etiquette she had ever been taught was somehow tarnished. "Infuriating Viking."

She dumped her book on the bed and stood, abandoning any hope of reading Bellamy's fantasy novel. Connor kept intruding on her thoughts.

Oh, the man had no right to make her feel so unsettled. She paced to the windows, batting the drapes, the jade green brocade billowing in her wake. He stirred things inside of her, feelings she never realized existed until he popped into her life, feelings she was certain no proper lady would ever allow herself to feel.

These feelings were nothing but base urges. Primitive. Provocative. And she couldn't get them out of her mind.

She caught a glimpse of her image in the cheval mirror standing in one corner of her room. Golden light spilled from the brass-and-crystal fixture overhead, bathing her, slipping light into her unbound hair. She thought of Connor's hands in her hair, lifting it, sliding the strands through his fingers as though it were the finest silk.

Thoughts of that scandalous dream were best forgotten. Still, the images were impossible to erase from her memory. She shifted on her feet, watching the way her flannel gown swayed with her movement, the soft cloth stroking her skin, every nerve shimmering in response. When had her skin ever felt so sensitive?

The silk gown she had worn in her dreams had been a delicate confection that whispered across her skin, no more than a veil. How had she imagined such a garment?

She stared at her reflection in the mirror. Tiny pearl buttons started at her neck and marched primly down the white flannel to her waist. It was a proper garment, sensible, respectable. No doubt Connor would think it prudish. He was a Viking, after all. A man who took what he wanted. And he wanted her. Her breath escaped with that silent admission.

You're mine—his words whispered in her mind, dark, compelling, tugging at something buried deep inside of her.

She lifted her fingertips to her lips, pressing, closing her eyes as the memory of his kiss rippled through her. A warmth flickered deep inside of her, a delicious heat spreading upward across her belly, until her breasts tingled.

Such scandalous feelings. Wicked. Intriguing.

Although the fire had died in the hearth, the room seemed stifling. Her skin felt flushed, far too warm, as though she stood in the full rays of the sun. She flicked open the first three buttons of her gown, imagining Connor's hands, his long, tapering fingers moving against the white flannel.

A lady shouldn't consider the images blossoming like forbidden flowers in her mind. A lady shouldn't be thinking of broad, naked shoulders, golden skin damp from his bath. No, a lady definitely shouldn't imagine a man's naked chest, or his long, muscular legs—bare to her eyes.

She parted the gown, revealing the pale curves of her breasts, her skin moist beneath the soft flannel. A pulse fluttered low in her belly as she stared at her image and imagined the unthinkable. What would it be like to feel Connor's hands on her skin? What would it be like to surrender to the magic she felt when he touched her?

The woman in the mirror looked positively scandalous, her hair waving wildly around her shoulders, her gown open, her lips parted as though she were waiting for a lover.

"Oh, my gracious." She clutched her gown together, her cheeks flaming as though she had just been caught walking naked down Beacon Street.

The man had her teetering on the edge of complete moral degradation. She turned away from the mirror. She would not succumb. She would never fall under the Viking's spell.

Moonlight flowed through the windows of Connor's bedroom, the silver light streaming across the open journal he held. He stared at the words etched in black ink upon ivory parchment, each letter carefully shaped, as though the writer had been especially careful to preserve every nuance.

The journal of Rachel Paxton was a type of primer for the *Sidhe*, a step-by-step guideline for conjuring simple spells. If the power that flowed through his people could be thought of as a river, using this book would allow someone to skim the surface. Still, even though they were simple spells, he suspected only a person of the bloodline could make the enchantments work.

"Intriguing," he whispered, staring at an incantation. "To bring to you that which you most desire."

> *Hear me, Lady of the moon.*
> *Your pull is great.*
> *You move the tide.*
> *Now bring my beloved to my side.*

This spell was different from the others in the book. Although simple in cadence, he suspected it would have the ability to plunge below the surface of that shimmering river of power that flowed through his people. He suspected if spoken by one of the *Sidhe*, it could form a bridge between two people, a bridge that could span time itself.

Was this how he had been able to find Laura? His medallion had opened the portal of time, but without the bridge, he would have been forced to search through centuries to find her.

He closed the book. He stared at the red leather cover, contemplating mysteries. How did a book such as this come into existence? And how did it come to be in Sophie Chandler's possession? It was an intriguing mystery.

He snapped his fingers. The journal disappeared. He knew it would reappear in Sophie's bureau drawer. She would never realize the book had left her possession.

He leaned his shoulder against the window frame and stared out at the gardens below, watching the wind carve patterns into the snow, thinking of Laura. He closed his eyes, conjuring her face, the dark beauty of her eyes, the curve of her lips, each feature delicately etched upon his memory. They were bound in ways even he did not fully understand. Or was it so indiscernible? Perhaps there was a simple answer to the mystery.

"Laura, my love, there just might be another fact you will do your best to deny, as you do your best to deny your love for me."

Mist from the waterfalls swirled on the warm breeze, spinning sunlight into a golden veil that brushed Laura's face. She had not expected to come here again so soon. The full moon had passed, and still she had found her way to this secret valley of her dreams.

"I've been waiting for you."

Laura pivoted at the sound of Connor's voice. He was in the pool that spread out from the base of the waterfalls, standing near the smooth black stone that surrounded the shimmering crystalline water. For a moment she could do nothing but stare, a mortal woman stumbling upon a pagan god in the midst of his realm.

His thick hair was slicked back from his face, the ebony strands curling at his nape. Sunlight glistened on the wide expanse of his bare shoulders, glittered like gold dust on the water clinging to the black curls covering his broad chest. As he looked at her, she became aware of the sunlight touching her breasts through the delicate silk of her gown, warmth conjuring sensation to shimmer across her skin.

He smiled, as though he realized he commanded every tingle rippling through her. "Come, join me."

She hesitated only a moment, dismissing the nagging voice of propriety whispering in her mind. Propriety

131

had no place in this secluded realm. She paused on the edge of the pool, the smooth black stone cool beneath her bare feet in spite of the sun shimmering all around her.

A smile curved his lips as Connor watched her, the intensity in his eyes dragging the air from her lungs. Water lapped at his waist. He stood naked before her, but for the shimmering veil of crystalline water.

Laura drew air into her lungs, tasting the sweetness of wildflowers and meadow grass mingled with the mist that swirled from the base of the falls. She stared, unable to drag her gaze away from the compelling sight of his potent male body.

"Join me." He touched her ankle, slipping his wet hand around her warm skin.

Heat drifted upward like steam rising inside of her, draining resistance, making her weak and powerful all in the same instant. She stood for what seemed an eternity, caught between a fear of the unknown and a desire that rose inside of her like the tide at the moon's command.

"Come." He slid his hand upward along her leg, long fingers curving around her calf. "I want to feel you next to me."

She suspected what would happen if she entered that shimmering pool: she would not emerge the same. He would alter her in ways she had not even allowed herself to imagine. "Connor, we shouldn't—"

"Come, join me."

She could find no power within her to resist him. This was Connor, the man she had loved all of her life. She placed her hands on his shoulders, his smooth skin slick beneath her palms. He grasped her waist and lifted her, drawing her into the pool, allowing her to slide against his body on her slow descent into the water.

Laura's breath tangled in her throat at the first touch of his body against hers. He was all power and strength wrapped in a shimmering heat that seeped into her pores. Thick muscles shifted against her breasts, the sheer silk of her gown nothing more than a pale veil between them, the wet heat of his skin searing her. Cool water climbed her legs, licking her calves, her thighs, her hips, wrapping around her waist as he lowered her, until her feet touched the smooth stone bottom. She swayed against him, her legs as liquid as the shimmering water, and he was there to steady her with his strong arms.

Water rippled from the base of the falls, sliding against his body before curling around her in a heated stream. The water lapped against her, dissolving the white silk of her gown into a transparent sheen that hugged the curves of her breasts.

"Beautiful," he said, his voice brushing against her like deep, soft velvet.

"For you." She slid her hands upward along his arms, flexing her fingers against his taut muscles. "I want to be beautiful for you, only you."

"You are everything I've ever wanted."

Laura stared up into his eyes, entranced by the desire for her shimmering in the endless blue depths.

He touched her breast through the sheer cloth, drawing her nipple between his thumb and forefinger.

Laura gasped, tipping back her head as sensation spiraled from her captured nipple.

"I've waited a lifetime to touch you like this."

She groaned deep in her throat. Bewitching. It was all she could think of as he rolled her nipple between his fingers.

She lowered her chin, staring through the water. Black curls formed a nest from which his thick organ soared, reaching for her. Fierce. Frightening. Fascinating. Could she possibly touch him, feel the smooth flesh, know him in this intimate way, if only for an instant?

"Touch me," he whispered, sliding his fingers around her wrist. "Feel how you command my body."

The heat of him shocked her as he pressed her fingers against his aroused flesh. She jerked back her hand.

"Touch me, Laura," he whispered, sliding his fingers across her cheek in a sleek caress of heat. "Know me. Know there is nothing to fear from me."

Laura stared at that part of him that was so exclusively male, so incredibly tempting. She touched him, a soft brush of her fingertips over the tip of him. He stirred beneath her touch, like a fierce, wild beast seeking a gentle touch, reaching for her. She stroked him.

Connor sucked in his breath.

She glanced up, seeing the intensity in his blue eyes, the mischief in the grin that curved his lips. Water oiled her skin as she explored the length and breadth of him, sliding up and down, discovering each subtle shading of texture and heat, reveling in the way the beast gentled to her touch. "I've never felt anything like this," she whispered, closing her hand around him.

He clenched his jaw as though he were in pain. Still, she knew in some deep, primal place inside of her that this was pleasure, a pleasure sinking so deep inside of him it was nearly impossible to endure.

"I want you." He flicked open the buttons of her gown, his dark hand moving across the sheer silk. "Every inch of you."

Heart. Body. Soul. There would be no turning back if she surrendered to him.

Laura stared as he peeled the silk from her skin, the sight of his dark hand against her pale breast riveting. Sunlight flickered on the pink buds that beaded and pleaded for his touch. She arched against the strong arm he slid around her waist, offering her breasts in silent supplication to this summer god.

He lowered his head, his lips brushing her nipple before he took her breast into his mouth. A soft moan rose from deep inside of her as he tugged at her sensitive flesh, flicking his tongue against the crest, nipping gently with his teeth.

She sank her hands into his midnight hair, the wet strands curling around her fingers. Water slid between her legs, a cool brush against flesh that wept hot tears for want of him.

He abandoned her breast, only to take the other with exquisite torture. She pressed against him, lifting her hips, the hard thrust of his arousal sliding sinuously against her belly.

He had always been here for her. He had always understood her, known her better than anyone. And she wanted to know him in every way possible for a woman to know a man. Still, she wondered what price she would pay for this glorious surrender.

"Tell me." He slid his hands through her hair, cradling her head, holding her captive as he stared down into her eyes. "Tell me you'll be mine, now and always. For eternity."

Fear prickled deep inside of her. Fear he would draw her away from her world and everything she had ever known. "Please," she whispered, suddenly unsure of herself.

"You're frightened." He slid his arms around her waist, holding her in a warm embrace. "Tell me what's wrong."

"I don't know." She stared up into his eyes, seeing the promise of eternity. Yet that promise both beguiled and terrified her.

He drew in his breath, then released it on a long sigh that brushed her damp face with heat. If he pressed her she would surrender all she had to give. She knew it. And so did he. She could see it in his eyes.

He stepped back, freeing her from the bewitching circle of his arms. "Come swim with me. The cool water should do wonders for both of us."

Chapter Eleven

Connor had a feeling Laura would not approve of his exploration, but he was not a man to be kept prisoner in his room, especially after the dream he had shared with her the night before. He had awakened restless, every muscle taut with need. A fist of desire curled in his loins, pounding against his flesh when he thought of Laura lying alone in her bed, so close he could sense her every breath.

He drew a deep breath and marched in the opposite direction from her room. The Laura he knew in his dreams might be warm and yielding, but the Bostonian Laura could freeze a man with a glance. All he needed was a little time, he assured himself, time to melt the ice.

The scent of fresh-baked cinnamon rolls and brewed coffee drifted from the main floor, teasing his senses as he descended the back staircase. He followed that delicious aroma and discovered the kitchen.

Bright winter sunlight spilled through the windows, reflecting on the copper kettles suspended from a wrought-iron fixture above the table, setting the room aglow with a golden light. Fiona stood beside the big oak table that dominated the center of the room. She was tucking a napkin into the collar of a dark-haired girl of six or seven who sat at the table.

"Good morning," Connor said, smiling when Fiona turned to face him.

"And good morning to you, sir. My, but you're looking fine today."

"And you too are looking fine, Fiona."

Fiona giggled, a blush rising to stain her cheeks.

"Who's that, Grandma?" the little girl asked, tugging on Fiona's light gray sleeve.

"It's Mr. Connor Paxton, Megan. Miss Laura and Miss Sophie's cousin from England."

Megan turned her head toward the doorway where Connor stood, but there was a distant look in her big blue eyes, as though she were looking past him. "You sound tall."

Connor's chest tightened as he looked at this delicate little girl and realized why her pretty eyes seemed so distant.

"He is tall, Megan." Fiona patted the girl's small shoulder. "And very handsome."

Megan smiled at Connor. "Will you have your breakfast with me?"

"Now, Megan. He'll be having his breakfast in the dining room."

"But Miss Laura has her breakfast with me lots of times. Why can't he eat with me?"

"Now, Megan, you can't be—"

"I would be honored to have breakfast with such a lovely young lady."

"He's nice too," Megan said, a smile lighting her little face.

Fiona looked at Connor, her gratitude reflected in her dark eyes. "Now you sit right here, sir," she said, pulling out the chair at the head of the table, to the left of Megan. "And I'll be fixing you the best breakfast you ever had."

Laura stared at the early morning sunlight slipping into her bedroom, her mind wandering through her dream from the night before. Wisps of images haunted her—Connor holding her, touching her in ways she had never imagined possible. "Oh, my gracious," she whispered.

She closed her eyes, hugging her pillow to her shamefully aching breasts, trying to forget the feel of his body moving against hers. Somehow she would rid herself of those images. She certainly couldn't allow such wicked thoughts to take root in her mind.

She threw back the covers. Somehow she would get her life back in order. On most mornings she rose with the sun, and this morning she intended to follow some semblance of her normal life, that is, her life before an infuriating Viking barged into her world.

After dressing in a gown of mint green wool she began her usual pilgrimage to the kitchen. It was her habit every morning to eat a roll or a slice of bread covered with jam before taking a long walk. Right now she needed to hold on to that routine, to remind herself that her entire world had not disintegrated into disorder.

The aroma of fried bacon mixed with the heady fragrance of fresh cinnamon rolls teased Laura's senses as she descended the back staircase. She paused in the doorway of the kitchen, stunned by what she saw. Connor sat at the head of the big oak table beside Megan, while Fiona fixed breakfast.

"I would never have taken you for an Englishman," Fiona said.

"I lived for a while in Ireland." Connor smiled when he noticed her in the doorway, a smile filled with such honest warmth, such genuine affection, Laura forgot to breathe.

He was dressed in one of the ready-made shirts and trousers they had purchased for him the day before. How could he manage to look so regal with the first few buttons of his starched white shirt unfastened and his cuffs rolled up to his elbows? Laura wondered.

Hadn't she told him how improper it was for a gentleman to go about revealing so much of his person? And there he sat, exposing the hollow of his neck, where those intriguing masculine curls shaded his smooth skin. She trembled with the memory of those black curls brushing her breasts through sheer, wet silk.

It was only a dream, she assured herself. A scandalous dream that must be forgotten.

"Now I was thinking there was a bit of the sod in your voice." Fiona shoveled scrambled eggs from an iron skillet onto a platter that was already piled high with slices of bacon. "I'm supposing it's in Ireland where you found your love for the past and Irish Vikings."

"I suppose."

Laura shivered in the warm room. They were talking about his life, a life they had sketched together on paper the day before, a life that could be pulled apart as easily as the warm cinnamon rolls piled high on a platter before him.

"Good morning," he said, rising from his chair when Laura entered the room "Did you sleep well?"

Laura stiffened at the question. Could he possibly know what had happened in her dream last night?

"What are you doing here?" she asked, the sharp tone in her voice drawing a curious glance from Fiona.

"Having breakfast with a charming lady," Connor said, tugging on one of Megan's long, dark curls.

"Miss Laura!" Megan shouted as she jumped from her chair.

Megan ran across the oak planks that lined the floor as though she could see every step of the way. Laura bent to meet her and the little girl ran straight into her arms.

"Good morning, sweetie," Laura said, hugging Megan close, breathing in the sweet scent of lavender clinging to her glossy dark curls.

Megan pulled back in Laura's arms, her little face serious. "Are you mad at me 'cause I asked Connor to eat in the kitchen?" she whispered.

"Of course not," Laura said, keeping her voice as soft as Megan's.

"But you sounded so mad."

"Never at you, sweetie." Laura kissed Megan's brow. "I was just surprised to see Connor here."

Megan smiled. "He said he'd be honored to have breakfast with me."

"And so am I."

"Do you think he'd let me see what he looks like? Grandma says he's real handsome."

"Why don't you ask him?"

Megan crinkled her nose. "Would you ask him for me?"

Laura looked up at Connor, each beat of her heart thudding at the base of her throat. "Megan would like to see what you look like. Would you mind if she touched your face?"

Laura saw the emotion in Connor's eyes, the softness as he looked at the blind little girl. He came around the table and knelt beside Megan and Laura. He took Megan's little hands in his gentle grasp and placed her fingers on his chin. Laura watched them, following Megan's small white hands as they roamed upward over his sun-drenched skin.

"You like to smile," Megan said, tracing the curve of his smile with her fingertips.

"So do you," he said, his smile growing wider.

He kept smiling as Megan explored the slim line of his nose, the curves of his cheeks, the thick fringes of his black lashes. And somehow, Laura felt as though she too were touching that smooth golden skin, learning every curve, every line, each silky lash of his eyes. She watched, breathless at the way he knelt quiet and gentle beneath a little girl's touch, like a powerful wild stallion allowing the touch of a butterfly.

"Grandma was right," Megan said, smiling as she patted his broad shoulders. "You are handsome."

Connor kissed the tip of her nose. "Thank you, gentle lady."

Laura clenched her jaw, fighting the tears she felt sting her eyes.

Fiona cleared her voice, her dark eyes moist. "Now you sit and eat, sir. We don't want your food getting cold."

Connor lifted Megan in his arms and deposited the giggling child in the chair to his left as Fiona set a plate filled with eggs and bacon in front of him.

"Has my father had his breakfast yet, Fiona?" Laura asked.

"Hours ago. He was up before dawn and out the door with a roll in his hand."

"I see." Laura drew the fragrant air into her lungs, trying to ease the sudden tightening in her chest. Her father had a business to run. He couldn't be expected to sit around the house waiting to have breakfast with his daughter.

"Come now, Miss Laura, eat something. You need a little more flesh on your bones. No man will be wanting a wife who is nothing but a hank of hair and a bag of bones."

"Fiona, really." Laura glanced at Connor, feeling the heat of her blush rise in her cheeks.

"I don't know about that, Fiona." Connor sipped his coffee, watching Laura as she sat in the chair to his right. "I can think of one or two men who might take the lady just the way she is."

She saw compassion in his eyes, and something more, something heated that touched her deep inside, like smoldering coal dropped into an icy pool. Under the heat of his gaze the air evaporated from Laura's lungs.

"More than one or two gentlemen, I'm thinking." Fiona used a pair of tongs to plop a cinnamon roll on a plate. She set the plate in front of Laura. "Our Miss Laura has Boston in a stir, she does. Why, you should see the young gentlemen coming to call."

"Miss Laura's real pretty," Megan said, turning to face Connor. "Like a fairy princess."

"Yes, she is," Connor said, smiling at Laura.

"A smart man would be snatching her up right away, he would," Fiona said.

Laura sent Fiona a chilling stare. Fiona grinned, deep creases flaring out from her brown eyes.

"But first he must win the lady's heart," Connor said. "He must show her he's worthy of her love. He must prove nothing could ever make him leave her side."

Why did he have to look at her that way, as though she were the most beautiful woman on God's green earth? It made it so hard to breathe, so hard to resist a man who was not even of her world.

"He reminds me of the prince in one of the fairy tales you read to me, Miss Laura," Megan said, grinning at

Laura from across the table. "The handsome prince who woke up the princess who was sleeping for a hundred years."

A handsome prince who had traveled a thousand years through time, Laura thought. A long way to come just to drive her to distraction.

The barber had trimmed his hair so it fell in neat waves that just brushed the collar of his shirt. Still, an unruly lock tumbled in a black wave across his brow, tempting her to smooth it back into place. She remembered the silky feel of his hair sliding through her fingers. All she had to do was lean forward, just a few inches, and she could slide her fingers into his hair.

Good heavens, what was she thinking!

Laura tore a roll with her fingers, the soft dough sticky with butter and cinnamon. She would not fall under this barbarian's spell.

"I'm glad to see the rules governing this century can sometimes be broken." Connor lifted a cinnamon roll from the platter. He winked at Laura when she met his gaze.

Laura glanced down at her sticky fingers. The man was the most infuriating creature she had ever met. Now he was implying her manners were not proper.

"Why, Mr. Paxton, you talk as though you were a stranger to this century," Fiona said, filling his coffee cup.

Laura glared at the man. He had to guard his tongue much more closely.

"I've spent so much time studying the past that sometimes I feel as though I'm from a different century." He grinned at Laura. "It's sometimes difficult to remember all of the rules of polite society."

"Aye." Fiona nodded. "There be a long list of rules."

"I would like to think a few can be broken. It makes me feel more at ease to see everything is not always so

144

rigid," he said, his voice soft and deep, like down wrapped in warm velvet.

Did he feel ill at ease? Laura glanced at him, seeing vulnerability in those blue eyes, a man lost from everything he knew, thrust into a confusing world. Yet there was no fear in his eyes. Instead she saw determination, a will of iron, and a need she recognized because she had seen it far too often when she glanced in a mirror.

Edaina, soul mate—the words echoed in her mind. Was it possible? Were they truly joined in some unimaginable way? How seductive, to believe their love could have crossed time. It was a fairy tale. A fantasy. A dream come true.

It was a nightmare.

She glanced down at her roll, staring at the cinnamon swirling through the soft dough. She could not allow herself to be drawn into this web. For all she knew, the man could disappear, with or without Sophie's help. The next full moon could draw him back to his own time. She could not allow herself to love him; that emotion would bring her nothing but disaster.

"I'm sorry if you're uncomfortable here." Laura stared at her roll, afraid of revealing far too much to this man.

"Every day I find something more I like about Boston." He touched Laura's chin, a soft brush of his fingers across her skin as he coaxed her to look at him. "There is much to be gained in this time and place, all I have ever wanted."

The breath stilled in her lungs. His touch had the uncanny way of making her forget where she was and who she was and why she couldn't possibly fall in love with him. When he touched her everything seemed possible.

She stared into eyes as blue as the sky in the secret valley of her dreams, feeling the gentle press of his fingers on her skin. He couldn't stay. They were worlds apart. Yet she wanted this moment to last, to stretch and expand until the world dissolved and all that remained was this man and the promise of forever she saw in his eyes.

"Come for a walk with me," he said, sliding his thumb over the plump curve of her lower lip. "I wish to see some of your Boston."

Boston.

Reality.

Laura sat back, pulling away from him. "I don't think that's a good idea."

"You don't like to go walking?"

"Why, the lass goes walking most every morning, don't you, Miss Laura?"

Laura glanced to where the plump little housekeeper was standing by the sink. For a moment she had forgotten Fiona and Megan were still there. She had the feeling Connor could make her forget nearly everything, including her own name. "I don't think Connor is up to walking around Boston just yet."

Connor grinned. "I'm feeling more than fit for a walk."

That's exactly what she was afraid of. "I would rather not."

Connor shrugged. "Then I'll go exploring on my own."

"You can't." The idea of a Viking roaming around unsuspecting Boston terrified her. "There are things we need to do today."

Connor frowned. "More rules?"

"Yes. And you still don't know how to dance."

"It's early. I'll only be gone a few hours."

"You could . . . get lost."

The curve of his smile tilted into a devilish grin. "I'm very good at finding my way around."

The stubborn barbarian was going with or without her. She cringed when she thought of the havoc the brute might cause wandering around her city. "All right, but only for a little while."

"I look forward to seeing Boston with such a lovely guide."

Laura looked away from him. She drew in a deep breath and tried to convince her heart to cease its ridiculously fast pace.

Chapter Twelve

"Where are Megan's parents?" Connor asked as they walked away from the house.

"Megan's mother died in childbirth." Laura glanced around, relieved Mrs. Gardner was nowhere in sight. More than once Laura had encountered Philip's mother on one of her early walks. Mrs. Gardner liked to stroll Beacon Street like a queen surveying her kingdom, or a gossip looking for fodder. "Megan's father left soon afterward. He didn't want the responsibility of raising a little girl alone."

"And Megan's mother, she was Fiona's daughter?"

Laura nodded, remembering the shy young woman who had been her friend for a few short years. "Her name was Arleen."

Connor glanced around him as though fascinated by the towering stone houses lining one side of the street. "Was Megan born without sight?"

"No." She paused on the snow-covered sidewalk,

waiting for a carriage to pass before crossing Beacon Street. "She came down with a fever four years ago, when she was three. It took her sight. She can see shadows, that's all."

"And the doctors, have they given any hope of her ever regaining her sight?"

Laura's eyes narrowed against the glare of sunlight on the snow that spread like a field of glittering white diamonds across Boston Common. "They said it was possible in time, but not likely. And now, after so many years, I doubt it will ever happen."

He was quiet, gazing out over the rolling drifts of white that covered the common, lost in thoughts he chose not to share.

"She is a happy little girl, in spite of her lack of sight."

"Yes." He smiled as he looked down at her. "Her warmth has touched me."

As his warmth had touched her own soul, Laura thought. She shivered with that realization.

Snow crunched beneath her boots as she walked beside Connor. Elms lifted arching branches, forming a silvery white canopy above their heads. They were the only people in the park, the only people in this glittering world of silver and white. And somehow, in a way she didn't want to understand, it seemed right, being here with him. In ways, he had been with her most of her life.

"When I was a child, my brothers and I would build fortresses in the snow." The crisp breeze ruffled his black hair. "We would divide into armies and have glorious battles."

"I suppose little Vikings are expected to have fine battles."

"I suppose all children love to play in the snow."

"Do they?" Laura glanced away from him, a memory stirring inside of her, bringing with it a chill, as though the cover had been pried from a dark, empty space inside of her.

"Didn't you enjoy playing in the snow?" Connor asked.

How dare you play in the snow!—the words echoed in her memory. They had been spoken on a morning like this, after a strong, fresh snow had fallen when Laura was only six. The gardens behind her house had looked so beautiful, as if the sun had scattered diamonds across the snow. After donning her coat and gloves and boots, she had slipped out of the house to play in that field of sparkling diamonds.

Laura remembered the crisp chill against her cheeks as she had tossed handfuls of snow toward the sun, watching as it rained over her in a shower of diamonds. Then Ridley had come for her. She remembered the sadness in his dark eyes as he had ushered her back into the house and to her mother's sitting room.

What were you thinking, you reckless child? her mother had demanded. *Do you wish to take ill? Do you wish to bring sickness into this house? Your carelessness will cause the death of me yet.*

Laura drew a deep breath, catching the bitter taste of burning wood and coal that drifted upward from hundreds of chimneys, feeling a sting of guilt as strong as it had been that morning so long ago. She had promised her mother she would never again play in the snow. And she never had.

"Laura?" Connor touched her arm.

She glanced up at him. "What?"

Connor smiled, a gentle curve of his lips that made her feel exposed, as though he could perceive her every thought and emotion. "Did you enjoy playing in the snow as a child?"

She looked away from him. "Playing in the snow is really a foolish thing to do."

"I see."

The man saw far too much with those beautiful blue eyes. She trudged through the snow, several inches deep on the path that had been shoveled yesterday, three and four feet deep where it had drifted for weeks. "We really should go back. You still must learn how to dance and—"

Something plopped against her back. She turned to find Connor standing a few yards behind her, grinning. "What did you just do?"

"I hit you with a ball of snow."

"You hit me with a snowball?"

"That's right." Connor bent and snatched a handful of snow from a drift that reached his knees.

She watched as he slowly packed the snow into a ball. "Put that down immediately."

"All right." With a flick of his wrist he sent the snowball flying.

Laura gasped as the soft-packed ball hit her chest, splashing snow into her face. "Why you . . . you . . ."

"Barbarian?"

"Yes!" she shouted, scrubbing at the snow plastered to the emerald green wool of her coat.

"I suggest you prepare to defend yourself." He scooped up a handful of snow. "I intend to throw another one."

"A gentleman does not—"

"I warned you." He lobbed this one. It arched, a glittering ball of silver that hit the top of her green velvet hat, wilting black ostrich feathers, raining snow on her shoulders.

Laura shrieked. "How dare you!"

"You will find a barbarian will dare anything." He bent to scoop up snow.

She brushed a damp ostrich feather away from her eyes. "Stop this childishness!"

151

"The snow is not as wet as I prefer," he said, packing the snow into a ball. "The best balls are made from nice, heavy snow."

Laura glanced around, hoping no one was near to see this spectacle. The common was deserted.

"But this snow will do." He threw the snowball, hitting her hip. Something cracked inside of her: the ice surrounding her self-control. "Stop this immediately!"

"Grab some snow and hit me."

"At the moment I could strangle you."

He laughed, the deep, rich sound of a man who was fond of laughter. "Come and get me," he shouted, spreading open his arms.

"Oooo . . ." She snatched a handful of snow and tossed it at him, the loose flakes falling in a shower of diamond dust.

"Pack it," he said, patting snow into a nice round ball.

"I have no intention of getting into a—" The snowball hit her shoulder, splintering the ice inside of her. "Why you . . ." She snatched up a handful of snow, packed it, and hurled it straight at his head.

He ducked, grinning at her. "Nice try."

She would show the arrogant buffoon, she thought, packing snow into a nice big ball. As she turned to throw it, he hit her arm with a well-aimed snowball.

"Villain!" she shouted, hurling her snowball. It hit his chest, spraying snow in all directions.

"Nice shot!" he said, wiping snow from his chin.

Laura bounced on her toes, giggling. "I did it!"

The next snowball hit her chest, spraying her face with frozen flakes.

"Oh, you . . . monster!" She packed a snowball and ran toward him, improving her chances for a direct hit.

He backpedaled as she ran toward him, his laughter filling the crisp air until her snowball hit him smack in the face. He blinked, snow clinging to his thick lashes.

Laura laughed, pure, sweet laughter that bubbled up from a well hidden deep inside of her. It had been a long, long time since she had felt this free.

A deep growl ripped through the air. She squeaked as he lunged for her. He tackled her, wrapping his arms around her waist, taking her with him into a snowdrift. Snow flew in silvery plumes around them as he settled on top of her.

"Viking!" She laughed, pushing on his shoulders.

"Enchantress," he said, smiling down at her.

Snowflakes drifted over them, glittering in the sunlight, dusting his hair with diamonds, painting his black brows with silver, kissing his smiling lips. Laura fell still beneath him, aware suddenly of the heat of his body where he pressed against her—a summer oasis in a frozen world.

A small voice screamed in her mind; she shouldn't be here. She shouldn't be this close to him. This was not at all proper. No, this was dangerous. Far too dangerous. And yet she couldn't find the words to tell him to leave her alone. She had been alone for so very long, except for Connor, only Connor.

"You have wonderful laughter inside of you," he said, brushing the snow from her cheek, his black leather glove cold and smooth against her skin, making her long for the heat of his fingers. "You should share it more often."

Snowflakes melted on his smiling lips, crystal droplets falling to touch her lips, warm from his kiss. She remembered the feel of his lips against hers: firm, warm, infinitely alluring. Had it only been yesterday when he had kissed her? It seemed a lifetime since she had felt his lips against hers.

Without conscious thought, she slipped her tongue between her lips, catching the melted snow that had kissed his lips, tasting him. Connor drew a sharp breath.

Thick black lashes lowered as he stared at her lips. She knew what he was thinking. He wanted to kiss her. He would kiss her if she didn't stop him. She should stop him, she thought, watching his lips as they drew near. Oh my, yes, she should stop him.

"Laura," he whispered, his lips brushing hers. "My beautiful Laura."

His breath warmed her chilled cheek as he kissed her, a slow slide of his lips against hers. She should push him away. She should not allow such liberties. Yet when she tried to push him away, her fingers curled against his wide shoulders, seeking to draw him near.

He was summer in a life filled with winter. He was every smile she had ever known, every note of laughter, every hope and dream. And she wanted his warmth, needed his smiles, craved his laughter.

He growled deep in his chest, opening his mouth over hers. He traced the seam of her lips with the tip of his tongue. She remembered the feel of him filling her mouth, the delicious taste and texture as he had dueled with her tongue. She knew she wanted all of this and more, so much more.

She parted her lips, welcoming the slick thrust of his tongue. He tasted of cinnamon and coffee and a spice she would always think of as Connor, only Connor.

She slipped her arms around his neck, needing to get closer to this man. Yet no matter how close she held him it wasn't enough, not nearly enough. Layers of clothes got in her way.

Images from an illicit dream flickered in her mind. Every nerve in her body retained the memory of his skin sliding against hers, his body touching her, claiming a place of mystery hidden deep inside of her.

She wiggled beneath him, trying to snuggle closer to

his warmth. She felt him stiffen, heard him groan as if in pain, and then he was lifting away from her.

He looked down at her, his breath warm puffs of steam against her lips. She stared up into the incredible blue of his eyes, longing for his kiss, wondering why he had stopped.

He swallowed hard. "You'll catch a chill lying here."

Too late, she thought, reality seeping like ice water into her veins. Laura closed her eyes, blocking out the compelling beauty of his face. This had to stop. She couldn't confuse dreams with reality. Heaven help her, she had to end this self-destructive fascination with this Viking.

She felt him pull away from her and it was all she could do to keep from reaching for him. If she didn't gain control over her wayward emotions . . . she shivered as she thought of the consequences. Yet she couldn't be sure if it was a shiver of fear or a shiver of anticipation.

She stood, ignoring his hand when he tried to help her. "You must stop this."

"What?"

"This unseemly behavior." She scrubbed at the snow on her coat. "A gentleman would never catch a lady unaware as you did me."

He slipped his hand under her chin, coaxing her to look at him. He was smiling with his lips and his eyes, a warm, gentle smile that spoke of everything she longed and dreaded to hear. "Is that what I did just now, catch you unaware?"

"Yes." She pushed his hand aside. "You most certainly did."

"And here I thought all I did was kiss you."

"That was catching me unaware." Laura drew a deep draft of cold air into her lungs. "A gentleman would never presume to kiss a lady in that . . . that heated fashion."

He grinned, mischief lighting his eyes. "Please show me how a gentleman would kiss a lady."

"He wouldn't!"

"Never?"

"Only after they are engaged." She pushed the ostrich feather out of her eyes. "And then only on the cheek."

Connor frowned. "Are you certain of this?"

"Quite certain."

One corner of his lips quirked upward. "Even when the lady wishes to be kissed?"

Laura released her breath in a hiss between her teeth. "If you think for one moment I wanted you to kiss me, you are very much mistaken."

"Was there someone else here just now with her arms around my neck?"

Laura pivoted and marched toward her house. She would not allow this man to humiliate her further.

"Wait a minute." He grabbed her arm, pulling her up short.

She froze beneath his touch. "Kindly remove your hand."

"Are you angry at me?" he asked, holding her in a firm grip. "Or angry at yourself because you enjoyed kissing me?"

"I did not enjoy kissing you!"

"I think you did." He grabbed her upper arms, holding her when she tried to break away from him. "I think for the first time in your life, your emotions are getting out of control and it scares you half to death."

She closed her eyes. "Will you please stop this?"

"Laura, don't you see? You can't keep everything bottled up inside of you."

"A woman of good breeding does not hang her emotions out like laundry."

"In this century a well-bred woman is supposed to keep all her emotions buried in some dark little tomb inside of her, is that it?"

She stared up at him, trying to maintain her dignity while looking past the limp ostrich feather dangling from her hat. "Well-bred individuals certainly do not parade their emotions around for everyone to see."

"I suppose it's improper to feel anger?"

"Anger is a base emotion."

"Indecent to laugh?"

Never allow your laughter to become vulgar—her mother's words rang in her ears. "You must keep your laughter to a moderate tone."

"And no doubt it's a hanging offense to feel anything remotely resembling desire."

Laura lifted her chin, a black ostrich feather bobbing before her eyes. "You are being quite vulgar."

"Am I?" He tightened his grip on her arms, jerking her toward him. "And is this vulgar?" he asked, before sealing his lips to hers.

This kiss was nothing like the other two she had experienced with this man. He kissed her with a raw passion that arced from him and ripped through her like lightning. He slanted his lips over hers as though he wanted to absorb her, devour her, consume her.

Laura gasped from the sheer intensity of him, the emotion that ran like a swollen river through this man. She struggled to free herself, afraid he would tap the spring of desire hidden deep inside of her, knowing she would drown if it ever joined with his.

He held her tighter, wrapping his strong arms around her, clamping her to his hard chest. He thrust his tongue into her mouth, then retreated only to thrust again, dancing to a rhythm that whispered low in her belly, taunting her in some mysterious way her mind could not comprehend, but her body knew.

Logic waged a battle with instinct within her. In spite of a warning voice that shouted in her brain, she felt her body yielding, melting against him. She tried to stifle the moan of pleasure rising in her throat, and failed, the soft sound sighing against his lips.

"It can't be wrong to feel this way, Laura," he whispered, his lips brushing hers. "This powerful pull that brought me to your side is a gift we share. Don't deny it. Don't deny me."

"Let go of me," she said, her words a harsh whisper.

"We belong to one another," he said, dropping his hands from her arms. "We always have."

She stumbled back, pressing her hand to her lips, the cold black leather chilling the lingering warmth of his kiss. "You must stop this!"

The breeze tossed a lock of black hair across his brow as he stared down at her, his blue eyes touching her soul. "How can I stop loving you when you are a part of me?"

"I'm not!"

"You are. And I'm a part of you."

There was truth lingering in his words, truth lurking inside of her, a truth far too frightening to acknowledge. A life with this man was impossible.

She knew what her father expected of her. For heaven's sake, she had responsibilities. No matter how attracted she was to this man, there was no place in her life for Connor, even if by some miracle he remained after the full moon had come and gone.

"You must stop saying these things." She turned and started running toward her house.

"You're running away like a frightened rabbit."

"A rabbit." She pivoted to face him, pushing the feather from her eyes. "I'm not frightened of you."

He held her in the taut tether of his gaze, his lips—

so accustomed to a smile—now a grim line. "You're terrified of me, and the way I make you feel."

Laura huffed, her breath condensing into a white puff. "Don't be ridiculous."

"Fine. Since you aren't frightened of me, then there is no reason you can't show me some of your city."

"I can think of one reason." She batted the feather out of her eyes. "I don't care to spend time with you."

He drew in a deep breath, his broad shoulders rising beneath the black wool of his overcoat. "All right."

She frowned as he turned and started walking away from her, in the opposite direction from the house. "Where are you going?"

"To see Boston," he said without glancing over his shoulder.

"Alone?"

"It looks that way."

"You could get lost."

"Maybe." He shoved his hands into his pockets, his long strides carrying him farther and farther away from her.

"There are dangerous parts of this city!" she shouted.

He didn't respond. He just kept walking away from her, a tall, broad-shouldered man who was all alone in the world.

He knew no one. He knew nothing of streetcars, and railroads. What if he stepped out in front of a train? He was in ways a child wandering through a foreign and hostile world. "Wait!"

He kept walking as though he didn't hear her.

She started after him, walking at first, then increasing her pace until she was running to catch him. "Wait!"

He pivoted, halting in the middle of the narrow path. She skidded to a stop, thrusting her hands against his hard chest as she plowed into him. "Sorry," she murmured, stepping back.

"What do you want?"

She pushed the feather out of her eyes. "In all good conscience I cannot allow a Viking to roam the streets of Boston unattended."

He lifted one black brow. "Do you think you can protect Boston from the rabid Viking raider?"

The feather flopped across her nose. "If he gets out of hand I suppose I can always stuff a snowball down his back."

"I think that will stop him." He smiled as he plucked the ruined feather from her hat.

Laura gazed up into his smiling face, realizing how much more she preferred his smile over his frown. "From the history books you've read of Boston, is there anything you would like to see in particular?"

"I would like to see the library."

"The library?"

His lips tipped into a devilish grin. "Every good Viking likes to pillage the library first."

Chapter Thirteen

Sunlight flowed in glowing gold columns through the arched windows of Bates Hall, the main reading room of the public library. Laura plopped a stack of books on the reading table in front of Connor, the thud echoing in the cavernous room.

The man had flown through every newspaper published in Boston during the past ten years before leaving the newspaper room to lay waste to stacks of reference, literature, and history books. The library runners could not keep up with his consumption, so Laura had started lugging stacks of books from the shelves, feeding Connor books like a railroad fireman stoking the engines of a steam locomotive with wood.

Yet he wasn't reading now. He was staring at the closed cover of the book he had just finished, as though the dark green leather could tell him more than the printed words had told him.

"Did you run out of steam?"

161

"Steam?" He looked up at her, one black brow arching upward in question.

"It's an expression of speech. You've been charging through these books like a steam locomotive racing down the tracks. And now you're sitting here as though all of the fuel is spent."

"These expressions are what I find most surprising about this language." He glanced down at the green leather book, sadness settling around his broad shoulders like a shroud.

"Is something wrong?" she asked, suddenly realizing how accustomed she had become to his smiles. "Are you ill?"

"No, I'm not ill." He looked up at her, giving her a smile. Yet the curve of his lips did not ease the sorrow lurking in the blue depths of his eyes. "I thought perhaps I could learn of my family in the pages of these books."

Laura glanced at the title tooled in gold on the green leather: *A History of Ireland.* "And did you find out what happened to them?"

"No. There is only a sketchy history of my time. But it does say Scandinavian power in Ireland came to an end during the first years of the eleventh century." Connor drew his fingertip over the title, tracing each letter. "The Norsemen were assimilated, or destroyed."

Laura wondered what would have happened to Connor if he had remained in his century. Would he have survived the bloodshed? An unexpected feeling of protectiveness washed over her when she thought of the fate that might await him in his time. "Are you wondering if your family survived?"

"My family is strong, with strong alliances. My mother is an Irish princess. I must believe they survived. There might even be descendants of my family living today." He opened his hand, resting his palm on the cover of the book. "But it's difficult knowing I shall never see my parents, my brothers, my sisters again. They live only as memories to me now."

She sensed his pain, like a finger of frost sliding down her spine. In some way she felt responsible for bringing him here, for tearing his life into shreds. She rested her hand on his broad shoulder, hoping in some way to ease the chill wrapping around this prince of summer.

He glanced up at her. Understanding shimmered in his blue eyes, as though he could feel every conflicting emotion swirling inside of her, as though he knew her better than she knew herself, as though he were the one who wanted to give her comfort.

"I'm sorry," she whispered. *Sorry for believing in a dream that could never come true.*

"Don't be sorry. A man can live with only memories of his family." His lips slowly curved into a smile as he lifted her hand from his shoulder and held her palm over his heart. "But he cannot survive without his heart. I'm where I most want to be."

"Oh," she whispered, staring down into those incredible blue eyes. The warmth of his skin radiated through the linen of his shirt, throbbing with the strong beat of his heart against her palm. He was warm and real and here, in her time.

Be mine. For eternity, my love—the words whispered in her mind, a siren call luring her to disaster. It was impossible to consider a future with a man who had no place in this century.

Slowly, far too reluctantly, she drew her hand from his light grasp, her skin suddenly cool where it had been warm nestled between his hand and chest. "I thought you weren't going to say such things to me."

His smile tipped into a devilish grin. "Are you always so frightened of the truth?"

163

"Don't be ridiculous I'm certainly not frightened of the truth."

"And yet you want to run and hide each time I confess how much you mean to me."

"Please keep your voice down." Laura glanced around the huge room, wondering if she knew any of the few people she saw sitting at the tables and wandering through the stacks. She recognized no one.

"Are you safe? Or has someone you know seen you with the horrible barbarian?"

Laura gave Connor a look designed to freeze him in his chair. He laughed, deep, rich laughter that echoed against the arched ceiling and rumbled like thunder down the length of the room. Heads turned, the other people who shared the huge room casting disapproving looks in their direction.

"Quiet," she whispered, sinking into the chair beside Connor, hiding behind a stack of books.

Connor drew his face into a serious mask. "I forgot; it's against the law to laugh in Boston."

Laura released her breath in a hiss between her teeth. "Now that you've pillaged the library, I suggest we go home."

"For more of your rules?"

Laura clasped her hands at her waist and stared at him, the way her tutor, Mr. Bixby, used to stare at her when he had caught her daydreaming. "I know you don't approve of all the social requirements of our time. Still, since we aren't altogether certain how long you will be trapped in this century, you must learn to conform while you are here."

Connor nodded. "Show me your city. There's no better way to teach me about your century."

No one had ever looked at her the way he did, as though she were a key that would unlock all of the riches in the world. She was the teacher, and he the student eager to explore all of life, his blue eyes burning with excitement and expectancy. How tempting. How very dangerous.

"From one of the maps of Boston, I noticed there was a train station nearby. I would like very much to see a steam locomotive."

"I think it would be better to go home."

"All right." He pushed back his chair. "I'll be back in time for dinner."

"I don't think you should be wandering about this town alone."

He grinned. "I'm glad you changed your mind. I'm always happy for your company."

"Oh, you are the most infuriating—"

"Please keep your voice down," he whispered, giving her a disapproving stare that would have rivaled any of Mr. Bixby's, except for the mischief sparkling in his blue eyes.

She drummed her fingers on the table, silently debating her choices, realizing he left her only one. "I'll call Aunt Sophie and tell her we won't be home for lunch."

The train house that ran along the back of the station seemed a giant man-made cave, iron tresses arching along the roof, iron poles plunging from the roof to the ground. A chill breeze blew in from the far mouth of the train's lair, rippling the legs of Connor's trousers as he moved toward the tall iron fence that imprisoned the huge iron beast beyond.

"You've seen your train. Now I suggest we leave." Laura glanced over her shoulder, staring back up the wide, sloping ramp leading to the main hall of the station. "Before someone sees us here."

"What harm is there in standing here?"

Laura pursed her lips. "The train isn't scheduled to

leave for another two hours."

"And it's against one of your rules to stand here and look at it?"

She clasped her hands at her waist and pinned him in one of those chilly stares she was so fond of giving. "No one in Boston stands around a platform staring at a train."

He grinned. "I do."

She released her breath in a hiss between her teeth. "Yes, I know."

How could he explain his need to see this creation? The steam engine had helped bring about the Industrial Revolution, forever altering the world, changing it from what Connor knew to something he must now discover.

"Look at it, Laura; it's magnificent." He rested his hand on the cold iron gate, testing the barrier. It was locked.

She frowned as she stared through the bars. "You must realize trains are commonplace. No one looks at a train with wonder any longer."

The train stood on iron rails, like a monster at rest. The other rails that led from a wooden platform to the opposite end of the huge iron cave were empty, the iron beasts having made good their escape. "How unfortunate they cannot see the wonder of this creation."

"What do you mean?"

"When we stop seeing wonder in something as magnificent as this mechanical marvel, we stop seeing wonder in everything around us."

"Nonsense." Laura looked away from him, staring at the train, her brow tugged into a frown. "Adults do not look at the commonplace and see miracles."

"And yet there are miracles around us every day."

Laura glanced up at him, one finely arched brow lifting. "I can think of one miracle I could certainly have done without."

"If you didn't want me here, why did you call to me?" Connor passed his hand over the latch, sensing the locking mechanism in the gate.

Laura stiffened, her chin jutting upward. "I didn't call you."

"It was your voice I heard calling to me. Your voice that beckoned me to your side."

"It can't be." Laura stepped back as though the truth grew in twisted thorns between them, and she feared getting tangled in them. "Aunt Sophie brought you here."

"Are you so certain of that?"

"Of course." Laura gripped one of the iron bars of the fence, her black glove growing tight across her knuckles. "I couldn't possibly have brought you here."

"Because it would mean you want me here?"

"Exactly."

"Is that what frightens you? Or is it the possibility you might have magic in your blood?"

"It's ridiculous to even think such a thing." She lowered her voice to a whisper, as though she were afraid someone in the distant station might hear her. "I certainly don't have magic in my blood."

Connor sighed, realizing he was a long way from being able to tell her the truth about himself.

"Now please come along."

"In a moment." He pulled open the gate, iron scraping against iron.

"That's odd." Laura stared at the gate as though it had suddenly spoken to her. "It should have been locked."

"Perhaps they knew I was coming."

"Trust me, Connor, no one could have imagined you would ever be in Boston."

"Ah, but I'm enjoying this place." He passed through the gate and stepped onto a wide wooden platform.

"You can't go out there. I'm certain passengers are

not allowed on the platform unattended."

"I didn't see a sign that said I couldn't." He moved toward the train, fascinated by the huge machine.

"Connor, come back here immediately."

He glanced back at her, smiling in the face of her fury. "Has anyone ever told you that you would make a good general?"

She frowned. "Why?"

"You like giving orders." He turned and walked along the platform toward the engine.

"Connor!" Laura shouted. "You can't do this. You'll get in trouble."

He glanced over his shoulder to where she stood outside the gate, as though the open portal were still barred and locked. She was staring at him, a general furious with her disobedient soldier. "I'll only be a few minutes."

"Stubborn barbarian!"

He smiled at her anger, understanding the chains that bound her. One day he would break those chains.

He glanced through the windows of the passenger cars as he passed them. Wooden benches lined both sides of the aisle in the first two cars, but the rest of the cars were much different. Red velvet covered narrow sofas that formed lines on either side of a narrow aisle in several cars, wicker chairs sat facing each other in several others, and dining tables and chairs marched down either side of the last car. Obviously there was a difference in class in these cars, a separation of the nobility from the peasants.

He paused beside the huge locomotive and pressed his hand against the cold black iron, the skin of this artificial beast of burden. The power of the machine thrummed through him, primitive yet potent. He had read of accidents with these trains, animals slaughtered on the rails, people killed when cars jumped the tracks. So this was modern magic.

"Here now, you can't be out here, sir."

Connor glanced over his shoulder. A tall, stout man dressed in dark blue trousers and a dark blue coat with shiny brass buttons was running toward him from the gate. He looked past the large man to where Laura stood, her hand tight on an iron bar of the gate, her expression proclaiming her every fear had just come true.

The station man halted beside Connor, breathing like a draft horse who has been forced to run in a derby. "Sir . . . I'm going . . . to have to ask you . . . to return to the station."

"I'm afraid you'll have to excuse my enthusiasm." Connor smiled. "I've never seen a train before."

The man cocked his head, eyeing Connor with suspicion in his dark eyes. "Never?"

"Never."

"Well, I'm afraid you can't be on the platform without a ticket. And even with a ticket, you can't be here this early before a train is to leave." He gestured toward the station. "Now, if you'll just be . . ."

Connor stared straight into the man's dark eyes and planted a single thought—*Would you like a closer look, sir?*

The plump man hesitated, a dazed look entering his eyes. "Would you like a closer look, sir?"

"Yes, I would. Thank you."

Laura took a deep breath of the crisp air as she left the station. "I don't understand it." She walked beside Connor, away from the imposing stone structure, snow crunching beneath her feet. "Why did that man give you a tour of the train?"

"I told him I had never seen a train before."

169

"That's all?" She stared up at Connor, still not believing what she had seen. It was as though he had taken control of the station man's will. "You mean you simply told him you had never seen a train before and he decided to give you a tour?"

"He was a most pleasant gentleman."

"Extraordinary." She released her breath in a steamy cloud. "We were lucky he was so agreeable."

"Yes." Connor glanced over his shoulder, frowning as he scanned the sidewalk.

"What's wrong?"

"Nothing. I just had a feeling we were being watched."

Laura glanced over her shoulder, seeing nothing amiss in the few people who strolled along the snow-covered sidewalk. "It's probably the stationmaster, making sure you're well on your way."

He smiled, his eyes lighting with a warmth she felt wrap around her like powerful arms. "Anytime I'm with you, I'm well on my way."

"Save your flattery for someone who wants it."

"I thought all women enjoyed flattery."

"You might have been able to bring all the ladies of the ninth century to their knees with your practiced ways, but you will find I'm quite immune to your dubious charm."

He tipped his lips into a devilish grin that added an extra beat to her heart. He winked. "One day, my love, you will be mine."

"When horses fly." She glanced away from him, trying to ease the thunderous pounding of her heart. The man was a rogue, a worldly man, even if that world was considerably different than her own. She would not fall under his spell. She most certainly could not surrender to the beguiling promises she saw in his eyes, no matter how tempting.

She stared into the window of the store they were passing, her attention snagged by the array of chocolates displayed with peppermint twists and caramel squares on the shelf behind the glass.

"What kind of shop is this?" Connor asked, pausing beside her on the sidewalk.

"It's Mr. Halloran's sweetshop." Laura stared through the window glass at the big sign posted on the wall behind the counter at the back of the store, where the current flavors of ice cream were posted. She could almost taste the rich, creamy treat melting on her tongue. "He makes some of the most delicious chocolate ice cream I've ever eaten."

"I'd like to try some of this." He turned and walked back to the entrance.

She stared into the window, her mouth growing moist. They couldn't possibly eat ice cream now, before lunch.

A small bell jangled as Connor opened the door. He stood aside, gesturing for Laura to enter the shop before him.

Laura hesitated, thinking of the ice cream and all the reasons she shouldn't indulge. It was ridiculous to think of eating ice cream now. Still, there was no reason why they couldn't buy some lemon drops for Megan, was there?

She entered the shop, armed with a worthy mission. Sweetness hovered in the warm air of the confectionery, born of chocolate and peppermint and maple taffy.

"Good afternoon, Miss Sullivan, and to you, sir." Mr. Halloran rested his pudgy hands on the wooden countertop, his white head barely rising a foot above the polished surface. "Will you be wanting your regular, miss?"

"What is your regular?" Connor asked, smiling as he looked at Laura.

Laura moistened her lips. "Chocolate ice cream."

"What is ice cream?" Connor asked the little man behind the counter.

"It's cream and sugar and eggs mixed with different flavors." Halloran popped open a lid beneath the counter and bent to dig into a silver bucket. "We freeze it and it comes out like this."

Connor took the spoon the man offered him, staring at the dark substance piled on the silver.

"That there's chocolate."

"Some of the best in the world," Laura whispered.

Connor slipped the spoon into his mouth, smiling as he tasted the sweet, creamy treat. "I'll have some of each flavor."

Laura tugged on his coat sleeve. "We haven't eaten lunch yet."

"We can eat here." Connor gestured to the three white wrought-iron tables near the windows. "We can have ice cream."

Laura shook her head. "We couldn't possibly eat ice cream for lunch."

"Then we'll eat ice cream and have lunch later."

"We can't eat ice cream before lunch." Laura clasped her hands at her waist, thinking of all the logical reasons they could not indulge in her favorite treat. "Ice cream is for dessert."

Connor frowned. "This is another rule?"

Laura pursed her lips. "It's only sensible to eat dessert after you've eaten your meal."

"Why?" Connor asked.

"Because it's . . ." Laura glanced at Mr. Halloran, who stood watching them, his round face crinkled with a big grin. "You could get too full to eat your proper meal."

"And if I eat my proper meal, I might get too full to eat ice cream." Connor glanced at his empty spoon as though he thought it was one of the saddest sights he had ever seen. "I think I'll have the ice cream, and take my chances with lunch."

There was simply no reasoning with the man. "All right. But not six scoops." She held up her hand when Connor started to speak. "Six scoops on an empty stomach will make you ill."

"That's a good reason." He grinned at her. "What do you suggest I have?"

"A scoop of chocolate, vanilla, and"—Laura looked up at the sign behind the counter—"a scoop of peach."

"You realize this is childish." Laura sat with Connor at one of the round wrought-iron tables near the windows of the little shop, sinking her spoon into a plump scoop of chocolate ice cream. "No responsible adult would be eating ice cream before lunch."

"I've never tasted anything like this." Connor dredged his spoon through a scoop of peach. "It's wonderful."

Laura couldn't suppress her smile as she watched his face light with pleasure. "There are those who only like to eat ice cream in the summer."

Connor pointed to her dish with his empty spoon. "You don't agree with them."

"I have to confess, I could eat ice cream every day of the year."

"If you want to, you should." Connor lifted a spoonful of vanilla to his lips, slipping the ice cream into his mouth, his smile reflecting his pleasure.

"We cannot always do what we want to do." She glanced down at her bowl, feeling a prick of guilt for her breach of decorum. "My mother would think I had lost my mind if she saw me now."

"There are rules that cannot be broken, this I agree." Connor blotted his lips with his napkin, the simple gesture made elegant by the graceful movement of his long-fingered hand. "But there are some rules designed solely to take away our freedom. These rules aren't worthy of respect."

"And if everyone felt that way, the world would fall to anarchy."

"Because we're eating ice cream before lunch?"

"Of course not." Laura jabbed her spoon into her ice cream. The man made the rules by which she had lived her entire life seem silly. "I wouldn't expect you to understand."

"Because I'm a marauding Viking?"

Laura looked up from her ice cream straight into a pair of endless blue eyes, eyes that startled her time and time again with the warmth of their beauty. She drew a breath, hoping to ease the sudden pounding of her heart, but the air only trickled past her tight throat.

Except for his tousled black mane, Connor looked every inch a Victorian gentleman in his white shirt and tie, his light gray coat molding his broad shoulders. Yet there was something about him, something smoldering beneath the elegant facade, an untamed spirit, a potent power that radiated from him and wrapped around her like the warmth of the sun, threatening to burn her if she came too close. Still, a part of her, that foolish girl who dwelled deep inside her soul, wondered what it would be like to feel the flames lick across her skin. She shivered, frightened by the wicked thoughts flickering in her mind.

"Does anything frighten you?"

He frowned, seemingly surprised by the turn of her thoughts. "I wouldn't be human if I were fearless."

"You don't seem frightened of anything. You approach everything as though it were a wonderful new discovery you had to claim as your own."

"This century is full of new discoveries for me."

"Yes, I know. But most people would be frightened

of so much change in so little time."

Connor turned his head to look out the window. Sunlight bathed his face, touching the tips of his thick black lashes with gold—an offering to this breathtaking god of summer who was lost for the moment in the depths of winter. "Have you ever seen a unicorn?"

"Of course not. There are no such things as unicorns."

"Not any longer." He looked at her, smiling, his eyes filled with a mischievous light. "But at one time, unicorns roamed the hills of a great island nation. They were the favorite mounts of the *Tuatha De Danann*, the people who ruled Atlantis."

"Atlantis?" Laura slipped a spoonful of ice cream into her mouth, the creamy chocolate melting over her tongue. Yet the taste of an exotic spice lingered in her memory, haunting her, warming her deep inside; a spice she would forever remember as the taste of Connor's mouth. She swallowed hard. "I'm a little old to believe in fairy tales."

"Considering all that has happened in the past few days, is it really so difficult to believe Atlantis and unicorns once existed?" He took a bite of ice cream, the spoon leaving a moist mist of cream lingering along the full curve of his lower lip.

"All right." Laura followed the slide of his tongue as he swiped the cream from his lips, her mouth growing dry as she remembered the feel of that slick tongue sliding between her lips. "So what happened to the unicorns of Atlantis?"

"The king's sorcerer warned him of the cataclysm that would destroy the island. Preparations were made to save as many people and animals as possible. Great ships were built and the exodus began. Yet when it came time for the unicorns to board the ships, they refused. No one could coax the animals to leave the island that was their home."

"Why didn't they simply force the unicorns onto the ships?"

"They did. But the unicorns that were forced upon the ships died before they reached the new land. The fear of change had broken their spirits and their hearts."

She caught herself staring at his lips, watching as he slipped a spoonful of ice cream into his mouth, wondering what it might be like to taste chocolate ice cream mingled with the spice of his mouth. "I suppose the moral to this little story is that those who do not change, who do not adapt, do not survive."

Connor nodded. "We must have the strength to bend, the courage to change, and the wisdom to know when to adapt."

Laura glanced away from Connor, disturbed by the wisdom she saw in his eyes; the wisdom that made her feel as though all the structure and rules she had obeyed all of her life were nothing more than iron bars designed to keep her a prisoner of propriety.

The man was a Viking, for heaven's sake. She couldn't expect him to respect the rules of society. And she certainly couldn't start breaking those rules. She shoved her spoon into her melting ice cream. This was all his fault. If he hadn't kissed her, she wouldn't be sitting here now, thinking scandalous thoughts. He had no right to make her thoughts travel down paths no lady should ever travel. No right at all.

Chapter Fourteen

"My mother was quite shocked to see Laura and Mr. Paxton leaving the common this morning." Philip Gardner sipped his tea, frowning as though it were bitter to his taste. "I must say, Miss Chandler, I'm surprised you allowed Laura to go walking alone with Mr. Paxton."

The warmth of sunlight spilling through the drawing-room windows behind Sophie chilled beneath Philip's dark glare. He sat on the edge of the Empire sofa beside her, like a stone statue perched on the green-and-gold-striped velvet.

"I'm certain Connor is quite capable of protecting Laura from harm." Sophie lifted a plate of sliced pound cake from the tea cart beside her. "Cake?"

"No, thank you." Philip pursed his lips. "I'm afraid you miss my meaning, Miss Chandler."

No, she hadn't. "More sugar?"

He shook his head. "Your cousin is a rather unusual man."

"Yes." Sophie stirred sugar into her tea. "You're quite perceptive to notice how exceptional he is. Why, he's brilliant, a genius, really."

"I seem to recall reading somewhere that genius is frightfully close to insanity."

"Did you?"

He nodded, his expression grave. "Surely you don't think a well-bred gentleman would go about with his hair down to his shoulders, wearing leather breeches?"

"Are you suggesting my cousin is ill bred, Mr. Gardner?"

"I think you must judge him for yourself. But as much as I hate to say this, I feel I must." He held her in an icy stare. "I believe you're being quite reckless with Laura's reputation, allowing this man to spend time alone with her."

"I see." Sophie forced her lips to maintain her smile. "Not only is my cousin ill bred, but I'm negligent in the care of my niece."

Philip sighed. "I say this only because I am deeply concerned for Laura. I think you realize I intend to make her my wife."

Sophie's spine stiffened at the thought of Laura married to this man. "She mentioned she was considering your proposal."

"In the future I would suggest you not allow Laura to spend time alone with a gentleman to whom she is not engaged. People may get the wrong impression. It could damage her reputation."

"And of course you wouldn't want a bride with a damaged reputation."

"I doubt any respectable man would want a bride with a damaged reputation." Philip cocked his head as he stared at her. "And I doubt Mr. Sullivan would be pleased if somehow Laura's reputation were sullied."

Sophie managed to keep the smile plastered to her lips as she wondered how Daniel would accept her meddling. "How fortunate I am to have you to tell me how I should behave."

Philip smiled, obviously pleased with himself. "I feel it my duty, Miss Chandler. You are, after all, naive to the ways of men."

Sophie's skin prickled under his cold gaze. "Because I'm a spinster?"

He cleared his throat. "It does imply a certain lack of experience."

Would she ever get used to the label society had scrawled across her forehead? Although she had received a number of offers in her youth, she had chosen to live her life without marriage. Yet it was there in that look of Philip's, a look she had often seen in the glances of so many others: the suggestion that she had never been quite good enough to cross that all-important bridge from maiden to married woman.

"I do hope you see the importance of maintaining Laura's untarnished reputation." Philip smiled, a smug twisting of his lips. "We wouldn't want to see her in the same situation in which you find yourself."

"I want to see Laura happily married. To the right man."

"As do I."

The arrogant boor. Oh, how she would dearly love to bring him down a few pegs. Sophie concentrated on his cup as Philip lifted the china teacup to his smug mouth. *China of ivory, listen to me, tip just a bit, as the man takes a sip.*

Philip sipped his tea; the teapot tipped on the tea cart beside her, sending tea splashing in all directions.

"Oh, bother!" Sophie snatched the teapot upright.

"How very odd." Philip stared at the teapot as though

it were a rare specimen of malachite he had just discovered. "I wonder what could have caused it to tip."

"I wonder." Sophie dabbed at the mess with her napkin, feeling like a failure in more ways than she wanted to admit.

Connor crossed his arms over his chest, staring up at the bronze statue of Leif, son of Eric, that the people of Boston had erected on one of their wide boulevards. "Now isn't this interesting."

"You needn't look so pleased with yourself," Laura said.

"But I am pleased." Connor looked down into her frowning face, her cheeks blushed a dusky rose from the cold. "Here I find a statue of a Norseman in the heart of Boston, complete with a dragon ship. It seems there is a place for Vikings in your city."

"Yes, there is." She smiled, her green gaze glittering with an anger he had seen glowing in her eyes since they had left the confectionery. "As long as they are made of bronze and chained to a pedestal."

"Is that what you would like to do to me, Laura? Chain me to a block of granite?"

"I would like to send you back where you belong."

"So you say."

"Because I mean it," she said, her voice lacking the conviction he sensed she wished it had.

He followed her as she marched away from the statue, her footsteps crunching against the snow. They walked down a wide, tree-lined mall that sliced the boulevard in half, carriages moving in opposite directions along the two roadways.

He studied the delicate curve of her profile, the slim line of her nose, the mutinous thrust of her plump lower lip. "Tell me, what would you be doing if I weren't here?"

"I'd be . . ." She hesitated, pursing her lips, staring straight ahead as though the answer were written in the snow that drifted between the trees lining the boulevard. "I usually spend the afternoons reading."

He suspected she had spent her entire life between the pages of books. "And so you're angry because I've taken you away from your books."

"I'm not angry." Laura paused on the path, glaring up at him as though she would dearly love to strangle him. Still, when she spoke her voice remained restrained. "And you needn't make it sound as though I lead a boring life."

"I didn't realize I had."

"I happen to like to read; it broadens the mind."

"It certainly does. I've found the books of this century fascinating."

"And just because I've spent most of my life at home reading, doesn't mean I don't know anything of the world." She looked away from him, her chin rising with her defenses. "I've traveled to the far reaches of the world through books."

He wanted so much more for her than the life she had found in books and dreams. The cold breeze rattled through the bare limbs of the elms arching overhead, ruffling the wispy curls at her nape, tempting him. He drew the glove from his hand and touched the silky curls, smiling when she cast him a startled look. "If you could do anything on this glorious day, what would it be?"

She swatted away his hand as though he were a pesky fly. "What's so glorious about this day?"

"Take a look around you," he said, gesturing with his arm toward the snow-swept mall surrounding them. "And see the beauty."

She glanced away from him, staring out across waves of undisturbed snow to where the carriages had plowed ugly ridges into the snow-covered street. "I see snow. Cold, inhospitable snow."

He sighed, searching for a way to reach the woman he knew from his dreams, the woman locked deep within Laura, hidden beneath a thick mantle of ice. "Look at the way the wind has carved patterns into the snow between the trees, as though it were an artist. See the crest of a breaking wave there, and over there the outline of a gull taking flight."

"I see swirls in the snow. It's hardly extraordinary."

Connor drew cold air into his lungs. "See how the sunlight glitters on the snow, turning it into a field of diamonds."

She stiffened as though he had touched an open sore, the muscles growing tight in her cheek as she clenched her jaw. "Only children look at snow as a field of diamonds."

"Children, and adults who have never lost the magic of childhood."

"You mean adults who have never really matured into responsible individuals."

"Is it so irresponsible to see beauty in the world around us?"

She glanced up at him, and in her dark green eyes he saw the scars cut deeply into her soul, scars sliced by discipline and neglect. "It's irresponsible to be out strolling when there is work that should be done."

He wanted to hold her, to take her in his arms and fill her with warmth and light until she smiled. But he knew she wouldn't smile for him, not yet. "What work needs tending, Laura?"

"You. There are a hundred things you must learn before the Gardner party."

He tugged on his glove, defending his hand against the cold. "You're right."

182

Laura frowned, suspicion narrowing her eyes. "I am?"

"I need to learn. I need to see things." Connor gestured toward the buildings rising on either side of the boulevard. The tall stone structures stretched as far as he could see, standing shoulder to shoulder. "I need to do more than read to understand this century."

Laura released her breath in a cloud of steam as she stared up at him. "That's right, you need to go right up to a locomotive and touch it, even when I told you it wasn't at all proper."

"Did I cause a problem?"

"You could have."

"But I didn't."

"Not this time." She crossed her arms at her waist, hugging herself as though she were cold. "But next time we might not be so fortunate."

"I don't want to make you unhappy." He rested his hands on her shoulders, feeling the tension within her, the emotions swirling inside of her like a whirlpool—anger, fear, longing, all colliding, confusing her. "But you can't lock me in the house, feed me facts, and expect me to understand this century."

"I'm not sure what to do with you." She pulled away from him as though the touch of his hands could burn her through the layers of her clothes. "You pop into my life and turn it completely upside down."

"Is change so threatening to you?"

"My life is fine the way it is." She backed away from him as though he were advancing with a drawn broadsword. "I don't need you to change it."

He looked into the forest green depths of her eyes, seeing the uncertainty that mixed uneasily with the conviction she tried to convey. "Are you certain?"

"Yes, of course, I'm quite certain."

She turned away from him, her back straight, her

shoulders rigid, as though she were going to war. Except he suspected the war was as much within her as it was with him. He followed her crisp footsteps, wondering how in the world he was ever going to reach the woman he loved.

Laura forced cold air into her lungs, trying to ease the tension squeezing her chest. The man made everything so difficult. It was as though he kept hacking at her, stripping away her defenses, laying her bare to his assault. She couldn't look at him without remembering the strength of his arms as he had held her against the warmth of his body. And his lips, good heavens, she wanted to feel the slow slide of his firm lips against hers again. She wanted to feel his magic flowing through her like a glittering flow of gold. What was happening to her?

Something moved to her right, a shift of white amid white. She halted and turned toward the trees. An animal stood beside the base of the tree, a huge beast staring at her with pale eyes.

"It's a wolf." The hair at the nape of her neck bristled. She reached for Connor, instinctively seeking shelter in his strength. "How could there be a wolf in Boston?"

"It's not a wolf, but a dog." Connor slipped his arm around her shoulders, drawing her close to his side. "There's no need to be frightened."

She hooked her hand in his lapel. The dog tilted her head, staring at Laura with pale blue eyes. "It looks hungry."

"Yes, she looks as though she hasn't eaten a good meal in a long time." He extended his hand toward the animal. "Come here, girl."

Laura twisted her hand in his lapel as the beast crept toward them. "What are you doing?"

"She means us no harm."

Laura refrained from asking how he could be so certain when the dog dipped her head, staring up at Laura and Connor as though she feared they might strike her. "I think she's afraid of us."

Connor gently pried Laura's hand from his lapel. "It's hard to say when she last felt a gentle touch."

As the dog drew closer, Laura saw she was nothing more than bones and fur and large pale eyes. She stared down into those gentle eyes and felt her fear drain away from her.

"It's all right, girl," Connor whispered, dropping to one knee. The dog hesitated a moment before slinking close enough for Connor to touch her head. "No one is going to hurt you."

Just as her own fear had fled, Laura sensed the animal's fear dissipating beneath Connor's gentle touch. "Is she wearing a collar?"

Connor stroked the dog's neck, his hand sinking into her thick white fur. "No."

The animal lifted her head and flicked her long pink tongue against his cheek. "Looks as though you've made a friend."

"We all need friends." Connor smiled up at Laura, color brushed high on his cheeks from the cold. "And she needs a home."

"Oh no." Laura stepped back from Connor and the stray. "She can't come home with us."

"She has nowhere else to go."

"Dogs bring fleas into the house. Dirt, disease," Laura said, recalling her mother's argument when she had asked for a puppy.

Connor frowned. "You've never owned a dog, have you?"

Laura stiffened. "What does that have to do with anything?"

"If you had ever had a dog, you would know they

bring affection, and the kind of loyalty rare in a human being."

The dog cocked her head and stared up at her, and Laura could have sworn the animal understood everything that was being said. "She must have a home."

"Look at her, Laura." Connor rubbed the dog's neck. "She's no more than skin stretched over bones."

"I don't think we should . . ." Laura hesitated, staring into those gentle eyes. "We couldn't possibly take her home."

"I doubt she can survive much longer on her own." Connor looked up at her with faith in his eyes, faith she would do the right thing.

Laura shivered, imagining what it must be like for the dog—cold, hungry, trying to make a place for itself in this world all alone. "I'm not certain my father would approve."

"Is your father the type of man who would allow an animal to suffer?"

"Of course not." Laura hugged her arms to her waist, wondering what her father would truly think of what she was about to do. "I suppose she could stay, just until we can find her owners."

Connor smiled as though she had just given him a wonderful present—his faith in her justified. She pressed her fingers to her lips, hiding the smile she couldn't suppress, not when faced with the happiness she saw in Connor's eyes.

"Come on, girl," he said, rising to his feet. "My lady has granted you shelter."

Laura tried to ignore the warmth surging through her limbs as she looked up into Connor's smiling face. "I'm not your lady."

Connor winked at her. "It's only a matter of time."

Chapter Fifteen

The hair prickled at the nape of Connor's neck; a warmth crept over his skin. He glanced over his shoulder. Beacon Street sloped down away from him, elegant homes lining one side of the street, Boston Common stretching out from the other. The street was empty. No one walked on the snow-covered sidewalk behind him. Yet he couldn't shake the feeling he was being followed.

"I'm surprised she's still with us." Laura stared at the animal who walked beside Connor. "I thought a dog would only stay with you if it were on a leash."

"I've never put a leash on any of my animals." Connor stroked the dog's head, wondering how long it would be before Laura touched the animal. "And I've never had one run away from me."

Laura stared at the dog as though it were a rare specimen she had never seen before. "I suppose she can tell you're accustomed to handling animals."

"She can sense I'm her friend." Connor ruffled the thick fur on the dog's neck, smiling as the dog looked up at him with adoring eyes. "One of the nice things about dogs is how much they like to make friends."

"Do they?" Laura paused as they reached the gate in front of her house. She stared up at the three-story structure as though she were afraid the granite walls would come crashing down around her if she entered.

"Are you worried your father won't approve of your houseguest?"

Laura glanced up at him, her lips tipping into a grin. "Which one?"

"The four-legged one." The dog sat on the walkway beside Connor, leaning against his leg, her white head reaching midway to his hip.

"To tell you the truth, I'm not certain how my father will react. I know my mother wouldn't allow a dog near the house." Laura sighed, her warm breath condensing to steam in the cold air. "Somehow I feel as though I'm going against her wishes."

Connor had a feeling those wishes had kept Laura from ever enjoying all the things little girls were meant to enjoy. "Your mother is gone, Laura. It's your decision." He dropped his hand to the dog's head, scratching behind one pointed ear. "You can turn her away or offer her shelter."

Laura stared down at the dog, frowning as she debated the animal's fate. The dog cocked her head and held Laura's look, a silent offer of companionship. Connor watched, sensing the conflicting emotions of this woman who had never known the simple friendship of a dog.

"You're really very pretty." Laura lifted her hand, and for one moment Connor expected her to touch the dog. Instead, she curled her fingers into her palm and brought her hand to her waist, as though she had suddenly remembered a rule against touching stray animals. "You can stay. But I'll expect you to behave like a lady."

"You can teach her proper manners." Connor grinned as Laura looked up at him. "If you can teach a barbarian to be a gentleman, think what you can do with her."

Laura smiled, a mischievous twinkle entering her green eyes. "If I can teach you to be a gentleman, I can teach her to recite the Gettysburg Address."

"So it seems you've finally decided to come home."

Laura jumped at the sound of Philip Gardner's voice. She turned and found him standing at the top of the flight of stone steps leading to Laura's front door. Philip was staring at Connor as though the Viking were a serpent he intended to slaughter.

"Philip." Laura fussed with her hat, wondering if it was on straight. "I didn't realize you were going to visit this afternoon."

"I would hope not." Philip descended the steps, his smile as stiff as his back. "It would severely wound my pride if I thought you left knowing I was coming."

"Connor wanted to see some of the city." Laura glanced at Connor, silently asking him to leave. The less time the man spent with Philip the better. "I felt I should show him around."

Connor leaned against the iron gate, smiling at her. The man had no intention of quietly retreating into the house.

Philip paused beside Laura, glaring at Connor. "So it seems you have overcome your fear of barbers."

Connor ran a hand through his hair, plowing ridges into the thick black mane. "Laura has a positive influence on me."

"So it would seem." Philip frowned as he noticed the

dog sitting beside Connor. "Good lord, what is that beast doing here?"

"We found her," Connor said, stroking the dog's head.

"And you expect to thrust this creature on the hospitality of your hosts?" Philip stared at the poor dog as though she were a leper.

"She's cold and hungry," Laura said, feeling as though she needed to defend the stray and her own actions. "She needs a place to stay."

"The pound is the place for this beast." Gardner patted Laura's shoulder. "Don't worry, I'll have one of my footmen take care of it."

"There's really no need. I've already told her she could stay."

Philip lifted one dark brow as he stared at Laura, the look coaxing the heat to rise in her cold cheeks. "You told the dog she could stay?"

Laura shifted on her feet, realizing how ridiculous she must sound. "Yes."

"You mean to keep this mongrel?"

"I intend to have Ridley put an ad in each of the newspapers. I'm certain we will find her owner."

Philip shook his head. "Do you really imagine anyone would want this animal back?"

Laura looked down at the dog, meeting gentle eyes that were filled with trust. "Yes, I can well imagine someone wanting her."

"You have a kind heart, Laura," Philip said, taking her hand. "Even if at times it is misdirected."

She had the uneasy feeling Gardner intended to steer her in the right direction if she decided to become his wife.

"Miss Laura and I have a surprise for you." Connor took Megan's hand and led her toward the dog who stood in one corner of the kitchen. He paused beside the dog and lifted Megan's hand toward the animal, emotion squeezing his heart as he sensed the girl's complete trust in him.

"What is it?" Megan asked, as she flexed her little hand in the soft fur.

"A dog."

"A dog!" Megan wrapped her arms around the dog's neck and pressed her face into the thick white fur, the animal bearing the lavish show of affection with stoic calm. "I've never touched a dog before. It's so soft and warm."

Laura stood in the shadows of the doorway, as though she needed to stay apart from the sunlight that poured through the windows to flood the room. "Megan, the dog might not be able to stay."

"Why?" Megan asked, turning her face toward Laura, her expression reflecting her concern.

"She might belong to someone." Laura hugged her arms to her waist. "We might have to give her back to her proper owners."

"But can I play with her until then?"

"Of course." Laura glanced at Connor, and he could see the questions in her eyes, the fear this was all a horrible mistake. "But you must remember, sweetie, she might not be able to stay."

"I will." Megan turned her face toward the dog, her expression far too solemn for a seven-year-old. "We'll play until you have to go away."

"We can't play with her now, Megan." Connor lifted the little girl in his arms. "She wants to eat."

"The poor dear looks as though she hasn't eaten in days." Sophie stood in the doorway beside Laura, watching Megan and their furry guest.

"Do you think I did the right thing?" Laura asked, without taking her gaze from the dog.

"Of course you did." Sophie patted Laura's arm. "Why, I'm certain Daniel will think she's a sweetheart."

"Not if she keeps eating the meat meant for the master's table, he won't." Fiona placed a plate of beef cut into chunks in front of the animal. "I'll be sending one of the boys to the market to be buying the proper food. And I think the little lady is in need of a bath before she joins the household."

The dog glanced up from the blue floral plate piled high with chunks of beef, looking at Fiona as though she understood every word the woman had spoken, and she wasn't at all certain she liked the idea of a bath.

"I'll take care of her bath." Connor sat at the table, with Megan in his lap.

"Now, sir, you won't be needing to be tending her." Fiona opened the oven door, the scent of freshly baked gingerbread billowing into the kitchen. "I can have one of the boys take care of the hound. You just stay here and have a nice piece of gingerbread."

Connor winked at the old woman. "I might have a piece before I take care of that bath."

"Do you think the dog will be able to stay?" Megan asked, looking up at him with big blue eyes that saw only shadows. Such pretty eyes to see so little.

"I don't know." Connor slipped his hand into the dark waves of her soft hair, touching the nape of her neck with his fingers, wondering if it were better not to know what he was about to discover. "But even if she's here for a little while, you can be friends."

She smiled, a big, innocent smile filled with the joy of childhood. "We can, can't we?"

"Yes, you can." He drew his fingers upward, touching her skull, sensing the damage wreaked by the fever. It was as he had suspected.

"I have something for you, Megan." Connor slipped his hand into his pocket and pulled out a bag of candy. "Miss Laura said lemon drops were your favorites."

"They are." She hugged the bag to her chest. "Thank you!"

He felt Megan's trust radiate against him as bright and warm as the sun flowing through the windowpanes to stroke against his back. As he watched her open the bag of candy, he drew in his breath, realizing the decision he must make: the damage to the nerves was not beyond his healing abilities. He could give Megan her sight.

He glanced up, meeting Laura's eyes. She was watching him, a smile tipping the corners of her lips, all anger washed from the green depths of eyes that regarded him with a warmth he had come a thousand years to claim.

Would she be looking at him with that sweet speculation in her eyes if she knew what he was? If he used his gifts, if he created what these people would think was a miracle, would he cause Laura to fear him even more than she feared him now?

"I'm not certain we should be doing this." Laura stood in the doorway of Connor's bathroom, watching as he rubbed soap into the dog's thick white fur, the tangy scent of pine and herbs spilling into the air.

"You don't think she needs a bath?" Connor knelt beside the bathtub in a shaft of sunlight streaming through the window of his bathroom, his white shirt-sleeves rolled up to his elbows, his black hair curling in damp waves from the steam rising from the tub.

"I don't think dogs are supposed to be bathed in the same bathtubs humans use."

He glanced at her, his lips curving into a devilish grin. "She isn't going to contaminate it."

The dog stood quietly in the tub, watching. Laura with those gentle eyes that seemed to reflect the intelligence of the ages. "How do you know what type of vermin she has hiding inside that thick white coat?"

"Fiona assures me this pine soap will dispatch any fleas she might have." Connor rubbed his hands along the dog's back and sides, working the soap into a frothy lather. "And leave her smelling like 'a breath of the forest.'"

The animal looked like a skeleton draped in white suds, her belly distended with the beef she had eaten. "Why didn't you want one of the footmen to bathe her?"

"I thought she would be more comfortable with me doing this the first time." Connor worked his fingers through the dog's thick white coat. "And I don't mind."

Laura hugged her arms to her waist as her mother's words echoed in her mind. *Dogs are filthy creatures, Laura. We shall never have one in this house.* "I thought dogs were supposed to hate baths. She looks as though she's enjoying it."

"Nice warm water, someone rubbing her back." Connor smiled as he glanced at Laura. "Of course she enjoys it."

Laura followed the swirling movement of his hands. He had such large hands, yet his touch was infinitely gentle. Unbidden memories teased her—those strong hands parting the wet silk of her gown, long fingers stroking her bare skin.

She shifted, leaning against the door frame, the steamy heat of the room penetrating the mint green wool of her gown, smoldering against her breasts. She imagined Connor's fingers sliding along her skin, soapy, slick, gliding along her neck, her shoulder, the curve of her—

"What would you like to name her?"

Laura flinched as she met his blue eyes. "Pardon me?"

He grinned, and she had the uncomfortable feeling

he knew her every wicked imagining. "The dog needs a name. What would you like to call her?"

"She doesn't belong to us."

Connor dipped a pan in the tub and drizzled water over the dog's back, melting the white lather. "We can't keep calling her Dog."

"I've asked Ridley to place ads in all of the newspapers. I'm certain we shall find her owner soon."

"Perhaps." Connor turned on the taps, allowing water to splash into the tin pan. "And perhaps we will never find her home."

Laura stared at the poor, emaciated beast as Connor poured warm water over her back; the dog's ribs sliced ridges along her sides, her backbone stuck out like a mountain range, and her eyes spoke of innocence and need.

Dogs are filthy creatures, Laura. We shall never . . . Laura ignored that distant voice echoing in her brain. The dog needed a home. She needed someone to love her. "Gypsy."

"Gypsy?" Connor glanced up at Laura.

"Because she wanders about." Laura hugged her arms to her waist. "You don't like it?"

"I do." He smiled. "It suits her."

"Yes." Laura allowed the warmth of his smile to penetrate deep inside of her, where her own smiles lay hidden. "It does, doesn't it?"

Gypsy chose that moment to jump from the bathtub. She shook, spraying water in all directions. Connor gasped. He crossed his arms over his face, bracing himself against the torrent. Laura jumped back out of range of the deluge. When Gypsy was done, water dripped from the marble walls, the ceiling, and the man who crouched beside the tub.

"Nice," Connor said, plucking his sodden shirt away from his chest. "Is this any way to treat a friend?"

The dog sauntered to a sunny corner of the bathroom, where she lay like a queen upon the cool white marble. A rare sound echoed against the marble walls, the sound of Laura's laughter. Connor had a way of tapping the laughter in her, making it bubble and flow like a sparkling spring.

Connor tilted his head as he looked at her. "You think this is funny, do you?"

Laura nodded, secretly enjoying the way the wet linen molded his broad shoulders. On impulse, she plucked a wet towel from the rack by the tub and tossed it over his head. "It looks as though Gypsy thought you needed a bath too."

Connor peeled the wet towel from his head and swept the black waves back from his face. He stood and faced Laura, his blue eyes narrowed, his lips curved into a smile. "Do you know what I think?"

"No." Laura stepped back, her gaze dipping to the damp white linen clinging to his chest, a white veil drawing attention to the intriguing black curls beneath. How would those intensely masculine curls feel against her fingers?

"I think you should join us." He moved toward her, each step filled with the slow, deliberate grace of a tiger about to pounce.

"Just stay right where you are." Laura backpedaled. She turned to run, squealing as he grabbed her arms and tugged her against his chest. "You're going to get me all wet!"

"Hmmm," he murmured, clamping one arm around her waist. "I hope so."

"Stop that!" She fought her giggles, pushing against his chest, struggling to free herself as he nuzzled the sensitive skin beneath her ear, sending shivers skimming along her skin. Heat flared inside of her as her imagination conjured images of his hands sliding along her bare skin. "Now let go of me before I'm soaked."

He nibbled her earlobe. "I can think of a hundred ways to get you all wet," he said, sliding his hands upward along the smooth wool covering her back, massaging her with his long fingers. "Care to explore the possibilities?"

"No!" The humor in his voice made her wonder if there was something beneath his words, a meaning she wasn't certain she wanted to understand.

Her breasts brushed against the damp heat of his chest, firm muscles shifting against her soft skin, scattering sparks in all directions. Still, instead of pulling away, her body leaned into his, craving a deeper contact. Suddenly she wondered what it would be like to feel his bare skin against hers. The impropriety of her wicked thoughts shocked her all the way down to her toes.

"Take your hands off of me." She pushed against his shoulders, knowing the man could snap her will like a piece of dry kindling if she wasn't careful.

"You're frightened." He pulled back, looking down at her, altering his touch from that teasing exploration to a gentle brush of his palms against her waist. "What's wrong?"

She stepped back, putting three feet of sunlight between them. "I don't care to be mauled by a Viking, that's what's wrong."

"You must realize this Viking would never do anything against your will."

"Still, you certainly do a good job of trying to bend my will."

"Do I?" He smiled, his lips tilting into a devilish grin that made her wonder what it might be like to feel him smile against her lips. "Now isn't that interesting."

"You needn't look so pleased with yourself."

He lifted one black brow, a pirate eyeing his bounty.

"Tell me, how close am I to bending your will?"

"A long way." She moistened her dry lips, realizing there was more hope than conviction in her words. "From here to the end of time."

He lowered his gaze, perusing her figure as though he were slipping buttons through wool, parting her gown, slipping it from her shoulders. "I've already come from the end of time, my beloved."

His deep voice slid over her, as warm as the sun streaming through the window, bathing him in a golden glow that glistened on the damp black waves curling around his exquisite face. "You shouldn't call me that."

"My beloved?"

She nodded, her words trapped by the emotions squeezing her throat.

"It's what you are to me." He looked into her eyes. "Is it really so difficult for you to hear my words?"

It was too easy, much too easy. Laura's breath grew still; her heart crept upward, until each beat throbbed against the collar of her gown. She looked up into his eyes, seeing eternity in the endless blue depths, an eternity he wanted to live with her.

Be mine, Laura.

He stood watching her, sunlight a golden glow around him, as though the light emanated from him, beckoning her to the warmth of his body. Desire flickered like awakening flames in his eyes, the same desire she could feel smoldering inside of her.

"Laura," he whispered, reaching for her. "Share your warmth with me."

No one had ever looked at her the way he did, as though she were every star shining in the sky.

She had obligations.

He was from a different world.

Her father expected her to marry Philip Gardner.

Still, one kiss, what harm could there be in one stolen kiss? She stepped into his arms, drawn by a need she didn't understand. Her breath escaped in a sigh that rose from deep within her as he touched his lips to hers.

Freedom—she tasted it on his lips, the blessed freedom to do exactly what she had longed to do from the first moment she had seen him standing in her library. No, it went further than that, deeper than that moment he had materialized from a bright silvery light.

She had wanted him for too many years. She had craved this feeling, this sublime awakening of a mind and body that had slept a fitful slumber until the day he had kissed her.

But where would it lead? Heaven help her, where would this horrible churning of heart and soul lead? Straight to disaster.

She stepped back, breaking the circle of his embrace, feeling as though she strained against an invisible tether that bound her to this man.

"What is it, my love?" He reached for her, brushing his hand along her arm.

"Please don't," she whispered, pulling away from his compelling touch.

"What's wrong?"

"This is wrong. We can't allow this to happen again."

He held her gaze, his blue eyes revealing every shred of the love he felt for her. "How can this feeling we share be wrong?"

"There can never be anything between us," she said, forcing the words past her tight throat.

"There already is something between us." Although he didn't move, she felt as though his arms were sliding around her, drawing her near. "There has been since the night you first came to me in my dreams."

Laura swallowed hard, silently denying the truth of his words. "It doesn't matter what came before. This is

199

the real world, Connor, not our dreams. We can't always do what we want in this world."

He drew in a breath, as though he were seeking the scent of her skin on the steamy air. "Tell me, what do you want, Laura?"

She stared at him—the thick black hair curling at his temples; the fine lines flaring out from his bluer-than-blue eyes, lines forged from laughter; the generous lips that were curved into a smile, lips that with a single kiss could make her forget who she was and what she must do. She could no longer evade the truth: she saw everything she had ever wanted when she looked at Connor, everything she could never have.

"It doesn't matter what I want." She turned and left him standing alone in the sunlight.

Chapter Sixteen

"I wonder what happened to that clock." Daniel tapped his pencil against a green leather desk pad as he stared across the library at the grandfather clock. "It was working perfectly a couple of days ago."

Sophie glanced away from the clock, but she could sense it, condemning her with its silence. She clasped her hands in her lap. Tonight, when everyone else was asleep, she would fix the damage. "I'm certain it can be fixed."

"Yes. I'm certain it can."

She watched the rise and fall of Daniel's pencil as he tapped the tip against his leather desk pad. Tap, tap, tap—he rapped the pencil as though he were marking the seconds that passed and stretched into silence between them. It seemed they had said little more than a handful of words to each other in three months. Was it because they had nothing to say? Or did they have far too much that should have been said long ago?

"I'm not sure I told you how grateful I am that you agreed to act as Laura's chaperon."

"I'm glad I was able to help." Sophie glanced up, her breath catching as she found him watching her, a speculative look in his eyes. How many nights had she dreamed of sitting like this, allowed the simple pleasure of looking into his beautiful dark eyes? "Laura is a fine young lady. I like to think of her as the daughter I never had."

He frowned, deep lines carving into his brow as he glanced down at his pencil. "I'm surprised you never married."

"Are you?" Did he know? Did he have any idea how much she had loved him? How much she loved him still?

"You had Boston at your feet." He drew in his breath, a slow filling of his lungs that lifted his shoulders beneath the black wool of his evening coat. "A steady stream of gentleman callers. I used to study them and wonder which one you would choose."

In spite of the few threads of silver streaking his thick dark hair, the lines flaring from his dark eyes—evidence that marked the passing of time—he looked the same to her as he had when she first realized he would always reside in her heart. She had been 13 then, a child in love with a handsome 20-year-old man, a man engaged to her sister.

"I always wondered why you never chose any of your eager young suitors." He glanced up from his restless tapping, meeting her eyes with the questions that had lingered between them for too many years.

"Father said I was a hopeless romantic." She glanced away from him, frightened of revealing too much. Even a spinster had her pride. "You see, I always believed the only reason to marry was for love."

"And you never met your true love?"

Sophie fidgeted with the golden lace at one cuff of her sapphire silk gown. What would he say if she confessed the truth? Would he be stunned? Appalled? Embarrassed? Or would he welcome the words?

"I suppose it really isn't any of my business." He released his breath in a sigh. "I'm afraid I've drifted from the subject I wanted to discuss with you."

Sophie clenched the lace between her fingers. The moment for confession had passed. Perhaps for the best, she thought. Confession could destroy any shred of dignity she had left.

"Philip Gardner came to see me this afternoon."

Sophie glanced up from the tortured lace she held between her fingers. Daniel was watching her, disapproval lurking in his eyes. "My, but he has been busy today. He must have gone to your office soon after seeing me."

"Yes."

Sophie squeezed the lace between her fingers. When Ridley had told her the master of the house would be home for dinner, she had taken extra pains with her appearance, donning one of her best silk dinner gowns. Now she realized she should have dressed in a hair shirt.

"Philip was concerned about Laura wandering around Boston unchaperoned."

"I know what has Philip concerned. Are you also concerned about my conduct as Laura's chaperon?"

Daniel rolled his pencil between his fingers. "I'm not certain it's wise to allow Laura to spend time alone with a young man. Especially a reckless young man like your cousin."

"Since you haven't yet met Connor, I'm not at all certain why you would think he is reckless."

Daniel looked at her over the pencil he held in a taut horizontal line between his fingers. "Philip provided an adequate description of the man."

Sophie smoothed the crushed lace with her fingertips. "I always thought you were a man who relied on his own judgment."

"Sophie, I don't mean to attack your conduct. I realize this is the first time you've ever been asked to act as a chaperon." He drew in a deep breath, rolling the pencil between his fingers. "I think in this case you may not have used proper judgment."

"Tell me something, Daniel. If Laura had gone for a walk alone with Philip Gardner, would you be questioning my judgment?"

"Philip Gardner wants to marry Laura."

Sophie squeezed her hands in her lap. "I don't have to ask whether or not he has your blessing."

Daniel frowned. "Of course he has my blessing. I intend to speak to Laura about setting the date for the wedding."

"And what if Laura doesn't want to marry him?"

Daniel leaned back in his chair, staring at her as though she had announced she was a witch. "Why in the world would Laura not want to marry Philip Gardner?"

"Perhaps she doesn't love him."

"He's from one of the best families in this town. He would make an excellent husband for her."

"Not if she doesn't love him."

Daniel tapped the tip of his pencil against the desk pad, the quick staccato rhythm echoing the rapid beat of her heart. "Few marriages are based on love, Sophie."

Sophie squeezed her hands together, staring at this man who looked exactly like the Daniel Sullivan she had loved·all of her life, wondering if she really knew him at all. "Is that what you want for Laura, a loveless marriage?"

He pursed his lips, keeping his gaze fixed on the pencil as though he were afraid of revealing too much if he looked at her. "I know what's best for her."

"Do you think a lifetime living a lie is what's best for her?"

"She deserves to marry into the finest family in this town."

"She deserves to marry a man with whom she wants to spend the rest of her life."

He clenched the pencil in his fingers. "She respects Philip."

"She doesn't love him."

Daniel stared at the tip of the pencil where he held it against the desk pad, the lead sinking into the emerald leather. "Is she in love with someone else?"

"I'm not certain. But I think she might be."

Daniel looked at her, his dark brows pulled together over the thin line of his nose. "You can't mean she's fallen in love with your cousin?"

Sophie thought of Connor, of the way Laura's eyes filled with light when she looked at him. Even when Laura was angry, there was something else in her eyes, something she suspected Laura would be the last to admit. "Yes, I think she is well on her way to loving him."

"She only just met the man."

Sophie held her breath, wondering what Daniel would say if she told him the truth. Of course he wouldn't believe her. No one would believe her. He would probably send her packing, straight to the lunatic hospital. "Sometimes all it takes is a glance."

He released his breath in a huff. "You really are a romantic."

"Yes, I don't deny it. I've always believed there was more to marriage than obligation, or a joining of two powerful houses."

Debra Dier

He turned away from her, staring across the room at the clock that stood frozen in time. "Following a whim of emotion can lead to disaster."

She studied his profile, seeking the strength that came from understanding. He had never been given the chance to find his own true love. "And would it not be a disaster if she married one man and discovered she loved another?"

Daniel clenched his hands into fists, the pencil snapping in his grasp. "I must think of Chandler Shipping as well as Laura's future. She must marry someone capable of taking over the business."

"I never realized the business meant so much to you."

"It didn't." He looked at her, his eyes fierce with an anger that had simmered for years. "Until I realized most of this town thought I would run the company into the ground."

"That's why you spend every waking moment working."

"I've doubled the business. Chandler Shipping is in better shape now than it has ever been."

At far too dear a cost, she thought. If only there were a spell for recapturing wasted years. "You've proved them wrong. You've proved you're more than their equal."

"Have I?" He smiled, yet there was no humor in the curve of his lips. "Do you have any idea what it's like to live in this town and have people look at you as though you're not quite good enough to sit at their dinner table?"

"Those people aren't worth a second thought."

"Those people control society in this town. And my daughter is going to prove to them she is every bit as good as any of them. When she marries Philip Gardner, no one will dare look down an aristocratic nose at her."

"At what price, Daniel?"

"Dammit, Sophie." Daniel tossed the broken pieces of the pencil on the desk. "You make it sound as though I'm selling her into slavery."

Sophie was quiet, staring at Daniel past the tears that misted her eyes. "I thought you of all people would understand how important it is to choose your own destiny."

"Do any of us choose our own destiny?"

"We all make choices that shape our destiny. Much of what we do, we do because of duty or responsibility." Sophie fought the emotion squeezing her heart like an icy claw. She refused to dissolve into tears for what the years had done to this man. Instead she would find a way to heal the ragged wounds she knew festered inside of him. "If you ask Laura to marry Philip Gardner, she will. Not because she loves him. Not because she wants the social position you crave for her. But because she loves you. Because she wants to please you. Because she wants to win your love."

"What do you mean she wants to win my love?" Daniel leaned his forearms on the desk. "She's my daughter; of course I love her."

"You might love her because she is your daughter. But I wonder if you really even know her."

"What's that supposed to mean?"

"How much time have you spent with Laura over the past twenty-five years?"

"I'm sure I've spent an adequate amount of time with my daughter."

Sophie held him in a steady gaze. "Have you?"

He balled his hands into fists. "I have a business to run. She should understand I can't spend every minute of every day with her."

"Laura thinks the sun rises and sets with you."

207

He looked down at the broken pieces of the pencil. "I want only the best for her."

"Then give her a chance to find her own happiness."

"With a man who wears his hair down to his shoulders and goes around in leather breeches?"

Sophie smiled as she thought of the extraordinary young man Daniel had yet to meet. "Perhaps you should use your own judgment rather than the prejudiced observations of a man who has a way of looking down his aristocratic nose at people."

A muscle in his cheek flickered as he clenched his jaw. "All right. I won't talk to Laura about wedding plans, at least not until I've had a chance to form an opinion of this Connor Paxton."

What would her father think of the Viking living under his roof? Laura wondered.

Stay calm.

If she only remained calm she could get through the coming ordeal, Laura assured herself. She drew in a deep breath before rapping on Connor's bedroom door. When he didn't answer immediately, she turned and paced toward the window at the end of the hall.

Moonlight shimmered on the panes, sliding silver along the frost that etched lacy patterns on the glass. The pull of the full moon had brought Connor to her side. Would the next full moon take him from her? She rubbed her arms, trying to ease the gooseflesh tingling beneath her sleeves. The man could disappear at any time, vanish like smoke in the wind. She must never lose sight of that fact.

"Laura."

She pivoted at the sound of Connor's voice, aqua silk swirling around her legs. He stood just outside of his room, his hair tousled and damp from his bath, the first few studs of his shirt unfastened, his black tie dangling around his neck.

Where was the Viking? Where was the infuriating barbarian who had invaded her life? A prince stood a few feet away from her. A man who might have graced the pages of a children's fairy tale. A dream made flesh and blood.

A future with him was impossible.

She had to stop wondering about things that could never be. "I thought you might need some help with your tie."

He fingered the ends of the black silk that dangled around his stiff white collar, smiling at her in a way that eased the air from her lungs, like a long hard hug. "I'm beginning to think it takes magic to tie one of these."

"Just a little practice." Still, would there be time for much practice? "I'll help."

He stood aside, allowing her to enter his room. She walked past him, so close she could catch the intriguing fragrance of his skin—soap and citrus, masculinity untarnished by cologne—a scent that made her want to press her face into the warm curve of his neck. Not at all proper thoughts. "Leave the door open, please."

"For propriety?"

She nodded, knowing propriety wouldn't even allow her to be in his room, with or without the door open. She turned away from him, afraid he might see too much in her eyes. "Where's Gypsy?"

"Megan wanted to play with her. The last time I saw them they were in the nursery upstairs."

"I hope she's not devastated if Gypsy has to leave." She sensed rather than heard his approach, felt the subtle shift in the air, his warmth wrapping around her as he stood behind her. She clenched her hands to keep them from trembling.

"It will be difficult, but at least they can enjoy the time they have together."

Even if it's only a few weeks, Laura thought, thinking of how many hours they would have before the next full moon.

"Do you want me to sit so you can tie this thing?"

"No." She took a moment, drawing breath into her constricted lungs, trying to find some defense against the emotions he evoked inside of her, some means to escape this maddening attraction. "I can manage with you standing."

She turned, resolved to keep her eyes focused on the business of tying his tie. Dark curls peeked from his open shirt, teasing her. She fastened the pearl studs in his shirt, the linen warm from his skin. Her fingers fell still against his shirt, hesitating at the last stud, as she stared at the hollow of his neck, knowing she shouldn't be thinking the thoughts flickering through her mind. Those thoughts were far too dangerous, far too tempting.

Still, she wondered what it might be like to press her lips against his skin, to breathe his scent deep into her lungs while his arms closed around her and held her forever. She closed his shirt, and fumbled with his black silk tie, her fingers trembling as she fashioned the bow.

He covered her hand with his, holding her curled fingers against the warmth of his neck. "Are you frightened I'll embarrass you?"

She hesitated a moment before looking up at him. "There are a hundred things you must remember, so many ways to make a mistake."

"Yes. In a way your rules are like vipers, coiling in my brain, waiting to strike should I make a wrong move."

He seemed so vulnerable in that moment, so open,

so utterly appealing. "If you're concerned about which fork to use, just look at me. I'll make sure you can see what I'm using."

He smiled. "I'll keep an eye on my teacher."

"Father may ask questions. You must remember that your father was a cousin of my great-grandmother's on my mother's side. You graduated from Cambridge. You've never been to Boston before. You—"

He touched his fingertip to her lips, her words halting with a soft exhale of her breath. "Have you considered telling him the truth?"

She blinked. "He would think we were insane."

"It's easy to get tangled in lies, Laura."

"How can I tell him you came from another time and place? I can't convince myself of the truth. I'm not even sure you're real."

He squeezed her hand. "I'm real. As real as anything in your world."

She stared at the back of his hand, where he held her fingers close against his neck. His hand was long and lean, his golden skin shaded lightly by dark hair. It was impossible to deny the reality of his existence while he held her this way, while she felt the heat and strength of his body, while she inhaled the fragrance of his skin with every breath. "You could disappear, vanish without warning."

"I'm not going anywhere without you." He lifted her hand, ivory lace spilling back from her wrist as he pressed his lips into the cup of her palm. "I love you enough to abandon everything else in my life."

She looked into his eyes like a woman lost in a winter storm, absorbing the warmth simmering in the blue depths. Her lips parted. She felt a shift inside her, almost imperceptible, but it was there, a subtle yielding that threatened her very existence.

Heaven help her, when he smiled at her, the winter faded into the warm days of summer. When he touched her, she believed in magic. And, in spite of her best judgment, she was beginning to wonder if all the things she once considered impossible were in some way possible.

"We'd better go." She drew her hand from his. She curled her fingers into her palm, wanting to enclose the warmth still lingering from his touch. "Father will be waiting."

Chapter Seventeen

Connor was accustomed to laughter at dinner. Conversation poured from his family like spring wine from a cask. Things were different at the Sullivan table. He dragged a piece of lobster through the white wine and butter sauce on his plate, watching the woman who sat across from him. Candlelight spilled across Laura's face, gilding the tips of her dark lashes.

Although the food was excellent, Laura had scarcely touched the oysters, and now she sat stirring a small piece of lobster on her plate. She had remained silent, sitting like a beautiful sculpture, as Connor parried her father's every thrust, doling out the details of his make-believe existence.

Laura lifted her dark lashes, glancing at him as though looking at him were a guilty pleasure. It was the only time her expression softened, when her eyes met his. He saw warmth in her eyes, curiosity and longing, enough to give him hope and the strength he needed to face any dragon threatening to drag him from her side.

"You have no idea how surprised Laura and I were when Connor showed up the other night." Sophie sipped from her water goblet. "Why, I can't recall the last time I set eyes on him."

"Strange," Daniel said, studying Connor, curiosity lurking with suspicion in his dark eyes. "I don't recall your family ever visiting Boston."

"They didn't." Sophie spoke before Connor had a chance to reply. "I visited them in England. The Paxtons were on my maternal grandmother's side. Connor is my cousin Blake's son. You remember Blake?"

Daniel frowned as he looked down the length of the table at Sophie. "No, I'm afraid I don't."

Laura stared at her aunt, and Connor could tell she was holding her breath.

"The poor dear died a few years ago. Typhoid fever, I'm afraid. The entire family was lost, except for Connor. He was doing research in Ireland at the time." Sophie looked at Connor, her smile disguising the anxiety he could sense churning inside of her. "He's the last of the Paxtons."

Daniel swirled the wine around his glass, the crystal catching the light of the candles glowing in the candelabra. "And what brings you to Boston, Mr. Paxton?"

"Well, he came to—" Sophie began.

"I came to meet your daughter."

Laura released her breath as though Connor had slapped her hard across the face.

Daniel looked from Sophie to Laura before fixing Connor with a steady gaze. "It seems a long way to come to meet a young lady."

"Is it?" Connor looked at Laura, smiling as he watched a blush creep up her cheeks, turning ivory to rose. "For some women a man would travel a thousand years and think it was well worth the trip simply to gaze upon their beauty."

"I can understand any man wanting to meet my daughter." Daniel stared at Connor as though he were trying to penetrate his mind. "I'm certain you will understand why I'm cautious about the men I allow near her."

"Your daughter is a jewel to be cherished." Connor held Daniel's steady gaze. "You would be a fool to allow someone unworthy to steal her."

"Yes, I would." Daniel glanced away from Connor, a muscle flaring in his cheek as he clenched his jaw. He stared at Sophie, who sat at the opposite end of the long table, as though he were seeking answers to mysteries he had only just discovered.

"Now you come back here!" Fiona shouted from somewhere beyond the swinging door of the butler's pantry.

"Fiona, stop the beast!" Ridley shouted.

The door flew open, crashing into the wall, rattling the crystal chimney of the wall sconce. Everyone in the dining room turned. Gypsy dashed through the open door, a streak of white followed by a gray cloud—Fiona, her dark gray skirts held in her plump hands as she chased the dog.

"What the devil!" Daniel muttered.

Gypsy bolted for the table. She snagged a length of damask cloth with the ham bone she carried, disappearing beneath the table, dragging the tablecloth with her.

Sophie screamed.

Laura gasped.

Dishes skidded across the table. Glasses tumbled. The candelabra rocked.

"Oh, my gracious!" Laura dove for her plate. She snatched it in midair, lobster flying in all directions.

Her chair tipped. She slipped, hitting the floor with a thump.

Connor snagged the candelabra. Plates tumbled to the floor across from him. Glasses rolled down the tablecloth, spilling unbroken across red and white roses stitched into the carpet. He stood, holding the candles high above the chaos, waiting for the next blow. It didn't come. As quickly as the storm had hit, it ended.

"May the saints preserve us," Fiona whispered, her voice a crack of thunder in the suddenly quiet room.

As he lowered the heavy silver candelabra to the bare table in front of him, Connor glanced across the table at Laura. She stared up at him, a dazed look in her eyes, as though she had just been swept up into the arms of a tornado and plopped down hard.

Laura sat on the floor in a puddle of aqua silk and white linen, her plate in one hand, an empty water goblet in the other. Butter-wine sauce dripped from her chin. Bits of lobster clung to the golden curls that had tumbled from tortoiseshell combs to cascade around her shoulders.

"This is dreadful." Ridley stood beside Fiona, a slim little man with a white towel draped across his arm, his dark eyes wide as he scanned the disaster that had been his carefully laid table.

"Will someone please tell me what just happened?" Daniel sat at the head of the table, spotless, his wineglass in his hand, a smooth expanse of polished mahogany before him.

"It was all my fault, it was!" Fiona said, snatching a water goblet that teetered on the edge of the table. "It was my job to be watching the animal. I should have known she'd be sniffing the bone after we carved the ham."

Sophie cleared her throat, covering what sounded suspiciously like a giggle. "It has been a long time since she's been around so much food."

Daniel frowned as he stared down at Laura. "Are you injured?"

Laura shook her head, dislodging a piece of lobster. The horrified look on her face triggered Connor's sense of the absurd. He clenched his jaw, fighting the laughter rising inside of him as he went to her aid.

"This isn't funny," Laura said, her voice a harsh whisper as Connor took the plate and glass from her hands.

"You have to look at it from my angle," he whispered close to her ear.

She glared at him.

He winked at her.

Daniel tilted his head and glanced under the table, then fixed Sophie with a dark stare. "I assume the wolf-like creature chomping on that bone is the dear little dog you said Laura brought home this afternoon."

"The poor dear was cold and hungry, with no place to go." Sophie smoothed the ripples in the tablecloth in front of her. "I assured Laura a man of your fine character would never turn an animal away to die."

Daniel set his glass on the table. "You did, did you?"

Sophie nodded, a smile curving her lips as she looked at him. "You're far too kind to turn away a helpless creature in need."

Daniel lifted one dark brow, staring at Sophie, a man fully aware he was being maneuvered into a corner.

"And you should see how sweet little Megan has taken to the animal." Sophie folded her hands in front of her, a picture of innocence. "It's a joy. You truly have made that child happy by allowing Gypsy to stay."

Daniel drew in his breath. He pursed his lips and turned his dark stare on Laura, a man about to pass judgment.

Connor felt Laura stiffen beside him as she stood and waited to hear the verdict.

217

"Since you brought this animal into the house, you're responsible for her." One corner of Daniel's lips twitched as though he were fighting a smile. "I trust you will make sure the animal has sufficient food to keep her out of the dining room while we eat."

Laura released her pent-up breath. "Yes, I will. You can be sure I will."

"The man is nothing short of infuriating." Laura dragged a brush through her hair, the freshly washed strands crackling with electricity. "Laughing at me as though I were an act in a sideshow."

A smile curved her lips as she replayed the disaster at dinner in her mind. A giggle started deep inside of her, welling until she couldn't retain the laughter. Good heavens, she must have looked perfectly ridiculous.

She stared at her reflection, seeing her smiling face, the color high on her cheeks. Yet it seemed the face of a stranger. When did the woman she knew as Laura Sullivan begin to change? When had logic and responsibility begun to feel like chains around her neck?

She laid the silver-handled brush on the embroidered linen covering the top of her rosewood vanity. She had made the delicate runner, fashioned each fragile pink rosebud and emerald leaf, crocheted the intricate white lace edging. It had occupied her time, filled empty hours. It seemed she was always trying to fill empty hours. All of her days had been empty before the moment Connor had popped into her life.

"Connor," she whispered, her pulse picking up speed at the mention of his name.

She crossed her arms, gripping her shoulders, longing for the feel of his arms around her. She closed her eyes, imagining the soft brush of his lips against hers, warmth whispering across her skin like a warm summer breeze.

218

"Foolish woman." She stared at the stranger in the mirror, color high on her cheeks. "What you're thinking is impossible. There is no future with Connor, only disaster."

She inhaled, slowly and steadily. Her soft intake of breath lifted her breasts, brushed the sensitive tips against the soft blue flannel of her gown, sending shivers skittering along her every nerve. He had awakened feelings inside of her, a hunger that threatened to consume her. "You must be careful," she said to the stranger in the mirror. "Very, very careful."

Something moved behind her, a white shadow pausing in one corner of the mirror. Laura turned and found Gypsy standing beside the bed, watching her as though she could read Laura's every thought.

"What are you doing here? I'm surprised you would show your face around me after the disaster you caused."

Gypsy trotted across the room and sat in front of her, staring up at her with those gentle eyes.

"You do realize you're lucky Father didn't toss you out on your pointed ear."

Gypsy poked at Laura, bumping her cold nose against her hand.

"I see, you want to apologize." Laura hesitated a moment before she touched the dog's head, her fingers sinking into the soft fur. "Your behavior really must improve if you want to stay here."

Gypsy made a sound deep in her throat, a plaintive little growl, as though she were answering, asking for forgiveness.

"All right. You're forgiven." Laura sighed, scratching the back of Gypsy's ears. "We all make mistakes."

Laura only hoped she could correct her own mistake, the very serious error of falling in love with the wrong man, before it could lead to disaster. She had to keep her distance from the man. Somehow she had to resist this dangerous attraction she felt for him.

"Please do as I say." Sophie moved the hands of the grandfather clock in the library, setting it to the current time: midnight. It seemed a perfect time to try to work a little magic. She glanced down at the journal that lay open across her palms. "Clock standing tall, but not working at all. Listen to me, please hear my plea. Go back to the time before you lost your chimes."

Sophie held her breath, waiting. Nothing happened.

"Pendulum of brass, do as I ask. Swing back to the time where you lost your chimes."

The pendulum twitched. It drew to one side, then the other, like an old man stretching after a long sleep. Slowly it found the proper rhythm, swinging back and forth, marking the seconds as they slipped away.

"Oh! I did it. I actually did it."

"Did what?" Daniel asked as he entered the room.

"Oh." She pivoted to face him, clutching the journal to her chest.

"I'm sorry, I didn't mean to startle you."

"I thought everyone was in bed."

"I couldn't sleep." He moved toward her, sapphire blue pajama legs peeking out from beneath his dark blue velvet dressing gown.

Sophie hugged the journal to her breasts, her skin growing flushed when she realized she had held those pajama bottoms in her hands. A proper lady would quickly retreat. A proper lady would never remain in the company of a gentleman who was dressed for bed, while she herself was dressed in nothing more than her nightgown and robe. Still, watching him move toward her, seeing the smile curving his lips, she discovered she had little care for being a proper lady.

He paused a foot away, so close she had to tip back

her head to look up into his dark eyes. "Is your guilty conscience keeping you awake?"

Sophie squeezed the journal to her chest. How much had he seen and heard? "Guilty conscience?"

"For the way you manipulated me into keeping that wolf. You gave me no choice, you know."

The room was cold, the fire long dead, and still she didn't feel the chill. Not with him standing so close, the warmth of his body radiating against her like a flame. "Did you want one?"

"No." He shook his head, smiling as though he had discovered something new and amusing in a world he had thought held no mysteries. "I'd like to think you were right about me; I don't think I could turn a helpless animal out into the cold."

"You couldn't." Strange how a man's face could change in a matter of hours, Sophie thought. Dark stubble shaded his cheeks, darkened the deep cleft in his chin. It made her wonder how his beard would feel against her fingertips. "The Daniel I knew was far too filled with a sense of honor and responsibility to do anything uncharitable."

"The Daniel you knew?" He frowned, a deep crease forming between his dark brows. "You make it sound as though I've died."

"Do I?" Sophie stared up into his dark eyes, feeling the years slip away, remembering the only time he had ever held her in his arms. Twenty-one years had passed. A lifetime since he had danced with her, one waltz, one moment she had pressed between the pages of her memory like a faded rose. Did he even remember that night? "It's been a long time since we were friends. We were children then. I suppose, in a way, it's as though we've both died. The people we were no longer exist."

He studied her face, his muscles tense, something fierce in his eyes, as though he struggled with a dark demon that had haunted him an eternity.

He drew in his breath.

She held hers.

"Sophie, I . . ."

She squeezed the journal to her chest, waiting, hoping for words that might roll away the years, words that might make her endless dream come true.

He turned away from her.

She felt the blood drain from her limbs. Foolish old maid, reaching for a dream.

Daniel snatched the drapes at one of the windows and tugged on the burgundy velvet, brass rings screaming against the brass rod. He shoved open the shutters as though he were a prisoner fighting to escape. Moonlight streamed through the frosted panes, illuminating the features of a man in pain.

"I've been thinking about what you said this afternoon. About Laura. You were right; I don't know my own daughter."

Sophie stood by the clock, where the pendulum ticked away the moments. "It isn't too late to become acquainted with her."

"She treats me with the quiet respect of a stranger."

"Spend time with her. Come with us tomorrow. We're going to the theater."

"The theater." He stared at the clock beside Sophie as though he were looking into the past, a past that brought a sad smile to his lips. "I haven't been to the theater in twenty-five years."

"It's an operetta, *The Pirates of Penzance*." Sophie held her breath, her heart pumping wildly at the thought of spending time with him. "I'm certain you would enjoy it."

"I doubt I can get away tomorrow."

Sophie stared at him, her heart squeezing with hurt and disappointment, not only for herself, but for a father who had no idea how much he was missing in this life.

He frowned, a muscle flickering in his cheek as he clenched his jaw. "I have a business to run."

She drew a deep breath. "Of course you do."

He shoved his hands into the pockets of his dressing gown, turning to stare out the window. "Laura is infatuated with Connor. I could see it when she looked at him."

"Connor loves her. He wants to marry her."

"What do you know of this young man?" He balled his hands into fists that pushed against the blue velvet of his dressing gown. "How do you know he isn't a fortune hunter? How do you know he won't destroy everything I've worked so hard to build?"

"Connor is a man of honor."

"You said yourself you hadn't seen the man in years." Daniel turned to face her. "How do you really know what he is made of?"

She smiled. "He comes from an excellent family."

"Every family can produce a scoundrel."

"He's a good man." Sophie pressed her hand over her heart. "I feel it here."

Daniel released his breath in a long sigh. "I have to admit, he wasn't exactly what I expected."

Sophie hugged the journal to her chest. "He's a very special young man."

Daniel rubbed the back of his neck. "He's direct, I'll give you that."

"It's only one of his qualities. Perhaps you should get to know him better."

"Philip Gardner won't wait around for Laura forever."

"If Philip loved her, truly loved her, he would wait a lifetime." Sophie gazed at him, seeing the pain and doubts in his dark eyes, wishing she could ease them with the love she had kept locked inside of her for an eternity. "Because if he loved her, no one else would be able to fill the empty places inside of him."

He stared at her from half a room away, and still she felt the intensity of his eyes. It was as if he were holding her, shaking her, seeking the truth hidden deep inside of her. Did he know? Did he even suspect her feelings for him?

"You must have loved him very much."

"Who?" she asked, her voice robbed of the breath he had stolen from her lungs.

"The man who caused you never to marry."

"Oh." She stared at the pendulum, watching the slow rise and fall and rise again, the brass capturing incandescent light like a hidden fire burning within. "Yes, I loved him very much."

"And do you still love him?"

In the corner of her eye she saw him, standing in thoughtful silence, watching her. She stared at the pendulum, unable to meet his eyes. She felt as though she stood on the edge of a precipice, too close to the edge, too close to revealing her soul to this man who could shatter her with a single word.

"I'm sorry. I seem to keep asking personal questions that I have no right to ask."

She squeezed the journal to her chest. What would he say if she confessed what was in her heart?

"I guess I'd better get to bed, try to get some sleep if I'm going to stay awake at the theater tomorrow night."

Sophie's heart hit the wall of her chest. "You're coming?"

"I think I'd better get to know the young man who has stolen my daughter's heart." He smiled, a dimple creasing his right cheek. It had been a long time since she had seen that dimple. "And I wonder if it's time you and I got to know each other again."

224

She held her breath.

"Good night."

She watched him cross the room, his head held in that proud way that defied anyone to look at him with anything but respect.

He turned at the door, looking at her as the pendulum marked the seconds and she fought the urge to run into his arms. "Sleep well."

"You too."

He started to leave, then paused, frowning as he looked at the clock. "That's strange; it's working."

"I set it when I came in, and it started working."

"It's working. But if you set it when you came in, it's losing time."

Sophie glanced at the clock; it read 11:45. She stared at it a moment, realizing it was running in reverse, erasing the minutes of the day. "Oh, bother. I thought it was fixed."

"Don't worry about it. I'll have someone see to it." He smiled at her, giving her a glimpse of his dimple. "See you tomorrow."

"See you tomorrow." She hugged the journal to her chest, feeling the chill of the room after he left. He wanted to get to know her all over again. "Perhaps dreams really can come true, even after so many years."

The sweet scent of talc and lavender settled around him as Connor entered Megan's room. Moonlight poured through the single window, slicing a wedge in the darkness, slanting across a sleeping little girl who could not be disturbed by the light.

When he considered the consequences of what he was about to do, his chest tightened. If Laura discovered what he was, he could lose her, just when she was beginning to warm to him.

Still, there really wasn't any choice, no chance to

225

avoid what he knew he would do from the first moment he had realized he could heal this child. He must accept the risks. He could not turn his back on Megan's innocence and trust.

A needlepoint carpet cushioned his footsteps as he moved toward her narrow bed, squares of spring flowers stitched on a dark red background. Megan looked like a sleeping cherub, snug beneath a thick down comforter and a white crocheted coverlet, her plump little cheeks as smooth and white as fresh cream, her dark hair curling around her face.

In the morning she would be able to see the golden-haired doll she cradled in her arms. That thought brought a smile to his lips and eased the anxiety in his heart. He took a deep breath, filling his lungs with the cold night air. He sat on the side of Megan's bed, careful not to disturb her slumber.

Deep within himself he tapped the power that rose and flowed through him like shimmering sunlight, warm and pure and healing sunlight. He touched her hair where the moonlight stroked her soft curls, feeling every texture against his sensitized skin. He closed his eyes, surrendering to the power within him, allowing the light to flow through him. He stroked her temples, a slow glide of his fingers, sensing scars that didn't show, easing them, erasing them beneath his touch.

"Are you an angel?"

Connor lifted his heavy lids, staring down into Megan's wide blue eyes, his breath catching when he realized he had been discovered.

"You glow like an angel."

"I'm not an angel. I'm a friend."

"Connor?" She touched his cheek with her soft little hand. "It's you. I can see you."

"The shadows are gone, Megan." He smiled, her wonder and joy flowing through him like a stream of glittering silver. "From now on you'll be able to see everything."

"Really and truly?"

He stroked the curls back from her face. "Really and truly."

"I could feel something warm inside my head. It felt so nice, like the sunlight on my face, only inside, behind my eyes." She smiled, looking past him to the window seat where a stuffed rabbit with long ears sat on a blue-striped pillow, flanked by two dark-haired dolls. "I can see Peter and Molly and Annie."

Tears pricked his eyes, tears for the gift he had been able to share with this little girl. Yet fear clutched at his heart, the fear of what would happen if Laura ever discovered the truth before she discovered her love for him.

He rested his fingertips against Megan's temple, wishing he could erase her memory of this night, but he knew he couldn't. His people always used caution in altering the thoughts of adults, and it was simply far too dangerous to meddle with a child's fragile mind. He might harm her in some subtle way. "Can you keep a secret, Megan?"

She nodded, gazing up at him with wide blue eyes.

"This must be our secret. No one must know I was ever here."

"But why? You fixed my eyes."

"Because people would think I'm strange if they knew I could do things like this. They might be afraid of me. They might force me to go away."

"But you're not scary. You're real nice."

"Promise me." He pressed his lips to her brow, breathing in the sweet lavender fragrance clinging to her hair. "Promise me this will be our secret."

She crossed her heart with her fingertip. "I promise."

"Thank you." He passed his hand over her eyes, closing her lids. "Sleep now."

"Promise me I can see in the morning?"

"I promise." He stroked her hair, humming softly until her breath resumed the slow, steady rhythm of sleep. He left her, praying she would not betray him.

Back in his room, he leaned against the window frame and stared out into the moonlight, each beat of his heart squeezing painfully in his chest. His future rested with one little girl and her promise to keep his secret.

"Laura, my love." He closed his eyes, leaning his brow against the cold pane. "Don't be frightened of me. Please don't turn away from me."

Chapter Eighteen

Laura smoothed the lace edge of her pillowcase, staring at the sunlight that crept through the crack of her drapes. She had been awake long before the sun had glowed upon her windowpanes, lying here, hiding from the world beyond the boundaries of her room. Reality lurked in the world outside of these four walls. A reality she couldn't escape. She drew a breath past her tight throat. With her father home, she knew the time for postponing destiny was quickly coming to an end.

Someone pounded on her door.

"Miss Laura!" Fiona shouted through the oak panel. "I have to see you!"

Laura tossed aside the sheets and comforter, ivory lace spilling across the foot of the bed and tumbling to the carpet. She jumped from her bed and ran to the door, wondering what disaster had transpired during the night. Fiona stood in the hallway, clasping Megan in front of her.

"What is it?" Laura looked from Fiona's pale face to Megan. "What's happened?"

"It's Megan." Fiona flexed her hands on Megan's shoulders. "Something's happened to her."

Laura's heart slammed into the wall of her chest. She knelt in front of the little girl, searching for signs of disaster. Sunlight poured through the window at the end of the hall, bathing Megan's little face. No blood. No sign of pain.

"I always knew you'd be real pretty, Miss Laura." Megan smiled and touched her face. "Just like a fairy princess."

Laura stared at Megan, seeing recognition in her eyes. "You can see. Can't you?"

Megan nodded, plump dark curls bouncing on her shoulders.

"I don't understand." Laura cupped Megan's face, staring into her big blue eyes. "How can this be?"

"It's a miracle, it is," Fiona whispered.

"A miracle." Laura felt the sting of tears in her eyes. "When did it happen? How?"

"Last night. An angel touched me, and then I could see."

Laura frowned. "An angel?"

Megan nodded.

"Lord, but it's a miracle. A dear, sweet miracle." Fiona slipped her arms around Megan and hugged her close. "If you don't mind, miss, I'd like to be taking Megan to my sister this morning. But it will be fine to be sharing the good news."

Laura drew in her breath, trying to gather her scattered wits. "Of course."

"Thank you, miss. You're a dear, you are."

Laura stood as Fiona ushered Megan down the hall. She stared long after both had disappeared around the corner leading to the back staircase.

"An angel," she whispered. Had Sophie found some way to cure Megan? The thought sent a chill through her. What type of power could Sophie wield?

"I've always thought it a terrible shame that the majority of the men in Boston either do not dance well, or do not dance at all." Sophie gathered handfuls of scarlet-and-gold-striped brocade and threw open the drapes at one of the windows in the music room, brass rings scraping against the brass rod. Sunlight rushed through the long window, slanting across the polished oak parquet floor.

Laura stayed by the door, watching her aunt, fighting the suspicion that had been gnawing at her all morning.

Connor pulled open the drapes at the next window. Sunlight spilled across him, as though the golden light were anxious to touch him. "Dancing is important?"

"Very. I've always admired a man who could lead his partner gracefully around a crowded dance floor. It shows a great deal of poise." Sophie threw open the drapes at another window. "I always hate to see so many young ladies languish on the fringe of the dance floor. It does make one feel terribly unattractive."

Connor grinned at her. "I have a feeling you never languished."

"Not often." Sophie made a slow turn on the dance floor, her skirt of pleated lavender wool swirling around her. "I always loved to dance."

Laura hugged her arms to her waist. It was difficult to believe this charming lady with the lovely face and bright smile could possibly be a witch, a woman who might have actually cured a little girl's blindness. Somehow that single act was far more powerful than transporting Vikings through time or making clocks whirl or creating feathers out of thin air. And far more frightening.

"I don't believe there has been a ball in this room since the night of my eighteenth birthday party." Sophie turned toward Laura. "Has there, Laura?"

Laura shook her head.

Sophie frowned as she moved toward her niece. "Laura, you scarcely touched your breakfast. Are you ill?"

"No." Laura took a deep breath. "I'm a little concerned, that's all."

"What is it, dear?"

Laura glanced past Sophie to Connor. He stood in the sunlight pouring through the windows, watching her, his face in shadows. Still, she knew there was no need to keep her suspicions from this man. "Aunt Sophie, did you do it? Did you cure Megan's blindness?"

"Me?" Sophie stared up at Laura. "Laura, dear, I wish I had. But I can't even fix a clock. How could I possibly have healed that little girl?"

"I didn't really think you had." Laura released her pent-up breath. "But Megan spoke of an angel visiting her last night."

"Yes." Sophie rubbed her arms. "It gave me shivers when Fiona told me."

"How could this happen?"

"I don't know." Sophie tapped her fingertip against her pursed lips. "The doctors did say it was possible she would regain her sight."

"After so many years?"

"It's a miracle." Sophie rested her hands on Laura's shoulders. "And miracles defy explanation."

"I suppose you're right. The doctors did say she could regain her sight."

"Still clinging to logic, dear?"

"With my fingertips."

Sophie nodded, a smile curving her lips. "Come, dear. I'll play while you teach Connor to dance."

Laura stared past Sophie, looking at Connor. Sunlight slipped into his ebony hair, stroked the width of his shoulders in silent adoration.

A pagan god able to command the sunlight. A prince straight out of the pages of a fairy tale. A man who could touch her deep inside with his warmth. That was Connor. If only she could step into his warm embrace. Yet she couldn't. It was better for both of them if she kept her distance. "I'll play while you teach him to dance."

"But, Laura—"

"Please." Laura stared down into her aunt's frowning face, hoping she would understand. "You're a much better dancer than I am."

Sophie sighed. "Very well, dear."

"Hop, three glides, and a short rest," Sophie said, smiling up at Connor as he led her through the steps of a mazurka polka. "Hop, three glides, and a short rest."

He had discovered something else he liked about this century, Connor thought—dancing. Ah, this polka, with its quick and lively steps, was more enjoyable than any of the dances in his own time.

"That's right, Connor. You're doing beautifully."

"Thanks to my teacher."

Sophie giggled as he led her around the floor of the music room, her feet tapping the polished oak planks.

Such riches, this dancing and the music. He had never heard any instrument so lovely as the voice of a piano. Connor glanced to where Laura sat playing the long, shiny black instrument near the windows, sunlight slipping golden fingers into her hair, brushing her cheek with a soft glow. Only one thing could add to the joy of discovering these treasures—having Laura in his arms.

She sat on the cushioned piano bench, rigid as a

statue, her face sculpted like smooth white marble, wiped clean of emotion. Yet emotion usually found some means to escape an icy prison. Her music flowed with feeling, lively and spirited, the notes crisp and precise, giving him a glimpse of the woman she tried to keep hidden.

Laura was filled with such intriguing contrasts. One moment she was a flame in his arms, scorching his skin, the next a beautiful ice sculpture, freezing him with a look. Still, he sensed what lay at her core, a fire that could consume him. And he was eager for the blaze.

"I'm exhausted." Sophie sank to the bench beside Laura, her hand still resting in Connor's grasp. "Connor, you've worn me to the bone."

Connor bowed, pressing his lips to the back of Sophie's hand. "You're a most charming partner."

Sophie blushed like a girl fresh out of the schoolroom. "Laura, dear, why don't you teach Connor the waltz?"

"Me?"

"Yes, dear. I'm far too tired."

Laura glanced up at him, a doe looking into the eyes of a lion. "You've gone through the steps of the german, the gallop, the reel, the polka. He doesn't really need to learn the waltz."

"Laura, most of the dances at the ball will be waltzes."

"I only just learned the waltz a few months ago." Laura toyed with the ivory lace dripping from the neck of her pale blue gown, flicking the scalloped silk between her fingers. "I'm certain I wouldn't be a good teacher."

"Nonsense, dear," Sophie said, patting Laura's arm. "You'll do just fine. Won't she, Connor?"

"Perhaps." Connor smiled as he issued the challenge.

"Then perhaps she is not very good at this dance."

One corner of Laura's mouth twitched.

"And then again, perhaps she is simply afraid to be near me, afraid she might succumb to my charm."

Fire flickered in Laura's green eyes. "The day horses sprout wings and fly like Pegasus will be the day I succumb to your dubious charm."

Horses with wings. He wondered what she would say if he told her this was not beyond his capabilities.

"What is it, Laura?" Connor rested his arms on the piano, leaning toward her until his face was level with hers. "Afraid I might break through all those icy defenses of yours?"

She clasped her hands in her lap as though she were trying to contain the emotion he sensed burgeoning within her. "I am not afraid of you."

He grinned. "Prove it."

"Fine."

Connor followed her as she marched to the center of the room. She pivoted to face him, her eyes sparkling with emerald fire. "Put your hand on the back of my waist," she said, resting her hand on his upper arm. She lifted her right hand. "And take my hand in a light grasp."

He felt her muscles stiffen as he touched her. He sensed the struggle within her, the emotions that screamed at him. With every ounce of strength she intended to resist the natural attraction she felt for him. And that was the last thing he intended to allow her to do.

"The dance is three-quarter time." She stood at arm's length, like a marionette whose strings had been caught at an odd angle. "You must lead your partner gracefully around the floor, taking care not to collide with any other dancer. Do you think you can manage that?"

Connor glanced around the empty dance floor. "I think I might."

She drew breath between her lips. "It will be different in a crowded room. You must make sure you never lift your partner so she must dance on the tips of her toes. With your height that won't be easy."

"Unless the woman fits as well as you do in my arms."

She moistened her lips. "Since you and I will not be dancing every dance, you must adjust for those women who are shorter than I am. I certainly can't dance with you more than twice."

"Only twice?"

"It would be most improper for us to dance more than twice." She curved her fingers against his arm, staring at his chin as though she were afraid to look into his eyes. "You must not ask any woman to dance more than twice."

"There is only one woman I want in my arms."

She closed her eyes, thick lashes brushing the crests of her cheeks. "You must ask other women to dance."

"If you wish for me to dance with other women, I shall."

"Of course I do." She squeezed his hand, a dark thread of jealousy coiling through her. "It's the proper thing to do."

"And we must be proper."

She glanced up at him, her chin tilting at a defiant angle. "With every step you must be smooth and graceful."

"And you don't believe a Viking can manage either."

She shrugged. "You seem to have managed adequately with the other dances."

"Under your guidance, I'm certain I will have no trouble."

She pursed her lips. "Aunt Sophie, we're ready to start."

"Yes, dear." Sophie began playing, the sparkling notes of the music filling the room like sunlight.

Laura stared up into his face, her lips a tight line. "Follow me until you have the rhythm."

"Lead the way, my beautiful teacher."

She moved through the steps, staying as far away from him as the length of her arm would allow. He was certain this was not how the waltz was meant to be danced. No, the glorious flow of this music demanded a communion between man and woman, graceful turns, sweeping steps.

Connor allowed the music to flow through him in a glittering stream. He stared down into the forest green of her eyes, seeing the struggle taking place as keenly as he felt her emotions flowing through him with the music—reluctance, anxiety, and a desire that glittered like a spring in the summer sun.

Let go of your fear, Laura. There is nothing to harm you here.

She frowned as she stared up at him. Yet he felt the tension in her relax. He pulled her closer as he learned the rhythm, as he made each step as natural as the ebb and flow of his own breath.

She lowered her gaze, staring at his lips. He sensed the memories flooding her, the memories of the kisses they had shared, the soft brush of her lips against his, breaths mingling, tongues touching. And the dreams. Images taunted him from the moments they had shared in their separate paradise.

He lowered his gaze, looking at her, the slim column of her neck, the soft swell of her breasts hidden beneath pale blue wool. In his mind he saw her as he had at the lake, her head tilted back, sunlight glowing on her damp skin, nipples drawn into pink pearls. He recalled her taste, the texture of her skin beneath his tongue. Low in his belly his muscles tightened, his need for her

237

pounding like a fist against his vitals.

He spread his hand against her waist, resenting the layers of cloth that kept him from touching her skin. She curled her fingers against his arm, her lips parting as she looked up at him.

I want you.

She drew in a breath that tangled in her throat. Desire rippled like a shimmering golden stream through her, into him. He felt it flow through him with the music that surrounded them. With each step her gown whispered against his legs, a soft, teasing caress.

He stared at her parted lips, wondering how much protest she would give if he kissed her, if he opened his lips over hers and filled her mouth with his tongue the way he wished to fill her body, in complete possession.

The music soared upward, notes growing bolder and stronger until they swelled and burst in a final crescendo. The last notes echoed on the walnut-lined walls. The dance was over, and still he held his beautiful partner. She stared up at him, confusion colliding with a hundred questions in her eyes.

"Connor, you are a marvel."

At the sound of Sophie's voice, Laura jerked in Connor's embrace. She stepped back from him, blinking, as though she were suddenly aware of where they were.

"Connor, I could believe you were born to dance the waltz," Sophie said.

Connor grinned as he looked down into Laura's wide, confused eyes. "Perhaps I have found the partner I was born to dance with."

The doubts he saw glittering in the forest green of Laura's eyes froze into certainties. "Then tell me why you were born a thousand years too early?"

Connor shrugged. "It doesn't matter. I'm here now. And here I shall stay."

"How can you be certain?" Laura stared at him,

doubts sparkling with tears in her eyes. "How do you know the next full moon won't pull you back to your own time?"

"Is that why you keep your distance?" He brushed the back of his fingers over the smooth curve of her cheek. "Are you frightened I'll disappear?"

She stepped back, lifting her hand to her cheek. "You don't belong in this time."

"I belong with you."

"Please don't," she whispered. "Please don't say such things to me."

Connor resisted the urge to run after her as she fled the room, her blue skirts flaring with the rustle of some mysterious feminine garment beneath the wool. He closed his eyes, breathing in the trace of spring flowers lingering in her wake. He felt her defenses slipping.

Soon, my love, he whispered into her mind.

Soon you will be mine.

Laura was nervous. Sophie could see the tension in the stiff line of her back as she followed her niece through the entrance hall of the theater. And she had good reason to feel tense. The poor dear was flanked by Connor *and* Philip Gardner. Thanks to Daniel.

Sophie saw the curious glances cast in her direction as she walked through the crowded room with Daniel. She couldn't allow her emotions to show. No matter how much she wanted to turn and slap the man walking beside her.

She had been a fool, a silly, simpering spinster to think Daniel had truly decided to come tonight for the chance to spend time with her. Sophie glanced up at the tall, dark-haired man walking beside her.

Incandescent light glowed against crystal overhead, sprinkling golden light across Daniel's smiling face. Oh, he looked so pleased with himself. How would he look if she planted a wart on the tip of his slim nose?

She slowed her pace, allowing the three young people to pull ahead several feet. "You didn't mention you were going to invite Philip to join us tonight." She kept her voice so low Daniel had to bend close to hear her, the scent of bay rum teasing her senses.

"I thought he deserved an equal chance to win Laura's affection."

"And if she prefers Connor?"

"She's only infatuated with Connor." Daniel frowned as he glanced at Connor. "Just look at the man. He's as handsome as the devil, charming as the serpent who tempted Eve. Any young woman would be infatuated with him."

She hesitated in the hall, while Laura and her two young gentlemen slipped past the gold velvet drapes into their private box. "And if it goes deeper than infatuation?"

"It doesn't."

"But if it does. What will you do?"

Daniel drew his lips into a thin line as he stared down at her. "I'm certain Laura will make the right choice in the end."

"The right choice being Philip Gardner."

He nodded. "Once she compares both men, I'm certain she'll see Philip's qualities."

Sophie shook her head. Daniel was blind when it came to that self-righteous snob. "You do realize you've put her in a rather awkward situation."

Daniel smiled as he took her arm to lead her into the box. "She'll thank me for it in the end."

Chapter Nineteen

Father had taken leave of his senses, Laura thought. It was the only possible explanation for finding herself in this situation. She glanced at Philip, who sat on her left. He was staring at Connor as though he were contemplating ways to pick him apart, piece by piece.

Connor sat on her right, seemingly oblivious to Philip. He was more interested in the six chandeliers dangling like clusters of shimmering icicles from the high ceiling; in the people flowing into the gold velvet seats below him; in the stage—the elaborate scrolls carved into the proscenium arch, the gold velvet drapes shielding the platform.

And when the musicians started tuning their instruments, notes rising, collecting with the conversation and laughter rising from the bubbling stream of people below, he stared at the orchestra as though he had never seen anything more fascinating.

Laura smiled as she watched Connor, catching a

glimmer of the innocent enthusiasm that radiated from him. In his company all things ordinary took on another light. The commonplace became the miraculous.

"Is there something you find particularly fascinating about this place, Mr. Paxton?" Philip cocked his head as he stared across Laura to Connor. "You're looking around as though you've never seen the inside of a theater before."

Connor met Philip's icy glare with a smile. "Perhaps because I have never been in a theater before."

Laura clasped her hands in her lap, praying Connor hadn't suddenly decided to reveal the truth. Looking for help, she glanced back to where Sophie sat behind her. Sophie smiled, content to allow Connor to ruin both of them.

"You've never been in a theater before?" Philip lifted his brows, staring at Connor as though he were certain that the man was luring him into some type of trap. "How very odd."

"Is it?" Connor held Philip's stare, a silent challenge in his eyes.

Under the force of Connor's will, Philip glanced away, ducking his head, a peasant chastised by a prince. Even in this century, men would bend to that powerful will, Laura thought. And a woman would surrender all she possessed just to be near him. She drew a deep breath, realizing how precariously close she was to that surrender.

"Look, Laura." Philip touched her arm, gesturing toward a man and woman who were taking seats in the private box directly across from them. "There's Lord Austin and Lady Sarah Sinclair."

Lord Sinclair was tall, broad shouldered, his hair as black as Connor's, his face carved with features handsome enough to cause women in the seats below to turn and stare. The lovely woman he escorted stood nearly as tall as his shoulder, her golden brown hair piled in thick curls on top of her head.

"What a handsome couple," Sophie said.

"Striking." Laura watched the way Lord Sinclair's hand lingered on his wife's shoulder as he helped her to her seat. Lady Sinclair smiled up at him, and Laura realized at that moment there was no one else in the world for these two; their love was that strong, that obvious, even at a distance.

Laura clenched her hands in her lap. An ache throbbed deep inside of her, a longing so powerful it felt like an open wound. She understood that type of love. She longed for it. Was it within her grasp?

She glanced at Connor, finding him watching her, a smile curving his lips as though he could read her every thought. Heaven help her, but she wished she could lean forward and touch his lips with her own.

He could disappear at any moment, she reminded herself. There were a thousand reasons why she shouldn't give her love to this man. And still, she wondered what it might be like to feel his arms around her, to surrender to the magic she felt when he touched her.

"Lord Austin Sinclair is from one of the most respected families in England. He holds the title of Marquess of Somerset. His father is the Duke of Daventry." Philip stared at the couple as though they were about to stand and bless the entire audience. He looked at Laura, a smug smile curving his lips. "And they are coming to my mother's party tomorrow night."

"Are they?" Laura glanced across the theater to Lord and Lady Sinclair, her skin growing cold when she wondered how much they would question a fellow Englishman.

Connor hummed one of the many tunes he had heard this evening as he left the theater with Laura at his side.

Ah, what music. The instruments had filled the huge room—violins and flutes and drums and all the others, lifting sweet voices, flowing through him like sunlight through water.

And Laura had been beside him, sharing every moment, smiling at him in that way that turned winter into the warmest summer. It was an evening to remember, an evening to slide between the pages of his memory and savor in years to come.

As they reached the bottom of the wide stone stairs descending from the main theater entrance, an old woman stepped out of the shadows into a pool of yellow light cast by a street lamp. Even with her battered straw hat with the bright red cherries around the brim, she stood no taller than the middle of Connor's chest.

She smiled up at him, lines crinkling around bright gray eyes. "Would ye like t'buy sum tarts, sir?" she asked, lifting a wicker basket covered by a faded red-and-white-striped cloth. "They be but a penny a one."

"Go away." Philip waved at the woman as though she were an annoying fly. "You should know better than to bother your betters."

"Here now." The old woman shoved back her shoulders, staring up at Philip, clutching the handle of her basket with both hands as though she were afraid he might steal it. "I'm only tryin' t'sell me tarts."

Philip stared down the length of his nose at her. "Sell them elsewhere."

Laura stiffened, glancing back at her father as though she expected him to intercede. Daniel stood with Sophie on the bottom step, frowning as he watched the old woman.

Connor looked at the little woman, her tattered gray gloves, her thin fingers poking through the ends of the wool. Her coat was patched in several places, bright splashes of white and green and red poking through the dark gray wool, the thin cloth hanging like a sack on her scrawny frame. Even in this splendid age of railroads and carriages and theaters, poverty still stalked the streets. He reached into his pocket, withdrawing one of the gold pieces Sophie had given him. "I'll take five."

The old woman stared at the coin that shimmered in the lamplight, her breath escaping, condensing into a stream of steam in the cold air. She licked her lips. "Ah, but I'm not having the coin ye be needing in change, sir."

"Since I'm anxious to taste your tarts, and I have no other coins"—Connor took her hand and pressed the gold piece into her palm, curving her bony fingers around the coin—"I guess it will have to do."

"Thank ye, sir." She smiled up at him, revealing the broken edges of her front teeth. "Ye be a saint, ye be. Ye take the lot of 'em, sir. Now go on. Take the basket and all."

Connor grinned, realizing he would insult the woman if he didn't accept her offering. "I'm sure we'll enjoy them."

"They be a taste of heaven, they be." The little woman winked at him. "If I don't mind sayin' so meself."

Connor smiled as he watched her strut away from him, a cocky little rooster in a battered straw hat. Daniel glanced at Connor as he passed him with Sophie on his arm, headed for the carriage that was waiting for them. There was a curious look in his dark eyes, as though Daniel were seeing something in Connor he hadn't expected to see.

"You really shouldn't encourage her type," Philip said, looking past Laura as they continued toward the waiting carriage. He stared at Connor as though he were chastising a servant. "Boston is full of those filthy Irish immigrants. It's getting so you can't pass a street corner without being accosted."

Connor felt Laura stiffen beside him. Daniel Sullivan glanced over his shoulder, staring at Philip, a startled look on his face. Yet Gardner didn't notice. Philip Gardner was a man who was accustomed to having his every order obeyed, his every opinion sanctioned by everyone around him.

"It seems the woman was only trying to make a living the best she could." Connor paused on the snow-covered sidewalk, watching as Daniel helped Sophie enter the carriage, noticing the way Laura's father held Sophie's gloved hand as though she were a precious piece of porcelain.

"The old hag should have stayed in Ireland with the rest of the peasants." Philip's face reflected his disgust, as though he had just bitten into a rotten apple. "How these people think they can leave their Irish bogs and make a decent living in Boston is beyond me."

Daniel drew in his breath. He stared at Philip a moment as though he meant to say something, before he turned and helped Laura into the carriage. He climbed in behind her, the carriage rocking with his swift movement. He took a place on the black leather seat between Sophie and Laura, staring straight ahead, his jaw tight. Laura stared down at her folded hands, her cheeks flushed a dusky rose.

Did Gardner have any idea how insulting he was being to both Laura and her father? Connor wondered. He resisted the urge to pick Gardner up by his ears and toss him in the gutter where he belonged.

Philip bumped Connor's shoulder as both men tried to enter the carriage at the same time. Connor stepped back, smiling at this stiff man who stared at him with murder in his dark eyes. Mr. Gardner would very likely hang himself with a noose of his own making. "After you."

The carriage rocked as Philip climbed inside. He sat across from Laura, forcing Connor to step over his feet as he entered. Connor settled on the seat, thinking he had met barbarians with better manners than Philip Gardner.

Connor looked at Laura. The lamp on the side of the carriage above her touched her black felt hat, gilding the tips of black ostrich feathers curling at the brim. Her thick, dark lashes cast shadows on her cheeks as she sat staring at her tightly clasped hands.

Connor leaned back in his seat, resisting the urge to take Laura in his arms. The carriage rocked beneath him, while injured pride settled like bitter ashes in the carriage.

Gardner glanced down at the basket sitting next to him on the seat. "You should get rid of that. For all we know the old woman has fleas."

Connor smiled at Gardner, a chilling twist of his lips that would have warned a man with more sense to hold his tongue. Gardner proved his arrogance far outweighed his sense.

"You'll probably contaminate us all with this," Philip said, wiggling his fingers at the basket. "You'll infest us all with fleas."

Not everyone, Connor thought, just one pompous ass. With a flick of his hand he jerked the cloth from the basket sitting beside him on the seat. In the same instant he whisked fleas from the nearest dog to the *gentleman* sitting beside him. He hoped the dog was grateful. He was certain the fleas wouldn't be.

Gardner flinched, a curious expression twisting his stiff features. He eased back against the seat, twitching his shoulders.

Connor smiled as he stared into the basket at the golden brown pastries piled high on a faded red-and-white cloth. "Ladies," he said, offering first Sophie then

Laura a choice of the pastries.

"Thank you." Sophie plucked a plump tart from the basket.

Laura kept her head down as she glanced at the tarts. "They look wonderful," she said, easing a pastry from the basket.

Daniel waved his hand as Connor offered him a tart. No doubt his jaw was too tight to eat, Connor thought, offering Philip Gardner his choice from the basket.

"You can't be serious." Philip stared down into the basket, scratching the back of his neck. "We have no idea what that Irish hag put in them."

Sophie gasped.

Daniel curled his hands into fists on his knees.

Laura stared at Philip, her lips parted in shock.

"We couldn't possibly eat that rubbish." Philip leaned back against the leather, a judge content that everyone would follow the law he had passed, his regal pose spoiled by the hand he stuck inside his coat to scratch his chest. "I wouldn't be surprised if they're filled with rotten potatoes."

Connor lifted a pastry and took a bite, bits of flaky crust spilling through his fingers. "Cherries. That's what she put in this one."

Laura stared at Connor, a smile tipping the corners of her lips. She took a bite of her tart, catching the crumbs in her gloved hand. "Apples. That's what she put in this one. And it's one of the most delicious pastries I've ever tasted."

Philip clenched his jaw so hard his teeth clicked. He twitched, rubbing his back against the seat.

Connor sat back against the leather seat, smiling as he enjoyed both his pastry and Philip Gardner's frantic squirming.

* * *

Austin Sinclair leaned back in a leather wing-back chair in Henry Thayer's library, looking over the rim of his brandy snifter at the last person he wanted to see in Boston. Fraser Bennett paced back and forth in front of the hearth, as he had been doing since Austin had entered the library 15 minutes ago.

"And you mustn't believe I don't have every right to come here. There is no law stating I can't investigate this matter." Bennett pivoted to face Henry Thayer. "Isn't that right, Henry?"

"As long as you realize one thing." Henry looked up from the pipe he was filling from the cherry humidor on his desk. "I'm in charge of this operation."

Fraser nodded. "Of course."

Austin swirled the brandy in his glass, inhaling the heady bouquet, marshaling his self-control. He had more than a few reasons to distrust Fraser Bennett. The man, and his political aspirations, had very nearly caused Austin's exile from Avallon two years ago. "Tell me, Fraser, just what do you hope to accomplish in Boston?"

"I want to see this young *Sidhe*." Fraser rested his arm on the carved mahogany mantel, keeping his gaze focused on the flames in the hearth. "I want to judge for myself just how much of a threat he really is."

"I see." Austin studied Fraser, sensing the fear hidden beneath his outward defenses. "And if you decide he is dangerous, what shall you do?"

Fraser's back stiffened; his hand drew into a tight ball against the mantel. "Nothing, of course. Unless Henry wishes my assistance in dealing with the matter."

Henry tapped the stem of his pipe against his lip, watching Fraser. "I'll decide what needs to be done."

"Of course." Fraser turned to face Henry Thayer, meeting that gentleman's steady stare with a smile designed to garner trust. "I'm here at your service."

He was here to influence Henry into doing exactly what he wanted, Austin thought.

"I assume my man was correct." Henry chomped on the stem of his unlit pipe. "Sophie Chandler reserved the box tonight to take the young man to the theater."

Austin nodded. "Connor was directly across from me."

"What did he look like?" Bennett asked.

"Tall, black hair. Sarah thought him quite handsome." Austin smiled at Bennett over the rim of his glass. "Except for the horns sticking up from the top of his head."

Bennett frowned. "Very amusing, Sinclair."

"Anything unusual happen?"

"No." Austin sipped his brandy, the amber warmth easing the anxiety squeezing his chest. "He looked like a gentleman enjoying the company of a beautiful woman."

"He's up to something." Fraser pivoted, pacing toward the windows. "No man travels a thousand years simply to enjoy the company of a beautiful woman."

Austin swirled the brandy in his glass, watching light swirl in the amber liquid, recalling the way Connor had looked at Laura Sullivan. Austin understood that look. Connor was a man in love. "I think it's possible the man came here for no other reason than to claim Laura Sullivan as his own."

"That's ridiculous!" Fraser swatted the drapes, blue-and-gold floral brocade swaying beneath his hand. "He must know we can no longer channel the power. He probably plans to take over Avallon."

Austin drew in a deep breath, inhaling the fragrance of brandy. "Then why is he here instead of Avallon?"

"I don't know." Fraser pivoted to face him. "But I do know the man is dangerous. We have to handle him carefully."

"I agree." Henry struck a match, sulfur spilling into the air. "The man is far too powerful to treat lightly. We must be prepared to defend ourselves in any situation."

"That's right. He might be able to channel the power." Fraser tapped his fist against his open palm. "But he can still be stopped by a bullet."

Austin clenched his glass. "I don't think there will be any need for violence."

"I believe Henry is in charge here, Sinclair."

"And I believe Henry has better judgment than to destroy this extraordinary young man unless there are no other alternatives."

Fraser stared at Austin, hatred and fear simmering in his eyes.

Henry cleared his throat. "We must examine this man closely."

"Of course." Fraser smiled at Henry. "I wouldn't suggest any other course of action."

Austin sipped his brandy, wondering how much influence Bennett could exert over the emissary. He would have to make sure it wasn't enough to get a young man killed for the simple crime of falling in love with a woman from a different time and place.

It only took a little practice, that was all, Sophie assured herself. She refused to believe she would always be a failure as a witch.

She stared at the porcelain pitcher standing in front of her on the kitchen counter. Moonlight spilled through the windows, reflecting on the glass-fronted cabinets. She hadn't turned on the lights. Somehow moonlight seemed much more fitting for practicing witchcraft.

She lifted her hand, pointing her finger at the pitcher. "Pour," she said, willing it to tip toward the mug poised in front of it.

The pitcher rocked on the oak counter.

"Pour from your spout." Sophie drew in her breath, her heart pounding as she reached deep inside of her for the magic. "Fill my cup."

The pitcher tipped, splashing milk into the mug.

Sophie clapped her hands. "I did it!"

"Sophie?"

Sophie pivoted, shielding the pitcher and mug from the man standing on the threshold of the kitchen. "Daniel! What are you doing here?"

"I couldn't sleep." He stepped into a wedge of moonlight that slanted through one of the windows. His dark hair was tousled, his blue dressing gown open as though he had thrown it on and marched out of his room. "I thought some warm milk might help."

"Warm milk?" Behind her the pitcher spilled milk from its spout, splashing into the full mug. "I was just about to make some hot chocolate. Why don't you wait in the library and I'll bring you some?"

"What's that noise?"

"Noise?" Milk streamed across the counter and dripped on the oak planks of the floor. She reached behind her, grabbing the handle of the enchanted pitcher, trying to force it upright. But it remained under her spell, sloshing milk into the mug. "What noise?"

Daniel frowned. "Are you all right, Sophie?"

Sophie jerked on the handle. "Fine."

Daniel shook his head. "We need some light in here." He turned toward the switch near the door.

Sophie turned toward the pitcher. "Stop," she whispered, tugging with both hands on the bewitched handle. Lights flickered overhead.

"I'm sorry, I didn't hear you," Daniel said as he moved toward her.

"I command you to stop," she whispered. The spell broke. The pitcher flew back in Sophie's grasp, the momentum taking her with it. She stumbled back, plowing into Daniel.

As Daniel caught her, preventing her fall, he stepped back, straight into a pool of milk.

"What the . . ." He slipped. He flew back, whacking the floor with a thud. The breath whooshed from his lungs, hitting Sophie's cheek as she sprawled back across him.

"Oh, bother!" She turned in Daniel's arms, smacking his shoulder with the pitcher she still clutched. "Sorry!"

He gave her a weak smile. "It's all right."

"Are you hurt?" She lifted her hand to touch his cheek, the pitcher bumping his chin. "Oh, dear. I'm so sorry."

"I think I'll feel better if you put that pitcher down," he said, prying the pitcher from her trembling hand.

"Oh, of course."

He set the pitcher on the floor beside them and rested his head back against the oak planks.

"Are you all right?"

"Bruised." He smiled, a dimple creasing his right cheek. "But fine."

Her heart seemed to do a slow tumble in her chest as she looked down into his handsome face. She became aware of each place her body touched his, the warmth of his body radiating through the layers of their clothing. She rose and fell with the rhythm of his breath, her breasts tingling against the firm muscles of his chest, her legs cradled between his.

He was so close she could trace each faint line that time had etched into his face, each line marking the years fate had stolen from her. So close she could feel each soft exhale of his breath against her cheek. So close she could lower her head just a bit and kiss him as she had dreamed of kissing him. Too close not to touch him.

She touched the deep crease of his dimple, tracing the cleft with her fingertip, his beard rasping against her skin.

"Sophie," he whispered, the dimple disappearing beneath her touch as his smile slipped away.

She saw realization dawn in his beautiful dark eyes and knew she had revealed far too much in one unguarded moment. "I'm sorry," she said, starting to pull away.

He slipped his arms around her, holding her when she would have run away from him and the truth she could no longer hide.

"Please." She stared at his shoulder, afraid to meet his eyes. "Let me go."

"Do you have any idea how long I've waited to hold you again?"

She looked at him then, straight into his eyes, seeing a warmth she had only seen in her dreams. "You have?"

"Since the night we danced at your birthday ball." He slid his hands upward along her back, the warmth of his palms seeping through the pink cashmere of her robe and the white flannel of her nightgown, soaking her skin. "Do you remember?"

She nodded, her voice tangled with emotion.

"I thought you were the most beautiful thing I'd ever seen. All white lace and silk." He lifted her braid, pressing his lips against the thick, dark coils. "You still wear the scent of roses. You always smelled like roses in the rain."

"You remember that too?"

"God, how I remember the scent of you. That night when I held you in my arms, when your perfume filled my senses and your skirts brushed my legs, it was all I could do to keep the proper distance between us. I wanted to press my lips against your neck, taste the roses clinging to your skin."

Sophie drew a breath that splintered in her tight throat. "You did?"

"I did." He tugged on the white satin ribbon securing the end of her braid, slowly working his fingers through the coils, releasing the heavy dark mass to tumble over her shoulders. "But that wasn't the night I fell in love with you."

"No?" It was all she could manage as he slid his hands through her hair, and the reality of his words hummed through her blood.

"I fell in love with you long before that night." He let her hair tumble around him, a silky dark curtain that locked them in their own private world. "When exactly, I can't be sure. But I loved you so much it hurt every time I looked at you."

"I thought I would die each time I saw you." She drew in her breath, taking the scent of bay rum deep into her lungs.

"I prayed the feelings would go away when you did." He stroked her cheek with his fingertips. "But they didn't."

"I couldn't stay here. I couldn't see you every day and know you were beyond my touch."

"Each day I wondered what you were doing. Who you were with. And I came to hate myself for the selfish bastard I'd become. Because I kept praying you would never allow another man to touch you."

Sophie smiled, tears misting her eyes. "I could never let another man touch me."

"Sophie," he whispered, slipping his hand into her hair. "I've never stopped loving you."

"There's never been anyone I've ever loved, only you."

"My beautiful Sophie." He cradled her head, easing her toward him until he could claim her lips for the first time.

255

Chapter Twenty

Laura stepped from the crystalline lake. Water streamed in shimmering rivulets across her skin, pooling on the black stones surrounding the lake as she strolled a few feet to where emerald grass danced in the breeze with bright wildflowers.

She sank to the fragrant bed of meadow grass and flowers, falling to her back, throwing her arms wide, offering her bare skin to the warm fingers of the sun, the delicate touch of the wind. The breeze licked across her nipples, nipped at her belly, her thighs, stirring embers inside of her, sparks of desire kindled by a handsome Irish Viking with eyes the color of a summer sky.

"Connor," she whispered, closing her eyes. She slid her hands through the grass, emerald strands streaming across her skin. "Where are you?"

"Here." A shadow fell across her face. "With you, my love."

She opened her eyes and found him standing beside

her, a towering figure draped in nothing more than golden sunlight. She stared, absorbing the power and strength etched into every line and curve of his magnificent body. This was a man who could inspire artists to struggle with marble and chisel, chipping, carving, striving to seize his beauty. But they would fail.

No mortal could capture the beauty of this man, for it dwelt deeper than the perfection of sculpted flesh and bone. It dwelt within. It sparkled in the pure blue of his eyes. It glowed in the warmth of his smile. The radiance of a gentle soul.

She lifted her arms, reaching for him, welcoming him as he covered her body with the warmth of his own. "I need you, Connor."

"And I'm here for the taking, my love." He smiled, his lips tipping into a crooked grin. "Totally, completely, at your service."

She slid her hand into the thick, cool waves at his nape, her fingers scraping the heat of his skin. "Kiss me," she whispered.

He lowered his head, his breath a warm pulse against her lips, his lips touching hers, brushing as softly as the breeze drifting across the wildflowers before sinking deeper against her.

The music of water tumbling over crystal-studded rocks sang with the blood pounding in her ears. All of the nights she had been drawn to this place were but links in a chain, a golden tether that connected her to this man, that bound them together and led them to this moment of splendid surrender.

"Laura," he whispered, drawing away from her. He sat on his heels between her long legs, looking at her, the hunger in his blue eyes feeding the desire pumping through every vessel of her body. "Do you realize how long I've waited to make love to you?"

"Too long," she said, the admission of her own wanton need releasing her from the remnants of restraint. "Make love to me. Now."

"It's been a lifetime of waiting." He plucked a white daisy from the sea of flowers and grass swaying around them. "I want to savor each moment."

Laura slid her fingers across the curls that spread like arching wings across his chest, absorbing the heat of his skin beneath the silky black hair. He brushed the flower down her neck, the soft petals kissing her skin. "I want to feel you against me," she whispered.

"I want to touch all of you." And still he touched her only with the petals of the daisy, drawing the flower lower, flicking the petals against her damp skin.

She held her breath, watching, drawn to the sight of the white petals flexing against her pale skin, drawing closer and closer to the pink bud of her breast. Petals whispered across her nipple, a feathery touch that unraveled her breath.

"The way you open for me," he said, sliding the daisy across her belly. "It's more beautiful than anything I've ever imagined."

Laura lifted her hips, a sigh escaping her lips as he brushed the flower up and down along her inner thighs. Desire pulled upon her vitals, drawing her taut inside.

"Please," she whispered, unsure of all that would pass between them, knowing she needed this, the completion of something started long ago—before she had taken her first breath.

"Anything for my beloved." He laid the flower between her thighs, the soft white petals resting against glistening feminine curls. He leaned toward her, sinking his hands into the grass on either side of her head, lowering himself until his chest brushed the crests of her breasts.

Laura arched her back, sighing at the intriguing rasp of black curls against the sensitive tips of her breasts.

"Beautiful enchantress," he whispered, pressing his lips to her neck. "You've bewitched me."

She felt bewitched, under some decadent spell that allowed her to feel as she had never felt before. Every nerve tingled and sang with pleasure as he followed the path he had traced with the soft petals of a daisy, kissing her, flicking his tongue against her, nibbling at her skin as though she were made of spun sugar and cream.

She moaned, arching beneath him as he drew her breast into his mouth. He lingered there, swirling his tongue across the tip while his hands roamed over her trembling body, conjuring magic to sparkle and flow through her until she shimmered inside, as bright and sparkling as the sunlight overhead.

He spread moist kisses across her belly, searching with his lips and tongue until he found the delicate petals of a daisy. He brushed the flower aside with his lips, seeking the moist petals beneath.

Laura clutched his arms as he touched her with the tip of his tongue. Never before had she even dreamed of this intimate kiss—the heat of his tongue, the soft brush of his lips, tasting her, devouring her—it was beyond imagining. With every illicit touch the magic rippled and shimmered inside of her until she felt she was dissolving, splintering into particles of light itself.

When she felt it impossible for this wicked pleasure to increase in intensity, he surged upward, claiming her lips beneath his own. She opened to him, and he filled her, his tongue plunging past her lips, retreating, plunging, in a rhythm that flowed and ebbed through her entire body. And then she felt the pressure against her moist threshold, the delicious heat of him as he slipped inside of her for the first time. She arched her hips, taking him as he gave himself to her.

Completion.

The joining of two halves once broken and now

whole once more. She lifted to meet him as he thrust against her, slow and steady, building faster and faster, surging like the sun rising in the dawn, climbing up over the mountains, rising, rising until it burst free of the darkness and shimmered across the valley.

Sophie had never in her life slept without a nightgown, and here she lay, covered with nothing more than a sheet, a comforter, and the warmth of a man's bare skin. Oh, my, was this really happening? Was she truly lying in Daniel's arms? Or was this a dream, like so many others? A magical moment that would vanish with the light of dawn?

Moonlight poured through the windowpanes, casting the shadows of a man and woman on the wall across from the bed. She flexed her hand on Daniel's chest, watching the shadow flow with her movement, testing the reality of firm muscles beneath her touch.

"Are you all right?" Daniel shifted beside her, raising on his elbow to look down into her face. "I didn't want to hurt you."

"You didn't." She touched his cheek where the moonlight kissed his skin, marveling at the scratchy texture of dark stubble, recalling the fascinating feel of his beard rubbing against her bare breasts. "I've never felt better in my life."

He brushed his lips across hers, his breath a warm whisper against her cheek. "I didn't mean to let it go this far."

"You didn't?" She stared up at him, her breath pausing in her throat. "Then you regret what we did?"

"I have only one regret." He lifted her dark hair away from her breast, allowing the silky strands to tumble through his fingers to the white linen sheet. "I regret we had to wait so long."

"Never look back, Daniel." She slid her hand over the

curve of his shoulder, his skin smooth and warm beneath her palm. "There's a great deal of life left to live."

"And I want to live the rest of my days with you, Sophie." He cupped her cheek in his big hand. "I want to wake up every morning and see your beautiful face. I want to go to bed each night and hold you in my arms."

Tears blurred her eyes even as a smile tipped her lips, as she looked up into the face of the man she had always loved.

"Marry me." He brushed his lips across the corner of her smile. "Come live your life with me."

"Yes." She slipped her arms around his shoulders, holding him close. "I want nothing more than to live with you all of my days."

"Sophie," he whispered, nestling between her thighs, pressing against her with the solid heat of his desire. "You're a dream come true."

"Reality is much better than dreams, my love," she whispered, welcoming him as he gently slid inside of her.

Laura stood by the windows in her room, staring at the moonlight shimmering against the frost that drew lacy patterns upon the windowpanes. She hugged her arms to her waist, feeling chilled where she had felt the warmth of Connor's skin in a dream that seemed more real than the reality she had awakened to.

How strange, to be both untouched maiden and scandalous wanton all in the same instant. She closed her eyes, drawing the cold air deep into her lungs, trying to cool the desire flickering like hungry flames inside of her.

Come to me, my love. She heard Connor's voice whisper in her mind, felt the dark tug on her vitals.

"Connor," she whispered.

She wanted him. She needed him. And he was here,

within her grasp, at least for these few moments in time. How could she waste these precious moments? How could she allow the shackles of propriety to chain her? Heaven help her, she felt bound by stronger chains.

Sophie tugged on the belt of her robe, backing away from the man who stalked her across the bedroom. "Daniel, I have to go."

"Not yet."

"It's late." Sophie hit the wall with her heel. "I can't stay any longer."

"It's early." Daniel placed his hands on the wall on either side of her head, leaning toward her until his nose brushed hers. "You can't leave yet."

She turned her head, avoiding his lips when he tried to kiss her. His kisses could steal every scrap of will she possessed. "It's nearly dawn."

"And what if I locked you in here and made love to you the entire day?"

She trembled with the heated promise in his voice. "We couldn't."

He nuzzled the soft skin beneath her ear. "What if we tell the rest of the world to go straight to hell?"

"Daniel, we have to think of Laura." Sophie leaned back against the wall, pushing against his chest, trying to gather her dissolving will. "What would she think if she knew I had spent the night with you?"

"She would think I was a scandalous libertine." He pulled back, smiling down into her face. "Forgive me, love. I never realized happiness could make a man forget everything except the woman he loves."

"This is the way it's meant to be, Daniel." She touched his cheek, his dimple creasing beneath her fingertips. "This is what I've waited for all of my life."

He kissed her brow. "I never realized just how good life could be until now."

Sophie drew in her breath. "And Laura, does she deserve less than what we shared these past few hours?"

Daniel stiffened. "What do you mean?"

She looked up into his eyes, fear for what she might lose pounding with the blood in her veins. "Laura deserves to find the same type of happiness we share."

He pulled back from her, a frown digging a single line between his dark brows. "And you think she can find that happiness with Connor?"

Sophie nodded.

"We're not even certain how the man plans to support her." Daniel walked toward the windows, stepping into the stream of moonlight. "He's an archaeologist. What does he know about shipping?"

Sophie smiled, wondering what Daniel would say if he knew the man he was discussing was actually a Viking. "I wouldn't underestimate Connor in anything he tried to accomplish. He's really quite remarkable."

"He might decide to marry her and take her back to England."

"I'm certain he plans to stay in Boston."

He shoved his hands into the pockets of his dressing gown as he stared out the windows for a long time, as though he were searching for answers in the snow-covered gardens. "Your father wanted Laura to marry into one of the finest families in Boston. I promised him she would."

"I admire your loyalty. But I think you owe Laura more than a promise you made to my father."

"I owe your father my life. If he hadn't taken me in, I wouldn't have survived on the streets."

"And what do you owe Laura?"

"I owe her the chance to lift her head in this town. I owe her a chance to prove she's every bit as good as any daughter of any blue blood in Boston."

"So what Laura wants doesn't matter to you."

"Dammit, Sophie." He turned to face her, pain etched in tight lines upon his face. "You don't understand."

"I do understand." She wanted to run to him, to throw her arms around him and hold him. But a chasm had opened between them, a dark abyss she might never be able to cross again. "I understand you think more about appearances than you do your daughter's happiness."

"That's not true."

"Isn't it?" Sophie fought the tears stinging her eyes. "How could you even imagine allowing Laura to marry Philip Gardner? You saw him last night; you heard what he thinks of the Irish. The man is a bigoted boor."

"Yes, he is. But he is no worse than most of Boston society."

"So tell Boston society to go jump in the Charles."

"It's easy for you to say, Sophie. You were born into this society. You've never had anyone look at you as though you had crawled from a bog."

"No, I never have." She felt the first tears fall, a warm trickle she couldn't prevent. "But I have had people look at me as though I wasn't quite good enough to win a man's affections, not quite good enough to become a wife."

"Sophie," he whispered, moving toward her. "Please try to understand."

"I do understand." She held up her hand, stopping him when he would have taken her into his warm embrace. "I understand you aren't the man I thought you were."

"Sophie, don't do this." He clenched his hands at his sides. "Please don't do this."

"I think it's best if we both forget what happened between us." Through her tears she stared at him, seeing her own pain reflected in his dark eyes, fighting the crippling need to run into his arms. "I'll stay as long as Laura needs me. Then I'm going back to New York." She turned, leaving behind the shattered remains of her dreams in his moonlit room.

Connor paused on the threshold of the kitchen, breathing in the scents of fresh-baked bread and brewing coffee. Even the food was more enticing in this century.

Fiona stood peering into the icebox, shaking her head. "I could have sworn there was a pitcher of milk in here last night," she muttered to herself.

"Good morning, Fiona."

Fiona flinched at the sound of his voice. She spun around to face him, eyes wide, lips parted as though she were face-to-face with a demon. " 'Tis you!"

Connor kept the smile on his face, even though suspicion crept like ice up his spine. It was possible Megan wasn't good at keeping secrets. "You look surprised to see me."

"Do I?" Fiona gripped an amber talisman she wore on a silver chain around her neck, holding it toward him. "Now why would I be surprised? You always like to be taking your breakfast early, sir."

He walked toward the table, keeping his anxiety hidden beneath his smile. Fiona pressed back against the counter as he passed, as though she might be burned if he touched her. There was no doubt in his mind— Fiona knew what he had done. He could see it in her eyes and in the way she held the talisman, as though it might ward off one of the Dark Folk. Now the question remained: What to do about it?

"Where's Megan this morning?" he asked, taking a place at the table.

"She's still abed." Fiona eased the icebox door closed, never looking away from him. Sunlight poured through the windows, reflecting like fire through the golden amber she held like a shield. "She was up late last night, looking at the stars."

"I imagine she is fascinated with seeing everything." Connor thought of Megan, recalling the look of wonder in her big blue eyes when she had looked up at him and realized she could see. He had made the right decision, no matter what the cost he must now pay. "You must enjoy the experience with her. While you watch her discover the world, you too will see the world through her innocent eyes. I hope you enjoy each moment."

Fiona stared at him, clutching her talisman, the icy fear he had seen lingering in the depths of her brown eyes softening. "In all the time you've spent in Ireland, have you ever heard any of the stories about the Shining Ones? They're also known as the *Sidhe*, or the gentry. They're the People of the Goddess, the *Tuatha De Danann*."

Connor smiled, sensing her fear turning into something else, something warm and pleasant and far less threatening. "Tell me about these people," he said.

"After their own home had been destroyed by a great flood, they came to Ireland aboard great glittering ships of metal and precious stones, back when the world was young and magic and mystery filled the air and every living thing." Fiona gazed down at the talisman she held in her open palm. "In that time the land had not truly been formed. And creatures we only dream of today roamed the earth."

Connor noticed Laura standing in the doorway. She smiled when he looked at her, the warmth he had glimpsed in a dream glowing in her eyes. He prayed he would always see that warmth, that acceptance. For the woman who stood clutching an amber talisman to protect her from evil could destroy him.

"Though they served the goddess of all living things, the Shining Ones were gods themselves." Fiona stared into her talisman, seemingly unaware of Laura standing behind her. "For many years, through generations, they ruled Erin with their power and magic, shaping the land, defeating enemies, casting out evil."

"What happened to these magical people?" Laura asked.

Fiona pivoted, clutching her talisman to her chest. "Oh, Miss Laura, sure but I didn't hear you come in."

"I see you're filling Mr. Paxton's head with tales of ancient Ireland."

"Aye, that I am." Fiona glanced at Connor, her keen brown eyes holding a conspiratorial gleam. "But I'll not be surprised if he already knows the story I'm telling, and knows it well."

"Do you?"

Connor drew in his breath, the truth pressing against his heart like a stone. "Yes. I have heard the legends."

Laura studied him a moment, curiosity in her eyes. "So tell me, Mr. Paxton, what happened to the Shining Ones?"

Connor hesitated, wondering how much of himself he would reveal in the story of his people. Yet perhaps in the telling, he could help prepare his *Edaina* for the truth he must eventually tell.

"Please." Fiona squeezed her talisman. "Tell us what you be thinking happened to them?"

"They spread their power beyond the borders of Erin, crossing the seas, flourishing where they settled," Connor said, recalling the lessons of his youth. "For ages they ruled the land. Yet they had one enemy they could not defeat—time. In time their power over the land dissolved like mist in the heat of the sun."

Laura frowned. "How was time their enemy?"

"You see, although the children of man worshiped the Shining Ones as gods, they were not divine. They were more than mortal, but not truly gods." Connor planted his elbows on the table and rested his chin on the steeple of his fingers. "And in time, as the children of man matured and they found the one God, they turned away from the Shining Ones. In time the people of the land came to fear the power the *Sidhe* possessed."

Laura stood watching him, seemingly entranced by the story. Did she think the history of his people no more than a fairy tale? Would she ever truly understand and accept him for what he was?

"Shunned and feared, the *Tuatha De Danann* retreated into sanctuaries—hidden mountaintops, secret valleys, protected isles. Yet there were many of the *Sidhe* who remained among the mortals of the world, and to this day they walk with the children of man." Connor looked at Fiona, holding her in a steady gaze, willing her to understand, to keep his secret. "But they are not to be feared. They mean no harm. They wish only to thrive in the world of man."

Fiona slipped the silver chain from around her neck. A smile curved her lips, tentative, a little shy as she moved toward him. "I was wondering if you might like to be taking a look at my pendant."

Connor extended his hand, palm up. The polished amber dangled from her silver chain, like a golden chestnut glittering in the sunlight that poured through the windows behind him. She eased the amber into his palm, keeping a grip on the chain.

He gazed down at the amber, reading the ancient runes carved into the gem, smiling at the simple words meant to cast away evil. On the other side, a crucifix had been etched into the amber. "It is a beautiful pendant."

Fiona released her pent-up breath. "It's been in my

family for generations. I've heard tell it was given to one of my ancestors by a *Sidhe* prince."

His people had often given tokens to ease the fears of mortals. He took the chain from her trembling fingers and slipped the pendant around her neck. "Wear it in good health, Fiona."

"Oh." Fiona closed her eyes a moment, as though in prayer. "Thank you, sir. Bless you."

Connor glanced past Fiona to where Laura stood in the doorway, a thoughtful look in her dark green eyes as she watched him. He only prayed he hadn't given himself away. For he feared she wasn't ready to accept him, not yet.

After breakfast, Connor walked with Laura down a snow-covered path weaving through Boston Common. He stared out across a frozen pond, sunlight glittering on the ice and snow entombing the water that lingered far below the surface. He would like to see this place in summer, when swans were free to glide atop the shimmering water.

"Fiona certainly was acting strangely this morning," Laura said.

"I didn't notice anything."

"You didn't?"

Connor smiled as he met her questioning green eyes. "No."

Laura frowned. "She served you as though you were royalty. I kept expecting her to fall to her knees before you."

"She was just being nice."

"Very nice." Laura sighed, a puff of steam condensing on the cold air. "The story she was telling you, the tale of the *Tuatha De Danann*, it's intriguing, isn't it?"

"It's intriguing to know these people have not been forgotten."

"Do you believe such people ever existed?"

A sparrow swooped across the path and landed on the back of a stone bench that stood in the snow a few feet away. He wished he could release the truth that dwelled within him, allow it to soar, but knew he must keep it locked inside of him. "They are the people I told you about, the rulers of Atlantis."

"I know." She paused on the path and looked up at him. "But do you truly believe the stories?"

"These stories were old in my time; even then they had become legends. And as with all legends, there are embellishments to the truth." Connor watched the little bird as it spread its wings and soaked up the sun that streamed through the naked branches of the trees overhead. "I believe the *Tuatha De Danann* were connected to the earth, and the sky, to the very essence of nature, in ways most people cannot imagine. This gave them abilities that made them seem like gods to the simple people outside of Atlantis."

"Years ago, when Fiona told me her Irish folktales, I thought they were all make-believe. Nothing but smoke. Fairy tales."

"And now?"

"And now . . ." She sighed, shaking her head. "And now I'm confronted with the impossible and find it not only possible, but reality. I look at my Aunt Sophie and doubt everything I have ever believed about the world in which I live. Magic. There really is magic in the world."

He slipped the glove from his hand and touched her cold cheek, tracing a ribbon of shadow cast by a slender branch overhead. "And is it so terrible to learn there is magic in the world?"

"It's frightening. Unsettling. It makes me feel unsure of myself." She hugged her arms to her waist. "I feel as though everything around me is not quite what it seems, not quite as solid as it once was."

"There is nothing to fear." He slipped his fingers beneath her chin, sliding his thumb over the corner of her mouth. "There is no darkness in this magic. Nothing to harm you."

She parted her lips, her sigh warming his hand as her need for him flowed through him, warming him deep inside. She stared up at him, confusion mingling with awakening desire in eyes the soft emerald green of the hills of Erin.

"I think we'd better go back." She stepped away from him as though she were straining against a chain. "Tonight is the Gardner party, and there are still so many things left for you to learn."

And perhaps one or two left for his beautiful *Edaina* to learn, he thought.

Chapter Twenty-one

"You realize, Aunt Sophie, this could be a disaster." Laura frowned at her reflection in the cheval mirror in her bedroom, fussing with the white silk roses stitched along one shoulder of her mint green ball gown. "There are a thousand things that could go wrong."

She smoothed the tight bodice and shifted a fold in the pale mint green brocade that draped the pleated white silk skirt. Nothing seemed to fit properly. Perhaps because her own skin seemed too tight. The dream from the night before had haunted her every waking hour. Every time she glanced at Connor, she remembered the feel of his lips on her skin. And more. So much more.

"I think it will be a good idea to keep Connor away from Lord and Lady Sinclair." Laura tugged on one of her gloves, smoothing the white kid above her elbow. "They might ask too many questions."

Sophie sat in the vanity chair behind her. In the mirror, Laura could see her aunt staring down at the delicate painted lace fan she held open across her lap, as though she hadn't heard a word Laura had said. More than once today Laura had found her aunt staring off into the distance as though unhappy memories were stealing her away from the world around her.

Laura turned, white and mint green silk rustling softly. "Aunt Sophie, are you all right?"

Sophie didn't respond. She sat staring at her open fan as though it held the secrets of the ages.

"Aunt Sophie," Laura said, touching her shoulder.

Sophie glanced up, her eyes wide and questioning. "I'm sorry, did you say something?"

"You've been so distant all day. Are you feeling ill?"

Sophie smiled, but her eyes lacked their usual sparkle. "I'm fine. A little tired, perhaps." She glanced down at the fan she held, staring at the watercolor scene painted below the embroidered lace trim: a man in court dress kneeling before his lady. "I didn't sleep well last night."

"Do you think tonight is going to be a disaster?" Laura squeezed a glove in her hand. "Mrs. Gardner, her friends, they could tear Connor to pieces."

"I'm certain he'll do just fine."

"How can we possibly expect him to be a perfect gentleman? He hasn't had enough time to learn everything he must know."

"Don't worry, dear." Sophie patted Laura's hand. "I have every faith Connor will charm them all."

"Well, I intend to make certain no one insults him." Laura tugged on her glove, determined to protect Connor.

Oh, she could strangle the man! Laura glanced past her partner's shoulder to where Connor was dancing nearby, leading Juliet Marsdale through the lively steps of a mazurka. The pretty little blonde was smiling up at Connor as though he were wearing shining armor.

"Your cousin certainly seems to be enjoying himself."

Laura managed a smile as she looked up at Lord Sinclair. "Yes, he does."

Connor had danced every dance since they arrived at the party, escorting one lady after another to the dance floor. Laura supposed she should be glad he was a success. Not one of the women who had danced with him had complained about his manners or his proud bearing, although a few had mentioned her cousin had an odd sense of humor.

"He's quite an excellent dancer."

Laura nodded. "It's really quite amazing, since his family never was very social. I doubt he's attended more than one or two balls his entire life."

"Really." Lord Sinclair glanced to where Connor and Juliet were dancing a few feet away, Juliet's laughter rippling with the violins. "He seems quite at ease on the dance floor."

"Yes. He does." Oh, she wanted to strangle the man! And here she was, thrust into the position of protecting the barbarian. "It's remarkable, considering the fact his father never entertained. Why, it's no wonder Connor is so unfamiliar with English society."

Austin looked down at her, smiling, his silvery blue eyes filled with a warmth that made her feel as though she had known this man all her life. "I suppose that's the reason we never met."

Laura nodded. "He spent his entire life in the country."

Austin frowned. "I thought your father mentioned Mr. Paxton attended Cambridge."

"Oh." Heaven help her, she had forgotten all about Cambridge. "Yes, yes he did."

"Mr. Paxton and I have something in common then.

I also attended Cambridge."

"Did you?" She missed a step, landing on Lord Sinclair's foot. He squeezed her hand, guiding her gently back into the graceful rhythm of the dance. "I'm terribly sorry."

"A gentleman never minds having a beautiful woman step on his toes."

She managed a smile as she looked up at him. It was difficult not to smile, looking up into his handsome face. He had a way about him, a warmth that radiated from him and ignited trust within her.

Lord Sinclair conjured images of knights who long ago in distant lands rescued fair damsels from fiery dragons. And for some odd reason, as she danced in his warm embrace and looked up into his silvery blue eyes, she had the almost uncontrollable urge to confess the truth. No doubt Lord Sinclair had never in his life lied to a woman. No doubt he had never professed his love one moment, then ignored her the next.

She glanced at Connor. He was smiling down at his pretty little partner, saying something that made Juliet tilt back her head and laugh.

Oh, she was going to strangle the man!

Such riches, this room, the dancing, and the music. Such wondrous music. Connor glanced at the orchestra perched high in a minstrels' galley at one end of the room. The voices of the instruments filled the room with a waltz, the notes flowing through him like a stream sparkling in the sun. And to have Laura in his arms, ah, it was the finest of all these treasures.

"You look pleased with yourself," Laura said.

"I'm enjoying this night."

Her eyes narrowed into emerald slits as she stared up at him. "I noticed."

"This is a feast for the senses." He frowned, confused

by the anger he sensed boiling inside of her. "How could you not enjoy every second?"

High over his head, hundreds of incandescent bulbs glowed against cut crystal, raining light upon the hundreds of men and women in this large room. Gilded mirrors attached to the white walls reflected the light, the flow of colors as the ladies in rainbow-colored gowns swirled by in the arms of dark-clad gentlemen. Perfume drifted from the ladies and from the vials placed high in the crystal chandeliers, mingling with the fragrance of cut white lilies and yellow roses standing in tall vases on each of the refreshment tables.

Only Laura did not seem to be enjoying any of this, especially being with him. She was as stiff as a wooden doll in his arms.

"Will you go in to supper with me?" When she hesitated he added, "Without your guidance I might use my oyster fork to eat my salad; just think of the scandal I could cause."

One corner of her lips twitched. "I suppose it would be better if I went in with you."

He traced the curve of her tightly pursed lips with his gaze, recalling the lure of her—her breath soft and warm against his cheek, her lips parting beneath his, her desire a siren singing in his blood. Yet now all he sensed was anger burning deep within her. "Have I done something to offend you?"

"Offend me?" She lifted her chin. "No, nothing."

"You're angry with me. Is it against the rules to tell me why?"

"I'm not angry."

"Yes, you are."

"No, I'm not."

"The corner of your mouth twitches when you're angry."

She frowned. "It does not."

"If you don't tell me what I've done to make you angry, how will I know not to do it again?"

"I'm not angry, I just . . ." She stared at his shoulder where her gloved hand rested, her fingers digging into the black wool of his coat. "I simply hate to think of unleashing a lusty Viking on the unsuspecting women of this town."

He pulled her closer as each step flowed from him as natural as the ebb and flow of his own breath. "There is only one woman this lusty Viking desires."

She looked up at him, anger sparkling in her eyes. "Are all Vikings as careless with the truth as you are?"

"You were the one who told me I must dance with other women. I believe you said I must not dance more than two dances with you or people would talk. I don't intend to waste my two chances to hold you with anything less than a waltz."

She tilted her chin. "It certainly doesn't matter to me how many women you dance with."

"I believe I have found the partner I was born to dance with."

"Such pretty words."

"Do you have any idea how beautiful you are to me?"

Laura dismissed his comment with a huff.

"Do you realize how the mint green of your gown highlights the forest green depths of your eyes?"

She moistened her lips. "Save the compliments for your other women."

"All other women fade into mist compared to you."

She rolled her eyes. "Have your other partners fallen for such blatant flattery?"

He sighed. "Tell me what I must do to win you, my love. Tell me how I can convince you I want only you."

She parted her lips as though to dismiss him. Yet she hesitated as she looked up into his eyes and saw what he knew was there for her, only her—his love.

She felt it too, the emotion shimmering between them, slipping golden links around them. Yet she fought it, as though the pull that drew them together might draw her into a deadly whirlpool.

Her skirts brushed his legs, a mist of frosted mint that whispered with every move she made, tempting him to peel away the silk, enticing him to discover each mysterious layer of femininity, luring him to the long, elegant legs beneath. Her lips parted on a soft exhale of warm breath. She curled her fingers against his shoulder. He felt her defenses shudder as she lowered her gaze to his lips.

Kiss me, Connor.

He heard her voice whisper in his mind. For one dizzying moment he was tempted to obey, to pull her close and kiss her as she longed to be kissed, as he craved to kiss her. Yet he knew the scandal he would cause in this crowded room, the humiliation she would suffer for one unguarded moment.

He drew in his breath. He tried to think of something other than her lips and the tempting lure of her body, fighting the pain that throbbed low in his belly.

The music soared and shattered into a final crescendo. The last notes rippled in the room. The dance was over, and still he held her. She stared up at him, desire shimmering with something more in her eyes, something he had waited a lifetime to see.

"It is customary for a gentleman to release his partner at the end of a dance, Mr. Paxton."

At the sound of Philip Gardner's voice, Laura jerked in Connor's embrace. She stepped back from Connor, blinking, suddenly aware they were not alone. On the contrary, they were in the middle of the dance floor, surrounded by at least 300 people. And she had been wishing Connor would kiss her. Heaven help her, the man had the most uncanny way of making her forget what she was about.

"I believe this dance is mine," Philip said, grasping Laura's upper arm as though he intended to drag her from Connor.

Laura stared up at Philip's taut features, stunned by the fury she saw in his brown eyes.

Connor slipped her free arm through his. "We were just going in to supper."

"I'm afraid you're mistaken," Philip said. Laura felt like a wishbone about to be snapped as he tugged on her arm. "She is having supper with me at midnight."

Connor's lips curved into a chilling smile. "Did you happen to ask the lady if she wanted to have supper with you?"

Color crept up from Philip's stiff white collar, staining his neck and his cheeks a dark scarlet. "Miss Sullivan and I have an understanding, Mr. Paxton."

"Do you?"

"That's right," Philip said, squeezing her arm, his long fingers biting into her skin.

The back of Laura's neck prickled. The man was acting as though she were a possession, and he didn't even have the excuse of being from the ninth century.

"I suggest you take your hand off of the lady's arm," Connor said, his voice low and deadly calm, the dark sound sending a chill through Laura.

Philip jerked back his hand as though he had been zapped by a bolt of lightning. He stared at Connor, an odd mixture of fear and indignation molding his features into a stiff mask.

"Philip, I told Connor I would go in to supper with him. Perhaps you would like to join us."

"Join you!" Philip stared down at her as though she had lost her wits.

Laura stiffened. "That's right."

Philip tugged on the bottom of his black silk waistcoat. "I prefer to go in later, at a much more civilized hour."

Laura chafed beneath the heated barb, even though she knew the comment was aimed at Connor.

"I trust we shall dance after you have had your supper." As though he needed no answer, Philip pivoted and began marching away from them.

She had never seen him like this. Why, the man had been positively rude, Laura thought, rubbing her arm where Philip's taut fingers had left red slashes on the skin below the scalloped ivory lace of her short sleeve.

Connor glanced at her tortured arm, then stared at Philip, his blue eyes narrowed, a man who could freeze water with a glance. "I don't like the way he touched you."

As the words left Connor's lips the ends of Philip's braces peeked out from the tail of his coat. His trousers drooped. With his nose elevated, Philip didn't notice.

"Philip," Laura said, intending to warn him.

Philip turned, his lips pulling into an arrogant smirk. "Have you changed your mind, Laura?"

In other words, had she come to her senses. Laura lifted her chin, meeting his arrogance with a touch of pride. "No. But you should know—"

Philip raised his hand, cutting off her words. "We shall discuss this later."

"Arrogant bastard," Connor whispered, aiming his glacial stare at Gardner.

Philip pivoted, his trousers sliding to his ankles, exposing baggy white linen drawers. Heads turned, ladies gasped, men snickered.

"What the . . ." Philip tripped, pitched forward, hitting the polished oak planks with his hands and knees, his linen-clad rear hoisted like a tent pole.

People surged around the edge of the dance floor like

ducks swarming scattered corn. Laughter started in a ripple and swelled to a cresting wave around the crowded room.

"Oh, my gracious!" Laura whispered. She tried to quell the giggles bubbling up inside of her and failed.

Philip scrambled to his feet, snatching at his trousers. He glared at Laura, his face purple with rage.

Laura pressed her hand to her lips, trying to catch the giggles. "I'm sorry," she mumbled through her laughter.

Philip clutched his trousers to his waist. The veins in his neck stood out like ropes. "This is not amusing, Laura."

"No." She bit her lower lip. "Of course it isn't."

Philip turned on his heel, trudging through his audience and out of sight.

"This is horrible," Laura said, her giggles spoiling the severity of her words. "He must be humiliated."

"Yes. And it couldn't happen to a more deserving snob." Connor smiled as he looked down at her. "Shall we go in to supper, my lady?"

Laura glanced up at her Viking. If she didn't know better, she would have sworn Connor had been the instrument of Philip's downfall. But how could that be?

She slipped her arm through his, noticing Sophie standing a few feet away. Her aunt was watching them, and impish grin on her lips. "It was rather odd, the way Philip's braces snapped."

"Was it?" Connor asked, the picture of innocence as he looked down at her.

"Yes. And his trousers, strange how they fell all the way to his knees. His buttons must have come undone at the same time his braces snapped." Laura frowned as she stared at her aunt. Perhaps someone had given those trousers a little nudge. She would have to have a little discussion with Sophie.

* * *

Connor stepped onto the terrace, escaping the heat and noise of the ballroom, seeking a moment's peace from the role of Mr. Connor Paxton. It was a glorious night, crisp and clear, a night when the stars seared the sky with their brilliant light.

Connor stood by the stone balustrade and lifted his face to the moonlight, taking a deep breath of the cold night air, clearing his senses of the mingled fragrances of a hundred perfumes. His trial was nearly over, and Laura was pleased with Mr. Connor Paxton. He frowned when he wondered what she would think if she knew he had snapped Philip Gardner's braces. He had an uneasy feeling it would turn his victory into defeat.

The music from the ballroom intensified as someone opened the door behind him. Connor turned and found Lord Austin Sinclair standing by the French doors.

"The room is getting a little stuffy, isn't it?" Austin closed the door, the music dissolving into a faded tapestry of notes.

"Yes, it is." Although Laura had warned Connor to stay away from Lord Sinclair, it was impossible to avoid the man without running like a coward. And he had never been a coward.

Austin smiled as he approached Connor. "I've been looking forward to meeting you, Mr. Paxton."

"Have you?"

"Yes. I believe we have a great deal in common."

"Do we?" How very strange, Connor thought as he shook Lord Sinclair's hand. He could perceive none of this man's emotions. It was as though Sinclair had erected a shield against him, a black curtain he could not penetrate. But how could this be?

"We come from the same country after all. Share the same ancestors, so to speak."

Connor frowned, instinct telling him this man meant more than he said. And instinct also told him it was Sinclair's intent to reveal more than shimmered on the surface.

Lord Sinclair turned toward the gardens, where the breeze rippled across the snow, lifting silvery veils. "I understand you have only recently come to Boston."

"Yes." Connor studied Sinclair's profile, experiencing an odd sense of familiarity with the man. It would be easy to believe they were actually from the same bloodline. "I've been here only a few days."

Sinclair glanced at him, an intensity burning in the silvery blue of his eyes, as though he were probing past this social facade Connor had fashioned to the man hidden beneath. "And have you come for business or pleasure?"

Connor studied Sinclair, the suspicion growing inside of him urging him to probe, to chip away until he found the truth hidden behind the dark curtain shielding this man. "I came to meet Miss Sullivan."

Sinclair smiled. "She is a lovely woman."

"She is beyond compare." Connor flexed his hand on the cold stone of the balustrade. "Perhaps you will understand when I say she is my *Edaina*."

Sinclair held Connor's look for a moment that stretched tautly between them. "I understand perfectly what you mean. She is your soul mate."

Connor's breath grew still in his lungs as he stared at Sinclair and realized who and what this man was. "And tell me what has brought you to Boston, Lord Sinclair? I would think you would be more comfortable in warmer climes. Perhaps that of Brazil."

Austin chuckled softly. "You are familiar with Avallon."

"I visited the sanctuary once. I found it far too confining."

Austin nodded. "There are many who prefer to live in the Outworld."

"How is it you knew who I was?"

"Your mother sent us a message." Austin glanced over his shoulder, looking into the shadows at the far end of the terrace. "She wanted the Inner Circle to send you back to your own time."

Connor frowned. "And this is your mission?"

Austin shook his head. "My mission is to observe you, to determine if you are in some way dangerous to the security of Avallon."

Connor studied the man a moment, trying to assess the power he might face if Lord Sinclair should prove an enemy. He saw nothing in the sculpted planes of his face, nothing in Sinclair's silvery blue eyes to betray any of his intentions. The man could be dangerous. "And if you find me dangerous?"

Austin looked straight into his eyes. "Then I am to eliminate the threat."

Connor cocked one black brow as he held Austin's steady gaze. "I have but one reason to be in this time. It has nothing at all to do with Avallon."

"I believe you." Austin drew a deep breath. "Still, I wonder if you would come back with me to Avallon. There are those who may not be so easily convinced."

"In time, I may visit the sanctuary again." Connor looked through the panes of the French doors, searching for Laura in the crowded room. She was standing at one of the refreshment tables with Sophie. "But at the moment I have no time to placate the Inner Circle of Avallon."

Austin released his breath, steam condensing on the cold air. "If there is anything you require, if you need assistance in anything, please don't hesitate to come to me."

Connor meet Sinclair's steady blue eyes, sensing the easing of the other man's defenses. There was honesty in these eyes. "Perhaps in time we may become friends."

"I would consider that an honor." Austin smiled. "Come, I would like to introduce you to my *Edaina*."

"I swear, Laura, I had nothing to do with Philip's tumble from his throne." Sophie lifted a glass of lemonade from a silver tray on the refreshment table beside her. "But I can't say I'm sorry it happened."

"It's odd the way it happened." With her thumb Laura stripped the moisture from her glass of lemonade. "I can't imagine how his braces gave way."

"No doubt he puffed his chest out so far he popped his braces."

"Aunt Sophie, you're terrible." Laura couldn't halt the smile tipping her lips. "The poor man must have been humiliated."

"Oh, bother."

Laura flinched. She glanced around, searching for white feathers or spinning clocks. "Did you just cast a spell?" she whispered.

"I wouldn't dare try something here." Sophie stared past Laura, her lips pulling into a tight line. "But it is tempting. If I weren't afraid we would end up with a confused penguin wandering the dance floor, I would zap the man coming toward us straight to the North Pole."

Laura cringed. "Philip?"

Sophie nodded. "And it looks as though he's managed to scrape together his dignity along with a healthy dose of his usual arrogance."

Laura didn't turn to face him as he drew near, but took the few precious seconds to compose her features into a calm mask.

"Laura, I need to speak with you."

Laura set her glass on the table and faced him, seeing Sophie had been correct. Philip was once again as stiff as an elegantly clothed scarecrow. "What is it?"

"I need to speak to you alone." Philip glanced at Sophie. "Please excuse us."

Laura's spine stiffened, an odd chill seeping into her blood as she wondered what he wanted to discuss. She glanced around, searching for Connor as Philip led her toward one corner of the room. Connor was on the dance floor, leading Lady Sarah Sinclair through the steps of a waltz, his movements bold, powerful, filled with the uncanny grace of a jungle cat.

Connor was a perfect counterpoint to Lady Sarah's delicate beauty, her gown of turquoise silk billowing, swaying as he swept her around the floor. Laura had promised the next waltz to Connor, the last she would be allowed to share with him this evening.

Laura watched his every move, wishing she could be Connor's partner this dance and every dance. When he held her in his arms, the rest of the world—

"I think tonight would be the ideal time to announce our engagement."

Chapter Twenty-two

Laura jumped, bumping a potted palm. The plant tipped. She grabbed for it, smacking Philip's jaw with the back of her hand as he dashed in front of her to grab it.

Philip stepped back, righting the palm with one hand, rubbing his jaw with the other.

"Sorry," Laura whispered.

"It's quite all right."

"It seems to be a night for accidents."

Philip tugged on the hem of his waistcoat. "I believe there's no need to mention that unfortunate incident."

Laura searched for some means of escape, some way to divert him from the subject he wanted to discuss. "Oh, dear, I'm afraid I've torn my hem. Please excuse me, I need—"

"It can wait," Philip said, grabbing her arm when she started to walk away.

"But I really should mend it before it gets worse."

Philip stared down at her gown. "I don't see a tear."

"It's really in my . . . petticoat," she whispered.

He frowned. "It can wait a few moments."

"But I—"

He heid up his hand, silencing her. "I believe we should announce our engagement tonight."

"But Father—"

"Has already given me permission." He smiled, a stiff twist of his lips that betrayed a man who was a stranger to laughter. "I must say, he was delighted with the match."

"I see." A jab of pain pierced her heart. She had known all along her father's intention to see her wed to Philip, and still, the realization of her fate twisted deep inside of her, a pain that threatened to drain the strength from her limbs.

"I'll have the musicians strike a fanfare and then we can announce our plans."

"No!"

Philip cocked one dark brow as he stared down at her. "No?"

"I'm not ready." She touched his arm. "Philip, you must give me some time."

"Time for what, Laura?"

"We scarcely know each other."

"We will have years to get better acquainted."

Laura stared at her hand resting on his arm, imagining what it might be like to touch his bare skin. She snatched back her hand, her stomach clenching into a knot.

"Now, Laura, I realize you must be concerned about being worthy enough to marry into the Gardner family, with your background."

Laura looked up at him. "My background?"

Philip nodded. "But I can assure you I've decided you would make a splendid wife. There's a cool reserve about you that is anything but Irish. You're like a beautiful marble sculpture of an ancient goddess. Cold. Aloof. Untouchable."

Laura stared at the man. "You could fall in love with someone you thought cold and aloof?"

"Love?" Philip frowned. "I assumed you were above those foolish females who insist on some mystical feelings of devotion. Anyone of good breeding realizes such intense emotions are to be avoided."

"I see. So you don't love me."

Philip released his breath in an agitated sigh. "I admire you. I respect you. I plan to take care of you for the rest of your life. I believe that is all any woman should expect from a marriage."

"I see." Heaven help her, was this all her future held? Were all the seasons to be washed from her life except one? Would she forever be trapped in the cold depths of winter, longing for the warmth of spring?

"Come now, Laura, let's end this childish game. We'll announce our engagement tonight."

"No!"

Philip drew in his breath, his dark brows meeting over the slim line of his nose. "Does your reluctance have anything to do with Connor Paxton?"

Heat crept into her cheeks as she held his angry gaze. Connor. How she longed to have him beside her, his strength sustaining her.

"It's obvious you have some infatuation with the man. I must say, I'm not at all happy with this, Laura. And I'm certain your father will be quite disappointed in you."

Laura felt the strength draining from her limbs as her choices drained like water through a sieve. "Please. I need some time to adjust to the idea of marrying you."

He pursed his lips, staring at her as though he were

a judge about to deliver a verdict. "So it seems you have come to your senses."

She forced her lips into a smile. "It's all so overwhelming, that's all."

"Yes. I know it is." He smiled, a smug grin that made her wish she had hit him with her clenched fist. "I'm certain you never imagined you would ever be fortunate enough to become a Gardner."

"I certainly never did."

"Very well. But don't take too long, Laura. I've never been a particularly patient man." He tugged on the hem of his waistcoat. "Excuse me; I've promised Juliet Marsdale this next dance."

Laura watched him walk away from her. She wanted to run and hide, but there were no safe places for her. She could not escape duty and responsibility. She would obey her father's wishes, even if those wishes destroyed her very soul.

She glanced at Connor, following his every move, seeing the light turn to sapphire in his thick black hair, tracing the curve of his smile, wishing she could touch him. He was everything she had ever wanted. And he was as far out of her reach now as he had been when he lived a thousand years before her.

Austin stood near one of the three pairs of French doors that lined one wall of the ballroom, watching his wife waltz with Connor. There was a time when Sarah would have been unsure of herself on a dance floor, and here she was, shining and beautiful, swirling in the arms of a man from a different time and place.

Pride glowed more brightly than the sun within him, pride for the lovely lady who had given him a son and more joy than he had ever imagined. And admiration for the young man who was the embodiment of all his people had once cherished. In a very real sense he and

Connor shared the same blood.

Connor was truly an amazing young man. He had been in this century less than a week and he had already assimilated the language and culture. More than that, Connor had conquered this century. He fit into this world more elegantly than most of the people filling this house.

"Isn't your wife expecting another child?"

Austin's muscles tensed as Fraser Bennett approached him. "That's right. The baby is due in August."

Fraser paused beside Austin, staring at Sarah and Connor. "Do you think it's wise to allow your wife to dance with that devil?"

"If I thought there were any danger, I wouldn't bring Sarah within a mile of the man."

"Those who practice the black arts have always had a penchant for young mothers." Fraser smiled as he looked at Austin. "Be careful, Austin; this man might bewitch your precious wife."

Austin sought the inner balance that would avert the anger rising within him. "There is only one woman Connor is interested in bewitching, Fraser."

Fraser rolled his eyes. "Do you still believe the man has come all this way for a woman?"

"I have no reason to believe otherwise." Austin held Fraser's icy stare. "The message we received from his mother, the behavior I've observed, all support the theory Connor came here to claim Laura Sullivan."

"If it is true, and I don't believe it is"—Fraser glanced away from Austin, his hands curling into fists at his sides as he stared at Connor—"what do you suppose a young sorcerer will do when he discovers the woman he desires is promised to another man? You have heard the rumors about her engagement to Philip Gardner?"

Austin nodded.

"I wouldn't care to be around the young man if he

were angered. He could prove deadly."

"I don't believe the man is dangerous."

"And I don't intend to allow your poor judgment to cause a disaster."

"You're here as an observer, Fraser." Austin smiled as he looked straight into Fraser's eyes. "I won't tolerate any interference."

Fraser flicked his tongue between his dry lips. "You can't intimidate me, Sinclair. I intend to do what I can to see that menace destroyed."

Austin watched Bennett march toward the refreshment table where Henry Thayer was standing alone, the emissary's brown eyes following Connor's every move. Austin didn't need to hear the conversation to know the malicious suspicions Bennett was spewing into Henry's ear. If he managed to turn Henry against Connor, it would be difficult to convince the governing council otherwise.

Austin glanced at Connor, wondering how he might be able to protect an Irish sorcerer from harm.

Connor felt Laura calling to him, a desperate plea tugging on his vitals. From a distance he sensed her pain: a deep, throbbing wound sliced across her heart. He paused in the middle of the dance floor, scanning the room, searching for Laura.

"Is there something wrong, Mr. Paxton?"

He glanced down into the lovely face of his partner. Lady Sarah Sinclair was looking up at him, concern shimmering in her hazel eyes. "I'm sorry. Please forgive me, but I must go to Miss Sullivan."

"Has something happened?"

"I'm not certain. But I know she needs me." He left Lady Sarah in the middle of the dance floor, amid the swirl of colorful gowns, unaware of how his actions had betrayed his heart. He only knew Laura needed him, and he must find her.

Laura stood against the wall near one corner of the room, hiding behind the fronds of a potted palm that rose from a brass pot on the floor beside her. She stood quiet and still as marble, her face as pale as the white roses that adorned one shoulder of her gown. When she noticed him approach, her lips parted, but not a word escaped, only a soft sound, like the strangled cry of a wounded swan.

"Laura," he whispered, touching her arm. The force of her emotions rushed through him like a river bursting through a dam, her pain taking his breath away. "What's wrong, love? What is it?"

"Please," she whispered. "Not in here. Not with all these people."

He slipped her arm through his and led her out of the ballroom.

Her legs trembled beneath her as Laura walked beside Connor down a hallway in the Gardner house, the music and laughter and conversation fading, dropping away from her like a dark shroud. He threw open a door and ushered her into a dark room that Laura had visited several times. She stood in the wedge of light pouring in from the open door, breathing in the scent of beeswax and lemon oil clinging to the cool air.

This was the drawing room where Esther Gardner held court for those privileged enough to be granted a place in her kingdom. One day Laura would be forced to sit beside the queen on her Empire sofa, a reluctant princess with no means of escape. She shivered as the image took hold of her.

Lights flickered overhead, exposing the gold fleurs-de-lis stitched into the royal-blue carpet below her feet. The door closed. She felt a strong hand touch her shoulder, Connor's warmth flooding her, blessed sunlight in the heart of winter.

"Tell me what's troubling you, love. Tell me how I can make you smile."

She turned to face him, looking up into his intense blue eyes. If only fate were more kind. If only she could gaze into his beautiful eyes every day of her life. But fate was not kind. They had so little time together.

She reached for him, touching his cheek, seeing the dark pinpoints of his beard sheathed beneath his smooth skin. "Hold me. Please hold me."

"For eternity," he whispered, sliding his arms around her waist.

She threw her arms around his neck, holding him, absorbing the heat and strength of him like a dying woman seeking one last chance at life. She pressed her face against his neck, breathing in the warm scent of musk and citrus. "I love you," she whispered. "I want you to know, no matter what happens to separate us, I do love you."

"I'm not going to leave you, my love." He tightened his arms around her, and then he was pulling away, far enough to look down into her face. "No matter how many full moons come and go. No matter how many spells Sophie casts, nothing can take me from your side."

Except the responsibility she felt wrapped like a noose around her neck. She cupped his face in her hands, looking up at him, trying to capture his image for the lonely years to come. Yet it wasn't enough to look at him.

With her fingertips she traced the smooth arch of his black brows, the thick black lashes that fluttered beneath her touch. He stood quiet and steady, like a pagan god welcoming the curious touch of a mortal woman. She lingered along the curve of his smiling lips, brushing his skin with her fingertips, staring up at him, pressing his features between the pages of her memory for safekeeping. No one could take away her memories of Connor.

"You're beautiful," she whispered. "A dream made flesh and blood."

He lowered his head and she rose on her toes, reaching for his kiss, meeting his lips with all the love and passion she had kept pent up inside of her since the first moment she had seen him. She slid her arms around his neck, holding him, welcoming the slick thrust of his tongue as he slipped between her lips.

This was what life was meant to be—a joyous joining of man and woman, two hearts finding the same rhythm, two lives touched by the same glorious light. She snuggled against him, trying to get closer, pressing her aching breasts against his hard chest.

He groaned deep in his throat. He slid his hands over her back, spreading a heat that seeped through the silk of her gown and made her long for the touch of his hands on her bare skin.

"Laura," he whispered, sliding his lips across her cheek. "Let me love you as I was meant to love you, with my heart, and my soul, and my body."

She tunneled her hands into his thick hair, clutching the silky strands as he nuzzled the sensitive skin beneath her ear. Dreams mingled with reality, forging a desire stronger than any she had ever imagined. This was what she had searched for all of her life—love and acceptance, a passion so strong it threatened to consume her.

She had responsibilities.

She was promised to another man.

She couldn't surrender to this glorious promise.

She tugged on his hair, drawing his lips away from her neck. She stared up into the endless blue of his eyes, seeing his love, his desire burning for her. A lifetime of winter stretched out before her, and summer was within her grasp.

He flexed his hands on her waist, his features drawn into lines of pain, his need for her naked in his eyes. "I want you, Laura. Here. Now."

She parted her lips, but her words of protest were swept away by need before they could even form. What justice existed in this life if she and Connor would forever be denied the joy of sharing heart, body, and soul?

He slid his hands upward along her back, spreading warmth. "Be mine, my love."

One splendid moment of heat and light, that was all she would steal. One moment to sustain her the rest of her life. She tugged him to her, capturing his lips beneath her own, tasting eternity.

Nothing mattered in this moment. Nothing but the feel of his lips on hers, the heat of his body radiating against her, promising an endless summer.

He slid his hands up her back, hooks coming undone beneath his touch as though by magic. Green silk slipped from her shoulders as he lifted her in his arms and lowered her to the thick carpet emblazoned with royal symbols stitched in gold. He covered her, kissing her lips, her cheeks, her eyes, tugging at his clothes, casting off his coat, his tie, his waistcoat, releasing the Viking hidden beneath the social trappings.

Laura clawed at the studs lining his shirt, ripping them from the white linen, seeking the warmth of his skin beneath. She plunged her hands inside his shirt, sliding her palms across silky black curls, warm skin. She felt a stranger to herself, free, unencumbered by the rules and responsibilities that had shackled her like iron bands. These ties were stronger. This chain that linked her to this man was more powerful than any forged of iron or steel.

Laura gasped, tossing back her head as he pushed her camisole down, releasing her breasts, her tight corset lifting the pale globes to the heat of his lips and tongue. The medallion he wore brushed her camisole as he lowered his head.

"Oh, my gracious," she whispered. This was more potent than any dream, this delicious tugging of his mouth upon skin that shimmered with sensation.

"So beautiful," he murmured, gazing down at her. He cupped her breasts, brushing his thumbs over the tips that had drawn tight and tingling. Slowly he paid tribute to each, flicking his tongue over the tiny pink pearls, nibbling, tugging, until she was gasping with the sheer intensity of the pleasure he sent spiraling through her.

He pushed her skirts out of his way, silk and linen tumbling around her waist, spilling over the blue and gold carpet. "So many layers," he said, tugging at the pale blue ribbon at her waist.

Laura shifted her hips, watching him, riveted by the sight of his dark hands against her white linen drawers.

"But I find these very pretty." He plucked open the three pearl buttons, flicking open the linen from her waist down. Desire shimmered in his eyes. "All these feminine layers are very teasing."

Laura bit her lower lip as he slid the drawers from her hips, her thighs, stripping them from her completely, exposing her shamelessly to his gaze. Yet she felt no shame. She felt bewitched, as though he had taken control of her, completely, irrevocably.

"It's like unwrapping a precious jewel." He touched her, a soft brush of his fingers upward along her inner thighs. "Sparkling, beguiling."

Laura held her breath, remembering the way he had touched her once in a dream, there in her most secret place; he had touched her with his lips and his tongue. Did such shocking intimacy happen beyond that cherished realm of their secret valley? Yet even as the question formed in her mind, he answered with a soft kiss.

"Oh, my . . ." She sucked in her breath. She slipped her hands into his soft, black waves, holding him, absorbing every wicked tingle that trembled through her. With his lips and his tongue he proved that reality could be so much more than fantasy.

Yet even as the delicious sensations built within her, she wanted more. She wanted him inside of her, as he had been once in a fantasy. She wanted to know the true joy of their joining.

He surged above her as though he understood her need. He watched her as he flicked open his trousers and released his potent heat and power.

"We belong to one another," he whispered, pressing against her. "We always have. We always will."

She trembled with the truth of his words, the warmth that flickered and flared like a thousand tiny flames inside of her at the touch of his arousal against her moist flesh. She tilted her hips, welcoming him as he pressed inside of her.

She felt the easing of her virginal sheath, the slow stretch as he eased deeper inside of her. In all of her life she had only imagined one man ever touching her this way. In all of her life no man would ever possess her as Connor did in this one moment.

Responsibilities lurked in her future. Nights of duty in the bed of another man loomed like monsters waiting to devour her. But she would have this one moment in time. She would have this memory to hold and cherish and sustain her through all the empty years to come.

"I love you," she whispered, slipping her hands inside his shirt, sliding her fingertips over the pebble-hard nipples hidden beneath silky black curls.

"You are my life." He watched her as though he

needed to see in her eyes the moment she crossed over the threshold from which there was no return.

She felt a sharp stab of pain as he reached her maiden barrier. He closed his eyes, sucking in his breath as though he felt her pain. And then the pain was dissolving, melting in the warmth pulsing from Connor, so vibrant he seemed to glow with its radiance.

Nothing but pleasure remained. Pleasure and the slow easing of his body into hers, the altering of her being from sleeping maiden into a woman fully awakened.

"Connor," she whispered, exalting in the joy of total possession.

He kissed her, slanting his lips across hers, slipping his tongue into her mouth as his body filled her so deeply, so completely, they seemed fused by the heat and power throbbing between them. Gold warmed by his skin brushed her breasts as he moved above her, his ancient medallion caressing her with heat.

With her arms and her legs she held him, moving to the rhythm that built and expanded until the world coalesced into this urgent rhythm, this giving and taking of man and woman. With all of her heart and soul she surrendered to the glorious fate that had been destined from the beginning of time, shuddering in Connor's arms, whispering his name as she felt his body tense and surge against her, as she heard her name escape his lips like the deep-throated growl of a contented lion.

She sighed as he eased against her, his warm breath stirring the damp curls beneath her ear. If only she could hold him like this until the end of time. She shuddered when she thought of what she would face in place of this joy she had found in Connor's arms.

He lifted away from her, leaning on his forearm as he looked down into her face. "What is it, love? You're frightened suddenly."

She touched his neck, his skin warm and damp against her palm. The truth lurked like a demon between them, threatening to shred the happiness they had stolen in these few treasured moments. She couldn't tell him she had been promised to another man, not now, not when she could feel his body still warm within her. "Someone might come."

He smiled. "This is not proper behavior for a ball?"

She traced the curve of his smile with her fingertip. "I'm afraid we would cause quite a scandal if anyone even suspected what we have just done."

"Propriety can be a nuisance."

She smiled up into his beautiful eyes. "Yes."

For a moment he seemed to struggle with the need to ease her fears of discovery and his desire to stay right where they were and make love to her over and over again.

It was tempting—the idea of making love with him again, the danger of being caught. Such scandal would end Philip's suit. Such scandal would also destroy her father. "Please, Connor. We have to get back to the ball."

He released his breath in a sigh that warmed her fingertips. "Let's see how well I can put all these layers back together again."

She moaned as he eased away from her, robbing her of the delicious heat and weight of his body.

"No more of that." He kissed her, a sweet brush of breath and lips. "Or I'll forget my good intentions."

With Connor's help she fit together the pieces of her garments, repaired the damage to her coiffure. When they were done, she glanced around Esther Gardner's throne room, her gaze lingering on the blue velvet sofa where she would one day sit and pretend to be the perfect wife to a man she would never love.

"Don't look so sad, my love." Connor stroked her

cheek with his fingertips. "This is just our beginning. We'll have a lifetime to share."

She looked up into his beautiful eyes, seeing his love for her, a love that could endure an eternity. A love she was not free to share.

Chapter Twenty-three

"Oh, bother," Sophie whispered as Daniel marched toward her, wending his way through the people milling around the refreshment table like moths around a flame. She felt the room grow warm, far too warm, so warm she could scarcely breathe. Although she had managed to avoid him the entire day, she couldn't keep avoiding him her entire life. One day she would have to face him. But not today. She turned toward the door leading to the adjoining drawing room as he drew near, her mind on escape.

"Only cowards run away from trouble," Daniel said, his voice carrying only as far as the three feet of warm air separating them.

Sophie froze at the sound of his deep voice. She took a long, steadying breath before she turned to face him. It was a mistake, looking at him, seeing the pain in his eyes as keenly as she felt it in her heart. It made her want to forget everything except the feel of his arms around her. "Trouble? I suppose there is little doubt you are that."

He sighed, a smile tipping one corner of his lips. "We need to talk."

She shook her head. "There's nothing left to be said."

"You're wrong."

He closed the distance between them, stepping so close she could catch the scent of bay rum rising with the heat of his skin. "I can't let you walk out of my life, Sophie."

She closed her eyes, fighting the lure of him, the need in his dark eyes. "Daniel, I—"

"I would like a few words with you, Mr. Sullivan."

Sophie's eyes snapped open to find Esther Gardner standing beside Daniel. She stood with her head tilted so she could stare down her nose at him, even though he stood a foot taller than she did.

Daniel frowned. "I'm afraid it will have to wait. Miss Chandler and I—"

"This cannot wait." Esther clasped her hands at her waist, staring at Daniel like a queen addressing a peasant. "What I have to say is of extreme importance."

Sophie saw her chance for escape and grabbed it. "It's all right. We were done with our discussion."

Daniel looked at her, his lips pulled into a taut line. "Not by a long shot, Miss Chandler."

Sophie released her breath as she watched Daniel follow Esther Gardner through the crowded room. And what would they have to discuss if not wedding plans? Sophie shivered. She fixed her thoughts on the horrible way Daniel was about to sell his daughter to Philip Gardner. It was the only way she could keep from falling like a beggar into his arms.

"Aunt Sophie."

Sophie turned, frowning when she saw her niece.

Laura's cheeks were flushed, her eyes wide and misty. "Laura, are you ill?"

Laura shook her head. "I would just like to go home."

Sophie slipped her arm around Laura's slender shoulders. "I'll have our carriage brought around."

This meeting was inevitable, Daniel supposed, as he followed Esther Gardner into her library. Still, he didn't care to be summoned like a peasant by a queen. As he strolled to the fireplace, he stared up at the mineral deposits and various rocks sitting on mahogany shelves rising above the mantel. He searched inside for the self-control that had served him for so many years, finding it brittle and crumbling.

The library door closed with a click. "I feel we really must discuss this situation," Esther said.

He turned to face her. "By situation I assume you mean your son's interest in marrying my daughter."

Esther's mouth twisted into a grim line. "Exactly."

He watched the egret plumes of white and lavender bob in her dark hair as she approached him, strutting like a plump hen, ready to assert her mastery over the barnyard. All of his life this woman had looked upon him as though he weren't fit to clean her shoes. Now she found herself in the rather indelicate position of becoming his relative.

He should be amused. Yet he could find no joy in this moment, none of the satisfaction he always imagined would come with this victory. All the joy had been drained from him in one night of splendid passion and stunning defeat.

She paused two feet away from him, cocking her head to look at him down the length of her Roman nose. "I must say I'm rather surprised the matter has not been dealt with in a more expedient manner."

He drew in his breath, the cloying sweet scent of her

perfume mixing with the smoke smoldering from the fire on the hearth. "You mean you're surprised my daughter didn't leap at the chance of becoming part of your family."

She pursed her lips. "Naturally I would assume your daughter would be thrilled with the prospect of becoming my son's wife."

"Naturally."

"There is little doubt most of the single young women in town would sell their souls for the chance to marry my son." She tapped her fan against her gloved palm, white and lavender feathers trembling at her touch. "Still, it seems your daughter does not possess the insight to realize she is in the enviable position of making the most desirable match in Boston."

He looked down into her cold, dark eyes, a chill crawling across the base of his spine when he thought of Laura facing this woman across the breakfast table every morning. "I can't imagine how Laura could possibly not see what life with Philip would bring her."

She smiled, a queen pleased with the actions of one of her peasants. "I'll be frank with you. I wasn't entirely pleased to learn my son's intentions. Still, he is a man who is not easily swayed from a course of action."

"He seems quite determined to have her."

"Yes." Esther shook her head as though she couldn't quite fathom her son's behavior. "I believe part of the reason is how cool she is to him. Most women fawn at his feet."

Daniel stared at the glass-fronted mahogany bookcases that flanked the fireplace, the shelves covered with rocks and colorful stones. He had the feeling Philip didn't love Laura, only saw her as a trophy, a prize he would take home, like the rocks he kept in his collection.

"We can announce the engagement this evening."

"This evening?"

She nodded, the feathers bobbing in her hair. "Three months should give us sufficient time to prepare the wedding. Although I would prefer the traditional year-long engagement, Philip wants the wedding held this spring."

Apparently it didn't matter what Laura wanted. Emotions wrapped around his heart, squeezing until his chest ached as he imagined the life Laura would lead: an endless purgatory of days under this woman's thumb, and nights locked in the arms of a man she didn't love. He knew that type of life. He had lived it.

"We'll have the ceremony in the music room of the Chandler house."

Unbidden images of Sophie taunted him, her words echoing in his mind—*And Laura, does she deserve less than what we shared these past few hours?*

"I think we'll—"

"I think we'll wait to see what Laura decides she wants to do."

Esther stared up at him. "You mean to say you intend to allow the girl to decide her own wedding arrangements?"

"I mean to say I intend to allow my daughter to decide the man she intends to spend the rest of her life with."

Esther's eyes narrowed, her nostrils flaring as she glared at him. "The cousin from England. He has her affection, doesn't he?"

Daniel smiled, feeling as though a weight had been lifted from his chest. "I believe he does."

"She can choose no better than my son."

"We'll let Laura make the final decision."

"Listen to me, Sullivan." She grabbed his arm as he started to leave. "This town believes your daughter is going to marry my son. I will not have him made a laughingstock."

"In the future, I would caution your son to refrain from boasting of his conquests before they are made." He pried her gloved fingers from his arm.

"I'm warning you, Sullivan," she said as he walked toward the door. "I will not allow that silly chit of yours to hold this family up for ridicule."

Daniel paused at the door, turning to face her, stunned by the venom in her eyes. "You have no choice in what my daughter does, Mrs. Gardner."

"We shall see." She smiled, a cold twisting of her lips. "No one crosses me."

"As far as I'm concerned, you can take a jump in the Charles, Mrs. Gardner."

He turned, smiling at the sound of her muttered curse.

"Sophie." Daniel rapped lightly on her bedroom door. "Let me in."

Sophie clutched the covers to her neck, staring through the moonlight at her locked door, praying Daniel would just leave her alone.

"Sophie," he said, jiggling at the door handle. "I have to talk to you."

"Go away."

"Not until you hear what I have to say." He rattled the door handle. "Now are you going to let me in, or do I wake everyone in this house by breaking down this door?"

She pressed her hand to the base of her neck, her fingers resting on the pulse beating wildly in her throat. "You wouldn't dare."

"I'll give you until the count of five, and then I'm coming through this door.

"One."

He was stubborn enough to do it. "You'll hurt yourself."

"Open the door."

"No."

"Two."

Sophie tossed aside the covers, the blue silk counterpane spilling to the floor. "You're acting like a child."

"Three."

"Just go away." She hurried to the door, shivering in the cold room.

"Four."

She rested her hand on the handle. "Go away."

"Five."

"You're being foolish!"

"Stand away from the door, Sophie."

"Oh, you stubborn . . ." She flipped the lock and pulled open the door, catching Daniel just as he was lunging forward, one foot braced like a battering ram. "Oh, my!"

She jumped to the side. Daniel hit thin air with the force meant to knock a door off its hinges. He soared past her, still dressed in his evening clothes, flapping his arms like a fledgling pushed from his nest, before he crashed with a *thwack* against the carpet.

"Oh, bother!" Sophie ran to his side, dropping to her knees on the carpet. "Daniel!"

He lay crumpled on his side in a pool of light spilling through the open door from the lamp outside her room.

"Oh, my darling," she said, pushing the hair back from his brow. "Are you hurt?"

He moaned, thick lashes fluttering against his cheeks.

"Daniel, speak to me. Please, darling, speak to me."

He opened his eyes, frowning as he stared up at her. "Now you want to talk."

She sat back on her heels, pressing her fingers to her

lips, nervous laughter bubbling up inside of her.

Daniel cocked one dark brow. "You think this is amusing?"

"No." She slapped her hand across her mouth, trying to catch her giggles. "Of course not," she murmured between her fingers.

Daniel planted his elbow in the carpet and propped his cheek in his hand, a smile curving his lips as he watched her try to control her wayward laughter. "You have this strange way of knocking me right off my feet."

He touched her, brushing her cheek with a soft slide of his fingers that rippled deep within her. A warm tide of desire crested over her, drowning her laughter, dredging the need for him she had tried so hard to bury.

"Don't," she whispered, drawing away from him.

"Sophie, I can't let you walk out of my life. Not now. Not when I've finally found what I've been looking for all of my life."

She scrambled to her feet and backed away from him, seeking some distance from the longing in his eyes. But she couldn't escape the longing that dwelled deep within her. "I told you it was over."

He stood, rubbing his hip. "You told me many things. Only I wasn't ready to listen."

"I think you'd better leave."

"Not yet," he said, moving toward her, lowering his eyes to sweep her slender figure with a heated gaze.

Sophie hugged her arms to her chest, aware suddenly of her pulse throbbing in each tip of her breasts.

"I've come to realize something." He paused in front of her, so close she could feel his heat radiate against her, an inviting warmth in the cold room. "What we share is rare and beautiful."

Sophie shook her head. "I won't be swayed by words, Daniel. I could never live with you, knowing how you forced Laura into a loveless marriage."

"And if I told Esther Gardner to go jump in the Charles, could you live with me?"

Sophie stared at him. "You didn't?"

"I did." He smiled, the dimple creasing his right cheek. "As far as I'm concerned, she and her precious, pompous son can take a flying leap."

"Oh," she whispered. "And Laura . . ."

"Can marry that handsome young cousin of yours if she wants him."

"Daniel!" She threw her arms around his shoulders. "You're wonderful."

"If you think I'm wonderful now, just wait until I get this nightgown off of you." He pressed his lips against her neck. "I'll show you something wonderful, my love."

Connor turned in bed at the sound of his bedroom door opening. He knew who would enter before he saw Laura step into the moonlight that streamed through his windows and captured her in a silvery column of light. He could sense her, feel her emotions as keenly as he felt the hunger for her throb in his loins.

She closed the door, leaning back against it, her lips parted, her breath lifting her breasts beneath the white flannel of her nightgown. For an eternity she stood with her back pressed against the door, her breath held tight in her throat, her beautiful eyes fixed on him, caught between her need for him and every rule by which she had lived every day of her life.

Without a word, he pulled back the thick down comforter and the soft white linen sheet, revealing the place beside him, the empty place she had been fashioned to fill. Laura closed her eyes as if she sought to resist temptation. A soft moan slipped from her lips. And then she was running toward him, her bare feet silent against the thick wool of the carpet.

"Laura," he whispered, taking her in his arms as she

scrambled into bed beside him.

"Hold me," she whispered, throwing her arms around his neck. "Warm me."

He knelt on the bed, drawing her close to the heat of his naked body, burying his face in her fragrant hair, breathing in the scent of spring flowers, while she trembled with the chill of winter in his arms. He rubbed her back through the soft white flannel of her gown, sliding his hands beneath the unbound waves that tumbled to her waist, absorbing her shivers.

Soon she warmed beneath his touch. Her shivers subsided, her muscles relaxed until she released her tight hold around his neck, until she drew back, sitting on her heels.

"I shouldn't be here." She slid her hands over his shoulders, a light brush of cool palms that whispered like a summer breeze across the fires flickering deep within him. "I'm not sure why I came."

He touched her lips, absorbing the warmth of her breath against his fingertip. "Aren't you?"

She smiled, a curve of her lips that spoke of a battle hard fought, and a victory found only in surrender. "Perhaps I am."

He brushed his fingertips over her cheek. She appeared sculpted in the moonlight that kissed her face, her skin smooth white marble. Yet she was warm and soft beneath his touch.

"I thought once with you might be enough." She slid her hands down his chest, spreading her fingers wide, as though she wanted to absorb him through her skin.

He sighed as she drew her nails lightly over his nipples, his muscles tensing with pleasure beneath her touch.

"But now I find I want you more than before." She drew in her breath, flexing her fingers along the curve of muscle above each nipple. "You're like some magical potion. One taste and I've come alive. One taste and I'm left craving you, until I fear I should wither and die if denied you."

He smiled, sliding his hand over her soft hair. "I'm here for you, always for you."

She closed her eyes, her features twisting with the pain he felt surge through her.

"Laura," he whispered, cupping her cheek. He slid his thumb over a corner of her lips. "What is it, love?"

"Nothing." She leaned forward, the warmth of her skin radiating through soft white flannel, teasing him, before he felt the lush press of her breasts against his chest. She kissed his shoulder. "Except my thirst for you."

"Then quench that thirst, my love. Take what you want of me."

She parted her lips against his shoulder, touching him with the damp heat of her tongue. Her hair tumbled over her shoulders, sliding across his chest, pooling on his thighs and in between, a cool brush of silk against his aroused flesh. "I want all of you. Now and always."

Connor tossed back his head, his breath escaping on a heated sigh as she flowed against him, sliding her hands across his ribs, spreading kisses along his neck, his chest, flicking her tongue against his skin as though she needed to fill her senses with him.

She swirled her tongue around his nipple, nipped at the sensitive nub with her teeth as her hands trailed over his belly. "I want every inch of you."

A growl twisted deep in his chest at the first touch of her cool hand against his heated sex. A dark sound escaped his throat, melding with the whisper of wind against the windowpanes.

"Intriguing," she whispered, stroking the long length of him. His muscles clenched. Sensation spiraled through him like fiery arrows. "To imagine this part of you inside of me."

He gripped her arms, needing to feel the delicious heat of her closing around him. Yet she drew back from him. She sat on her heels, drawing in her breath, looking at him as though she needed to memorize every fierce line and curve of his aroused body. He clenched his jaw, fighting the desire that pounded like a fist low in his belly, forcing his body to remain steady and still beneath her hot gaze.

"Perhaps it isn't a word meant for a man, but I find you beautiful." Slowly she slipped pearl buttons through the small loops running down the front of her gown. "Like a jungle cat, all sleek muscle and power."

Connor followed her trembling fingers as she unfastened her gown, white flannel parting, revealing glimpses of the treasures beneath—the hollow of her neck, the pale curves of her breasts, the shadow of her navel. She dropped her hands to her lap, her breasts lifting with each quick breath, tempting him. She watched him, as though she needed a word from him, permission perhaps to continue along this scandalous path.

He waved his hand before the garment, resisting the urge to strip it from her shoulders. "Take it off."

She moistened her lips. In one elegant movement, she grabbed the hem of her gown and drew it upward, over her head, exposing her skin to the moonlight and his eyes. Her hair tumbled wildly around her shoulders, covering her breasts, the pink tips peeking at him through shimmering golden silk.

"Only you, Connor," she whispered, grasping the medallion he wore around his neck. She pulled him toward her. "I want only you."

Her words humbled him, exalted him. The love he saw burning in her eyes drew him more fiercely than the golden chain around his neck.

"Kiss me," she demanded, tugging on the medallion, the gold chain nipping his neck.

He slipped his arms around her, meeting her as she lifted to kiss him. She slanted her open mouth against his as though she were dying and he were a life-giving fount. Her emotions flowed through him, her desire pumping into him, flooding the desire rising like a raging river inside of him. Yet he sensed something more, currents of fear and pain that rippled through her with every breath.

"It's all right," he whispered against her lips. "There's nothing to fear. I'll never leave you. Never."

Laura moaned. She slipped her arms around his neck, plunging her hands into his hair, holding him, kissing him, her need for him pouring over him like sheets of hot summer rain. She wiggled against him, brushing smooth skin and silken waves across his skin. He groaned with pleasure.

They tumbled back onto the bed, her precious body burning him like a pale flame in the moonlight. He rolled, taking her beneath him. With his lips and his hands and his tongue, he promised her a lifetime of joy, seeking to quell the fear he sensed deep within her, lurking beneath her pleasure.

He spread kisses across her collarbone, and lower, tasting the first swell of her breast with the tip of his tongue, easing his mouth over the pink tip. She whimpered. She sank her hands into his hair, holding him close to her as he tugged on the delicious little pearl of flesh. Moonlight slanted across her body, glistening on her damp nipple as he rose above her.

The intoxicating scent of her arousal rose with the heat of her skin, tingling his senses. She lay still, expectant, the muscles in her thighs taut as she waited for the first touch of his hardened sex upon her damp heat.

He slid against her moist nether lips. She twisted her hands into the white sheets, her hips arching toward him in a silent plea he could not resist. His medallion brushed her skin with ancient gold, the key that had unlocked the portal of time and delivered him to her side.

He slipped his arms around her and rolled to his back, taking her with him in a tumble of golden hair and ivory limbs. She sat up, soft feminine curls brushing his belly, large green eyes filled with questions.

"My beautiful *Edaina*," he said, lifting her hair, allowing the golden strands to glide through his fingers, to brush his chest with cool silk. "Take me."

She looked shocked, her eyes wide, her lips parted. But her shock soon dissolved into an intriguing blend of curiosity and expectation, tinged with a subtle sense of power. Ah, she was learning. She was discovering the possibilities, her own delight in taking control of his body.

A smile curved her lips as she shifted her lush body over his. He sighed at the first touch of damp curls against his aroused flesh. Slowly she lowered herself, easing his hardened sex into her slick cleft, her sleek feminine sheath stretching, accommodating the length and breadth of him as only Laura could.

"Oh, my gracious," she whispered, staring down to where the moonlight etched their bodies from the shadows, a man and woman joined as destiny had proclaimed.

His skin was kissed by sunlight, a golden brown lingering from the long days of summer; hers was as pale as the moonlit snow beyond the windowpanes. And when she moved against him, they found the season of their hearts. He thrust beneath her, lifting her, drawing

315

a soft moan of pleasure from her lips.

He lowered his head, watching her pale breasts bob softly with each flex of his hips. He lifted the firm, pale mounds in his hands, took one pink tip into his mouth, swirling his tongue over the tight little bud as she arched against him, as she moved her hips and allowed him the pleasure of touching her deep inside.

As though they had all the time in the world, they gave one to the other, slow, deep thrusts, long, leisurely feasting of mouths and tongues and the sensuous friction of flesh against the most intimate of flesh. In time, Connor sensed the splendor sparkle within her, and he responded, giving her what she needed, what he desired.

He thrust harder, lifting his hips to meet her downward plunge. He felt the tightening of slick muscles around him, the quiver that started deep within and spiraled in all directions, the sweet exotic pulsing of feminine release.

She tossed back her head, a ragged cry escaping her throat as she shattered around him, as her body tensed and her emotions flared through him. He thrust upward, possessing her completely as he gave himself unconditionally to this woman he had always loved.

Chapter Twenty-four

Laura closed her eyes. Yet she couldn't dismiss the gray light glowing at the windows. It was dawn. They had made love through the fleeting hours when the moon ruled the sky. Yet the sun was rising. And her night with Connor was at an end.

"I have to leave." Still, she couldn't draw away from the warmth of his body radiating against her side. She couldn't tear herself from the strong arm nestled across her waist.

"Propriety again." He slid his hand upward across her ribs. "When will propriety be on our side?"

Never. The reality of their situation stabbed her, the pain searing her chest.

"Laura," he whispered, concern naked in his dark voice. "Such pain. Why, my love?"

"I don't want to leave you." She turned toward him, burying her face in the warm curve of his neck, holding

317

him, her hand a fist against his back. "I never want to leave you."

"We'll be married today." He slid his hair-roughened thigh over hers, wrapping her in a cocoon of warmth and power. "We'll never have to part like this again."

Pain sliced through her, the slow burn of ice seeping into her veins. She clutched him to her. "If only we could."

"We shall find a priest to perform the rites." He smoothed his warm hand over her bare shoulder. "And we shall tell propriety to take a jump over the moon."

She pressed her lips to his neck, breathing in the dark, musky scent of him, tasting the salt of his skin upon her tongue. The time for dreams and fantasy had passed. Reality had crept up on them until there was no chance for escape. "I can't marry you, Connor. Not now. Not ever."

She felt his muscles grow tense, his breath still in his lungs. He grasped her chin, forcing her to look at him. He was frowning, his beautiful eyes filled with questions. "Have things changed so dramatically in this century? Do people in love no longer marry and have children?"

"They do." She forced the words past the emotions squeezing her throat—the longing for a future she could never share with him. "But it isn't to be. Not for us."

His fingers tightened on her chin. "Why?"

There was no escape from the truth, no reprieve from the words that would tear them apart forever. "I must marry Philip."

He released her as though she had burned him. "What nonsense is this?"

"Father has arranged it. He has promised me to Philip."

Connor's eyes narrowed. "You belong to me."

"Yes." She rested her trembling fingers against his cheek. Thick black hair tumbled around his face in unruly waves. With the dark shadow of his beard shading his lean cheeks, he looked wild, untamed, and so vulnerable her heart ached. "In my heart I will always belong to you. But I must do as Father wishes."

He gripped her shoulder. "I will not allow it."

"My love." She stroked his hard cheek, his beard rasping her fingertips, sending chills rippling through her as she recalled the feel of his rough cheeks against her breasts. "What type of life could we have knowing it was forged on my father's broken promises?"

"He has no right."

"He is my father."

He clenched his hand on her shoulder, his fingers biting into her skin. "I can't let you do this."

"Please." Through her tears she saw the pain in his eyes, the same desperation she felt coiling around her heart like a steel band. "Try to understand what this marriage means to my father."

"I do understand." He released her, clenching his hand into a fist as he drew away from her. "Your father wants to buy a place in this society and he's willing to sell you to that bigoted ass to obtain it."

Laura shook her head. "He wants only what's best for me."

Connor clenched his jaw. "And is Philip Gardner what is best for you? Do you also wish to become a queen of this Boston society?"

"Of course not."

"Then marry me," he said, his voice a deep command that tugged on her vitals.

She shook her head, tears spilling over her lashes, burning her cheeks. "I can't."

"I see." He stared down at her, the warmth in his eyes

319

turning to ice. "I'm good enough to bed, but not quite good enough to marry."

"Connor, it's not like that." She reached for him and he pulled away. "Please understand. I can't turn my back on my father."

"Get out."

Although his voice was soft, his words hit her with the force of a clenched fist. "Connor . . ."

"Get out." He tossed the covers from her, exposing her to the chill of the room. "You are not the woman I thought I loved."

She gasped with the pain, the sharp searing pain his words inflicted on her soul. She scrambled from the bed, her knees threatening to buckle as her feet touched the floor. With trembling hands she snatched her gown from the floor and covered herself, seeking some shelter from the anger burning in his eyes.

It couldn't end this way, she thought as she stumbled to the door. Somehow she had to make him understand this was tearing her into pieces. She paused at the door, her hand on the cold brass handle. "Connor, please try to—"

"Get out."

There was a finality to his words, a sharp note in his voice that pierced her like a blade. She opened the door and escaped. Yet she could not escape the pain that burned like white-hot coals in her heart.

Snow crunched beneath his feet; a bitter chill licked at his cheeks as Connor prowled the paths of Boston Common. He drew the cold air into his lungs, trying to quell the burning in his chest. He couldn't allow Laura to do this. He couldn't allow her to give herself to another man.

Please understand. Her words echoed in his mind.

He clenched his hands into fists at his sides, resisting

the urge to toss back his head and howl in rage. He did understand. He understood the bond of honor that forced Laura to obey her father's wishes. And still he fought against the inevitable tide. He could not allow this to happen.

Connor rested his hands on an iron fence, staring into the burial ground beyond, his eyes narrowing against the glare of early morning sunlight on snow. Granite tombstones poked their heads above the sheet of drifting white snow, winter flowers marking the resting places of the dead. He didn't need Aisling's gift of divination to see the future he would live without Laura—cold, devoid of the fire that was the very spark of life.

He curled his bare hands around the cold iron. There were a hundred things he might do. With a snap of his fingers he could whisk Laura away from this place. Yet how could he force her to betray the ties of blood?

He closed his eyes. Beneath his clothes, the medallion glowed against his skin, a warmth spun from ancient gold. With a pass of his hand and a whisper of words he could leave this place; he could return to the embrace of his family. And leave behind his heart.

"Damn!" he whispered, his breath a puff of steam on the early morning air. He could not accept defeat. He would—

A loud crack exploded behind him. He felt something plow into his back, a searing of flesh that buckled his knees. He sank to the snow, pain surging like liquid fire through his veins, searing away his strength.

Laura stared down at the man who lay so still upon his bed, his hair a tumble of black waves against the white pillowcase. It was Connor, and yet this man seemed a stranger, a beautiful husk drained of life.

"I have to be frank with you, Mr. Sullivan." Dr. Hasting's whisper carried like thunder in the quiet room. "I doubt the young man will survive the day."

"No!" Laura pivoted to face the doctor, who stood beside her father at the door. Hasting peered at her through the small round lenses of his glasses, bushy white brows drawn together over the thick bridge of his nose. "He is going to be all right."

"Now, Miss Sullivan." Hasting fiddled with the chain of his pocket watch, the gold links tapping the green brocade waistcoat that stretched across his plump middle. "I don't think it would be wise to get your hopes up."

Laura felt a shaking inside of her, a fear that went deeper than flesh and sinew. "He is going to be all right."

Hasting drew breath between his clenched teeth. "I'm sorry, Miss Sullivan, but—"

"Thank you, Doctor," Daniel said, throwing open the bedroom door. "Please wait in the drawing room down the hall. I'll be right with you."

Hasting nodded. He cast Laura a look of sympathy before leaving the room.

"That man has obviously given up trying to help Connor." Laura turned toward the bed, staring down at Connor, his face as still and pale as carved ivory. "We should send for another physician."

Daniel moved toward her, his face reflecting his concern. "Hasting is one of the best in the city."

"He isn't good enough. Connor needs someone who hasn't given up hope. He needs . . ." Her voice cracked, a pitiful sound she couldn't prevent escaping her lips. "Dear God."

"Laura." Daniel slipped his arm around her shoulders.

"He has to be all right." Laura couldn't halt the shaking that spiraled from deep inside of her to tremble along every nerve. "He has to."

"I'll send for another physician." Daniel rubbed his hand up and down her arm. "We'll do everything possible."

"Who would have done this?" She looked up at her father, tears burning her eyes. "Who would have shot him?"

Daniel shook his head. "The police think it might have been an attempted robbery."

"I hope they find him." Laura sank to the edge of Connor's bed. She lifted his hand and pressed her lips against his palm. "I hope they hang the blackguard who did this."

"Do you need anything?"

"A miracle."

Daniel squeezed her shoulder. "I need to talk to the doctor." He turned and left her alone with Connor.

Laura pressed her fingertips against the pulse point in Connor's neck, holding her breath, absorbing each thready throb beneath her touch. She watched the rise and fall of his chest, each inhale—slow, shallow, barely lifting the white sheet that lay across him, each exhale threatening to be his last.

"Connor," she whispered, brushing the cool black waves back from his brow. "I never meant to hurt you."

He lay still beneath her touch, beyond her reach. Grief surged inside of her like a searing tide of acid, eating at her heart, burning her throat when she realized he might remain forever beyond her touch.

"I love you." She leaned over him, kissing his closed eyes, his cheeks, each corner of his lips, tears falling from her eyes to glisten in shimmering droplets against his skin. "Forgive me, my love."

Something bumped her arm. She glanced away from Connor to find Gypsy sitting beside the bed. "What are you doing in here?"

Gypsy rested her paw on Laura's knee. She regarded Laura with those pale eyes, as though she understood everything this human woman was feeling, as though she meant to give comfort.

Laura ran her hands over the dog's head, sinking her fingers into the soft white fur. "You're worried about him too, aren't you?"

Gypsy cocked her head.

Laura swiped at her tears. "He'll be all right. He has to be."

Henry Thayer tapped his spoon against the edge of his coffee cup, the ping of silver striking china pealing in his library. "So you say when you went to visit the Sullivan house this morning, you discovered the young *Sidhe* had been shot."

"That's right." Austin stood before Henry's desk, watching the emissary, searching for signs of guilt, sensing only the darkness of his defenses. "Apparently someone shot him in the back."

Henry tugged on the edge of his drooping white mustache. "Will he survive?"

"According to Daniel Sullivan, the doctor doesn't expect him to last through the day."

Henry shook his head. "This is dreadful."

"I've sent for your physician."

"Austin, we can't have one of our physicians tending to this man; our abilities are centuries ahead of the physicians in the Outworld. An apparent miracle would raise too many questions."

"I don't intend to let that young man die."

"But we—"

"We have an obligation to do everything within our power to preserve this young man." Austin rested his palms on Henry's desk, leaning toward the older man. Henry sat back in his chair, springs creaking with his weight. "He is one of our people, the finest of what we ever were."

Henry glanced down at his coffee. "Of course."

Austin searched for his control, easing back away from the desk. "Where is Bennett?"

"I haven't seen him this morning."

"When I find him, I certainly hope he can prove he didn't put a bullet in that young man's back."

Henry glanced up at him. "You suspect Fraser?"

Austin stared down at the emissary. "Right now he is only one of several people I suspect."

Henry nodded. "Fraser did believe the young man to be a threat."

"That young man is no threat to anyone except perhaps Philip Gardner." Austin reached deep within himself, searching for balance, for the control he needed to contain the anger swelling inside of him. "And I'm going to do everything I can to see Connor survives."

"Connor."

Warmth flowed through Connor, deep, penetrating, a radiance that saturated every pore.

"Open your eyes."

A woman's voice, dark, compelling. Soft hands brushed across his cheeks, a scent of heather and spices spilling over him.

"Awaken, dark warrior."

He opened his eyes. Light, a soft glow like the first rays of sun touching the morning sky. He blinked. He drew in his breath, a twinge of pain rippling from a place just below his right shoulder blade.

"I'm afraid you're still going to experience a small amount of pain."

His blurry eyes focused on the face suspended above him. A woman with light blue eyes leaned over him, her silvery blond hair tumbling over her shoulders in a shimmering cascade that spilled against the dark blue velvet of the comforter. "Aisling?"

She smiled. "Surprised to see me?"

He sat up, blood swimming before his eyes.

"Easy." Aisling touched his shoulder, easing him back to his pillow. "I couldn't heal the wound completely; these mortals would pose far too many questions if you showed no signs of injury."

Connor settled against the soft pillow with a sigh. "What happened to me?"

"You were shot."

"Shot?"

"Yes." She patted his cheek. "From what I've been able to gather, a small piece of metal is projected from a device called a pistol. It can prove deadly. And it very nearly was."

"Who did it?"

"I'm afraid I don't know. You showed up on the front doorstep with a wound in your back."

"How did you know I was in trouble?"

"Oh, I've been keeping my eye on you." She sat beside him, smiling in a way that made him think she had a secret she intended to keep. "Just in case you needed a little bit of help. We can thank the stars I was nearby."

"You've been here all along?"

"Here and about." She smoothed the wide sleeves of her white silk gown, the small golden stars sprinkled across the fabric shimmering in the sunlight that flooded the room. "Close enough to watch your progress. And I must say, you've done splendidly since arriving in this century. I believe you've swept Laura right off of her feet, as they like to say in this century."

"Have I?" Connor glanced away from his aunt, unwilling to allow her to see the pain in his eyes, his gaze resting on Laura. She sat in an upholstered armchair beside the bed, her golden head tilted to one side against the dark blue velvet, her lips parted, her eyes closed in slumber.

"Don't worry; she won't awaken until after I leave."

"I assume no one else is going to interrupt us?"

"We're quite safe." Aisling stood and strolled to Laura's side, where she studied the sleeping woman for a moment. "She's a lovely girl. Though a bit headstrong." She grinned at him. "But then, I would think the two of you should get along splendidly."

"We do." Connor drew in his breath, pain sparking with the deep inhalation. "But I'm afraid she feels an obligation to do as her father wishes."

Aisling lifted one golden brow. "And he still wants her to marry that insipid Philip Gardner?"

Connor nodded.

"I could alter his thinking." Aisling pursed her lips. "I'm surprised you haven't already done it."

"It's tempting. But I want to win this fight without any magic."

"Without magic?" Aisling marched toward him, a thin line forming between the wings of her golden brows. "I didn't send you here for you to abandon your heritage, Connor."

"Why did you send me here, Aisling?"

"Oh." Aisling lowered her lashes, hiding her eyes. "I have my reasons."

"Which are?"

"Mine to know." She flicked her skirts, golden stars glittering around her. "Yours when the time is right."

"Aisling, I—"

"I must be going." She pressed her fingertips to her lips, then blew him a kiss. "Don't worry, dark warrior. I won't be far."

"Wait!" Connor struggled to sit. "I—"

"Later, darling." Aisling lifted her arms and snapped

her fingers. She vanished in a swirl of white silk and glittering golden stars.

Connor fell against his pillow, groaning as a dull pain ripped through his back. He glanced at Laura, watching as she awakened, thick lashes fluttering on her cheeks. She drew in a deep breath and opened her eyes. She blinked.

"Connor." Laura sat up in the chair, staring at him as though he had just stepped from a tomb. "You're awake."

He smiled. "I'm feeling much better."

"Dear lord!" She came off the chair like a marionette whose strings have been jerked by her puppetmaster. She sank on the bed beside him, cupping his cheeks in trembling hands. "Are you really all right? You are going to be all right, aren't you?"

"I'm going to be fine." He covered her hands with his, holding her palms against his cheeks. "You mustn't worry."

Laura closed her eyes, her breath escaping her parted lips in a long sigh that warmed his cheek. "The doctor said you wouldn't survive the day."

He moved his head, pressing his lips against one soft palm. "The doctor was mistaken."

She looked down at him, tears shimmering in her eyes. "I feel as though I've been granted a second chance."

Connor lay still beneath her touch, allowing her emotions to stream through him, cleansing away the pain of her rejection. For what flowed through him was the pure, undiluted love she had for him.

"If you'll still have me, I want to marry you, Connor."

Connor smoothed a wayward curl of gold back from her cheek and tucked the silky strands behind her ear. "And what about your father?"

Tears trembled on her thick, dark lashes. "I'll find

some way to make him understand."

"And if he doesn't? You'll be faced with a choice."

"I know." She swallowed hard. "And I know I don't want to live without you."

Chapter Twenty-five

"It's amazing the way that young man has recovered." Daniel stood near the windows of the second-floor drawing room, his face lifted to the sunlight that poured through the panes in columns of gold. "It was good of Lord Sinclair to bring his physician to see Connor, but it doesn't look as though there is much for the man to do."

"It seems Dr. Hasting gave up on his patient a little too soon." Laura sat on the edge of the Empire sofa, tracing her finger over a green stripe in the stiff cushion beside her. "Thank heaven he was mistaken about the severity of the injury."

Daniel nodded. He stood for a moment staring out the windows, while Laura searched for ways to approach the subject of her choice of a husband.

"Laura, I think we should—"

"Father, I need to tell you—" she began, her words overlapping her father's.

"Sorry," they said in unison.

She looked up at him, grateful for a moment's reprieve. "You wanted to say something, Father?"

Daniel rubbed the back of his neck. "I've been thinking lately of how little time we've spent together over the years."

"I understand." Laura glanced down to where her hand rested against stripes of gold and green velvet, refusing to allow him to see the hurt in her eyes, the pain of old wounds that had never healed. "You had a business to run."

"I also had a daughter who needed me." Daniel cleared his throat. "And the truth is, I used my office as a refuge. For me, this house never truly felt like my home."

"Even after you married Mother?"

"Yes. Perhaps more so after I married Eleanor."

Laura laced her fingers together, resting her hands on her lap. "Your marriage was arranged, wasn't it?"

"Your grandfather expected me to marry his eldest daughter. He expected me to take over the business."

Just as her father expected her to marry Philip Gardner. Heaven help her, how could she tell him she was going to marry Connor? "Did you ever regret doing what was expected of you?"

"I owed your grandfather my life. He gave me his daughter, and the helm of a powerful shipping company. And I felt like a traitor because I wanted to throw it all away. I wanted a life of my own." Daniel was quiet a moment. Laura could feel him watching her, perhaps weighing what her reaction would be to the truth. "I wanted a woman I had been denied by a twist of fate."

Laura drew her teeth over her lower lip. "Aunt Sophie?"

"I didn't realize I was that obvious."

Laura peeked at him. He stood with his head bowed,

his hands shoved into the pockets of his dark gray trousers, tapping the claw-footed leg of the wing-back chair with the tip of his shoe. In that moment he looked like a little boy who had been caught stealing apples. "I think she cares for you too."

"I think she does." He kept his head down, but she could see the grin that spread across his lips, the smile of a man enjoying an amusing secret. "But believe me, neither one of us ever betrayed your mother."

"I believe you." Laura smiled as she wondered if there was perhaps still time for her father to find happiness with her cherished aunt.

Daniel moved toward her, pausing a foot away. Laura stared at a small scuff mark on one tip of his shiny black shoes, wishing she could throw her arms around him and hug him, wondering if he would permit it.

"Laura, I want you to know how much I regret that I wasn't here for you when you needed me."

He was quiet a moment, watching her, and she sensed he was looking for some sign. She clasped her hands tighter, unsure of herself. Her entire life she had been taught to suppress her emotions, all of them. There had never been any outward show of affection in this house. And now she wasn't certain of what to do.

"Can you forgive me?"

"It's all right," Laura said, staring at that one little scuff mark on his shoe. "I understand."

"I've wasted twenty-five years." He touched her chin, coaxing her to look at him. He was smiling, his dark eyes filled with a warmth she had never thought to see. "I love you, daughter."

Laura's throat tightened with emotion, so that the words she spoke escaped in a husky whisper. "I love you too, Father."

He sat beside her and slipped his arm around her shoulders, a tentative touch, both hopeful and filled with regret. She wanted to turn to him, to hug him, to tell him everything was all right. And still, she sat stiff beneath his touch, frightened by what was yet to come.

"What did you want to tell me?"

Laura tried to swallow but her mouth had turned to dust. She stared at her clenched hands, unable to look at her father. "It's about Philip Gardner."

He flexed his hand on her arm. "What about him?"

"I know how much you want me to marry the man, but . . . I firmly believe . . ." She hesitated, trying to find the words, recalling the words Sophie had spoken a lifetime ago. "I believe there is one special person in the world for each of us. Two halves separated before birth. And if we are somehow fortunate enough to find that person, we should hold on with both hands and never let go."

"And have you found your special person?"

"Yes." Laura glanced up at her father, her breath stilling in her lungs as she saw the curve of his smile. "I'm in love with Connor. And he's in love with me."

Daniel nodded. "Then I suppose there's only one thing to do?"

"What?"

"Arrange a wedding."

Laura stopped breathing. "Do you mean a wedding for Connor and me?"

He chuckled softly. "That's who you want to marry, isn't it?"

"You don't mind?"

"How could I mind?" He hugged her against his side. "All I want is for you to be happy."

"Oh!" She threw her arms around his neck.

He hugged her, strong arms tight around her, before he pulled back, smiling down into her tear-filled eyes. "Sophie said it would be this way."

Laura smiled in spite of the tears trickling in warm

rivulets down her cheeks. "She is an exceptional lady."

"I'm glad you think so." Daniel smoothed his thumb across Laura's cheek, brushing away her tears. "Because I've asked Sophie to be my wife."

"Oh! I'm so happy for you." With her arms around his neck, she squeezed him as she had often longed to hug him. She pulled back, her tears vanishing in the joy pumping through her veins. "Do you think we could have a double ceremony?"

Daniel smiled, his dark eyes growing misty as he looked down into her eyes. "I'd like that very much."

Connor leaned back against the pillows propped behind his back as the physician from Avallon left the room. He looked up at the tall, dark-haired man who stood beside his bed. "The medicine your physician gave me has already helped ease the pain."

"I'm glad he could help." Austin Sinclair smiled. "I expected to find you on your deathbed."

"The wound could have been fatal."

"For someone who could not channel the power?"

Connor nodded, deciding there was no need to mention Aisling. Apparently this Lord of the Inner Circle was unaware of the limitations of Connor's healing abilities, the limitations of all the *Sidhe*. "Before you came, I wondered if you had something to do with the shooting."

Austin frowned, his eyes flickering with an anger Connor sensed was not directed toward him. "I'm not a man who would shoot someone in the back."

"No. I can sense you are a man of integrity."

"Still, I fear, the shooting could have been done by one of our people." Austin curled his hands into fists at his sides. "Someone who fears your abilities."

"Because he does not possess these abilities?"

"Exactly." Austin glanced toward the windows, sunlight falling full upon his face, illuminating the determination etched into his chiseled features. "And I intend to take care of him."

He felt a kinship with this man. Although Austin Sinclair had been born a thousand years after Connor, they were brothers in a sense; the blood of the *Tuatha De Danann* flowed through their veins. Yet Connor sensed a thousand years had altered his people. "I noticed your physician relies on medicine instead of the natural healing ability of our people."

Austin frowned. "He does not possess the healing ability."

"So it is as a wise sorceress once predicted." Connor smoothed the dark blue velvet comforter that lay across his lap. The blue cashmere robe he wore kept the chill of the room from his skin, but it couldn't relieve the chill that crept into his blood when he realized how much his people had lost. "The Inner Circle can no longer channel the power."

"We have lost most of our abilities."

In a thousand years, there will exist only a handful who truly understand the ancient ways, and a scattering of children who do not even know they possess the power of Mother Earth. Aisling's words echoed in his memory.

"I wonder if your abilities have been lost. Or if they are only sleeping." Connor looked up at Austin, offering his hand. "Lower your defenses against me."

Austin stared at Connor, a moment of suspicion, perhaps a thread of fear, holding him back, a fear for what Connor might sense inside of him.

"Are you so reluctant to face the truth inside of you?"

Austin drew in his breath and gripped Connor's hand. "All right."

Connor closed his eyes, reaching for the power that dwelled deep inside, feeling it stir and shimmer as it

335

flowed through him. "Do you feel it?"

"Yes," Austin whispered.

"Reach for it deep inside of you. Open yourself to the pulse that throbs from the earth. Let it possess you, fill you, until each beat of your heart throbs in rhythm with the earth."

Austin gripped his hand tighter.

"Allow the light to pour over you and through you, the light of the sun, of the moon, of the stars. Let it slide through every vessel of your body. Let it saturate your soul."

Austin dragged air into his lungs, the sound as loud as the wind whipping through a tunnel to Connor's acute ears.

"Don't fight it. Welcome the warmth. It is your legacy."

Austin loosened his hold on Connor's hand.

"Open yourself to the light." Connor could sense the easing of Austin's muscles as the light seeped into him. "Allow the light to pour through you. That's it, you're doing well."

"Beautiful." Austin's breath escaped in a ragged sigh. "So beautiful."

Connor opened his eyes, looking up at Austin, who stood with his head tilted back, his eyes closed, his skin glowing in the sunlight, a look of bliss on his features. He released him, smiling as Austin looked down at him with the wonder of a child in his eyes. "I would say the power is only sleeping in you, my brother."

"Will you come back with me to Avallon? Teach us, help us regain what we have lost?"

"It's tempting, but you should know I'm to be married soon. And my future bride does not yet know what I am."

"Do you plan to tell her?"

"I feel I must." Connor felt a tightening in his chest

when he thought of how Laura might react to his confession. "And yet I fear what might happen should I reveal the truth."

Austin rested his hand on Connor's shoulder. "Trust me, my brother, there is no room for deceptions between a man and the woman he loves."

"Yes. I feel this also. I must believe that if she loves me, she will accept me for what I am."

Laura paused with her hand on the brass handle of the drawing-room door, smiling as she watched her father take Sophie into his arms. She slipped out of the room, closing the door behind her. In three weeks two couples would stand together and speak the vows that would forever bind them. Now all she had to do was tell her handsome husband-to-be about the arrangements.

"Miss Laura," Megan said.

Laura turned to find Megan standing a few feet away, her little hands clasped in front of her, tugging on the pale blue wool of her dress. She looked like a little girl who had found her favorite doll shattered on the pavement. "What is it, sweetie?"

Megan looked up at her, tears lurking in her huge blue eyes. "Grandma told me Mr. Connor was hurt."

"Don't be sad." Laura knelt in front of the girl, resting her hand on Megan's shoulder. "He's going to be better soon."

"For real?"

Laura kissed Megan's soft cheek, breathing in the sweet scent of lavender. "For real."

Megan clapped her hands, smiling as though Laura had given her the best present in the whole world. "I knew he'd get better."

Laura smiled. "You were sure of it?"

Megan nodded, thick dark curls bouncing on her

small shoulders. "I knew he'd get better, 'cause angels can't die."

Laura tugged on one of Megan's glossy dark curls. "Do you think Mr. Connor is an angel?"

Megan nodded, her expression growing serious. "I know he is."

Laura thought of the gentle man with the heavenly blue eyes waiting for her in the room down the hall. "I know he is too."

"Then he told you about fixing my eyes?"

Laura's breath halted in her throat. "Your eyes?"

Megan nodded. "He touched my head, and his hands were real warm. When I opened my eyes I saw him. And I knew he was an angel."

It couldn't be. It just couldn't be. "He fixed your eyes?"

"He told me it was our secret." Megan frowned. "I thought you knew it too."

Laura felt as though she had been slammed hard to the ground. Her skin grew moist and cold beneath the peach-and-yellow-striped wool of her gown.

"Did I do a bad thing? Did I tell a secret?"

"No." Laura sucked air into her burning lungs like a drowning woman fighting for life. "No, you did a good thing, Megan."

Megan touched her cheek, her small hand warm against Laura's cool skin. "You look sad."

Laura forced a smile to her lips. "I'm fine." She stood, her legs trembling beneath her. "I have to go now. I have to talk to Mr. Connor."

Laura moved toward Connor's room as though she were wandering through a thick mist. Questions swirled in her brain along with the answers that were too horrifying to acknowledge. Yet she couldn't avoid the truth. If what she suspected was indeed reality, then everything that had happened since Connor's arrival, including her own scandalous behavior, made sense, a horrible, twisted logic she was loath to face.

Connor was standing by the windows when she entered his bedroom, Gypsy lying on the carpet by his feet. He turned in a column of sunlight that poured through the windowpanes, smiling as he saw Laura. "You've been gone too long, my love."

Laura pressed her back against the closed door, staring at him, the perfection of his features illuminated by sunlight, the height and strength of him draped in soft blue cashmere. He was a dream made flesh and blood. A prince who had stepped from the pages of a fairy tale. A Viking who had journeyed a thousand years to claim her. But was he human?

"Laura, what is it, love?" He moved toward her, a frown digging lines into his brow. "What's wrong?"

How could any human being have survived the wound she had seen in his back? And here he was, walking toward her in long, graceful strides, like a lion who had suffered no more than a scratch.

She held up her hand as he drew near. "Please don't touch me." She couldn't think when he touched her.

He paused a few feet away from her. "What's wrong?"

She moistened her dry lips. "I need to know if . . ." Dear heaven, it couldn't be true.

"What is it?"

"Megan told me you healed her eyes."

He held her in a steady gaze, unflinching, a man who faced a judgment he long suspected would come.

"Is it true?" *Please say it isn't true. Please tell me nothing has changed between us.*

"It's true."

Laura's stomach clenched with the force of a blow. "What are you?"

"I'm a man, Laura. A man who loves you with all of my heart and soul."

339

Laura shook her head. "You aren't human, are you?"

He drew in his breath, then released it in a long sigh. "I'm human, but different."

"You're a witch." She pressed her shoulders back against the solid oak door. "Or warlock, or whatever they call a man who conjures magic."

"I'm one of the *Sidhe*. My people are the *Tuatha De Danann*."

"Dear heaven." Laura pressed her hand to her lips, trying to catch the moan of pain that started deep in her chest and clawed its way up her throat.

"Laura, there is nothing to fear with me."

She flinched at the soft touch of his hand against her arm. "Don't touch me."

A look of pain twisted his features. He stepped back, as though increasing the distance between them might help ease her fear. "I would never do anything to harm you," he whispered, his dark voice strained by emotion. "You are my heart."

"You've been manipulating me, haven't you?"

"Never."

"You've influenced my thoughts, bewitched me."

He smiled, yet his eyes remained filled with a pain that touched her as keenly as the pain throbbing in her tight chest. "I have cast no spells upon you, my love."

"I've felt something strange from the moment you appeared in this house, a pull, here." She thumped her clenched fist against her heart. "As though I were being drawn to you against my will. Now I know why."

"What you felt is the same pull that brought me to your side. It is a spell as old as time. A spell more beautiful than any my people could conjure. The spell of love."

"The spell of a monster."

"Look at me, Laura." Connor spread his arms at his

340

sides, palms open, his long fingers curved toward her. "Am I a monster?"

His black hair was tousled around his face, a lock falling over his smooth brow, the silky strands curling wildly at his neck. He watched her with vivid blue eyes—so beautiful, far too beautiful for any mortal man. "Get out of this house. Out of my life."

"Laura, you don't mean this."

"Go back to where you came from. And stay out of my dreams!"

She pulled open the door and escaped, slamming the door behind her. Yet she couldn't escape, not truly escape. The pain was there, deep inside of her, as though she had been shattered into so many pieces they could never again be fitted back together. She ran down the hall, seeking the sanctuary of her bedroom, where she fell upon the soft comforter covering her bed and wept.

Connor stood staring at the door, unable to move. He felt as though all the strength were draining from his body, his life force ebbing with the pain that pierced his heart. A breeze rippled in the air with a soft sound, like leaves whispering on a warm summer day. A fragrance of spices and heather brushed his senses. And he knew he was no longer alone.

"I thought she would accept you," Aisling whispered, resting her hand upon his arm. "I was wrong."

"I need more time, that's all."

"Come, dark warrior, it's time to go home."

"No." He looked down at her, seeing the compassion in her blue eyes, feeling her love for him flow through her. "I can't leave."

Aisling shook her head. "You will gain nothing if you stay."

"I will not accept defeat." Connor clenched his jaw. "Not in this, Aisling. I'm fighting for my future."

"You have lived a charmed life, my beautiful warrior." Aisling smiled, a sad curve of her lips that left her eyes filled with concern for him. "Never have you felt the cold touch of defeat. And in this matter, I know you want to stay and fight. I also know you must leave to have any chance at victory."

"Leave? You ask me to flee like a coward. How will this gain victory?"

"Stop thinking like a Viking and trust me," she whispered.

"I'm not leaving. Don't ask this of me."

"My blood is pure. You must realize your power is no match for mine."

"I must stay. I must show her I'm not a monster. I must show her how much I love her."

"Oh, my darling." Aisling cupped his cheeks in her hands. "You have given her your heart, your soul, the very best anyone could offer another. And still she turns away from you. She is not yet worthy of you."

"I know she loves me; I feel it here," he said, pressing his fist to his heart. "I haven't had enough time with her. It will only take a little longer to teach her to trust as well as to love."

"She will hurt you if you stay."

"I can't leave her."

"The way to victory is not always clear." Aisling slipped her arm through his. "Come."

The medallion grew warm against his chest, near the place where his heart was breaking. "No!"

Aisling snapped her fingers and they both vanished, leaving behind an empty sunlit room.

Chapter Twenty-six

Austin Sinclair stood on the flagstones in Henry Thayer's conservatory, staring down at a delicate white orchid, seeing the faint veins of pink running through each curving petal, noticing each speck of pollen on the delicate yellow tongue. It seemed he had never really seen an orchid before this moment.

The fragrance of the flower drifted to him on air that felt like damp silk against his skin. His senses were more acute than ever in his life, now that he felt the power flow inside of him, even though only a faint ripple remained of the lush river of heat and light he had felt when Connor had touched him.

"You say someone shot the *Sidhe*?" Fraser Bennett shifted in his chair, white wicker creaking beneath him. "Will he survive?"

"Yes, he will." Austin glanced at Fraser, who sat with Henry at a round wicker table a few feet away. "And

I'm certain he will be interested in discovering who shot him."

Fraser sipped his cup of tea. "Do you think he'll go searching for the man?"

Austin stroked his knuckles over the soft petals of the orchid. "Wouldn't you want to know who tried to murder you, Fraser?"

"Of course." A bead of sweat ran down Fraser's cheek. "Have you any ideas who might have done it?"

"A few." Austin smiled, staring at Fraser, trying to pierce the man's defenses. "Any idea who they might be?"

"It could be a thief." Fraser stared down into his cup. "Or perhaps Philip Gardner wanted to eliminate the competition."

"Or perhaps someone wanted to see 'the menace destroyed,'" Austin said, keeping his voice low and smooth.

Fraser's head snapped up, his eyes wide as he looked at Austin. "You can't believe I did this."

Austin's footsteps were soundless against the flagstones as he moved toward the table. "Where were you this morning, Fraser?"

Fraser glanced at Henry, who sat with his hands cupped beneath his chin, watching with emotionless eyes. "I was in bed."

"The housekeeper said she saw you leave the house just after dawn," Austin said.

"She did?" Fraser loosened his white tie. "I didn't realize I had left that early. I've been having trouble sleeping. I often walk when I'm disturbed about something."

Austin rested his hands on the back of a wicker chair, holding Fraser in a cold stare. "And you've been disturbed about a *Tuatha De Danann* in Boston."

"Yes, I have." Fraser pulled out his handkerchief and

blotted the sweat from his upper lip. "But I didn't try to murder him."

Austin curled his fingers against the white wicker chair. "Where did you go this morning?"

"I took a walk."

"Through Boston Common?"

"No." Fraser mopped his brow. "I walked to the river."

"Did you see Connor?"

Fraser shook his head.

Austin studied the man a moment, unable to perceive the emotions hidden behind a dark barricade inside of Fraser. "Connor possesses an amazing ability to read people. I'm certain he will want to meet you when he is completely recovered."

Fraser flicked his tongue over his lips. "I don't want to meet him."

"If he decides he wants to meet you, Fraser"—Austin smiled—"I doubt you'll have a choice."

"Henry, I thought you were running this operation." Fraser scooted to the edge of his chair as though he wanted to run. "Are you just going to sit there and allow this man to threaten me?"

"If you're innocent, Fraser, you have nothing to fear." Henry bowed his head, pressing his lips to his knuckles. "If you aren't, I doubt there is a place on earth where you can hide from a sorcerer."

"I won't be offered up as a sacrifice to this monster." Fraser stood, bumping the table, setting teacups rattling against saucers. "I'm going back to Avallon."

"I'm certain the governing council will have a few questions for you," Austin said. "Especially after they hear my report."

"I have nothing to fear from the council." Fraser pivoted and marched toward the door leading to Henry's library, plowing through the heavy foliage, banana and palm leaves shuddering in his wake.

Henry leaned back in his chair. "Do you really think he did it?"

"I'm not certain." Austin smiled. "But I know the governing council has ways to discover the truth. And I intend to find it."

"I don't understand." Sophie stared up at Laura. "Why have you changed your mind?"

"I realized . . ." Laura turned away from her aunt, searching for words to explain the unthinkable. How could she explain she had given herself to a man who wasn't even human? She sank to the burgundy velvet wing-back chair near the fireplace in the library and stared into the fire flickering on the hearth. "I realized I made a mistake."

"A mistake? This morning you were thrilled to be marrying Connor. This afternoon the wedding is off."

Logs crackled in the consuming flames, red and orange and yellow tongues licking at the charred pieces of wood. Laura held her hands toward the hearth, trying to warm the chill deep inside of her, the burn of ice that came from shreds of shattered dreams lying lifeless in her heart. "I simply realized Connor and I were not meant to be married."

Sophie slipped her warm hands around Laura's cold ones. "Look at me, dear."

Laura hesitated a moment before looking up at Sophie. Firelight flickered on Sophie's face, illuminating each line of worry etched into her brow. "Please don't look so concerned. I'm fine."

Sophie squeezed Laura's hands. "What has happened to change your mind?"

Laura stared at the ivory cameo pinned on the raspberry wool at the base of Sophie's neck. "I realized that

Connor doesn't belong in this century. He doesn't belong in my life."

Sophie frowned. "There is something more here."

Laura pulled her hands from Sophie's warm grasp. "I don't want to talk about it."

"I see." Sophie glanced away from Laura, staring at the grandfather clock across the room, her lower lip trembling. "You don't trust me."

"It's not that."

"I thought we had grown quite close."

Laura rubbed her fingertips against her temples, the blood throbbing beneath her touch. "I can't marry Connor because . . . he isn't human," she said, her voice dissolving to a whisper as she admitted the horrible truth.

"How can you say such a thing?"

"He admitted the truth to me. He's some type of sorcerer."

"A sorcerer?"

Laura nodded. "He healed Megan's eyes."

"Oh, my!" Sophie pressed her fingertips to her lips, her eyes as wide as a child's on Christmas morning. "He possesses a wonderful gift. Can you imagine being able to give a little girl back her sight?"

The wind whipped against the windowpanes, battering snow against the glass. Laura rubbed her arms. "He manipulated my mind."

"I don't believe it."

"It's true. He cast some type of spell that turned me into someone I don't even recognize. He invaded my dreams, placed all manner of scandalous images in my mind." Laura hugged her arms to her chest, her shoulders curling forward with the pain burning with memory deep inside of her. "You don't realize the shameful things I've done."

Sophie smoothed a strand of hair back from Laura's face, spilling the scent of summer roses that radiated with the warmth of her skin. "Perhaps I do."

Laura stared into the fire, ashamed to allow Sophie to look into her eyes, to see the truth that lingered inside of her—those moments with Connor had been the most glorious of her entire life. She fought to find the shame inside of her, and found only pain, a terrible ache for want of him. Proof of how far she had fallen under Connor's spell. "I've allowed him liberties no decent woman would allow. I am no longer . . . untouched."

Sophie rested her hand on Laura's shoulder. "What happened between you and Connor isn't shameful, not if you love each other, not if you intend to spend the rest of your lives together."

"Don't you see?" Laura fought the bitter bite of tears stinging her eyes. "He bewitched me. It's the only explanation for why I've behaved as I have these past few days. It's the only explanation for the way I feel now. As though I'm being ripped into pieces."

"I can think of another reason." Sophie stroked Laura's cold cheek with the back of her fingers.

"What?"

"Love."

What you felt is the same pull that brought me to your side . . . the spell of love. Connor's words rippled in her mind. Laura shut her eyes, trying to shut out the vision of his face, the pain she had inflicted glittering in his beautiful blue eyes. Yet his image burned in her memory. "This cannot be love."

"Why? Because it hurts?"

Laura nodded.

"That's love, my darling child. Nothing else burns the soul so intensely as the pain of love that has gone wrong."

"It's some type of enchantment. Some dark spell he cast upon me." Laura shuddered with the mournful sound of the wind upon the glass. "He's not human. He's a monster. He's some strange creature."

"A monster? Some strange creature?" Sophie stared at Laura. "How can you say such things about that gentle young man? You saw him this morning. You held him, felt the heat of his blood on your hand, wept when you thought he might die. How can you sit there and say he isn't human?"

"A human being would have died of that wound."

"Connor is different, I agree, with different abilities. Does that truly make him a monster?"

How could a monster touch her with such gentleness? How could a monster look at her with eyes the pure blue of heaven? She shook her head, dismissing everything except the way he made her feel at this moment—as though she would die if she couldn't be with him. "He has the ability to bewitch me."

"And what about me? Am I a monster?"

"You?" Laura stared at her aunt. "Of course you aren't a monster."

"But I too can cast spells." Sophie shrugged, a shy smile tipping her lips. "Perhaps not at all well, but I have been practicing."

"It's different."

"Is it? I wonder if I should confess my true nature to your father now, while he still has the chance to escape life with a witch."

"Aunt Sophie, no." Laura grabbed Sophie's arm. "You can't tell him the truth."

"I see." Sophie lifted her chin. "You think he might shun me."

"It's hard to say what he would do."

"If he loves me, he will accept me as I am." Sophie drew in a deep breath, her slender shoulders rising beneath the raspberry wool of her gown. "I don't think there is any place for lies in a marriage. I think it's time I tell him the truth."

"Please." Laura gripped Sophie's arm. "Don't do this."

"You wait right here." Sophie patted Laura's hand. "I want you to be with me for a little moral support."

"Daniel, I think you'd better sit," Sophie said, gesturing toward the armchair across from Laura, "while you hear what I have to say."

He hesitated, a frown digging lines into his brow. "Sophie, what is it?"

"Please, I think you should take a seat."

"All right." He settled on the ivory-and-burgundy-striped silk upholstery like a man who had been summoned to the witness box. "This sounds serious."

Sophie clutched the journal to her chest, silently praying Daniel would understand. Dear Lord, he had to understand. She couldn't lose him, not now, not after all of these years. "It is serious."

Daniel rubbed the back of his neck, glancing at Laura and then back at Sophie. "Having second thoughts, love?"

"Never!"

He smiled then, a generous curve of his lips, his dimple creasing his right cheek. "Then whatever it is, it can't be so terrible."

"I hope you're right." Sophie glanced at Laura, who was shaking her head, silently pleading for Sophie to remain quiet. "Don't worry, dear."

Daniel glanced at his daughter. Laura glanced down at her clenched hands, avoiding her father's curious look.

"I'm afraid I find it difficult to begin." Sophie wandered to the desk across from Daniel. She lifted a brass paperweight in the shape of a clipper ship from one corner of the polished mahogany. It had belonged to her father. She remembered staring at it the morning she had told her father she was leaving home, her futile attempt to escape. She had never been able to escape the prison her love for Daniel had forged around her heart.

"Sophie," Daniel said, his deep voice bringing her back from her memories. "No matter what it is, we can work through the difficulties."

She prayed he was right. She could lose everything; her entire future was at stake in the next few moments. Still, she could not marry Daniel without telling him the truth. She turned to face him, gripping the journal like a lifeline. "As you know, Daniel, my maternal grandmother was a Paxton."

"I remember her." Daniel leaned back in the chair and crossed his long legs, a man who had no idea a tornado was about to rip through his life. "You inherited her eyes."

"Yes." Sophie clutched the journal. "And a few other traits as well."

"Sophie, sweetheart, you look as though you're about to be burned at the stake."

Laura groaned. Daniel glanced at his daughter, one dark brow lifting in a silent question.

"Aunt Sophie, please don't."

"I must, dear."

Daniel looked at Sophie, his dark eyes filled with confusion. "Will someone please tell me what's going on?"

"I suppose the best way to say this is just to say it." Sophie moistened her dry lips. "I'm a witch."

Daniel smiled. "We all have a show of temper from time to time."

"No. I'm truly a witch."

"A witch?"

"That's right."

351

He frowned, studying her a moment. "Sophie, what type of game is this?"

"It isn't a game. I'm a witch."

"You're a witch?"

Sophie nodded. "It runs in my family."

"It does?" Daniel leaned forward, planting both feet on the floor. "Sophie, are you trying to get out of this marriage?"

"No. Of course not. I'm only trying to tell you the truth. I'm a witch, a real honest to goodness, spell-casting witch."

He stared at her a moment, his mouth drawn into a tight line, before he glanced at Laura. "What is this all about?"

"It's the truth," Laura said, her voice barely rising above the crackle of the fire. "She's a witch."

"All right." Daniel lifted his hands in surrender. "I don't know what this game is, or what the point of it might be, but I'm willing to play. You're a witch. So what part do I play? A warlock?"

"A warlock is a traitor to the coven," Sophie said, hugging the journal. "Witches are either male or female."

Daniel frowned. "You've been doing research into this?"

"It's all in this book." Sophie held out the journal. "The history of the Paxton clan. It contains lessons for learning to conjure magic."

"All right." Daniel smiled as he held out his hand. "Let me see the magical book," he said, his voice unusually deep, as though he were playing the role of a magician onstage.

Sophie sighed. "Yes. I think it is time you see." She stared down at the book she held, concentrating for all her worth. "Go!"

The book trembled in her hands.

"You want me to leave?" Daniel asked.

"No." Sophie stared at the book. "Do as I ask. Fly to his grasp."

The book shuddered, then leapt from her hands. It sailed across the room, headed straight for Daniel.

"What the—" The book slammed into his chest, dragging a groan from his lips.

"I did it!" Sophie said, bouncing on her toes. "Now do you think this is simply a game?"

Daniel stared down at the book that lay in his lap. "How did you do that?"

Sophie smiled. "Magic."

"No, I really want to know how you did that."

"Daniel, I can conjure magic. Though not very well. Not yet. But I'm certain with a little practice I'll master it. Oh, isn't it a wonderful surprise!"

Daniel stared at her. "A surprise?"

Sophie nodded. "It's really like a gift, when you think of it. Why, who knows what I'll be able to accomplish when I've actually mastered the use of magic."

Daniel turned away from her. "Laura, how did your aunt make this book fly?"

Laura chewed her lower lip. "She's been dabbling in magic."

"Magic?" Daniel came to his feet, the book tumbling from his lap. It thumped on his toes. "Damn!" he mumbled, shaking his injured foot.

"Are you all right, Daniel?"

"I've had enough of this nonsense. When the two of you are willing to tell me about this little parlor game, I'll be in my study."

"You always were a stubborn man," Sophie whispered as he marched across the room.

He opened the door.

She slammed it shut with a flick of her hand.

He turned, glaring at her, his lips pulled into a tight line.

She grinned. "I'm getting better at this already."

He tugged on the door handle. "How the devil did you lock it?"

"Believe me yet?"

He dragged air into his lungs. "Sophie, I'm past the point of being amused."

"I see you're still not convinced. Then watch this." Sophie turned toward the windows. "Shutters tucked away for the day, hear what I have to say—Close."

The shutters slammed together at one window, then the next, and the next, shutting out the sunlight.

"Oh, dear, we need some light." Sophie looked up at the light fixture and snapped her fingers. The lights flickered and glowed.

"Good God!" Daniel whispered.

Sophie turned, smiling at him. "I find my spells work best if I keep them simple."

"You're a witch?" He stared at her, the color draining from his face. "You're actually a witch."

Sophie nodded. "A fledgling, but I'm working at it."

Daniel sagged back against the door as though someone had sapped all the strength from his legs. "This can't be happening."

"Daniel, my darling, I'm sorry to have shocked you like this." Sophie hurried to his side. "But I really—"

He held up his hand as she reached for him. "Don't touch me."

Sophie stepped back, flinching as though he had slapped her. "Daniel, you're not afraid of me. Are you?"

"Dear God! You're a witch."

"I'm still who I always have been. I've just discovered I have a few . . . talents."

"Talents?" He stared at her, a muscle flaring in his cheek as he clenched and unclenched his jaw. "Playing the piano is a talent. Painting landscapes is a talent. Making books fly through the air is insane."

Sophie gasped. "You think I'm insane?"

"No." Daniel laughed, a harsh sound in the quiet room. "I think you're a witch. A witch!"

Tears burned a path upward in her throat, a slow, scalding, singeing the back of her nose, etching a searing trail to her eyes. "I thought you would understand."

"Understand?" He rubbed the back of his neck. "Understand? You're asking me to understand that the woman I plan to marry is an honest to God witch!"

Sophie nodded.

Daniel moaned. He tugged on the door handle. "Dammit!"

Sophie sniffed.

Daniel dug in his heels and jerked on the handle.

"Open," Sophie whispered.

The door popped open, sending Daniel flying. He crashed to the floor, sprawling across the urns and flowers stitched in shades of red and ivory.

"Oh, bother!" Sophie rushed to his side, falling to her knees. "Daniel, I didn't mean to hurt you," she whispered, resting her hand against his hard cheek.

He pushed her hand away.

"Daniel, please . . ."

He scooted away from her, staring at her as though she were a cobra about to strike.

"Daniel, please try to understand."

He scrambled to his feet. "Don't come near me."

Sophie sat back on her heels, the first tears falling from her eyes as she looked up at him. His handsome face was twisted into a mask of rage and revulsion. "Daniel, I'm still the same woman I've always been."

"The hell you are!"

"I love you," she whispered through the tears clawing at her tight throat.

"Dear God." He stood a moment, staring at her, shaking his head before he turned his back to her.

Sophie watched him storm from the room, each thump of his footsteps a nail driven into her heart. She sat in a heap of raspberry wool, tears streaming in hot trails down her cheeks. Shattered. Defeated.

Chapter Twenty-seven

For a moment Laura couldn't move. She sat like someone who had just emerged from the wreckage of a deadly train wreck. Horrified. Paralyzed.

Sophie struggled to rise from the floor, like a wren with a broken wing trying to take flight.

"Aunt Sophie." Laura rushed to her aunt's side.

"Thank you, dear," Sophie said as Laura took her arm. "I'm afraid I'm a little unsteady."

Laura helped Sophie to the wing-back chair, searching for some way to heal the wounds her father had so carelessly inflicted, finding only platitudes where she needed substance. "He needs a little time to get used to everything."

Sophie clasped her trembling hands in her lap, and somehow, even in this moment of defeat, she managed to smile. "At least the magic worked."

"It'll be all right," Laura whispered, wondering if anything would ever be all right again.

Sophie looked up, firelight glittering in her tear-filled eyes. "He thinks I'm a monster."

"He's shocked, that's all."

"Yes, shocked. And repulsed." Sophie smoothed her fingertips over her cheeks, wiping away her tears. "At least you haven't shunned me, my beautiful child."

"Never. I'll talk to him." Laura knelt beside Sophie, her throat growing tight with the tears she could feel rising inside of her. "I'm sure he'll come to understand you haven't changed, not really. You've simply discovered . . . hidden talents."

"Laura, there is someone else you need to talk to." Sophie cupped Laura's cheek in her soft hand. "Think of how Connor must be feeling right now."

"It's not the same."

"Isn't it?"

Laura stared at Sophie, seeing the pain her father had inflicted. Fear. Intolerance. Was she as guilty as her father? An image of Connor blossomed in her mind; she saw the pain in his blue eyes, heard the desperation in his dark voice: *I'm a man, Laura. A man who loves you with all of my heart and soul.* Was it all some type of magic? Or was it real?

"Aunt Sophie, you don't understand. Connor isn't like us. He's a *Tuatha De Danann*, an ancient race of people. I can't even imagine what he might be capable of doing."

"Do you honestly fear him?"

Laura stared into the fire, watching the logs shrivel beneath the flames. "I fear the influence he has over me."

"Go to him. Talk to him. Try to understand him." Sophie stroked Laura's cheek. "You share something very special with Connor, something I can't begin to understand. Don't throw it all away."

Laura used the arm of the chair to rise to her feet. "I

358

want my life back the way it was, before all this magic
and spells and Vikings traveling through time."

"I see. Then I suppose you don't want a witch in your
life either."

"Aunt Sophie, I never meant—"

Sophie raised her hand. "I'll be leaving on the first
train back to New York."

"You can't."

"I can't alter who I am, Laura." Sophie rose from the
chair with all the dignity of a queen rising from her
throne. "And I can't stay where there is no tolerance for
those of us who are a little different from the majority."

Laura stood beside the fire, watching as Sophie
walked across the room. She felt a twisting inside of
her, the awakening of a loneliness she had thought was
gone forever. "Aunt Sophie, please don't go."

Sophie hesitated at the door. "I'm sorry, Laura. I can't
stay." She glanced over her shoulder, a sad smile curving her lips. "I hope you realize how precious the gift
of love can be. I hope you learn before it's too late."

Laura hugged her arms to her waist, seeking to ease
the chill of loneliness, the icy despair that seeped into
her blood. Tears burned her eyes as she watched her
aunt leave the room. "You don't understand," she whispered to the empty room. "How can I be sure what I
feel is really love?"

"Father." Laura tapped on the door of his second-
floor study.

No answer.

She stood in the hall for a moment, torn by conflicting emotions, unsure of how he would receive her. They
had forged such a tenuous bond this morning. What
she was about to do might tear it to shreds. She turned
the handle and opened the door.

Daniel sat in the burgundy leather chair behind his

desk, one hand clenched into a fist on the polished rosewood top beside an empty brandy snifter. In the other hand he held his pocket watch.

"Father."

He didn't acknowledge her presence, but sat staring at his open watch.

Deep furrows were plowed into his hair, as though he had dragged his hands through the thick, dark waves. His tie was pulled to one side, the first few buttons of his shirt unfastened. There had never been a time before this moment when her father had ever appeared disheveled. He had always been impeccable. Remote. In complete command of his emotions and his world. That man had vanished with a snap of Sophie's fingers.

Laura leaned back against the door, allowing it to close with a soft click of the latch. "I think we should talk about what happened."

Daniel sat as though he had been turned to stone, deep lines carved into his brow. Sunlight flowed through the two floor-length windows behind the desk, surrounding him in a glowing light that mocked the darkness emanating from him, a darkness that touched the soul. She knew of this darkness; she was filled with the same shadows of pain and doubt.

She moved toward him, feeling each beat of her heart thud at the base of her throat. "Father, I realize what a shock this has been to you."

He didn't respond, but sat staring at his watch, a man frozen in time.

She lifted his dark gray coat from the floor and draped it over the back of a Chippendale armchair near the windows. "You must understand, Aunt Sophie is still the same woman she has always been."

A muscle flashed in his cheek as he clenched his jaw. Laura paused beside him, gazing down at him, his bowed head, the hand he held open on the desk, the watch lying open across his palm, its gold chain dangling over the edge of the desk, unattached. The crystal covering the watch face reflected the sunlight, obscuring the hands of the watch. But it was the photograph opposite the watch face that had bewitched her father. An oval cut from a larger photograph had been attached to the gold cover—the image of Sophie as she had been more than 20 years ago.

"Aunt Sophie hasn't changed much since that photograph was taken."

Daniel clicked the cover shut, clutching the watch in his hand. "How long have you known about . . ." He hesitated, tapping the back of his hand against the desk. "How long have you known about her . . . talents?"

"Just over a week. She didn't know until then either."

He looked up at her, his dark eyes raw with pain. "She didn't know she was a . . . a . . ." He cleared his throat. "She didn't know until a few days ago?"

"She discovered her abilities after Ridley discovered the journal in the wine cellar."

Daniel frowned. "As I recall, Ridley nearly broke his ankle that day. How appropriate."

"Father, I'm afraid Aunt Sophie is going to leave."

Daniel tapped his knuckles against the smooth, polished rosewood.

"Are you going to let her walk out of your life?"

"I suspect she'll be riding a broom."

Laura stared at him, seeing too much of herself reflected in his pain. "You've known Aunt Sophie since she was three years old. Have you ever known her to be unkind to anyone or anything?"

"No." He stared at his clenched hand, the watch chain spilling from his tight fist. "But it doesn't change the fact that she's a . . . witch," he said, his voice dissolving as he admitted the truth.

"Yes, she is a witch. But what does that really mean?"

"You saw what she can do." He waved his hand, the gold watch chain swishing in the sunlight. "She's a witch. A real honest to God witch."

"I can't explain why she's different than we are." She stared at her father's clenched fist, but in her mind she saw Connor, the pain in his beautiful blue eyes. Was he truly a master of illusion? Or was he merely a man with abilities she didn't understand?

She perceived a shaking deep inside of her, a trembling of doubt that threatened to destroy her if she peered too deeply into the truth. "You're Irish. That makes you different in the eyes of someone like Esther Gardner. But does it make you inferior?"

"It's not exactly the same. I can't make a book fly across the room by mumbling a few words."

"Do you believe Aunt Sophie would ever harm you with one of her spells?"

"No." He stared hard at his clenched hand. "Not intentionally, anyway."

"Neither do I." Unbidden, Connor's voice whispered in her memory: *I would never do anything to harm you. . . . You are my heart.* And somehow she knew those words had been sincere. In his own way, Connor would never harm her. "Father, you can't let Aunt Sophie leave. You love her, and she loves you."

Daniel shook his head. "I need some time to think about this."

"I hope you don't take too long, Father. You might lose everything." Even as she spoke the words, a sense of impending disaster settled around her like an icy shroud.

She turned and left her father. She needed time alone, time to sort through the conflicting emotions of heart and soul, time to unravel her tangled thoughts. Had she escaped a monster? Or had she thrown happiness away with both hands?

Fiona was waiting for her in the hall outside of the study. Laura froze in the hallway, staring at Fiona, fearing what the housekeeper would say even before she spoke.

"He's gone, Miss Laura."

Laura felt the blow, a hard thrust to her chest that threatened to buckle her knees. She pressed her hand against the wall, steadying herself.

Fiona gripped Laura's arm. "Are you all right, miss?"

Laura nodded, unable to use her voice, her throat closing with the sudden pain. Dear heaven, was she doomed to live the rest of her years bewitched by Connor's potent sorcery?

"A little while ago I came up with some broth and bread, a little tea. And he was gone." Fiona clutched her amber talisman in her hand. "I thought I'd best find you and tell you."

Had he truly gone? Laura walked toward his room like a puppet drawn by strings. She hesitated a moment on the threshold before plunging from the shadows into the sunlight that poured through the floor-length windows in Connor's room.

The bed covers were tossed to one side, revealing the white linen sheets, the haven she had found with Connor the night before. She touched his pillow, the white linen cool against her fingertips.

A trembling spiraled from deep inside of her, doubts mingling with memories conspiring to destroy her. *I'm here for you, always for you.* She heard his voice, felt a shimmer of heat flicker across her belly, her breasts, remembering the touch of his hands against her skin, the warm slide of his lips, his tongue.

"Connor," she whispered, clutching the pillow in her hand.

"He's gone, miss," Fiona said softly from the doorway.

Laura ran across the room. The bathroom door was open. "Connor," she shouted, staring into the bathroom.

"I've looked for him, miss," Fiona said as she moved to stand behind Laura. "But he's vanished."

Laura stared across Connor's room, sunlight stinging her eyes. "Perhaps he's downstairs. He could have . . . He might . . ." She hesitated, recognizing a truth she wanted to deny. "I didn't think he would leave without a word."

"It's the way of it sometimes. The *Sidhe* don't always stay with mortals. It's difficult for them, keeping their gifts a secret."

Laura stared at Fiona. "You know?"

"Aye." Fiona gazed at the windows, smiling as though she saw Connor standing in the sunlight. "Megan spoke of an angel healing her eyes with a touch of his hands. And when I questioned her about this angel, I came to realize she was describing Mr. Connor."

"And you weren't frightened of him?"

"At first I was. But I started thinking that none of the Dark Folk would be healing a little girl. And then I realized he wasn't one of the Dark Folk. No, not with that smile of his and the gentle touch of his hand." Fiona shook her head, her smile growing sad. "Aye, he was one of the Shining Ones, he was. And we should be grateful for the precious time we had with him."

Laura sank to the sofa near the fireplace, all the strength seeping from her limbs. "You know the legends of the *Tuatha De Danann* well, don't you?"

"Aye. The stories have been passed from one generation to the next. 'Tis our way of keeping the *Sidhe* with us."

Laura laced her trembling fingers together on her lap.

She stared at the twisted remains of a log on the hearth, the blackened wood whittled from the flames that had died before consuming it entirely, leaving charred chips scattered on the bricks.

She wanted the truth. Yet she feared it might sear the last of her defenses, leave her with no shield from the pain of losing Connor. "Have you ever heard of a *Sidhe* prince taking a mortal for a wife?"

"Aye. 'Tis common for one of the *Sidhe* to take a fancy to a comely mortal lass."

"Then it's common for a *Sidhe* prince to use enchantment to ensnare a woman's heart?"

"Never!"

Laura glanced up at her. "Never?"

Fiona tapped her fingertip against her lower lip, frowning as though she were trying to recall the old stories. "I have heard tale of a *Sidhe* lord who kidnapped a young bride; Eileen was her name. He took her from her home and carried her away to his realm. He enchanted her, made her life in the mortal world seem no more than a dream."

"He made her forget who she was." Laura stared down at her clasped hands, longing a tight fist in her chest. Even now a part of her wanted to believe everything she and Connor had shared had been real. "He bewitched her, until she couldn't even recognize herself."

"Aye, she wandered as if in a dream. But her husband—Niall, he was—fought for her and won."

"How could a mortal fight such a powerful being?"

"There are forces even stronger than the magic of the *Sidhe*. One of those forces is love."

Connor's words whispered in Laura's memory, chipping away at her defenses—*It is a spell as old as time. A spell more beautiful than any my people could conjure. The spell of love.*

"Through it all, the *Sidhe* lord came to realize that his spell could only keep Eileen enchanted for a wee bit of time. He could never really possess her because she had already given her heart to another. He knew the love Eileen and Niall shared would sustain the young couple their entire lives."

"Why didn't the *Sidhe* lord force her to fall in love with him?"

Fiona shook her head. "There's no spell for that."

Laura squeezed her hands together, trying to ease the shaking inside of her. "So you've never heard of a spell to make a woman fall in love with a *Sidhe*?"

"No. 'Tis well known that love must grow. It can't be stolen or forced."

An image of Connor blossomed in Laura's mind; she saw the pain in his blue eyes, heard the desperation in his dark voice: I'm a man, Laura. A man who loves you with all of my heart and soul. All the ugly things she had said to him, all the pain she had caused—understanding forged a blade inside of her, a sharp knife that twisted in her heart.

"And 'tis also well known that those of the *Sidhe* seldom need love potions or spells. They carry a beauty about them, more than the cast of their features. They have a light that shines from within."

"The light of a gentle soul," Laura whispered.

"Lucky is the mortal who catches the heart of a *Sidhe*. Even if they must leave behind the world as they know it."

Laura glanced up, staring at Fiona. "What do you mean, they must leave the world as they know it?"

"The *Sidhe* live in the *Tir na nOg*, the Land of Ever Young. Once you cross the border into their realm, you will remain as you are the day you leave this mortal world behind. But you must stay, or feel the cold touch of time."

She had sensed the truth of this in her dreams, in the valley where she had met Connor for so many years. The very essence of the place lured her, promising to shelter her, to nurture her for eternity—if she would only give up the world she knew.

"Still." Fiona lifted the talisman she wore and stared down into the golden amber that glowed like fire in the sunlight. "I'm thinking the legends don't tell all there is to know about the Shining Ones."

"Do you think he'll ever come back?" Laura whispered.

" 'Tis not likely, miss. The *Sidhe* prefer to live with their own kind, where they can be free to use their gifts without threats from mortals who might destroy them out of fear."

A hard hand squeeze Laura's heart when she realized she would never again see Connor's face. He was gone. And she had no one to blame except herself.

She was trapped in a cage of her own design, bars forged of propriety, planted by prejudice. She had held happiness in her hands, and then destroyed it, shattered it like crystal carelessly tossed against stone.

Still, she wondered if she would ever have found the courage to enter Connor's realm, to leave the world she knew far behind, even if she hadn't destroyed any chance they might have had of being together. She closed her eyes, immersing herself in the memory of Connor. Memories were all she had, all she deserved.

Chapter Twenty-eight

Waves pounded against the rugged stone face of the Cliffs of Moher, tossing spray into the air. Connor stood at the edge of the cliffs, like a prisoner up against the bars of his cell. Upon his return to Erin three weeks ago, Aisling had cast a spell confining him to the island, a spell revoking his ability to use his medallion; he could no longer open the portal of time.

The damp wind whipped at his hair, bathed his face in the salty scent of the sea; the cold penetrated the emerald wool of his tunic. His face and hands tingled with the cold as he stood 700 feet above the rolling gray water, staring into the mist that fell like a silvery veil from the gray sky to the darker gray of the ocean.

Laura was across that great expanse of gray water. At least she would be in a thousand years. Strange to love a woman who had not yet been born. He stiffened when he sensed another presence on the bluffs, knowing who it was even before she spoke.

"You're a long way from home, dark warrior," Aisling said, her voice ringing like a bell above the crash of the surf.

Connor drew in his breath, the damp, salty air leaving a tang on his tongue. "About a thousand years."

"You should not be out in this cold air, not so soon after healing." She touched him, resting her hand against his back, the heat of her palm warming him through the soft cashmere of his tunic. "And look at you, not even wearing a cloak."

Connor glanced down at her. The breeze tugged at the dark burgundy wool of the hood framing her beautiful face. She was smiling, yet he saw a hint of anxiety in her pale blue eyes. "If you're so concerned for my welfare, then release me from this prison."

"I can't allow you to go back to Boston, Connor."

"Dammit, Aisling. Why won't you let me fight for what belongs to me?"

"What do you plan to do? Kidnap the woman?"

"She's in love with me. I'm certain I can find a way to make her see we must be together."

Aisling shook her head. "If you would stop thinking like a Viking, you would understand why you must stay away from her."

"All right." He raised his hands in surrender. "Explain your reasoning to this poor, misguided Viking."

"First, you must know Laura regrets turning away from you."

"You've seen her?"

"Yes."

"If she regrets turning away from me, then why can't I go to her?"

Aisling pursed her lips, studying him a moment before she spoke. "Laura has agreed to marry Philip Gardner."

369

"No!" Connor gripped the handle of his sword. "I cannot allow this to happen."

Aisling rested her hand on his shoulder, and instantly he felt a healing warmth slide through his veins, like a soothing balm eased over an open wound. "Think like the *Sidhe* prince you are."

"This is my life, Aisling. My future. And you're playing some game with it."

"It isn't a game, I assure you." Aisling turned toward the sea, the wind whipping the hood back from her head. "If you and Laura are to be joined, she must recognize the ties that bind her to you. She must see them as stronger than any ties that bind her to her life in Boston."

"You want her to choose. Me or her life in Boston."

"She must choose." The wind eddied around her, lifting her cape, the hem flicking like the tail of an angry cat above the wind-blown clifftop. "It is the only way you can stay with her."

Connor stared down at the waves that crashed against the rocks, white foam swirling, disappearing as the water ebbed, before the next waves crashed into the rocks. "Nothing you have said convinces me of the wisdom of remaining here while that bastard is preparing to steal my woman."

"If Laura loves you, truly loves you with all of her heart and soul"—Aisling rested her hand on his arm—"she will find a way to reach you. You must trust in the power of your love."

Connor watched a white gull ride the wind, gliding with wings stretched across the vast expanse of gray. "And what if she discovers her love for me after she marries Gardner?"

Aisling slipped her hood over her pale hair. She turned to look up at him, her eyes filled with a steely resolve as cold as the sea. "Then she was not meant to be with you."

Connor stared into the mist, wondering if he would ever see Laura's face again. *Be mine, Laura. Now and for eternity.*

"I find it hard to accept." Austin stood on the stone terrace that stretched along the cliffs behind his parents' home, staring into the valley below. A city carved by his ancestors 6,000 years ago rose from the valley floor, black stones shaping the temple and surrounding buildings of ancient Avallon, crystals embedded in the chiseled stones sparkling in the sunlight. "How the devil did Fraser Bennett persuade the governing council there is no need to probe his mind for the truth?"

"There isn't sufficient evidence to warrant such an intrusion into his mind, Austin. You must know that as well as I do." Rhys leaned his hip against the stone balustrade and regarded his son. "Are you certain you aren't simply disappointed he is to be spared the indignity?"

"Perhaps." Austin smiled as he looked at the tall, broad-shouldered man standing beside him. Although 30 years his senior, Rhys Sinclair looked no older than Austin's 35 years, his black hair untouched by gray, his skin taut and unlined. It was the way of his people, a legacy from the past, a gift they could bestow.

"I have an uneasy feeling about this." Austin pressed his palms against the smooth black balustrade. "As much as I dislike Bennett, I'm not certain he shot Connor. He fears Connor's power too much to try to destroy him by his own hand. It would be far too dangerous if he should fail."

"Do you have any idea who did?"

"I have a few people in mind, one in particular. But I'm not certain there is anything I can do without proof, especially now that Connor is gone."

"Pity. As a result of your report, the council has issued an open invitation to Connor. And now he's gone." Rhys turned and stared out across the valley that cradled the ruins of ancient Avallon. "I regret I never had a chance to meet the young man."

"He had the ability to tap the power in us, Father." Austin took a deep breath, his senses filling with the fragrance of roses drifting from his mother's garden. In a few hours he would leave for the frozen climes of Boston, but for these few moments he would absorb the warmth of this mountaintop sanctuary. "Connor could have taught us to be all we once were."

"And you have no idea why he left?"

"When I spoke to him on that last day, he had no intention of leaving." Austin brushed his fingertip over a blue aquamarine embedded in the black stone of the balustrade, the gem glittering in the sunlight. "He told me he and Laura Sullivan were to be married."

"Do you know what happened between them?"

"I suspect the truth drove them apart." The laughter of children spilled through the balcony doors of the nursery on the second floor of the house, the sound of Austin's son playing with his brother Devlin's twin boys, safe under the watchful eye of their nurse. The last time he had checked, the boys were busy playing with blocks. "Connor was going to tell her about himself, confess the truth of his unusual heritage."

"It would seem she couldn't accept the truth."

"So it would seem." Austin turned toward the gardens that stretched from the house to the very edge of the cliff. He watched his wife as she strolled through the rose garden beside his mother.

Sarah's tunic of jade silk was belted at her waist by strands of braided gold and silver; her ivory silk trousers rippled in the breeze as she stopped to inhale the fragrance of a pink rose. He remembered the turmoil his wife had suffered when he had first brought her to Avallon. How difficult it had been to accept this distant city, so different from the world she knew. Yet their love had bridged the chasm. Their love had healed the wounds inflicted through the deceptions he had weaved around her. Austin believed that if love was strong enough, it could span time itself.

"The day she told me Connor had left Boston, I sensed a sadness in Laura Sullivan, a sharp pain of loss. I believe she loves him."

"Do you still plan to attend her wedding?"

Austin nodded. "Maybe Connor will come back. I keep hoping he will find some way to change Laura's mind."

"I've been thinking a great deal about Connor and his journey through time." The cool breeze ruffled his thick black hair as Rhys stared out across ancient Avallon. "I can think of only one way he would know of Laura Sullivan."

"What is it?"

"Think, Austin." Rhys glanced at his son, his blue-green eyes sparkling with mischief. "How would a mortal woman in Boston of 1889 be connected to a sorcerer in Ireland of 889?"

Sophie stood beside a window in her drawing room, holding aside the drape, staring out into the night. Snow fell in plump white flakes, turning gold in the light of the street lamp before settling on the sidewalk and street outside her Fifth Avenue town house. Was it snowing in Boston? Was Daniel looking through the windows of his study and watching the snow fall?

She turned away from the window, allowing the drape to fall across the panes, the heavy blue and ivory brocade rattling the brass curtain rings. It was more difficult than she thought to put back together the pieces of her life. This house seemed bigger than before, so many halls, so many rooms, all empty of life. It had never been easy living alone. But now, after having glimpsed the possibilities of her dreams, it felt like a prison.

She sank to the Sheraton sofa near the hearth, seeking the warmth of the fire, her gown of cinnamon wool spilling across the ivory roses in the blue brocade upholstery. A smile curved her lips as she looked at the photograph sitting on the round pedestal table beside the sofa, the image of her late aunt Millicent staring up at her.

"I wish you were here," Sophie said, running her fingertip over a scroll carved in the brass frame. Millicent had been gone three years, and still Sophie missed the woman who had been like a mother to her.

"Chin up, Sophie," she whispered to herself, imitating her aunt Millicent's husky voice. "Be thankful for all you have. Don't dwell on all you wish you had."

Millicent had never been blessed with a child. When Sophie came to live with her mother's older sister, she had become the daughter Millicent had always dreamed of having. Millicent had been the only person Sophie had confided her secret to, the horrible secret of her love for her sister's husband.

"It's funny, isn't it," she said to the picture. "I thought of Laura as the daughter I might have had. Now I'm not even going to her wedding."

"Why?"

Sophie started at the sound of a deep male voice, knocking the photograph from the table with the back of her hand. It plopped facedown on the carpet. She turned on the cushion, staring at the man who stood in the doorway, a ghost from the dreams that had died inside of her.

Why had he come?

Daniel stood before her, tall and real, no figment of her far too active imagination. His dark hair was tousled as though he had used his fingers as a comb. Purple smudges darkened the skin beneath his beautiful eyes, as though he hadn't slept well in weeks. And he looked thinner, his cheeks drawn, the dark gray coat and trousers not quite fitting his tall frame.

Daniel glanced at her butler, who stood beside him like a plump gray terrier protecting his bone, Daniel's coat over his arm, his hat dangling from his fingers. "That will be all."

Lyndley cocked his head, looking up at Daniel a moment before turning his dark gaze on Sophie. "The gentleman assured me you would receive him, miss," he said, lifting one bushy gray brow.

Sophie had to swallow hard before she could speak, a tangle of emotion lodging at the base of her neck. "Thank you, Lyndley. You may take your leave."

"I shan't be far if you need me, miss." Lyndley cast Daniel a dark glance before he marched out of the room, leaving the door open.

Daniel tapped the door, the solid oak swinging shut with a thud. "I think he believes I'm going to steal the silver."

Sophie fingered the cameo pinned on the wool below the lace that edged the high neck of her gown. "What are you doing here?"

Daniel glanced past her to the fire on the hearth as though he were cold and needed warmth. Yet he didn't move. "Laura is upset that you won't be at the wedding tomorrow."

Sophie released the breath she had been holding, the hope inside of her dissolving with the air vanishing from her lungs. What had she expected? A change of heart? Daniel down on one knee begging for her hand?

At her age she should realize that fairy tales didn't come true. "I assume she is still planning to marry Philip Gardner."

Daniel nodded, his lips pulled into a tight line. "This morning she told me about Connor. I think she was tired of evading my questions about him."

"Then you must be relieved to know she is going to marry Philip." Sophie spread the ivory lace that fell from her cuff across the back of her hand. "What a disaster if she had married Connor. Why, think of the scandal if anyone ever discovered he was really a Viking as well as a sorcerer."

"Sophie, I—"

"And Chandler Shipping, my goodness, can you imagine a Viking in charge of your precious shipping company?"

"Sophie, I've—"

"Why, it's hard to say what type of—"

"I've tried to talk her out of going through with the wedding."

Sophie glanced up at him. "Pardon me?"

"I said I've tried to talk her out of marrying Philip Gardner."

"You have?"

Daniel nodded. "I don't think she realizes just what it means to be locked in a marriage with someone who can't give her what she needs." From across the room, he stared into the fire as though he were looking into his past. "I don't want that type of life for her. Cold. Empty. It's not a life. It's existing day to day."

Sophie gripped the arm of the sofa, her fingers sliding across the smooth walnut trim. She couldn't go to him. She couldn't slip her arms around him and comfort him. No matter how much she longed to touch him. "She is afraid of causing a scandal."

"Boston society can go jump in the Charles, for all I care."

"Oh," she whispered. "You told her that?"

"Yes, for all the good it did. She has some misguided sense of duty. She thinks she has to give me an heir, and carry on the Chandler tradition." Daniel drew in his breath. "But I think there is more to it."

"What?"

"I'm not sure. There is something about her these days. She's distant, distracted, as though she were walking in a daze most of the time. It's almost as if part of her has died." Daniel looked at Sophie, uncertainty in his dark eyes, a hundred questions lingering there in the dark brown depths, and something more, something that whispered to the loneliness inside of her, the longing she felt for him. "I understand how she feels."

Did he at all regret turning away from her? "If Laura marries Philip, she surrenders her chance to live with the one person who can make her soul whole again."

"I know. But I haven't been able to make Laura see the truth."

He didn't move, and yet she felt as though he were reaching for her. Hope fluttered inside of her like a bird with a broken wing trying desperately to fly. "And you think I will have better success in convincing her not to marry Philip?"

"I doubt anyone can talk her out of the wedding, except perhaps Connor."

"But he isn't here."

"No, he isn't." Daniel shifted on his feet like an accused felon standing before a judge. "But Laura said you brought him to Boston. I thought you might be able to bring him back."

"Bring him back?" Sophie stared at him, his words soaking into the swirl of thoughts in her mind. "You want me to use magic to bring back a sorcerer so that your daughter can marry him? Is that what you're asking me to do?"

He released his breath in a slow exhale. "Yes. I suppose that's exactly what I'm asking you to do."

Sophie fingered the cameo at her neck, the present Daniel had given her on her eighteenth birthday. She stared at him, wondering, feeling hope lift delicate wings. If he could accept a sorcerer into his life, could he also accept a witch?

Daniel moved toward her, long strides that were slow and steady. He stood for a moment, looking at her, uncertainty lurking in his eyes. Sophie waited, her heart pounding at the base of her throat, the crackle of the fire roaring to her heightened senses.

He bent and retrieved the photograph of her aunt Millicent. "It didn't break."

"How fortunate," she whispered.

He set the frame on the embroidered lace doily that covered the top of the pedestal table by the sofa, staring at the photograph a moment, before he looked at Sophie. "I've missed you."

"I've missed you too."

He smiled then, the tension easing from his features, his dimple peeking out at her. "I think there is a cure for what ails us."

Sophie gripped the arm of the chair. "What?"

"Come live with me, Sophie." He knelt on one knee before her and lifted her trembling hand from the arm of the sofa. "Come share your joy with me. Come be my bride."

Sophie stared into his dark eyes, seeing a warmth that beckoned her like a cozy hearth beckoned to a frozen traveler. "I'm still a witch."

"I know." He pressed his lips to the back of her hand. "And I know I want the magic of you in my life. Now and always. I love you, Sophie."

She cupped his cheek in her hand, absorbing the warmth of his skin against her palm.

"Forgive me." He looked up at her, pain and need naked in his eyes. "Please come back to me."

Tears pricked her eyes, the sweet cleansing tears of joy. "Shall we go home, my love? I have a spell to cast."

He grinned up at her. "I only hope it's as potent as the spell you've cast over me."

Sophie thought of Laura and prayed she could bring Connor back in time to save Laura from her own misguided sense of honor.

There was a full moon tonight, but it was hidden in the snow-filled sky. Laura smoothed her finger across a windowpane, following the slow slide of a plump snowflake as it melted against the glass. Light from the library slanted through the windows, casting golden frames into the snow-covered garden. Snow drifted through the squares of light, plump flakes, heavy, full of moisture, perfect for snowballs.

"Such miserable weather," Philip said as he moved to her side. He twisted his lips into a downward curve, staring at the snow with contempt. "By this time tomorrow, we shall be well on our way to Italy, and away from all of this snow."

Philip had planned a trip to the continent for their honeymoon. But instead of lazy gondola rides along the canals of Venice, or strolls along the streets of Paris, he had already decided their itinerary would include all of the best museums. It seemed a museum in Rome had one of the finest collections of malachite in the world. How fascinating. How very fascinating—for Philip.

Silently she chided herself, knowing there was nothing to be gained in dwelling on regrets. It was better this way, Laura thought. It was better not to think of romance or passion or love—all the things beyond her reach. She had made a practical decision when she agreed to marry Philip. Still, the memories lingered.

When she heard laughter, she remembered Connor's smile. When she looked into a clear morning sky, she saw the vivid blue of his eyes. And when she went to bed at night, she remembered the warmth of his body pressed against hers. She would never forget him—memory was her salvation and her curse.

She sighed, her breath steaming the windowpanes. Perhaps there was more to this man she was going to marry. Perhaps there was a warmth inside of him. All she had to do was find it. "Have you ever played in the snow?"

"Played in the snow?"

Laura nodded. "Did you ever have snowball fights with your friends?"

Philip shrugged. "I suppose I did when I was a child."

"Come out with me, Philip," she said, touching his arm. "Let's play in the snow."

He looked at her as though she had just asked him to rob a bank. "You want to go out in the cold and play in the snow?"

"That's right." She squeezed his arm, hoping he might bend just a little. Perhaps then she could face the vows she would speak, binding her to this man, with less dread. "Please come with me into the gardens."

Philip regarded her a moment, his dark eyes touched with a hint of disdain. "No responsible adult would consider something so foolish."

"I see." She dropped her hand from his stiff arm. There was no chance of reaching a tender warmth hidden beyond Philip's icy facade because nothing resided within him, nothing but ice.

"Laura, I'm not at all certain what's gotten into you these days." Philip shook his head, releasing his breath in a way that shouted his disapproval. "Last week you stood for an hour staring at a train as though it were the most fascinating creation on earth. Yesterday you wanted to have ice cream before we had eaten lunch. Before lunch! Today you want to play in the snow."

Laura hugged herself, shivering with a cold that came from within. "I thought it would be fun."

"Fun?" Philip shook his head as though the concept of fun escaped him. "I know what's wrong with you."

She looked up at him, wondering if he had any suspicion of what she had shared with Connor. She stared straight into his cold, dark eyes, refusing to feel the slightest twinge of shame for the few hours of pleasure she had stolen. "What?"

"You're simply having a case of nerves before our wedding." He patted her shoulder. "Now, you're not to worry. I'll make certain you behave as you should. I shall help you. In time you'll feel quite comfortable carrying the Gardner name."

A stab of panic ripped through her heart. "Will I?"

"Of course." Philip twisted his lips into the stiff curve that served as his smile. "I'm certain once we're married, you will settle back into your former self without any problem."

"A marble sculpture? Cold? Aloof? Untouchable?"

"Well, not exactly untouchable." Philip chuckled, an awkward sound for a man unaccustomed to laughter. "We will be married, after all. I do expect children, if you understand what I mean."

"Yes." Bitter bile crept up the back of her throat when she thought of this man touching her. "I think I understand exactly what you mean."

"Well, I should be off. You need your sleep." He chucked her under the chin. "Tomorrow is a big day."

She watched him cross the room, feeling the ice thicken inside of her, numbing her. She had chosen this man. She had told all of Boston she would marry Philip. And now there was nothing left but to fulfill a destiny of her own making.

Philip paused as he reached the door, staring at the clock standing against the far wall. "That's strange." He took his pocket watch out and looked at the time, then glared at the grandfather clock. "The hands are moving in reverse."

If only she could make time run backward, she thought. If only she could erase the damage she had caused. If only she could go back to that moment in time before Connor had disappeared. Still, even if she could go back in time, she wasn't sure she possessed the courage to take what she wanted. No matter how much she loved Connor, she wasn't certain she had the courage to face a life with one beguiling Irish sorcerer.

"I'll leave you two alone." Daniel hesitated on the threshold of the library, smiling at Sophie as though the very sight of her brought him pleasure. "I'm sure you have a great deal to discuss." He turned and closed the door, leaving Laura and Sophie alone in the library.

"I kept hoping he would come to his senses," Laura said, hugging Sophie once more, the fragrance of summer roses filling her senses. She pulled back, smiling down into Sophie's dear face. "He's been miserable since you left."

Sophie smiled, her eyes filling with mischief. "That's certainly nice to hear."

"And he doesn't mind this?" Laura asked, tapping the journal her aunt held.

"I told him he must accept me as I am." Sophie stroked the red leather cover with her fingertips. "And he said he wouldn't have me any other way."

"Are you certain you don't want to turn the ceremony tomorrow into a double wedding?"

"Quite certain. I need time to have my mother's wedding gown altered. And . . ." She drew in a slow breath, looking up at Laura, all the laughter fading from her eyes. "I can't honestly say I want to share your wedding to Philip Gardner."

"Oh." Laura stepped back, all the warmth she had felt upon seeing her aunt chilled into the solid realization of what was to take place tomorrow morning. "I understand."

"Laura, you can't go through with this."

"I know it isn't the love match you would have liked for me." Laura turned away from her aunt. Slowly, as though her legs were made of wood, she crossed the room to where Gypsy was lying by the hearth. "But most marriages are not based on love. I'm sure in time you will see, as I do, that this is a suitable arrangement."

"Arrangement? Laura, you're talking about living the rest of your life with that man."

Laura rubbed her arms, trying to warm the chill that crept from deep inside of her. "I doubt my life with Philip shall be any worse than it would be should I marry any of the other young men of my acquaintance."

"If it's fear of scandal that has you going through with this marriage, then you should know your father doesn't want you to suffer because of a mistake you made while you were confused and upset."

"I know." Laura sank to the edge of the burgundy velvet wing-back chair beside the fireplace. "But there is no reason to cause a scandal. You see, it doesn't matter to me if I marry Philip. I must marry someone, give Father an heir for the company, carry on the Chandler bloodline. I can at least do that. And in a strange way Philip is ideal. You see, he doesn't expect me to love him."

"Laura, you can't spend your life with a man you don't love."

"It really doesn't matter." Laura leaned forward, reaching for Gypsy. The dog turned her head as Laura stroked the soft hair between her ears, bumping Laura's arm with her nose. "Connor's gone."

"And if he were here?"

"I can't keep thinking of what might have happened." Laura stroked Gypsy's head. "I can only try to make the best of a difficult situation."

"Well, there's something more I can do."

Laura stared as Sophie began leafing through pages in the journal. "What are you going to do?"

Sophie grinned. "I'm going to bring him to you."

"Connor?"

Sophie nodded. "We'll use the same incantation that brought him here in the first place."

The pulse of her heart throbbed against the high neck of her amethyst cashmere gown, excitement mixing with fear. What would she do if Connor suddenly appeared?

Sophie cleared her throat. "Hear me, Lady of the moon. Your pull is great. You move the tide. Now—"

"Aunt Sophie!" Laura came to her feet. "What would I say to him if he returned?"

"Tell him you love him."

"But Philip—"

"Not another word about Philip. We'll take care of him in the morning."

"You don't understand. Even if you can bring Connor here, I'm not certain we can have a life together."

Sophie glanced up from the journal. "Why?"

"His people live in a world separate from mortals. What if Connor wants me to leave Boston? What if he wants to take me back with him to his time, to the land of his people?"

"Do you really believe he would take you back to that barbarous century?"

Laura nodded. "I've always suspected Connor would take me away from the world as I know it."

"You can't be certain."

"It's in the legends. Those who want to live with one of the *Sidhe* must leave the mortal world behind." Laura stared down into the fire. "Connor would always be out of place here, always forced to hide his abilities. How could I ask him to stay? And how could I leave?"

"If the love you share is as strong as I believe it is, you'll find a way. When Connor returns, I'm certain everything will be just fine."

"I wish I could believe that."

"You'll see."

Laura balled her hands into fists as she stared at Sophie, fear warring with longing in her heart. There were so many doubts in her mind, a hundred reasons why Connor shouldn't return to this time, and only one reason why he should.

"Hear me, Lady of the moon," Sophie said, her voice strong and sure. "Your pull is great. You move the tide. Now bring Laura's beloved to her side."

Laura held her breath. The wind whispered against the windowpanes. She turned, staring at the windows, seeing nothing but darkness beyond the reflection of the room in the glass.

Sophie read the incantation over and over again. Each time the words throbbed with the blood pounding in Laura's temples. Each time Laura waited.

Tick, tick, tick, tick. The pendulum of the grandfather clock marked the passing of the seconds, each tick chipping at Laura's taut nerves. She stared at the windows, expecting the man of her dreams to materialize out of thin air.

Nothing. Not a glimmer of moonlight appeared.

Debra Dier

Sophie tried again, speaking the incantation, drawing the words from deep in her chest. She repeated the words over and over again as though she could summon Connor with the force of her will.

Nothing.

Laura moved to the windows. "He isn't going to come."

"Maybe it has something to do with the moon being blocked by clouds. Maybe we should try tomorrow night."

Laura shook her head. She stared past the golden squares of light tossed across the snow, looking into the darkness. A full moon glimmered somewhere beyond the dark clouds. Yet Connor wouldn't come to her tonight; she felt the certainty of it in her soul. Without the courage to turn her back on life as she knew it, she would never again see Connor. Not even in her dreams.

"It's for the best, Aunt Sophie." She had made the logical decision in accepting Philip, Laura assured herself. Still, her heart rebelled against the practical choice her mind had made; she could feel it twist in her chest, pain radiating through her. "We're from two different worlds, Connor and I. If I had never met him, I would have married Philip. And now that Connor is gone, I see no reason to postpone the ceremony."

Chapter Twenty-nine

Laura stared out one of the windows of her bedroom at the freshly fallen snow, sunlight turning the gardens into a field of diamonds. It was so beautiful. A perfect clear day for a wedding. Her wedding. Odd, but she felt nothing as she stood here in her wedding gown and waited as the last few moments of her freedom ticked away. It was as if she were numb, frozen inside.

"Laura, dear, I wish—"

"Aunt Sophie, please. Let it rest. There is nothing more to say."

"Laura, you can't do this."

"We have a house full of guests." Laura glanced over her shoulder to her aunt, her maid of honor, her only attendant. The gown of icy blue satin emphasized the dark blue of Sophie's eyes, the smooth ivory of her face. She looked beautiful, and as sad as a mother attending her daughter's funeral. "I can't possibly stop the wedding. Not now."

"Yes, you can."

Laura crossed the room, her train of ivory satin rippling across the intricate urns and flowers stitched in gold and green and ivory in the carpet. "Don't you worry about me," she said, giving Sophie a firm hug. "I'm going to be just fine."

Sophie touched her cheek. "I pray you can find some happiness, my beautiful child."

She had given up her chance for happiness, Laura thought. And now that Connor was gone, nothing mattered.

"You go on down." Laura slipped her arm through Sophie's and led her to the door. "I want a few minutes alone."

"Think about what lies ahead, Laura. And remember you can still escape."

Laura stared at the door a long moment after Sophie left, her words ringing with the truth in her brain. Pain seeped from the icy prison she had forged around her emotions, a searing pain that threatened her carefully fashioned facade of calm.

"There is no other way." She drew in a deep breath, trying to brace the walls of her defenses. "I can't change my mind. This is the right decision. It is."

A cold nose bumped her hand. Laura glanced down to find Gypsy sitting beside her.

"Don't look at me that way. I'm doing what must be done."

Gypsy tilted her head, looking at Laura as though she understood everything that was about to transpire.

"You're going to like living with my father and Aunt Sophie." Laura crouched in front of the dog, heedless of the wrinkles she was pressing into the Brussels lace that draped the entire front of her satin gown. "And I'll come visit you when I can."

Gypsy rested her big paw on the lace covering Laura's

knee, staring at Laura with somber eyes. Laura felt the affection the dog had for her, the honest friendship she had offered from the first moment Laura had seen her.

"I'm going to miss you too." Laura smoothed her hand over Gypsy's head, feeling the bite of tears in her eyes. "But you can't come to live with me. Philip doesn't like dogs."

Gypsy made a soft sound deep in her throat. She turned her head, bumping Laura's hand.

"I know. I don't want to go either." Laura felt a cracking inside of her, the icy walls of her defenses threatening to collapse. She couldn't allow emotion to rule her, not today.

Laura slipped Gypsy's paw from her knee and stood, shaking out the wrinkles in her gown. "You must understand," she whispered, looking down into Gypsy's sad eyes. "I'm only doing what I have to do."

The music of Mendelssohn drifted from the music room, the wedding march from his *Midsummer Night's Dream*. The notes of the string quartet shimmered around Laura as she stood frozen on the threshold. Sunlight poured through the six floor-length windows, casting everything in a soft golden glow, lending a strange surreal quality to the room. She felt numb, detached, as though she were viewing someone else's dream.

People turned on their seats as she crossed the threshold on her father's arm, murmurs of appreciation rippling through the crowd of 200 people, pounding like a drumroll with the roaring of blood in her ears. They stood as she passed, row after row of Boston's best.

Through the ivory tulle of her veil she saw Lord Austin Sinclair standing on the aisle watching her, his face reflecting the gravity she had seen the day she had told him Connor had left. And disapproval. She felt it. Sensed it. She glanced away from the truth she saw in his silvery blue eyes, staring at the arch of lacy white lilacs rising at the end of the aisle, Philip a blur in her vision.

"It isn't too late," Daniel whispered, pressing his hand over hers where she held his arm. "You can stop this."

Could she? Dear heaven, could she face all of these people and tell them she had made a dreadful mistake?

Turn back.

Turn back.

Turn back.

The words sang like a litany in her brain. And still she kept walking as though she were a mechanical doll, feet moving, touching the floor without feeling.

The fragrance of a thousand white lilacs enveloped her as she reached the altar. She tasted the sweetness on her tongue, drank it with every breath. Too sweet. Her empty stomach clenched, a stream of bitter bile etching a searing path up her throat. Philip touched her arm. She fought the urge to scream.

The voice of the minister droned in her ears like an annoying buzz amid the throb of her blood. In her mind she heard the distant notes of a piano, a Strauss waltz filling this room, Connor taking her in his arms.

Connor!

She became aware of silence, of people staring at her. Through her veil the shape of the minister was a dark outline against the bright sunlight behind him. Blood pounded behind her eyes.

They were waiting, everyone gathered for this union. There were words she must speak, vows she must make.

She glanced up at Philip, seeing his frown through the pinpoints of darkness clouding her eyes. She parted her lips, but no words escaped. And then she was sliding backward, inside of herself, sinking into a blessed dark void.

A warm breeze whispered through the valley, setting wildflowers dancing with long strands of emerald grass. Laura lifted her face to the sun, drinking in the warmth and light, issuing a silent prayer of gratitude. She had feared she would never find her way back here again.

She turned, daisies and buttercups bending beneath the sway of her white silk gown. The mountains rose as they always had in this hidden paradise, rugged black diamonds piercing the sky. Water tumbled down the face of one craggy cliff, cascading into a glittering crystal pool. Nothing had changed. Except she was alone.

"Connor!" Laura ran to the edge of the pool.

Sunlight shimmered on water so clear she could see color sparkling from the crystals embedded in the black stone lining the bottom of the natural pool—blue, green, pink, and yellow, glittering like stars in a black sky.

He wasn't here.

"Please, Connor, come to me." She turned in a circle, searching, finding no one. He had to come. He had to!

"Connor, I'm sorry." She closed her eyes, the first tears spilling from beneath her lashes, carving a hot stream across her cheek. "Please, Connor," she whispered. "I love you. I need you."

"Tell me, Laura, do you truly understand your love for Connor?"

Laura started at the sound of a woman's voice. She opened her eyes, staring at the tall, slender woman standing before her. "Who are you?"

"I am called Aisling. I am the sister of Connor's mother."

"Do you know where he is? Do you know how I can reach him?"

Aisling smiled, her pale blue eyes sparkling with humor. "The answer to both of your questions is yes."

"Tell me, please. You must tell me how I can find him."

"Are you ready to accept him for all he is?"

"Yes." Laura gripped Aisling's arm, the ruby silk of her gown warm against her palm. "Please tell me how I can find him."

"My dear child. You have always had the power to summon Connor to your side."

Laura stared into Aisling's eyes, seeing the answers, the truth of what slumbered deep in her own soul. "No."

"Can you truly deny your gifts? Do you not feel the truth deep inside your soul?"

Laura shook her head. "I'm not one of you. I'm not a witch."

"A witch is only one of many names we have been called, although we do not practice Wicca." She pushed her hair over her shoulder, the silvery blond curls tumbling to her knees, shimmering in the sunlight. "Mortals have devised a number of names for us, but I have always preferred to be called a sorceress."

"It doesn't matter what you're called." Laura backed away from this woman, trying to escape the truth. "I'm not one of you."

"You deny your heritage even now." Aisling shook her head, eyeing Laura with a measure of disappointment. "When I left you the journal, I had hoped you would come to accept all you were meant to be."

"You left the journal?"

"Yes. When Connor was a child, he told me about the little girl he had met in his dreams. I was curious about you. You see, I've heard of instances where two of our people were joined in such a way. But never have I known of a joining that could span such an enormous space of time. So I investigated. It took some time, but eventually I found you. And afterward I traced the thread of your bloodline." She smiled, her eyes filling with pride. "You, my lovely child, are a descendant of the great Alexis, who was once a king of Atlantis."

"No." Laura pressed her fingers to her lips, struggling to keep from screaming. "I can't be one of you."

"Be calm," Aisling whispered, touching her arm, the wide sleeve of her gown tumbling back from her slender wrist. "There's nothing to fear."

Laura felt a soothing heat flow into her, numbing the fear that threatened to buckle her knees.

Aisling smiled as though she knew the panic was under control. "That's much better."

Laura stared at Aisling, the perfection of her features heightened by the light that seemed to glow from within her. With her pale hair shimmering around her, she seemed an angel.

"Since my first journey into genealogy, I've become quite an expert on our descendants," Aisling said, continuing as though Laura were not staring at her like a lost little girl. "The weaving of our bloodline through the centuries is fascinating. You would be amazed if I told you the number of people wandering your world who have a drop of our blood. A few are gifted with heightened intuition and glimpses of second sight. Of course, most of them will never be able to channel the power. But I have great hopes for you."

Laura turned from Aisling. She stared into the glittering pool, seeing a stranger in her own reflection. "I don't want this."

"What you possess is a great gift."

Laura shook her head. "I'm frightened."

"There is nothing to fear." Aisling moved toward her,

her reflection shimmering gold and ruby beside Laura's pale image in the crystal pool. "There is no darkness to the power of the *Tuatha De Danann*, only light and warmth."

Laura sensed the truth of Aisling's words deep within her.

"Open yourself to the power. Feel the pulse of the earth beat in rhythm with the pulse of your heart," Aisling whispered, resting her hand on Laura's arm. "Allow the light and warmth to flow through you. The light of the sun, of the moon, and the stars."

Deep inside, Laura felt a stirring, a shimmer of light. She pulled away from Aisling's touch. "No!"

"I had such hopes for you." Aisling sighed, her lovely face reflecting her disappointment. "There are so few in your century with true potential. In time, I fear our people shall all but vanish from the world of man."

"Please," Laura whispered, unwilling to talk of magic and sorcery and the vanishing of a people she didn't really understand. There was only one thing she knew, one truth she could not deny. "I want to see Connor. I need to see him."

Aisling studied Laura a moment, one golden brow curving upward. "I wonder if you truly realize what Connor sacrificed to be with you? He gave up his home, his family, all he held dear for the chance of being with you. He came to your century and fought to become what you wanted him to become. He loved you with that type of conviction."

Every harsh word Laura had spoken to Connor shifted inside of her, pricking her like sharp thorns. "Is that what I must do? Must I too give up my home, my family, everything I hold dear to be with Connor?"

"Your love for him must be that strong. You must be prepared to sacrifice everything for him. And you must embrace the truth buried deep inside of you."

"Is this what Connor asks of me?"

Aisling smiled. "No. Connor would come to you now, if I allowed it. But I cannot. His power is strong. I must see him wed to a woman of the bloodline, a woman who does not fear the legacy of the *Sidhe*."

Laura pressed her hand to her heart at the sudden pain that sliced through her. "He is going to marry another woman?"

"In time."

Laura closed her eyes, emotions colliding inside of her, pain and need and fear she couldn't suppress.

"Did you think he would live his days without the warmth of a woman?" Aisling drew in her breath, then released it in a long sigh. "Do you truly wish that type of loneliness for him?"

Laura shook her head. "Please let me see him."

"When you have the courage to embrace the power within you, that is when you shall see Connor." Aisling walked toward the mountains, her gown of ruby silk rippling in the breeze.

"No, please, don't go!"

Aisling turned, smiling as she looked at Laura. "Search within your heart for the answers."

"Wait!"

Aisling kept walking, sunlight shimmering around her, as though the light were coming from her, her image growing lighter, lighter until there was nothing but sunlight.

"No! Please let me see him." Laura sank to her knees on the thick carpet of meadow grass and wildflowers, all of her doubts and fears coalescing into one undeniable fact—she didn't want to live without Connor. "I need you, my love."

Chapter Thirty

"Wake up, sweetheart." Someone brushed a damp cloth, cool and soft, over Laura's brow.

"Connor," Laura whispered.

"Wake up," a soft male voice commanded as strong fingers drew the damp cloth across her cheek.

Laura opened her eyes, blinking through her tears at the man who leaned over her. Sunlight glowed behind him, slipping golden fingers into his thick hair. He was frowning, deep lines carved between his brows, concern for her lingering in his dark eyes. It was a dear face, a face she loved, but it wasn't the face she longed to see. "Father."

Daniel released his breath in a long sigh. "You had us worried, sweetheart."

She was lying on the sofa in the library, a plump pillow beneath her head, her father sitting on the edge of the cushion beside her. She was back in her safe, little world. Yet a part of her, the very essence of her, remained lost in a different place and time.

"Laura, dear," Sophie said, appearing at Daniel's side, a crystal goblet trembling in her hand. "Take a few sips of water. It will help you feel better."

Laura struggled to sit. Daniel slipped his arm around her shoulders, steadying her as she reached for the glass.

"You gave us quite a fright." Sophie rested her hand on Daniel's shoulder. "We couldn't seem to reach you."

Laura looked from Sophie to her father, seeing their love for her, feeling it surround her, as solid and comforting as her father's arm around her. They were all she held dear in this world. And somehow she knew she must find the courage to leave them.

"I must say, Laura"—Esther Gardner's voice cracked like thunder in the quiet room—"you've managed to make quite a spectacle of yourself."

Laura looked past her father to where Esther Gardner was sitting on the burgundy wing-back chair near the fireplace, a queen on her throne, staring with intense disapproval at the peasant who dared disrupt her kingdom. "Thank you for your concern for my welfare."

Mrs. Gardner lifted her chin, glaring at Laura.

Philip stood beside his mother, his lips pulled into a tight line as he stared at Laura. He looked like a statue, cold white marble carved into a solid chunk of disdain.

"A case of nerves is hardly what I would expect of my future wife."

Laura tightened her fingers on the heavy crystal. She had the most insane notion to toss it at his frowning face.

"Our guests are waiting." Philip tugged on the hem of his gray-striped waistcoat. "I think we've taken enough time with this childish nonsense."

Daniel's hand flexed on her arm as he held Laura closer to his side. "I've had just about—"

"Father, please." Laura rested her hand on his chest, smiling up into his furious eyes. "I started this; let me finish it."

Daniel stared at her a moment, the fury draining from his face as understanding lit his eyes. He took the glass from her hand. "It will be my pleasure to see it."

With the help of her father's strong arm, Laura came to her feet. She crossed the room, her head held high, her hair tumbling around her shoulders, her gown a crumpled mass of ivory satin, Brussels lace, and crushed-silk orange blossoms. She paused a foot from Philip Gardner, staring up into his face, seeing the ice encrusted beneath the handsome features. In that instant she glimpsed the stark reality of the future she would have with this man if she didn't find the courage to face her true destiny.

"I think it is obvious I can't possibly hope to obtain the level of icy perfection you deserve in your wife." Laura squeezed her hands into fists at her sides. "I'm certain you are relieved to discover this before you made the tragic mistake of marrying me."

Philip's lips parted and he stared at her a moment, as though she had spoken a language he hadn't understood. "What are you saying?"

Laura smiled. "I'm saying you are free to find your perfect ice goddess, Philip."

"This is nonsense." Philip tugged on the hem of his waistcoat. "I certainly have no intention of calling off this wedding."

"You don't have to." Laura patted his chest just below the pearl stickpin nestled in the folds of his perfect white cravat. "I will."

"Young woman, I will not permit this." Mrs. Gardner rose indignantly from her throne, her apple-green satin gown rustling. "There is a room full of guests out there."

Laura faced Esther Gardner, sensing the murderous

rage emanating from her. And for some reason, Laura felt the urge to laugh. Dear heaven, she felt like tossing open the windows and singing. "I will certainly make sure they all take home a piece of cake."

Mrs. Gardner's nostrils flared as she drew an angry breath. "As much as I abhor the fact, you *will* marry my son."

Laura smiled. "Not in this lifetime."

"No one humiliates my son." Mrs. Gardner turned to face Daniel. "Tell your daughter she must uphold her engagement promise."

Daniel grinned at Mrs. Gardner. "My daughter must do what she thinks is best. All I want is her happiness."

Mrs. Gardner shook with anger, green and yellow ostrich plumes fluttering in her dark hair. "I'll see she's ruined in this town."

"There is more to this town than your closed little society." Daniel slipped his arm around Sophie's shoulders. "We don't need you or the bigoted boors you call friends."

Mrs. Gardner gasped. She snapped her jaw together so quickly her teeth clicked.

"I can see now how fortunate I am to escape the taint of this family." Philip took his mother's arm. "Come, Mother, let's leave them to their own vile company."

"You'll regret this." Esther Gardner marched toward the door, matching the stiff strides of her son.

Philip opened the door for his mother, then turned to glare at Laura. "You're smiling now, but when you find the doors to all the best houses in Boston closed to you, I'm certain you will think of this day and weep." He slammed the door behind him, rattling the crystal chimney of the wall sconce near the door.

Sophie crossed her arms, her eyes narrowing like those of a cat about to pounce. "I have half a notion to turn that young man into a frog."

Daniel frowned as he looked down into Sophie's face. "You could turn him into a frog?"

"I could try." Sophie smiled, a mischievous glint filling her eyes. "But he would probably end up with just a few warts on his nose."

Daniel shook his head as though he were still having trouble comprehending all the ramifications of marrying a witch. He looked at his daughter, his lips curving into a smile. "I should tell our guests about your change of plans."

"Thank you, Father." Laura took a deep breath, trying to ease the tension in her chest. "But I'll do it."

"I'm very proud of you." He smiled, the warmth of his love shining in his eyes. "You've shown a great deal of courage this day."

Laura thought of the courage she must find to gain what she needed to survive: Connor.

Austin swirled the brandy in his snifter, watching light twist in shimmering strands of gold through the amber liquid. His ancestors had used precious amber to pierce the mists of time, to peer into the future. But he knew, as the ancient ones had always known, that the future remained liquid, each vision as fragile and shifting as a reflection on water, each change in the past a ripple distorting that reflection. Still, he longed for the power of divination, the power to see what might come to pass. He needed to believe there was a chance Connor might return and bring with him the knowledge his people had long forgotten.

"I didn't think Miss Sullivan would go through with the wedding," Henry said. "Not with her link to Connor."

Austin glanced up from his glass. Henry Thayer stood at a window in his library, staring out at the common. They were alone in the room, free to speak of secrets.

"I didn't realize you believed there was a link between Connor and Laura Sullivan."

"Did you think you were the only one who could see the connection?" Henry turned to look at him, moonlight brushing soft silver across one half of his face. "Did you believe you alone could unravel the mystery of Miss Sullivan? It's obvious she is one of the *Sidhe*."

Austin held Henry's steady gaze, careful to keep his own thoughts and emotions carefully guarded. "Is that what you believe?"

"Don't play games with me, young man. You know as well as I do what the connection between Laura Sullivan and Connor implies—she is of the bloodline. And I would wager she will waste little time in bringing him back here."

"I hope she does. He can teach us a great deal."

"Yes, of course he can." A smile curved Henry's lips as he lifted his glass. "Let us make a toast: To Connor, and his swift return."

The back of Austin's neck prickled as he held Henry's emotionless gaze. "To Connor, and all he may teach us."

"Are you certain you won't come with us, dear?" Sophie asked.

"The two of you go along and have a nice time." Laura gave her aunt a hug, long and hard, breathing in the fragrance of roses. "Don't worry about me. I want some time to myself."

Daniel cupped his daughter's chin and lifted her face, frowning as he looked at her. "We don't have to go to the theater tonight. We can stay here with you."

"I don't want you to worry about me. I'm fine." Laura threw her arms around his neck and hugged him. "No matter what happens, always remember that I love you," She whispered into the collar of his evening coat. "Both of you."

401

Daniel hugged her hard, then pulled back. "Are you sure you're all right?"

Laura nodded, tears glittering in her eyes as she looked up at him and wondered how she would find the courage to leave him. "I love you both so much, that's all. Now you'd better go or you'll miss the beginning of the play."

Sophie glanced up at Daniel, uncertainty in her eyes.

Daniel frowned. "Laura, I think we should stay here with you tonight."

"I'm fine." Laura touched her father's cheek. "Go, have a good time."

Sophie squeezed Laura's hand. "Tomorrow we'll go for a sleigh ride in the country."

"Tomorrow." She walked with them to the door and stood watching as they walked down the hall, leaving her alone with her doubts.

Gypsy bumped Laura's hand with her cold nose. The dog was sitting beside her, looking up at her as though she wanted to give comfort. Laura patted the dog's head, smiling as she looked into Gypsy's wise face. There were moments when she believed the animal could sense her every emotion.

"Connor was right about you," she said, stroking Gypsy's head. "Affection and loyalty, that's what you've given me."

Gypsy tilted her head, perking her ears as though intent on Laura's every word.

"For the first time in my life I feel as though this house is truly my home. It just doesn't seem fair. Now, when I finally know the love of my father, Aunt Sophie, you, I must abandon everything." Laura glanced at the windows, where moonlight glowed against the panes. "Yet how can I stay without Connor? It's as though a part of me has been ripped away."

The journal lay on the velvet cushion of the wing-back chair near the fireplace, firelight flickering across the red leather cover. The book seemed to glow, red leather against dark burgundy velvet, beckoning her, luring her to the truth and the man she could only have if she faced that truth.

As though she had no conscious will, she crossed the room, drawn to the fire and her destiny. The book was warm to her touch, the leather soft against her fingers.

"I have to know the truth," she whispered, glancing at the dog who had curled into a ball on the carpet beside the chair. Laura sank to the chair, opened the cover, and began to read the history and magic of her people.

Three hours later, Laura closed the book. She stared into the flames on the hearth, words swirling in her brain. As much as she wanted to deny it, the stories she had read, the legends of an ancient civilization, the words written in the journal Aisling had left for her, all whispered to a truth hidden deep within her. It was all familiar and strange in the same instant, as though a part of her remembered a life lived long ago, a past too distant to be within her reckoning.

"It's all so hard to believe." She stood and moved past Gypsy, walking toward the fire, seeking the heat of the flames. "And yet I can't deny the feeling I have that everything I've read is true."

She watched the flames lick at the logs, orange and red tongues devouring the helpless wood, just as the flames of truth devoured all her denials. "I'm one of them, the *Sidhe*. I feel it."

"Yes. I suspect you are."

Laura jumped at the sound of a male voice. She turned, staring at the man who stood near the library door. "Mr. Thayer, what are you doing here?"

Henry moved away from the closed door, smiling as he walked toward her. "I've had my suspicions about you ever since I learned Connor had traveled through time to be with you."

She stared at him, her mind swirling with confusion. "How did you know about Connor?"

"That's a very long story." He slipped his hand into his pocket and withdrew a small pistol. "And I'm afraid there isn't any time to tell you."

Laura stepped back, staring at the pistol, the steel glinting red as it captured the firelight. "What are you doing?"

"I'm making certain Connor won't be able to find his way back to this time." Henry frowned as he looked down at her. "I do so hate to take your life, but there is no other way. I can't allow you to bring him back here."

Laura stared at the pistol, her mind refusing to accept the reality of steel glinting in the firelight. "I don't understand."

"Connor would upset the balance of things in this time. There would once again be those who could wield the power, and those who could not. Why, he could create a whole new dynasty of the *Sidhe*, disrupt everything. I'm afraid I can't allow it to happen." He lifted the pistol, pointing it at her heart. "I'm terribly sorry."

Laura tried to draw breath to scream, but the air caught in her throat. A dark growl pierced the silence. From the corner of her eye she saw Gypsy move, a streak of white headed for Thayer.

Henry caught the movement as well. He moved with the reflexes of a much younger man, pivoting, swinging the gun into position. Laura flinched with the explosion of the gunshot, but it was the dog who had been hit.

Gypsy yelped. She jerked back, then fell to the carpet, blood staining the white fur of her chest.

"Gypsy!" Laura rushed to the dog's side, falling to her knees beside the animal. A weak whimper escaped Gypsy as Laura stroked her head.

"I'm sorry about this. You have to realize I'm unaccustomed to violence."

Laura stared up at him, tears blurring her eyes. "Monster!"

"You don't understand." Thayer wiped his hand across his damp brow. "I must do this. I'm from a place called Avallon. Long ago we abandoned the power. Connor would turn us around. He would destroy everything as we know it. He is dangerous. You are dangerous."

"You're insane!"

"No." Henry raised the pistol, using both hands to steady his aim. "I'm doing this for the greater good."

Awaken the power inside of you—Aisling's voice whispered in Laura's mind. Laura turned, looking for the fair-haired sorceress, finding no one in the room except Thayer.

Henry looked around. "What are you doing?"

Reach deep inside of you. Feel the pulse of your heart, the pulse that throbs from the earth itself—Aisling's voice whispered.

Laura closed her eyes.

"Answer me!" Henry demanded.

Laura ignored him, listening only to the voice that whispered in her mind—*Feel the light that shimmers within you, the light of the sun, of the moon, of the stars.*

Laura drew in her breath, then let the air flow out of her in a long, slow exhale as she welcomed the light, embraced it, allowed it to fill her, until it seemed to saturate her very soul.

Call to Connor. Bring him to your side.

"I'll shoot. I swear! Tell me what you're doing."

Laura recalled the words that had brought Connor to her a lifetime ago.

Hear me, Lady of the moon.
Your pull is great.

You move the tide.
Now bring my beloved to my side.

In her mind Laura repeated the words over and over again, feeling the light shimmer inside of her.

"What's happening?" Thayer asked, his voice tinged with panic.

The wind whipped against the windows, rattling the panes. Laura opened her eyes, staring at the windows.

"What are you doing?" Henry jumped as the fire blazed on the hearth behind him, flames leaping upward. "Tell me what's happening!"

The air pressed against Laura. She welcomed the feel of it, like Connor's arms wrapping around her. A familiar fragrance drifted in the air, the smell of pine and herbs, the pungent scent of burning candles. This was the opening of the portal of time, the connection between this world and Connor's world.

"He's coming," Laura whispered.

"No!" Henry shouted as the electric lights in the crystal-and-brass fixture overhead flickered. The room pulsed with a brilliant glow before the lights faded to black. "Stop this!"

Laura rose to her feet, staring at the moonlight streaming through the windows, holding her breath as she waited. Particles of light gathered, glimmering, shimmering, coalescing, sculpting the figure of a man.

Henry whimpered behind her.

The moonlight faded. Electric lights flickered overhead, flooding the room with a golden glow. And Connor stood before her, pulsing with vitality. He smiled when he saw her, his eyes filling with a warmth that had haunted her dreams. Sapphire-blue wool hugged his shoulders, the shirt tucked into black leather breeches that molded his slim hips, the long muscular length of his legs. It seemed an eternity since she had gazed upon his potent male beauty.

"Connor," she whispered, emotion strangling her voice. She took a step toward him, needing to feel the warmth of him wrap around her.

Henry gripped her arm. He yanked her back against his chest, holding her like a shield. "Don't move."

"Let me go!" Laura struggled against Henry's grasp, until the cold steel of a pistol pressed against her cheek.

Chapter Thirty-one

Connor clenched his hands into fists at his sides, his eyes narrowing as he stared at the man holding Laura. "Take your hands off of her."

"I'll kill her if you come near me," Henry shouted. "In case you don't know what this is, it's a pistol. The one I used to shoot you. If you don't want her to end up like this dog, then do as I say."

Connor glanced at the dog lying near Laura's feet, blood staining her thick white fur. He knew so little about the weapons of this age. How quickly could Thayer use the pistol?

"I can shoot her before you have a chance to move," Henry said, prodding Laura's cheek with the pistol.

Connor looked into Laura's eyes, seeing her fear, feeling a steel band wrap around his heart when he realized he could lose her. "What do you want?"

"I want you to leave this time and promise you will never return."

"And you will let her go without harm?"

Henry smiled. "Yes."

"Connor, don't believe him," Laura shouted. "He wants to kill both of—"

"Quiet!" Thayer shouted, pushing the pistol hard against her cheek.

Laura's soft moan of pain ripped through Connor. He looked at Thayer, knowing he could not trust the man. He would have to pit his abilities against this modern sorcery. He directed his gaze at the deadly piece of metal in the man's hand.

Thayer screamed, jerking his hand away from the pistol, which suddenly felt like fire in his grip. He stumbled back from Laura. As the weapon tumbled to the floor, Connor waved his hand.

Thayer gasped as he left the floor, soaring upward until he bumped against the carved plaster ceiling. "Get me down from here!"

Connor ignored the man's screams, opening his arms as Laura ran toward him.

"Connor!" She threw her arms around his shoulders, and he lifted her against him, absorbing her shivers as she trembled in his arms.

He pressed his face into the soft curve of her neck and shoulder, breathing in the fragrance of spring flowers. Her love for him poured over him, flowing into him, saturating him with a shimmering light.

"I was afraid you wouldn't come." She pulled back in his arms, tears glittering in the forest green depths of her eyes. "Can you forgive me?"

"You are a part of me." He brushed his lips over hers. "How could I turn away from my heart?"

"Get me down from here!" Thayer shouted.

Connor lowered Laura, holding her close once her feet touched the floor. He glanced up at the man who was pressed flush against the ceiling, arms and legs spread against the scrolls molded in the white plaster, like a gray moth pinned to a board. "You'll stay there until I decide what to do with you."

"You don't understand. I'm afraid of heights! Please get me down from—"

Connor waved his hand. Henry's handkerchief flew from his coat pocket, slamming into his mouth, cutting off his words. "That's better."

"I'm very happy to see you, dark warrior," Aisling said, her voice weakened by pain.

Connor looked to where Gypsy had been lying. In the dog's place, Aisling lay upon the carpet, blood staining her white robe below her right shoulder.

"Connor, my darling," Aisling said. "I realize I've startled you, but I could use some help."

Her words snapped Connor out of his startled immobility. He rushed to her side and dropped to his knees beside her. "Aisling, what happened?"

"I didn't have time to alter my form. I tried to stop him the only way I could, in the form of Gypsy." She moaned as he lifted her, cradling her head and shoulders in his lap. "I'm afraid there are a few disadvantages in changing shape."

Connor shook his head as he looked down at her. "Your way of keeping an eye on me?"

Aisling smiled. "It seemed like a good idea at the time."

"Aisling?" Laura sank to the floor beside them, the emerald wool of her gown billowing around her. "It's really you."

Connor looked across his aunt at Laura. "How do you know my aunt?"

Laura smiled. "She saved my life."

"And now you can save mine, dear child."

"Me?" Laura stared at Aisling as though the other woman had lost her senses. "I can't."

"Yes, you can."

"You've lost a great deal of blood." Connor rested his hand against Aisling's pale cheek. "Let me help you."

"No." Aisling pushed aside his hand. She stared up at him, determination glowing along with pain in her silvery blue eyes. "Give Laura a chance to feel the best of her power."

Connor looked into Laura's eyes, seeing the glimmer of fear that remained with the last traces of uncertainty.

"Are you ready to accept your proper place beside Connor?" Aisling asked, her voice barely rising above a whisper.

Laura hesitated a moment before she touched Aisling's arm. "Tell me what I must do."

Aisling smiled. "Reach inside of you, touch the light within, allow the power to flow through you."

Connor watched as Laura closed her eyes. He sensed the power stir within her. He felt her fear burn away in the cleansing light that flowed through her, watched the soft glow come into her cheeks and her hands as she touched Aisling, resting her palm above the wound.

Connor glanced up as the door to the library opened. Daniel Sullivan stood on the threshold beside Sophie, both sharing a shocked expression as they took in the scene.

Don't speak, Connor whispered into their minds. *Don't move.*

Both Daniel and Sophie stayed where they were, staring as if mesmerized by the sight of Laura. Connor watched her, realizing she had cast away her fears, her doubts, for one reason alone. Within him, he felt the pure glow of Laura's power, the golden aura of her love for him. The connection he had felt with her from the time he was a boy culminated in this moment of acceptance. Gone were the secrets and fears. Only love remained.

411

* * *

"Well done, my dear," Aisling said, resting her hands over the hand Laura still held against her shoulder.

Laura opened her eyes and stared down at Aisling. Color had returned to her cheeks; the strain of pain had lifted from her beautiful features. "Are you going to be all right?"

"Look for yourself." Aisling smiled as she lifted Laura's hand away from her shoulder.

Through the bloody tear in the white silk of Aisling's robe, Laura could see the smooth, pale flesh beneath—whole, unscarred. "Oh, my gracious," she whispered, sitting back on her heels. "Did I really . . . did I do that?"

"You certainly did." Aisling sat up, frowning as she glanced down at her bloody gown. "But I look terrible." She snapped her fingers. The white gown disappeared in a heartbeat, replaced by a gown of ruby silk, gold threads weaving through the shimmering material. "That's better."

"Laura, is this lady a witch too?" Sophie asked.

Laura glanced over her shoulder, smiling when she saw her father and Sophie. "This is Connor's aunt, Aisling. And she prefers to be called a sorceress."

Aisling rose from the floor in a swirl of ruby silk. "How very nice to meet you."

Connor smiled as he offered Laura his hand, a wide, embracing smile that told her everything would now be as it should be, as it had been destined to be from the beginning of time. His strong fingers closed around her hand as he helped her to her feet.

Daniel released his breath in a long sigh. "I guess I'm the only one in the room who doesn't have any magic in his blood."

"You and Mr. Thayer," Aisling said, pointing toward the ceiling.

Daniel followed her gesture, staring a moment before

he found his voice. "Laura, do you mind telling me why Henry Thayer is plastered to the ceiling?"

"I'm not exactly certain." Laura looked at Connor, assuring herself he was still there. If she lived a thousand years, she would never tire of looking at him. "He said he's from a place called Avallon, and he wanted to stop me from bringing Connor back to this time."

"I see." Daniel rubbed the back of his neck. "So Henry Thayer isn't exactly what he appears to be."

"I think we should send for Lord Austin Sinclair," Connor said, slipping his arm around Laura's shoulders. "He'll have a good idea of what we should do with Mr. Thayer."

"Lord Sinclair?" Daniel shook his head. "I don't know why I should be surprised."

Laura slipped her arms around Connor's waist, snuggling close to his warmth, holding him, afraid someone might steal him from her. "I had a feeling Lord Sinclair knew about you."

Connor grinned. "I have a feeling he's a relative."

"Quite so," Aisling said. "His father Rhys can trace his ancestors back to the great Alexis, as can both you and Laura."

Connor grinned down at Laura. "You're a descendant of Alexis?"

"So it would seem," Laura whispered, still amazed by everything she had learned this day.

"But what I found truly interesting about Austin Sinclair is that his mother, Brianna, is a direct descendant of Connor's brother Brendan." Aisling tossed her hair over her shoulder, smiling as though she were pleased with herself as she faced Connor. "It would seem that although your brother displayed no talent, Viking that he is, Brendan was able to pass on the bloodline. Though I doubt Brianna is even aware of her heritage. Rhys, her husband, was drawn to her without knowing why."

"I get the impression you've been spying on these people," Connor said.

Aisling shrugged. "I prefer to say I've kept a vigil over our people for the past few centuries."

"Only a vigil?" Connor asked.

"In my studies, I have found that often two people of the bloodline are drawn together without even knowing the connection they share. In a few cases, I may have helped smooth out problems here and there." Aisling smiled in a way that made Laura wonder what type of matchmaking this beautiful sorceress had accomplished. "It was your connection with Laura that sparked my interest in this field. And I'm very glad to see you've managed to overcome your differences."

"Thank you." Laura rested her hand on Connor's chest, feeling the warmth of his skin radiate through the sapphire wool of his shirt, absorbing each strong beat of his heart. "For everything."

Aisling bowed her head. "My pleasure."

"I'm afraid I neglected to welcome you back, Connor." Daniel offered Connor his hand. "I'm happy you're going to be part of this family."

Tears welled in Laura's eyes as she watched Connor shake her father's hand. How could she tell her father they wouldn't be staying in this world?

"After I fetch Austin Sinclair, there are a few things I would like to discuss with you, my dear Sophie." Aisling slipped her arm through Sophie's and started walking toward the door.

"Do you suppose you can teach me to straighten out my magic?" Sophie asked, looking up at Aisling, hope shining in her blue eyes.

"Perhaps." Aisling paused after going only a few feet. She glanced past Sophie at Daniel. "Daniel, you and Sophie are planning to marry soon, are you not?"

"We plan to marry in three days." Daniel frowned,

looking at Aisling with an equal amount of caution and suspicion in his eyes. "Why do you ask?"

"Because your son and daughter will be born in eight full cycles of the moon."

Daniel's mouth dropped open. "My son and daughter?"

Aisling smiled, pleased with herself. "Yes."

Sophie stared up at Aisling, her eyes wide with wonder. "I'm going to have a baby?"

"You're going to have two." Aisling patted Sophie's arm. "Twins are quite common with our people."

"Oh, my." Sophie glanced back at Laura. "You're going to have a brother and a sister."

"That's wonderful." Laura squeezed Connor close, wondering if she would ever be allowed to see them.

"Daniel, think of it," Sophie said as she left the room with Aisling. "A son and a daughter."

Daniel paused in the doorway, looking at Laura, his love for her warming the depths of his dark eyes. "It looks as though we both have been blessed with magic."

"Yes." Laura closed her eyes as her father left the room. She turned her face into Connor's chest, breathing in the scent of citrus and musk, allowing the heat of his body to warm the chill deep inside of her.

"What's wrong, love?" Connor slid his hand down her back. "Why are you sad?"

"I'm sorry, I don't mean to color the joy of being with you again with sadness, but . . . I'm going to miss them."

"Miss them?"

"My father, Aunt Sophie." Laura held him closer, her arms cinched around his waist. "I know what I must do. Aisling told me I must abandon my home and family if I wanted to be with you. And I will." She tried to steady her voice. "I promise I'll go with you, no matter where."

He brushed his cheek against her hair. "You would go anywhere with me?"

She nodded, the soft wool of his shirt absorbing her tears. "Anywhere."

He rested his palm against the curve of her neck, his long fingers curving against her nape. "Even back to my own time?"

She shivered with the fear of returning to that brutal time. "Yes."

With long, soft strokes, he brushed his fingertips over her neck, the warmth of his touch soaking into her skin. "You do know you will have to learn to eat with your fingers."

She sniffed. "I'll manage."

His chest rose beneath her cheek as he inhaled, slowly and long. He slipped his fingers beneath her chin and tipped back her head, smiling at her. "There isn't any chocolate ice cream in my time."

She stared through her tears into his smiling face, seeing the mischief sparkling in his blue eyes. "Are you teasing me?"

"I'm afraid I am." He slid his thumb over her cheek, wiping away her tears. "I have no intention of taking you back to my time."

His words hit her like a hard fist to her jaw. "You're going to leave me here?"

"Laura," he whispered, cupping her face in his hands. "You're my heart; how could I ever leave you?"

"But—"

He kissed her, sipping the words she might have spoken from her lips. He slid his lips across hers, soft and gentle. She slipped her arms around his neck, holding him close, absorbing the warmth of his body like the first flowers of spring absorbed the heat of the sun. All her fear withered under the heat of his kiss. All her sadness melted into a simmering pool of need.

"I was meant to come to you," he whispered against her lips. "I was meant to live in this time."

She slid her fingers down his cheek, his skin smooth and warm beneath her touch. "You're going to stay?"

He turned his head, pressing his lips against her fingertips. "For eternity, my love."

Someone cleared his throat.

Connor glanced over Laura's head, smiling as he saw Lord Austin Sinclair on the threshold of the library. "Come in."

"I'm sorry to interrupt." Austin smiled as he looked from Laura to Connor. "But Aisling told me I would find Henry Thayer in here."

Connor gestured toward the ceiling. "I don't think he's going to cause any trouble for the moment."

Austin glanced up, his eyes growing wide as he saw Henry plastered against the ceiling. "You were curious about the power Connor might be able to channel, Henry. Now it looks as though you're getting a taste of it."

Henry groaned against the handkerchief stuffed in his mouth.

"I suspected he might be responsible for shooting you, but there was nothing I could do without proof." Austin rubbed his temple. "I was careless this evening. He slipped a drug into my brandy. If Aisling hadn't come for me, I would still be sound asleep in his library. I'm sorry I couldn't prevent this."

"I understand." Connor slipped his arm around Laura's shoulders, needing to keep her close. "What shall you do with him?"

"Take him back to Avallon. We have ways of rehabilitating people." Austin studied Connor a moment. "I was hoping you would also come back with me. There is so much you can teach us."

Connor felt Laura stiffen beside him. He stroked her

arm, silently reassuring her, even though he wanted this chance to bring his people out of the darkness. "I'm not certain that will be possible."

"I believe there was more than one reason you were brought to this place in time." Austin glanced at Laura, then back at Connor, his eyes revealing his total understanding of the reason behind Connor's reluctance. "We come from the same wellspring, you and I. But the power has been drained over the centuries, forced deep inside of us, like a stream running far beneath the earth. With your help, we may learn to channel the power once more. Without your help, I fear the abilities we once nourished will turn to dust."

Connor tightened his hand on Laura's arm. "My life is here with Laura."

Laura touched his cheek, her hand soft against his skin. There were no tears in her eyes as she looked up at him, only the glow of her love for him. "I think we should go to Avallon. I too have much to learn of my ancestors."

Connor covered her hand with his own, holding her palm against his cheek. "You would go to Avallon with me?"

"I would go to the end of time with you. I've waited a lifetime for you." She kissed the hand he held over hers. "You are my love, my heart, the man who has made my dreams a reality."

Connor turned his face, pressing his lips against the palm of her hand, knowing at last he had found his place in this world.

Laura stood at the bow of Lord Austin Sinclair's private yacht. It had been only a few hours since they had left Boston and the powerful vessel had already carried them into warmer climes. Waves crashed over the sleek steel bow, tossing mist into the warm air that brushed her cheeks with the tang of the sea. She watched the sun paint pink and gold streaks across the clouds as it sank toward the horizon, and recalled the events of this, her wedding day.

The morning had bloomed with sunlight, the golden light surrounding her as Laura had stood beside Connor, beneath an arch of white roses in the music room, her voice ringing clearly as she spoke the vows that confirmed the joining of their souls. Sophie had stood in her mother's wedding gown, between Laura and Daniel, sharing vows with her first and only love. A crowd of people had filled the room, applauding this joining of hearts and souls, friends who ignored the dictates of Boston's tarnished queen of society.

"We'll return often." Connor slipped his arms around her waist and rested his cheek against her hair. "And your family will always be welcome in Avallon."

Laura turned in her husband's arms, looking up into his handsome face. The setting sun painted gold along the high crests of his cheeks, gilded the tips of his thick black lashes. "Teach me how to make magic."

He pressed his lips against her brow and she felt the curve of his smile. "You've already bewitched me, my beautiful enchantress."

She slid her hands across his broad shoulders, feeling the warmth of firm muscles beneath the white linen of his shirt, the full sleeves billowing in the wind. "I want to know all of your secrets."

He looked down at her with mischief sparkling in his eyes, the warm wind whipping at his thick black hair. "And what shall you give in return, my lady?"

She traced the curve of his smile with her fingertip, feeling the damp warmth of his breath against her skin. "I thought a Viking always took what he wanted."

He winked at her. "Not if he can win what he so desires."

She slipped her arms around his neck. "And do I have what you want?"

He pulled her close, pressing the hard length of his body against her. "You are everything I have always wanted."

"Then take what you want, my love." She stared up into his eyes, seeing eternity in the endless blue depths. "My heart, my soul, all I am and ever will be."

"Edaina." He lowered his lips to hers and sealed the vows they had made in a thousand lifetimes. "Forever, my love."

Epilogue

Avallon, Brazil, 1895

"I should be the one to teach the children how to fly," Ciara said, lifting her chin as she stared at her sister. "After all, I am their grandmother."

Aisling planted her hands on her slim hips. "As I recall, Ciara, you didn't even want Connor to come to this century, and now you spend as much time here as you do in Erin. Aren't you afraid your Viking will miss you?"

Connor sat in a burgundy leather wing-back chair in the library of his house in Avallon, watching his mother and his aunt. They stood face-to-face in a pool of sunlight spilling through the open French doors, oblivious to the soft breeze that carried the scent of roses from the garden and stirred the sapphire and scarlet silk of their gowns.

His children sat on the carpet nearby—Quinn, his five-year-old son, and Glenna, his three-year-old daughter. A castle the children had fashioned from blocks stood on the green-and-gold carpet between them, but Quinn and Glenna both sat with their dark heads tipped back, staring at the bickering women.

"I would think it's about time you found a mate, Aisling," Ciara said, smoothing the wide sleeve of her sapphire silk robe. "If you had children of your own, you just might leave my grandchildren alone."

Aisling twitched her pendant between her fingers, the emerald eye of the bird carved into the ancient gold medallion winking in the sunlight. "If it hadn't been for me, Connor would never have found Laura in the first place, and you wouldn't have these lovely children to fawn over."

"How dare you—" Ciara's words ended in a gasp as she floated from the floor.

"Great Alexis!" Aisling followed her, her gown of scarlet silk fluttering around her.

Quinn clapped his hands. Glenna giggled.

"Connor!" both women shouted.

Connor shrugged his shoulders, smiling up at the women who floated five feet off the floor. "I didn't do a thing."

"But if you didn't," Aisling said, looking down at the children, "then . . ."

"That means . . ." Ciara smiled as she gazed down at her grandchildren. "How very talented you are, my darlings. Now let Grandmama down."

Glenna shook her head, giggling.

"Glenna, Quinn. I'm very proud of you, but you must let me down," Aisling said.

Quinn lifted a block and placed it on top of his castle. "When you promise not to fight."

"We weren't really fighting, darling," Aisling said. "We were just having a little disagreement."

Quinn shook his head. "Sounded like fightin' to me."

"Connor, do something with your children!" Ciara demanded.

Connor rose from his chair and bent on one knee beside his children. Quinn looked at his father, his forest green eyes filled with sudden doubts. Glenna looked up at Connor with her summer blue eyes, looking as innocent as an angel. Both children were holding their breaths, waiting to hear what he would say.

"That's a nice castle," Connor said, placing a block on the wing Quinn had started. "I'm very proud of both of you."

Glenna linked her fingers and grinned. Quinn winked at his father. It was all Connor could do to keep from laughing.

"Connor, tell them to get us down!" Aisling shouted as Connor strolled toward the open French doors.

"I wouldn't dream of interfering with your lessons." Connor turned as he reached the doors leading to the gardens, smiling up at his aunt and mother. "Look how much they've learned." He left the room, chuckling softly as the voices of his aunt and his mother tumbled into the gardens.

"Quinn, Glenna, let me down, my sweet angels," Aisling said.

"I'll give you a nice piece of gingerbread if you let Grandmama down."

Connor found his wife in the gardens. Laura was sitting on a black stone bench in the center of a five-pointed star fashioned from colorful roses. She was holding a bowl of ice cream, staring out across the ruins of ancient Avallon that stood nestled in the valley below.

Although his booted footsteps were silent against the black stones that shaped the paths between the roses, Laura turned when he drew near, as though she could sense his presence. She smiled, the warmth in her eyes beckoning him.

"Ice cream before lunch?" he asked as he walked toward her, blossoms of red and white and pink bobbing as he passed.

"I find I've been terribly corrupted." She smiled up at him, mischief glittering in the forest green depths of her eyes. "Want some?"

"Please." He knelt before her, easing between her knees, the emerald silk of her trousers sliding against the black linen of his own. Laura had long ago abandoned stiff corsets and gowns for the soft, flowing tunics and trousers popular with the women of Avallon. Only on their frequent trips to Boston did she don the trappings of a proper Victorian lady.

She dipped her spoon in the creamy confection and lifted it toward his lips. "Have a taste."

He parted his lips, allowing her to slip the spoon into his mouth, the sweet, creamy chocolate melting over his tongue. "I can think of a better way to taste it," he said, taking the spoon from her fingers.

The rose-scented breeze ruffled her unbound hair, brushing the silky strands against his bare arm, where he had rolled the sleeves of his white shirt up to his elbows. "Can you?"

"Trust me." He set the silver spoon on the bench beside her and dipped the tip of his forefinger into the chocolate ice cream in her bowl.

"Still eating with your fingers?"

"Some treats are better eaten with your fingers." He slid his fingertip over her lips, leaving a trail of ice cream in his wake. "And your tongue."

"Wicked barbarian." She smiled as he slid his hand into the golden hair at her nape and drew her close.

"Luscious lady," he whispered before pressing his lips to hers.

Cool ice cream. Warm lips. Soft. Sweet. Enticing.

He traced the curve of her lips with his tongue, licking away the ice cream, seeking the sweet nectar of her mouth. She opened to him, sliding her hand into the thick hair that tumbled over the collar of his white silk shirt in unruly waves.

"I can think of even better ways to eat ice cream," she whispered against his mouth. "Let's go upstairs to our room."

He nipped her chin. "You wouldn't have anything wicked in mind, would you?"

"Only something a marauding Viking once taught me to do with honey."

He smiled against her neck. "I'm your slave, my lady; do with me as you wish."

Laura giggled and snapped her fingers. They disappeared with a whisper of wind, leaving behind a silver spoon glittering in the sunlight. And in a bedroom overlooking the roses and an ancient city their ancestors had carved from stone, the sorcerer and his lady found their own enchanted paradise.

Author's Note

When I read myths and legends I often wonder if there isn't a measure of fact mixed in with the fantasy. Although Connor was conceived in my imagination, he has a basis in Irish legend.

While doing research for *A Quest of Dreams,* the book that first introduced the people of Avallon, I discovered some interesting theories linking Atlantis to the *Tuatha De Danann* of Irish legend. Although the very existence of Atlantis has been disputed over the years, I prefer to believe the island nation did exist. Perhaps it's because my mother's maiden name is McTigue, and we of Irish blood tend to believe there is more to the world than what we can see, but I prefer to believe magic exists. Do the *Tuatha De Danann* live today? Think of the possibilities.

My thanks to all of you who have written to tell me how much you enjoyed the previous novels involving the people of Avallon, *A Quest of Dreams* and *Decep-*

426

tions and Dreams. I hope you enjoyed the time you spent with Connor and Laura. Perhaps one day we will return to Avallon.

My next novel from Leisure, *Scoundrel,* is set in Regency England. It's the story of a woman who invents a husband only to have her fictitious mate march into her life. Although Emily Maitland believes the man posing as her husband is a fortune-hunting scoundrel, Simon St. James is actually a spy for England in search of a traitor. I had a great time with Emily and Simon, plunging them into adventure with smugglers and spies. and watching them fall in love.

I love to hear from readers. Please enclose a self-addressed, stamped envelope with your letter.

Debra Dier
P.O. Box 4147
Hazelwood, MO 63042-0747

SPECIAL SNEAK PREVIEW FOLLOWS!

Madeline Baker writing as Amanda Ashley

Cursed by the darkness, he searches through the ages for the redeeming light, the one woman who can save him. A creature of moonlight and fancy, she fears the handsome stranger whose eyes promise endless ecstasy even while his mouth whispers dark secrets. They are two people longing for fulfillment, yearning for a love like no other. Alone, they will face a desolate destiny. Together, they will share undying passion, defy eternity, and embrace the night.

He walked the streets for hours after he left the orphanage, his thoughts filled with Sara, her fragile beauty, her sweet innocence, her unwavering trust. She had accepted him into her life without question, and the knowledge cut him to the quick. He did not like deceiving her, hiding the dark secret of what he was, nor did he like to think about how badly she would be hurt when his nighttime visits ceased, as they surely must.

He had loved her from the moment he first saw her, but always from a distance, worshiping her as the moon might worship the sun, basking in her heat, her light, but wisely staying away lest he be burned.

And foolishly, he had strayed too close. He had soothed her tears, held her in his arms, and now he was paying the price. He was burning, like a moth drawn to a flame. Burning with need. With desire. With an unholy lust, not for her body, but for the very essence of her life.

It sickened him that he should want her that way, that he could even consider such a despicable thing. And yet he could think of little else. Ah, to hold her in his arms, to feel his body become one with hers as he drank of her sweetness. . . .

For a moment, he closed his eyes and let himself imagine it, and then he swore a long vile oath filled with pain and longing.

Hands clenched, he turned down a dark street, his self-anger turning to loathing, and the loathing to rage. He felt the need to kill, to strike out, to make someone else suffer as he was suffering.

Pity the poor mortal who next crossed his path, he thought. Then he gave himself over to the hunger pounding through him.

She woke covered with perspiration, Gabriel's name on her lips. Shivering, she drew the covers up to her chin.

It had only been a dream. Only a dream.

She spoke the words aloud, finding comfort in the sound of her own voice. A distant bell chimed the hour. Four o'clock.

Gradually, her breathing returned to normal. Only a dream, she said again, but it had been so real. She had felt the cold breath of the night, smelled the rank odor of fear rising from the body of the faceless man cowering in the shadows. She had sensed a deep anger, a wild uncontrollable evil personified by a being in a flowing black cloak. Even now, she could feel his anguish, his loneliness, the alienation that cut him off from the rest of humanity.

It had all been so clear in the dream, but now it made no sense. No sense at all.

With a slight shake of her head, she snuggled deeper under the covers and closed her eyes.

It was just a dream, nothing more.

Sunk in the depths of despair, Gabriel prowled the deserted abbey. What had happened to his self-control? Not for centuries had he taken enough blood to kill, only enough to assuage the pain of the hunger, to ease his unholy thirst.

A low groan rose in his throat. Sara had happened. He wanted her and he couldn't have her. Somehow, his desire and his frustration had gotten tangled up with his lust for blood.

It couldn't happen again. It had taken him centuries to learn to control the hunger, to give himself the illusion that he was more man than monster.

Had he been able, he would have prayed for forgiveness, but he had forfeited the right to divine intervention long ago.

"Where will we go tonight?"

Gabriel stared at her. She'd been waiting for him again, clothed in her new dress, her eyes bright with anticipation. Her goodness drew him, soothed him, calmed his dark side even as her beauty, her innocence, teased his desire.

He stared at the pulse throbbing in her throat. "Go?"

Sara nodded.

With an effort, he lifted his gaze to her face. "Where would you like to go?"

"I don't suppose you have a horse?"

"A horse?"

"I've always wanted to ride."

He bowed from the waist. "Whatever you wish, milady," he said. "I'll not be gone long."

It was like having found a magic wand, Sara mused

as she waited for him to return. She had only to voice her desire, and he produced it.

Twenty minutes later, she was seated before him on a prancing black stallion. It was a beautiful animal, tall and muscular, with a flowing mane and tail.

She leaned forward to stroke the stallion's neck. His coat felt like velvet beneath her hand. "What's his name?"

"Necromancer," Gabriel replied, pride and affection evident in his tone.

"Necromancer? What does it mean?"

"One who communicates with the spirits of the dead."

Sara glanced at him over her shoulder. "That seems an odd name for a horse."

"Odd, perhaps," Gabriel replied cryptically, "but fitting."

"Fitting? In what way?"

"Do you want to ride, Sara, or spend the night asking foolish questions?"

She pouted prettily for a moment and then grinned at him. "Ride!"

A word from Gabriel and they were cantering through the dark night, heading into the countryside.

"Faster," Sara urged.

"You're not afraid?"

"Not with you."

"You should be afraid, Sara Jayne," he muttered under his breath, "especially with me."

He squeezed the stallion's flanks with his knees and the horse shot forward, his powerful hooves skimming across the ground.

Sara shrieked with delight as they raced through the darkness. This was power, she thought, the surging body of the horse, the man's strong arm wrapped securely around her waist. The wind whipped through

434

her hair, stinging her cheeks and making her eyes water, but she only threw back her head and laughed.

"Faster!" she cried, reveling in the sense of freedom that surged within her.

Hedges and trees and sleeping farmhouses passed by in a blur. Once, they jumped a four-foot hedge, and she felt as if she were flying. Sounds and scents blended together: the chirping of crickets, the bark of a dog, the smell of damp earth and lathered horseflesh, and over all the touch of Gabriel's breath upon her cheek, the steadying strength of his arm around her waist.

Gabriel let the horse run until the animal's sides were heaving and covered with foamy lather, and then he drew back on the reins, gently but firmly, and the stallion slowed, then stopped.

"That was wonderful!" Sara exclaimed.

She turned to face him, and in the bright light of the moon, he saw that her cheeks were flushed, her lips parted, her eyes shining like the sun.

How beautiful she was! His Sara, so full of life. What cruel fate had decreed that she should be bound to a wheelchair? She was a vivacious girl on the brink of womanhood. She should be clothed in silks and satins, surrounded by gallant young men.

Dismounting, he lifted her from the back of the horse. Carrying her across the damp grass, he sat down on a large boulder, settling her in his lap.

"Thank you, Gabriel," she murmured.

"It was my pleasure, milady."

"Hardly that," she replied with a saucy grin. "I'm sure ladies don't ride pell-mell through the dark astride a big black devil horse."

"No," he said, his gray eyes glinting with amusement, "they don't."

"Have you known many ladies?"

"A few." He stroked her cheek with his forefinger, his

435

touch as light as thistledown.

"And were they accomplished and beautiful?"

Gabriel nodded. "But none so beautiful as you."

She basked in his words, in the silent affirmation she read in his eyes.

"Who are you, Gabriel?" she asked, her voice soft and dreamy. "Are you man or magician?"

"Neither."

"But still my angel?"

"Always, *cara*."

With a sigh, she rested her head against his shoulder and closed her eyes. How wonderful, to sit here in the dark of night with his arms around her. She could almost forget that she was crippled. Almost.

She lost all track of time as she sat there, secure in his arms. She heard the chirp of crickets, the sighing of the wind through the trees, the pounding of Gabriel's heart beneath her cheek.

Her breath caught in her throat as she felt the touch of his hand in her hair and then the brush of his lips.

Abruptly, he stood up. Before she quite knew what was happening, she was on the horse's back and Gabriel was swinging up behind her. He moved with the lithe grace of a cat vaulting a fence.

She sensed a change in him, a tension she didn't understand. A moment later, his arm was locked around her waist and they were riding through the night.

She leaned back against him, braced against the solid wall of his chest. She felt his arm tighten around her, felt his breath on her cheek.

Pleasure surged through her at his touch and she placed her hand over his forearm, drawing his arm more securely around her, tacitly telling him that she enjoyed his nearness.

She thought she heard a gasp, as if he was in pain, but she shook the notion aside, telling herself it was

436

probably just the wind crying through the trees.

Too soon, they were back at the orphanage.

"You'll come tomorrow?" she asked as he settled her in her bed, covering her as if she were a child.

"Tomorrow," he promised. "Sleep well, *cara.*"

"Dream of me," she murmured.

With a nod, he turned away. Dream of her, he thought. If only he could!

"Where would you like to go tonight?" Gabriel asked the following evening.

"I don't care, so long as it's with you."

Moments later, he was carrying her along a pathway in the park across from the orphanage.

Sara marveled that he held her so effortlessly, that it felt so right to be carried in his arms. She rested her head on his shoulder, content. A faint breeze played hide and seek with the leaves of the trees. A lover's moon hung low in the sky. The air was fragrant with night blooming flowers, but it was Gabriel's scent that rose all around her—warm and musky, reminiscent of aged wine and expensive cologne.

He moved lightly along the pathway, his footsteps making hardly a sound. When they came to a stone bench near a quiet pool, he sat down, placing her on the bench beside him.

It was a lovely place, a fairy place. Elegant ferns, tall and lacy, grew in wild profusion near the pool. In the distance, she heard the questioning hoot of an owl.

"What did you do all day?" she asked, turning to look at him.

Gabriel shrugged. "Nothing to speak of. And you?"

"I read to the children. Sister Mary Josepha has been giving me more and more responsibility."

"And does that make you happy?"

"Yes. I've grown very fond of my little charges. They

437

so need to be loved. To be touched. I had never realized how important it was to be held, until—" A faint flush stained her cheeks. "Until you held me. There's such comfort in the touch of a human hand."

Gabriel grunted softly. Human, indeed, he thought bleakly.

Sara smiled. "They seem to like me, the children. I don't know why."

But he knew why. She had so much love to give, and no outlet for it.

"I hate to think of all the time I wasted wallowing in self-pity," Sara remarked. "I spent so much time sitting in my room, sulking because I couldn't walk, when I could have been helping the children, loving them." She glanced up at Gabriel. "They're so easy to love."

"So are you." He had not meant to speak the words aloud, but they slipped out. "I mean, it must be easy for the children to love you. You have so much to give."

She smiled, but it was a sad kind of smile. "Perhaps that's because no one else wants it."

"Sara—"

"It's all right. Maybe that's why I was put here, to comfort the little lost lambs that no one else wants."

I want you. The words thundered in his mind, in his heart, in his soul.

Abruptly, he stood up and moved away from the bench. He couldn't sit beside her, feel her warmth, hear the blood humming in her veins, sense the sadness dragging at her heart, and not touch her, take her.

He stared into the depths of the dark pool, the water as black as the emptiness of his soul. He'd been alone for so long, yearning for someone who would share his life, needing someone to see him for what he was and love him anyway.

A low groan rose in his throat as the centuries of lone-liness wrapped around him.

"Gabriel?" Her voice called out to him, soft, warm, caring.

With a cry, he whirled around and knelt at her feet. Hesitantly, he took her hands in his.

"Sara, can you pretend I'm one of the children? Can you hold me, and comfort me, just for tonight?"

"I don't understand."

"Don't ask questions, *cara*. Please just hold me. Touch me."

She gazed down at him, into the fathomless depths of his dark gray eyes, and the loneliness she saw there pierced her heart. Tears stung her eyes as she reached for him.

He buried his face in her lap, ashamed of the need that he could no longer deny. And then he felt her hand stroke his hair, light as a summer breeze. Ah, the touch of a human hand, warm, fragile, pulsing with life.

Time ceased to have meaning as he knelt there, his head cradled in her lap, her hand moving in his hair, caressing his nape, feathering across his cheek. No wonder the children loved her. There was tranquility in her touch, serenity in her hand. A sense of peace settled over him, stilling his hunger. He felt the tension drain out of him, to be replaced with a nearly forgotten sense of calm. It was a feeling as close to forgiveness as he would ever know.

After a time, he lifted his head. Slightly embarrassed, he gazed up at her, but there was no censure in her eyes, no disdain, only a wealth of understanding.

"Why are you so alone, my angel?" she asked quietly.

"I have always been alone," he replied, and even now, when he was nearer to peace of spirit than he had been for centuries, he was aware of the vast gulf that separated him, not only from Sara, but from all of humanity as well.

Gently, she cupped his cheek with her hand. "Is there no one to love you then?"

"No one."

"I would love you, Gabriel."

"No!"

Stricken by the force of his denial, she let her hand fall into her lap. "Is the thought of my love so revolting?"

"No, don't ever think that." He sat back on his heels, wishing that he could sit at her feet forever, that he could spend the rest of his existence worshiping her beauty, the generosity of her spirit. "I'm not worthy of you, *cara*. I would not have you waste your love on me."

"Why, Gabriel? What have you done that you feel unworthy of love?"

Filled with the guilt of a thousand lifetimes, he closed his eyes and his mind filled with an image of blood. Rivers of blood. Oceans of death. Centuries of killing, of bloodletting. Damned. The Dark Gift had given him eternal life—and eternal damnation.

Thinking to frighten her away, he let her look deep into his eyes, knowing that what she saw within his soul would speak more eloquently than words.

He clenched his hands, waiting for the compassion in her eyes to turn to revulsion. But it didn't happen.

She gazed down at his upturned face for an endless moment, and then he felt the touch of her hand in his hair.

"My poor angel," she whispered. "Can't you tell me what it is that haunts you so?"

He shook his head, unable to speak past the lump in his throat.

"Gabriel." His name, nothing more, and then she leaned forward and kissed him.

It was no more than a feathering of her lips across his, but it exploded through him like concentrated sun-

440

light. Hotter than a midsummer day, brighter than lightning, it burned through him and for a moment he felt whole again. Clean again.

Humbled to the core of his being, he bowed his head so she couldn't see his tears.

"I will love you, Gabriel," she said, still stroking his hair. "I can't help myself."

"Sara—"

"You don't have to love me back," she said quickly. "I just wanted you to know that you're not alone anymore."

A long shuddering sigh coursed through him, and then he took her hands in his, holding them tightly, feeling the heat of her blood, the pulse of her heart. Gently, he kissed her fingertips, and then, gaining his feet, he swung her into his arms.

"It's late," he said, his voice thick with the tide of emotions roiling within him. "We should go before you catch a chill."

"You're not angry?"

"No, *cara*."

How could he be angry with her? She was light and life, hope and innocence. He was tempted to fall to his knees and beg her forgiveness for his whole miserable existence.

But he couldn't burden her with the knowledge of what he was. He couldn't tarnish her love with the truth.

It was near dawn when they reached the orphanage. Once he had her settled in bed, he knelt beside her. "Thank you, Sara."

She turned on her side, a slight smile lifting the corners of her mouth as she took his hand in hers. "For what?"

"For your sweetness. For your words of love. I'll treasure them always."

441

"Gabriel." The smile faded from her lips. "You're not trying to tell me good-bye, are you?"

He stared down at their joined hands: hers small and pale and fragile, pulsing with the energy of life; his large and cold, indelibly stained with blood and death.

If he had a shred of honor left, he would tell her good-bye and never see her again.

But then, even when he had been a mortal man, he'd always had trouble doing the honorable thing when it conflicted with something he wanted. And he wanted— no, needed—Sara. Needed her as he'd never needed anything else in his accursed life. And perhaps, in a way, she needed him. And even if it wasn't so, it eased his conscience to think it true.

"Gabriel?"

"No, *cara*, I'm not planning to tell you good-bye. Not now. Not ever."

The sweet relief in her eyes stabbed him to the heart. And he, cold, selfish monster that he was, was glad of it. Right or wrong, he couldn't let her go.

"Till tomorrow then?" she said, smiling once more.

"Till tomorrow, *cara mia*," he murmured. And for all the tomorrows of your life.

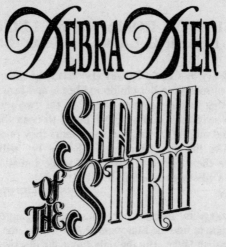

DEBRA DIER

SHADOW OF THE STORM

He is her dashing childhood hero, the man to whom she will willingly surrender her innocence in a night of blazing ecstasy. But when Ian Tremayne cruelly abandons her after a bitter misunderstanding, Sabrina O'Neill vows to have revenge on the handsome Yankee. But the virile Tremayne is more than ready for the challenge. Together, they will enter a high-stakes game of deadly illusion and sizzling desire that will shatter Sabrina's well-crafted facade.

___4397-1 $5.99 US/$6.99 CAN

PASSIONATE ROMANCE BY LEISURE'S LEADING LADIES OF LOVE!

Noble & Ivy by Carole Howey. Ivy has long since given up dreams of marrying her childhood beau, and bears a secret sorrow that haunts her past. Now, as the two reunite in a quest to save their siblings, Ivy burns to coax the embers to life and melt in the passion she swears they once shared. But before that can happen, Noble and Ivy will have to reconcile their past and learn that noble intentions mean nothing without everlasting love.

_4118-9 $5.50 US/$6.50 CAN

Lord Savage by Debra Dier. Elizabeth Barrington is sent to Colorado to find the Marquess of Angelstone, the grandson of an English Duke. But the only thing she discovers is Ash MacGregor, a bounty-hunting rogue who takes great pleasure residing in the back of a bawdy house. Convinced that his rugged good looks resemble those of the noble family, Elizabeth vows she will prove to him that aristocratic blood does pulse through his veins. But the more she tries to show him which fork to use or how to help a lady into her carriage, the more she yearns to be caressed by Lord Savage.

_4119-7 $4.99 US/$5.99 CAN

Dorchester Publishing Co., Inc.
P.O. Box 6640
Wayne, PA 19087-8640

Please add $1.75 for shipping and handling for the first book and $.50 for each book thereafter. NY, NYC, and PA residents, please add appropriate sales tax. No cash, stamps, or C.O.D.s. All orders shipped within 6 weeks via postal service book rate. Canadian orders require $2.00 extra postage and must be paid in U.S. dollars through a U.S. banking facility.

Name_____

Address_____

City_____State_____Zip_____

I have enclosed $_____ in payment for the checked book(s).

Payment <u>must</u> accompany all orders. ☐ Please send a free catalog.

SAINT'S Temptation

DEBRA DIER

Seven years after breaking off her engagement to Clayton Trevelyan, Marisa Grantham overhears two men plotting to murder her still-beloved Earl of Huntingdon. No longer the naive young woman who had allowed her one and only love to walk away, Marisa will do anything to keep from losing him a second time.

___4459-5 $5.99 US/$6.99 CAN

Dorchester Publishing Co., Inc.
P.O. Box 6640
Wayne, PA 19087-8640

Please add $1.75 for shipping and handling for the first book and $.50 for each book thereafter. NY, NYC, and PA residents, please add appropriate sales tax. No cash, stamps, or C.O.D.s. All orders shipped within 6 weeks via postal service book rate. Canadian orders require $2.00 extra postage and must be paid in U.S. dollars through a U.S. banking facility.

Name_____
Address_____
City_____ State_____ Zip_____
I have enclosed $_____ in payment for the checked book(s).
Payment <u>must</u> accompany all orders. ❏ Please send a free catalog.

YESTERDAY'S GOLD
BOBBY HUTCHINSON

BESTSELLING AUTHOR OF
A DISTANT ECHO

With her wedding to Mr. Right only two weeks away, Hannah Gilmore has more on her mind than traveling to a ghost town. Yet here she is, driving her widowed mother, an incontinent poodle, and a bossy nurse through a torrential downpour. Then she turns onto a road that leads her back to the days of Canada's gold rush—and into the heated embrace of Mr. Wrong.

Logan McGraw has every fault that Hannah hates in a man. But after one scorching kiss, Hannah swears that nothing will stop her from sharing with Logan a passion that is far more precious than yesterday's gold.

___4311-4 $5.50 US/$6.50 CAN

A Love Beyond Forever

Diana Haviland

In the solace of slumber he first tempts her—a dark-haired stranger with a feral green gaze—and Kristy Sinclair sees the promise of paradise reflected in his eyes. She swears it is only a dream. But in a New Age boutique, an antique hand mirror shows the beautiful executive more than mussed lipstick—that magnificent man, and a land she has never before known. Suddenly, Kristy is in Cromwell's England. And when an ill-advised remark turns into a brush with the Lord Protector's police, Kristy finds a haven in the solid arms of Jared Ramsey—the literal man of her dreams. But after one rousing kiss from the rogue royalist, Kristy is certain she is awake—and she knows she must learn of the powers that rule her destiny.

___52293-4 $4.99 US/$5.99 CAN

Dorchester Publishing Co., Inc.
P.O. Box 6640
Wayne, PA 19087-8640

Please add $1.75 for shipping and handling for the first book and $.50 for each book thereafter. NY, NYC, and PA residents, please add appropriate sales tax. No cash, stamps, or C.O.D.s. All orders shipped within 6 weeks via postal service book rate. Canadian orders require $2.00 extra postage and must be paid in U.S. dollars through a U.S. banking facility.

Name_____

Address_____

City_____ State_____ Zip_____

I have enclosed $_____ in payment for the checked book(s).

Payment <u>must</u> accompany all orders. ❑ Please send a free catalog.

CHECK OUT OUR WEBSITE! www.dorchesterpub.com